Francis Henry Stauffer

The Queer, the Quaint, the Quizzical

A cabinet for the curious

Francis Henry Stauffer

The Queer, the Quaint, the Quizzical
A cabinet for the curious

ISBN/EAN: 9783337321932

Printed in Europe, USA, Canada, Australia, Japan

Cover: Foto ©Andreas Hilbeck / pixelio.de

More available books at **www.hansebooks.com**

THE QUEER, THE QUAINT

AND

THE QUIZZICAL

A CABINET FOR THE CURIOUS

"The company is mixed."—*Byron*

BY

FRANK H. STAUFFER

PHILADELPHIA

DAVID McKAY, Publisher

1022 MARKET STREET

Oddities and wonders,
  Antiquities and blunders.
    Omens dire, mystic fire,
Strange customs, cranks and freaks.
With philosophy in streaks.

INTRODUCTION.

Custom doth often reason overrule,
And only serves for reason to the fool.—*Rochester.*

A moon dial, with Napier's bones,
And sev'ral constellation stones.—*Butler.*

He shows, on holidays, a sacred pin,
That touch'd the ruff that touch'd Queen Bess's chin.
—*Wolcot's Peter Pindar.*

Stretching away on the one hand into the deep gloom of barbaric ignorance, and on the other hand into the full radiance of Christian intelligence, and, grounding itself strongly in the instinctive recognition by all men of the intimate relations between the seen and the unseen, the empire of SUPERSTITION possesses all ages of human history and all stages of human progress.—*Nimmo.*

Matrons who toss the cup, and see
The grounds of *fate* in *grounds* of *tea.*—*Churchill.*

I have known the shooting of a star to spoil a night's rest; I have seen a man in love grow pale upon the plucking of a merry-thought. There is nothing so inconsiderable which may not appear dreadful to an imagination that is filled with omens and prognostics.—*Addison.*

(5)

Books with Unpronounceable Names.

In the seventeenth century there was a book published entitled: "Crononhotonthologos, the most tragical tragedy that ever was tragedized by any company of tragedians." The first two lines of this effusion read—

"Aldeborontiphoscophosnio!
Where left you Chrononhotonthologos?"

We might name another singular title of a work published in 1661 by Robert Lovell, entitled: "Panzoologicomineralogia; a complete history of animals and minerals, contain'g the summs of all authors, Galenical and Chymicall, with the anatomie of man, &c."—*Salad for the Solitary.*

Most Curious Book in the World.

The most singular bibliographic curiosity is that which belonged to the family of the Prince de Ligne, and is now in France. It is neither written nor printed. All of the letters of the text are cut out of each folio upon the finest vellum; and, being interlaced with blue paper, it is read as easily as the best print. The labor and patience bestowed upon it must have been excessive, especially when the precision and minuteness of the letters are considered. The general execution is admirable in every respect, and the vellum is of the most delicate and costly kind. Rodolphus II., of Germany, offered for it, in 1640, eleven thousand ducats, which was probably equal to sixty thousand at this day. The most remarkable circumstance connected with this literary treasure is that it bears the royal arms of England, but it cannot be shown that it was ever in that country. The book is entitled: *Liber Passionis Domini Nostri Jesu Christi cum Characteribus Nulla Materia Compositis.*

A Long Lost Book Recovered.

The book called "The Ascension of Isaiah the Prophet" had been known to exist in former ages, but had disappeared after the fifth century. During the present century Dr. Richard Laurence, the professor of Hebrew at Oxford, and afterwards Archbishop of Cassel, accidentally met with an Æthiopic MS. at the shop of a bookseller in Drury Lane, which proved to be this apocryphal book. There was something remarkable in the discovery, in a small bookseller's shop, of a book which had been lost to the learned for more than a thousand years.

The Bug Bible.

Among the literary curiosities in the Southampton library, England, is an old Bible known as the "Bug Bible," printed by John Daye, 1551, with a prologue by Tyndall. It derives its name from the peculiar rendering of the fifth verse in the 91st Psalm, which reads thus: "So that thou shalt not need to be afraid for any bugs by night."

Illuminated Manuscript Bible.

Guido de Jars devoted half a century to the production of a manuscript copy of the Bible, with illuminated letters. He began it in his fortieth year, and did not finish it until his ninetieth (1294). It is of exceeding beauty.

The Mazarine Bible.

This is so called from its having been found in the Cardinal's library. It was the first book printed with metal types, and cost $2,500.

A Book without Words.

A literary curiosity exists in England in the shape of "A Wordless Book," so called because, after the title page, it contains not a single word. It is a religious allegory devised by a religious enthusiast, and the thought is in the symbolic color of its leaves, of which two are black, two crimson, two pure white, two pure gold. The black symbolizes the unregenerate heart of man; the crimson, the blessed redemption; the white, the purity of the soul "washed in the blood of the Lamb;" the gold, the radiant joy of eternal felicity.

Wierix's Bible.

The edition of this Bible contains a plate by John Wierix, representing the feast of Dives, with Lazarus at his door. In the rich man's banqueting room there is a dwarf playing with a monkey, to contribute to the merriment of the company, according to the custom among people of rank in the sixteenth century.

Gilt Beards.

There was a French Bible printed in Paris in 1538, by Anthony Bonnemere, wherein is related "that the ashes of the golden calf which Moses caused to be burnt, and mixed with the water that was drank by the Israelites, stuck to the beards of such as had fallen down before it, by which they appeared with gilt beards, as a peculiar mark to distinguish those who had worshipped the calf." This idle story is actually interwoven with the 32d chapter of Exodus.

Printed in Gold Letters.

Bede speaks of a magnificent copy of the Gospels in letters of the purest gold, upon leaves of purple parchment.

Magnificent Latin Bible.

Amongst the rare and costly relics in the library of the Vatican, is the magnificent Latin Bible of the Duke of Urbino. It consists of two large folios, embellished by numerous figures and landscapes, in the ancient arabesque.

Interesting Manuscript Bibles.

In the British Museum there are two copies of the Scriptures which are peculiarly calculated to interest the pious visitors, from the circumstances under which they were transcribed. The elder manuscript contains "The Old and New Testaments, in short hand, in 1686," which were copied, during many a wakeful night, by a zealous Protestant, in the reign of James II., who feared that the attempts of that monarch to re-establish Popery would terminate in the suppression of the sacred Scriptures.

The other manuscript contains the book of Psalms and the New Testament, in 15 volumes, folio, written in characters an inch long, with white ink, on black paper manufactured for the purpose. This perfectly unique copy was written in 1745, at the cost of a Mr. Harries, a London tradesman. His sight having failed with age so as to prevent his reading the Scriptures, though printed in the largest type, he incurred the expense of this transcription that he might enjoy those sources of comfort which "are more to be desired than gold, yea, than much fine gold."

The British Museum paid $3750 for the manuscript Bible made by Alcuin, in the eighth century, for the Emperor Charlemagne, whose instructor and friend he was.

The Vinegar Bible.

This Bible derives its title from an edition which contained an error in the heading to the twentieth chapter of St. Luke, in which "Parable of the Vineyard" is printed "Parable of the Vinegar." The edition was issued in the year 1717, by the University of Oxford, at their Clarendon Press.

Queen Elizabeth's "Oone Gospell Booke."

This book is a precious object to the virtuoso. It was the work of Queen Catherine Parr, and was enclosed in solid gold. It hung by a gold chain at her side, and was the frequent companion of the "Virgin Queen." In her own handwriting, at the beginning of the volume, the following quaint lines appear—

"I walke many times into the pleasaunt fieldes of the Holie Scriptures, where I plucke up the goodliesome herbes of sentences by pruning; eate them by readinge; chawe them by musing; and laye them up at length in ye state of memorie by gathering them together; that so, having tasted their sweetness, I may the lesse perceave the bitterness of this miserable life."

This was penned by the Queen, probably while she was in captivity at Woodstock, as the spirit it breathed affords a singular contrast to the towering haughtiness of her ordinary deportment.

Eliot's Indian Bible.

At the age of 42, John Eliot, pastor of a church at Roxbury, Mass., began the study of the Natick Indian dialect, with a view of translating the Bible into that language. He completed the translation in 1658, after a labor of eight years, and the book was issued in 1663. Upwards of one thousand copies were printed, of which twenty copies were dedicated to King Charles. The latter copies are so rare that one of them was sold in the U. S., in 1862, for $1000, and six years later for $1150. Among the many points of interest which Eliot's Indian Bible possesses, not the least is the fact that it is the language of a nation no longer in existence, and is almost the only monument of the race; another, that it is the first edition of the Bible published in this country.

Silver Book.

In the library of Upsal, in Sweden, there is preserved a translation of the four Gospels, printed with metal type upon violet-colored vellum. The letters are silver, and hence it has received the name of *Codex Argenteus*. The initial letters are in gold. It is supposed that the whole was printed in the same manner as book-binders letter the titles of books on the back. It was a very near approach to the art of printing, but it is not known how old it is.

Huge Copy of the Koran.

D'Israeli mentions a huge copy of the Koran—probably without a parallel, as to its *size*, in the annals of *letters*. The characters are described as three inches long; the book itself is a foot in thickness, and its other dimensions five feet by three.

A Lost Book.

Celsus wrote a book against the Magi, which was not preserved. He was an Epicurian philosopher, and lived in the second century. Much regret has been expressed over the loss of the work. He is mentioned with respect by Lucian, who derived from him the account which he gives of Alexander the imposter. Even Origen treated him with consideration.

Book of Riddles.

The Book of Riddles, alluded to by Shakespeare in the Merry Wives of Windsor (Act 1st, scene 1st), is mentioned by Laneham, 1575, and in the English Courtier, 1586. The earliest edition now preserved is dated 1629. It is entitled "The Booke of Merry Riddles, together with proper Questions and with Proverbs to make pleasant pastime; no less usefull and behovefull for any young man or child, to know if he be quick-witted or no."

Unique Library.

A singular library existed in 1535, at Warsenstein, near Cassel. The books composing it, or rather the substitutes for them, were made of wood, and every one of them is a specimen of a different tree. The back is formed of its bark, and the sides are constructed of polished pieces of the same stock. When put together, the whole forms a box, and inside of it are stored the fruit, seed and leaves, together with the moss which grows on its trunk and the insects which feed upon the tree. Every volume corresponds in size, and the collection altogether has an excellent effect.

The New England Primer.

After the horn-book, the children of the incipient United States were furnished with primers, among the most noted of which was "The New England Primer for the more easy attaining the reading of English, to which is added the Assembly of Divines and Mr. Cotton's Catechisms." This primer had in it the alphabet, syllables of two letters, and many a pious distich, such as—

> Young Timothy
> Learn'd sin to fly.
>
> Whales in the sea
> God's voice obey.
>
> In Adam's fall
> We sinned all.
>
> Vashti for pride
> Was set aside.

These puritanic verses were accompanied with illustrations fully as bad as the rhymes, which were occasionally stretched to a triplet, as—

> Young Obadias,
> David, Josias,
> All were pious.

The Bedford Missal.

One of the most celebrated books in the annals of bibliography is the richly illuminated Missal executed by John, Duke of Bedford, Regent of France under Henry VI., and presented by him to the king in 1430. This rare volume is eleven inches long, seven and a half inches wide, and two and a half inches thick. It contains fifty-nine large miniatures, which nearly occupy the whole page, and above a thousand small ones, in circles of about an inch and a half in diameter, displayed in brilliant borders of golden foliage, with variegated flowers, etc. At the bottom of every page are two lines in blue and gold letters, which explain the subject of each miniature. This relic, after passing through various hands, descended to the Duchess of Portland, whose valuable collection was sold by auction in 1786. Among its many attractions was the Bedford Missal. A knowledge of the sale coming to the ears of George III., he sent for his bookseller, and expressed his intention to become the purchaser. The bookseller ventured to submit to his Majesty the probable high price it would bring. "How high?" asked the king. "Probably two hundred guineas," replied the bookseller. "Two hundred guineas for a missal!" exclaimed the Queen, who was present, and lifted her hands in astonishment. "Well, well, I'll have it still," said his majesty; "but since the Queen thinks two hundred guineas so enormous a price for a missal, I'll go no higher." The bidding for the royal library actually stopped at that point, and a celebrated collector, Mr. Edwards, became the purchaser by adding three pounds more. The same missal was afterwards sold at Mr. Edwards' sale, in 1815, and purchased by the Duke of Marlborough for the enormous sum of £637 15*s*. sterling.

Lord Kingsborough's Mexico.

The most costly undertaking of a literary character ever undertaken by a single individual is the magnificent work on "Mexico," by Lord Kingsborough. This stupendous work is said to have been produced at an enormtous cost to the author. It is comprised in seven immense folio volumes, embellished by about one thousand colored illustrations. He spent more than $300,000 in its production, his enthusiasm carrying him so far that he ultimately died in debt.

Imperishable Prison Literature.

Bœthius composed his excellent "Consolations of Philosophy" in prison. Grotius wrote his "Commentary" while
in prison. Cervantes, it is said, wrote that masterpiece of
Spanish romance, "Don Quixote," on board one of the gal-
leys, in Barbara. Sir Walter Raleigh compiled his "History
of the World" in his prison-chamber in the Tower. Bunyan
composed his immortal allegory in Bedford jail. Luther gave
the Bible to Germany, having translated it in Wartburg castle.

Puffing their own Books.

Authors of the olden time used to puff their own works by
affixing "taking titles" to them; such as "A right merrie and
wittie interlude, verie pleasant to reade, &c.;" "A marvellous
wittie treatise, &c.;" "A Delectable, Pithie and Righte Profitable Worke, &c."

Sibylline Books.

The Sibylline prophecies were of early Trojan descent, and
the most celebrated of the Sibyls, or priestesses, plays an
important part in the tales of Æneas. Her prophecies were
supposed to be heard in dark caverns and apertures in rocks.
They are thought by Varro to have been written upon palm
leaves in Greek hexameters. They were largely circulated in
he time of Crœsus, and the promises which they made of
future empire to Æneas escaping from the flames of Troy into
Italy, were remarkably realized by Rome. Of the nine books
offered for sale by a Sibyl to Tarquinius Superbus, six were
burnt, after which he purchased the remaining three for the
price originally demanded for the nine. They were kept in a
stone chest under ground in the temple of Jupiter Capitolinus,

in the custody of certain officers, who only consulted the books at the special command of the Senate. Some Sibylline books appear to have been consulted until the tenth century.

Prophetic Almanacs.

The fame of the celebrated astrologer, Nostradamus, who prophesied minutely the death of Henry II. of France, the execution of Charles I. of England, the great fire of London, the Restoration, &c., gåve such an impulse to predictions that, in 1579, Henry III. of France prohibited the insertion of any political prophecies in almanacs, a prohibition which was renewed by Louis XIII., in 1628. In the reign of Charles IX. a royal edict required every almanac to be stamped with the approval of the diocesan bishop. Prophetic almanacs still circulate to an incredible extent in the rural districts of France, and among the uneducated. The most popular of all these is the "Almanac Liègeois," a venerable remnant of superstition, first issued in 1636. It is a most convenient almanac for those who are unable to read, for by certain symbols attached to certain dates the most unlettered persons can follow its instructions. A rude representation of a phial announces the proper phase of the moon under which a draught of medicine should be taken; a pair of scissors points out the proper period for cutting hair; a lancet, for letting blood, &c.

Diaries.

Marcus Antonius' celebrated work, entitled "Of the Things which Concern Himself," would be a good definition of the use and purpose of a diary. Shaftesbury calls a diary "A Fault-book," intended for self-correction; and a Colonel Hardwood, in the reign of Charles I., kept a diary which, in the spirit of the times, he entitled "Slips, Infirmities and Passages of Providence." One old writer quaintly observes that "the ancients used to take their stomach-pill of self-examination every night. Some used little books or tablets, tied at their girdles, in which they kept a memorial of what they did, against their night-reckoning." We know that Titus, the delight of mankind, as he has been called, kept a diary of all his actions, and when at night he found that he had performed nothing memorable, he would exclaim: "Friends, we have lost a day." Edward VI. kept a diary, while that left by James II., so full of facts and reflections, furnished excellent material for history. Richard Baxter, author of one hundred and forty-five distinct works, left a diary extending from 1615 to 1648, which, when published, formed a folio of seven hundred closely-printed pages. Valuable diaries were also left by Whitelock and Henry Earl of Clarendon.

Literary Ingenuity.

Odo tenet mulum, madidam mappam tenet anna.

The above line is said, in an old book, to have "cost the inventor much foolish labor, for it is perfect verse, and every word is the very same both backward and forward."

Supposed to be a Genuine Island.

When the Utopia of Sir Thomas More was first published, it occasioned quite a complimentary blunder. This political romance represents a perfect but visionary republic, in an island supposed to have been newly discovered in America. As this was the age of discovery (says Granger), the learned Budæus, and others, took it for a genuine history, and considered it as highly expedient that missionaries should be sent thither, in order to convert so wise a nation to Christianity.

King of India's Library.

Dabshelim, King of India, had so numerous a library, that a hundred brachmans were scarcely sufficient to keep it in order, and it required a thousand dromedaries to transport it from one place to another. As he was not able to read all these books, he proposed to the brachmans to make extracts from them of the best and most useful of their contents. These learned personages went so heartily to work, that in less than twenty years they had compiled of all these extracts a little encyclopædia of twelve thousand volumes, which thirty camels could carry with ease. They presented them to the king, but what was their amazement to hear him say that it was impossible for him to read thirty camel-loads of books. They therefore reduced their extracts to fifteen, afterwards to ten, then to four, then to two dromedaries, and at last there remained only enough to load a mule of ordinary size.

Unfortunately, Dabshelim, during this process of melting down his library, grew old, and saw no probability of living long enough to exhaust its quintessence to the last volume. "Illustrious Sultan," said his vizier, "though I have but a very imperfect knowledge of your royal library, yet I will undertake to deliver you a very brief and satisfactory abstract of it. You shall read it through in one minute, and yet you will find matter in it to reflect upon throughout the rest of your life." Having said this, Pilpay took a palm leaf, and wrote upon it with a golden style the four following paragraphs:

1. The greater part of the sciences comprise but one single word—*Perhaps*, and the whole history of mankind contains no more than three—they are *born, suffer, die*.

2. Love nothing but what is good, and do all that thou lovest to do; think nothing but what is true, and speak not all that thou thinkest.

3. O kings! tame your passions, govern yourselves, and it will be only child's play to govern the world.

4. O kings! O people! it can never be often enough repeated to you, what the half-witted venture to doubt, that there is no happiness without virtue, and no virtue without God.

Palindromes.

One of the most remarkable palindromes is the following—

SATOR AREPO TENET OPERA ROTAS.

Its distinguishing peculiarity is that the first letter of each successive word writes to spell the first word; the second letter of each the second word, and so on throughout; and the same will be found as precisely true upon reversal. But the neatest and prettiest that has yet appeared comes from a highly cultivated lady who was attached to the court of Queen Elizabeth. Having been banished from the court on suspicion of too great familiarity with a nobleman in high favor, the lady adopted this device—*a moon covered by a cloud*—and the following palindrome for a motto—

ABLATA ATALBA. (Secluded but Pure.)

The merit of this kind of composition was never in any example so heightened by appropriateness and delicacy of sentiment.

Chronogram.

Such was the name given to a whimsical device of the later Romans, resuscitated during the *renaissance* period, by which a date is given by selecting certain letters amongst those which form an inscription, and printing them larger than the others. The principle will be understood from the following chronogram made from the name of George Villiers, the first Duke of Buckingham—

Georg IVs. DVX. bVCkIngaMIæ.

The date MDCXVVVIII (1628), is that of the year in which the Duke was murdered by Felton, at Portsmouth.

Instance of Remarkable Perseverance.

The Rev. Wm. Davy, a Devonshire curate, in the year 1795, begun a most desperate undertaking, viz: that of himself printing twenty-six volumes of sermons, which he actually did, working off page by page, for fourteen copies, and continued the almost hopeless task for twelve years, in the midst of poverty. Such wonderful perseverance almost amounts to a ruling passion.

Alliterative Whims.

Mrs. Crawford says she wrote one line in her song, "Kathleen Mavourneen," for the express purpose of confounding the cockney wablers, who sing it thus—

> "The 'orn of the 'unter is 'eard on the 'ill."

Moore has laid the same trap in the *Woodpecker*—

> "A 'eart that is 'umble might 'ope for it 'ere."

And the elephant confounds them the other way—

> "A helephant heasily heats at his hease,
> Hunder humbrageous humbrella trees."

Alliterations carried to Absurd Excess.

In the early part of the seventeenth century the fashion of hunting after alliterations was carried to an absurd excess. Even from the pulpit the chosen people were addressed as "the *c*hickens of the *c*hurch, the *s*parrows of the *s*pirit, and the *s*weet *s*wallows of *s*alvation." "Ane New-Year Gift," or address, presented to Mary Queen of Scots by the poet **Alexander Scot**, concludes with a stanza running thus—

> "Fresh, fulgent, flourist, fragrant flower formose,
> Lantern to love, of ladies lamp and lot,
> Cherry maist chaste, chief, carbuncle and chose, &c."

Vacillating Newspapers.

The newspapers of Paris, under censorship of the press, in 1815, announced in the following manner Bonaparte's departure from the Isle of Elba, his march across France and his entrance into the French Capital:—

"9th March.—The Cannibal has escaped from his den. 10th.—The Corsican Ogre has just landed at Cape Juan. 11th.—The Tiger has arrived at Gap. 12th.—The Monster has passed the night at Grenoble. 13th.—The Tyrant has crossed Lyons. 14th—The Usurper is directing his course toward Dijon, but the brave and loyal Burgundians have risen in a body and they surround him on all sides. 18th.—Bonaparte is sixty leagues from the Capital; he has had skill enough to escape from the hands of his pursuers. 19th—Bonaparte advances rapidly, but he will never enter Paris. 20th.—To-morrow *Napoleon* will be under our ramparts. 21st.—The *Emperor* is at Fontainebleau. 22d.—His *Imperial* and *Royal Majesty* last evening made his entrance into his Palace of the Tuileries, amidst the *joyous* acclamations of an *adoring* and *faithful people*."

Dr. Johnson's Blunders.

Considering that Doctor Johnson was himself a severe verbal critic, it might be expected that his own writings would be correct. But he wrote: "Every monumental inscription

. should be in Latin; for that being a *dead* language it will always *live*." Another Johnsonian lapsus is palpable in the lines—

> "Nor yet perceived the vital spirit fled,
> But still fought on, *nor knew that he was dead.*"

It would puzzle the reader to understand how a warrior could continue fighting after he was dead.

Blunders of Painters.

Tintoret, an Italian painter, in a picture of the Children of Israel gathering manna, represents them armed with guns. In Cigoli's painting of the circumcision of the infant Saviour, the aged Simeon has a pair of spectacles on his nose. In a picture by Verrio of Christ healing the sick, the by-standers have periwigs on their heads. A Dutch painter, in a picture of the Wise Men worshipping the Holy Child, has drawn one of them in a white surplice, and in boots and spurs, and he is in the act of presenting to the children a model of a Dutch man-of-war. In a Dutch picture of Abraham offering up his son, instead of the patriarch "stretching forth and taking the knife," he is represented as holding a blunderbuss to Isaac's head. Berlin represents in a picture the Virgin and Child listening to a violin. A French artist, in a painting of the Lord's Supper, has the table ornamented with tumblers filled with cigar lighters. Another French painting exhibits Adam and Eve in all their primeval simplicity, while near them, in full costume, is seen a hunter with a gun, shooting ducks.

Thackeray's Geographical Blunders.

The novelist, in "The Virginians," makes Madam Esmond, of Castlewood, in Westmoreland county, a neighbor of Washington at Mt. Vernon, on the Potomac, fifty miles distant, and a regular attendant at public worship at Williamsburg, half-way between the York and James rivers, fully one hundred and twenty-five miles from Mt. Vernon; and so "immensely affected" are the colored hearers of a young preacher at Williamsburg "that there was such a negro chorus about the house as might be heard across the Potomac," the nearest bank of which is fifty-seven miles away.

He makes General Braddock ride out from Williamsburg (he never was there) in "his own coach, a ponderous, emblazoned vehicle," with Dr. Franklin, "the little postmaster of Philadelphia" (Franklin's average weight was 160 pounds), over a muddy road, in March, through a half-wilderness country of more than one hundred miles, to dine with Madam Esmond, in Westmoreland county, near Mt. Vernon.

A Stupid Critic.

Commentators are sometimes stupid, and their criticisms so absurd as to be amusing. A German critic, in explaining the text of Shakespeare's comedy "As You Like It," came to the following passage—

> "Tongues in trees, books in the running brooks,
> Sermons in stones, and good in every thing."

He made this comment upon it: "The lines as they now stand are manifestly wrong. No one ever found books in the running brooks, or sermons in stones. But a slight transposition of words reduces the passage to sense. Shakespeare's meaning is clear, and what he meant he must have written. The passage should read thus—

> "Stones in the running brooks,
> Sermons in books, and good in every thing."

Crooked Coincidences.

A pamphlet published in the year 1703, has the following strange title—

"The *Deformity* of Sin Cured, a sermon preached at St. Michael's, *Crooked* Lane, before the Prince of Orange, by the Rev. James *Crook*shanks. Sold by Matthew Dowton, at the *Crooked* Billet, near *Cripple*gate, and by all other Booksellers." The words of the text are, "Every *crooked* path shall be made straight," and the Prince before whom it was preached was *crooked*, i. e., deformed.

The Bride of Abydos.

In this poem of Byron's there is no *bride*, for the heroine dies heart-broken and unwedded.

Grandiloquent Outbursts.

There is a volume printed at Amsterdam, 1657, entitled: "Jesus, Maria, Joseph; or the Devout Pilgrim of the Everlasting Blessed Virgin Mary, in his Holy Exercises, Affections and Elevations, upon the sacred Mysteries of Jesus, Maria and Joseph." We append a few extracts from this curious book, as a specimen of the language employed at that time in addressing the Virgin—

"You, O Mother of God, are the Spiritual Paradise of the second Adam; the bright cloud carrying him who hath the cherubims for his chariot; the fleece of wool filled with the sweet dew of heaven, whereof was made that admirable robe of our royal shepherd, in which he vouchsafed to look after his sheep; you are pleasing and comely as Jerusalem, and the aromatical odours issuing from your garments outvie all the delights of Mount Lebanon; you are the sacred pix of celestial perfumes, whose sweet exhalations shall never be exhausted; you are the holy oil, the unextinguishable lamp, the unfading flower, the divinely-woven purple, the royal vestment, the imperial diadem, the throne of the divinity, the gate of Paradise, the queen of the universe, the cabinet of life, the fountain ever flowing with celestial illustrations."

"All hail! the divine lantern encompassing that crystal lamp whose light outshines the sun in its midday splendour; the spiritual sea whence the world's richest pearl was extracted; the radiant sphere, the well-fenced orchard, the fruitful border, the fair and delicate garden, the nuptial bed of the eternal world, the odoriferous and happy City of God, etc., etc."

Dialect Rhyme.

The subjoined is a specimen of the dialect spoken in the county of Lancashire, England. The verse is a description of a lost baby, by the town-crier, or bell-man, who still plies his trade in out-of-the-way parts of England—

> Law-st oather [either] to-day or else some toime to morn,
> As pratty a babby as ever wur born;
> It has checks like red roses, two bonny blue een,
> Had it meauth daubed wi' traycle th' last toime it were seen;
> It's just cuttin' it teeth, an' has very sore gums,
> An' it's gettin' a habit o' suckin' it thumbs;
> Thoose at foind it may keep it, there's nob'dy 'll care,
> For thoose at hav lost it, hav lots moor to spare!

In Search of a Rhyme.

Luttrell made this couplet on the wife of "Anastatius" Hope, famous for his wealth and her own jewels—

> "Of diamond, emerald and topaz,
> Such as the charming Mrs. Hope has!"

Noted Anachronisms.

Shakespeare makes Lear, an early Anglo-Saxon King, speak of not wanting spectacles, which were not known until the fourteenth century. Cannon were first used in the year 1346, but in relating Macbeth's death, in 1054, and King John's reign in 1200, he mentions cannon. In his Julius Cæsar, he makes the "clock" strike three.

Schiller, in his "Piccolomini," speaks of a "lightning-conductor" as existing about 150 years before its invention.

Diogenes and his Tub.

Modern scepticism about the practical stoicism of the ancients is surely brought to a climax by a living writer, M. Fournier, who maintains that the so-called tub of Diogenes was in reality a commodious little dwelling—neat but not gorgeous. It must be supposed, then, that he spoke of his tub much as an English country gentleman does of his "box."
—*The Book Hunter, by Burton.*

Slave Advertisements.

The following announcements are curious, showing the merchandise light in which the negro was regarded in America while yet a colony of Great Britain:

Francis Lewis, has for Sale,

A Choice Parcel of Muscovado and Powder Sugars, Tierces and Barrels; Ravens, Ducks and a Negro Woman and Negro Boy. The Coach-House and Stables, with or without the Garden Spot, formerly the property of Joseph Murray, Esq.; in the Broadway, to be let separately or together:—Inquire of said Francis Lewis.—*New York Gazette*, April 25th, 1765.

This Day Run away from JOHN McCOMB, Junier, an Indian Woman, about 17 Years of Age, Pitted in the Face, of a middle Stature and Indifferent fatt, having on her a Drugat, Wastcoat, and Kersey Petticoat, of a Light Collour.   If any Person or Persons shall bring the said Girle to her said Master, shall be Rewarded for their Trouble to their Content.—*American Weekly Mercury*, May 24th. 1726.

A Female Negro Child (of an extraordinary good Breed) to be given away.   Inquire of Edes and Gill.—*Boston Gazette*, Feb. 25th, 1765.

TO BE SOLD, FOR WANT OF EMPLOY,

A Likely Negro Fellow, about 25 Years of Age.   He is an extraordinary good Cook, and understands setting or tending a table very well, likewise all kind of House Work, such as washing, scouring, scrubbing, &c.   Also, a Negro Wench, his Wife, about 17 Years old, born in this City, and understands all Sorts of House Work.   For farther Particulars, inquire of the Printer.—*New York Gazette*, March 21st, 1765.

Sir John Moore not Buried at Night.

It has been generally supposed that the burial of Sir John Moore, who fell at the battle of Corunna, in 1809, took place during the night, an error which doubtless arose from the statement to that effect in Wolf's celebrated lines.   Rev. Mr. Symons, who was the clergyman on the occasion, states, however, in Notes and Queries, that the burial took place in the morning, in broad day-light.

Cleopatra a Myth.

Commentators of no mean standing insist that Cleopatra

> " Star-eyed Egyptian,
> Glorious sorceress of the Nile,"

is merely a creature of the imagination; in plain words, that
the Cleopatra of history never existed, though there were two
or three women who bore the name.

Abelard and Heloise.

Though they may have lived about the same time, the
romance of their love is now gravely denied by scholars and
antiquarians.

Odd Titles of Old Books.

In "Gleanings for the Curious" we find the following list
of odd titles to books, most of which were published in the
time of Cromwell :—.

A Shot aimed at the Devil's Head-Quarters through the
Tube of the Cannon of the Covenant.

Crumbs of Comfort for the Chickens of the Covenant.

Eggs of Charity, layed by the Chickens of the Covenant,
and boiled with the Water of Divine Love.   Take Ye and eat.

High-heeled Shoes for Dwarfs in Holiness.

Hooks and Eyes for Believers' Breeches.

Matches lighted by the Divine Fire.

Seven Sobs of a Sorrowful Soul for Sin; or, the Seven Peni-
tential Psalms of the Princely Prophet David; whereunto are
also added William Humius' Handful of Honeysuckles, and
Divers Godly and Pithy Ditties, now newly augmented.

Spiritual Milk for Babes, drawn out of the Breasts of both
Testaments for their Souls' Nourishment: a catechism.

The Bank of Faith.

The Christian Sodality; or, Catholic Hive of Bees, sucking
the Honey of the Churches' Prayer from the Blossoms of the

Word of God, blowne out of the Epistles and Gospels of the Divine Service throughout the yeare.   Collected by the Puny Bee of all the Hive not worthy to be named otherwise than by these elements of his Name, F. P.

The Gun of Penitence.

The Innocent Love; or, the Holy Knight: a description of the ardors of a saint for the Virgin.

The Shop of the Spiritual Apothecary; or, a collection of passages from the fathers.

The Sixpennyworth of Divine Spirit.

The Snuffers of Divine Love.

The Sound of the Trumpet: a work on the day of judgment.

The Spiritual Mustard Pot, to make the Soul Sneeze with Devotion.

The Three Daughters of Job: a treatise on patience, fortitude and pain.

Tobacco battered, and the Pipes shattered about their Ears that idly idolize so loathsome a Vanity, by a Volley of holy shot thundered from Mount Helicon: a poem against the use of tobacco, by Joshua Sylvester.

A Fan to drive away Flies: a theological treatise on Purgatory.

A most Delectable Sweet Perfumed Nosegay for God's Saints to Smell at.

A Pair of Bellows to blow off the Dust cast upon John Fry.

A Proper Project to Startle Fools: Printed in a Land where Self's cry'd up and Zeal's cry'd down.

A Reaping-Hook, well tempered, for the Stubborn Ears of the coming Crop; or, Biscuit baked in the Oven of Charity, carefully conserved for the Chickens of the Church, the Sparrows of the Spirit, and the sweet Swallows of Salvation.

A Sigh of Sorrow for the Sinners of Zion, breathed out of a Hole in the Wall of an Earthly Vessel, known among Men by the Name of Samuel Fish (a Quaker who had been imprisoned).

Title-Pages which Mislead.

The title-page is not always a distinct intimation of what is to follow. "The Diversions of Purley" is one of the toughest books in existence. "Apes Urbanæ" (Urban bees), by the great scholar, Leo Allatius, is not about bees, but is devoted to the great men who flourished during the Pontificate of Urban VIII., whose family carried bees on their coat-armorial. "Marmontel's Moral Tales" has been found to give disappointment to parents in search of the absolutely correct and improving; and Edgeworth's "Essay on Irish Bulls" has been counted money absolutely thrown away by eminent breeders. "MacEwen on the Types" is not a book for printers, but for theologians. Ruskin's treatise "On the Construction of Sheepfolds" treats about Popery and Protestantism.—*The Book Hunter.*

A Carmelite Friar's Poem.

In the seventeenth century a carmelite friar named Jean Louis Barthelemi, but who always called himself Pierre de St. Louis, composed (in twelve books) a poem entitled, "The Magdaleneide; or, Mary Magdalen at the Desert of the Sainte Beaume in Provence, a Spiritual and Christian Poem." Some idea of it may be obtained from a literally translated extract. Having treated at large of the Magdelen's irregular conduct in the early part of her life, and of her subsequent conversion, he says:—

"But God at length changed this coal into a ruby, this crow into a dove, this wolf into a sheep, this hell into a heaven, this nothing into something, this thistle into a lily, this thorn into a rose, this impotence into power, this vice into virtue, this caldron into a mirror."

The poem cost him five years of close application, and he

concludes it by egotistically saying: "If you desire grace and sweetness in verses, in mine will you find them."

Striking Parallel Passages between Shakspeare and the Bible.

Othello.—Rude am I in speech.—I. 3.

But though I be rude in speech.—2 Cor. xi. 6.

Witches.—Show his eyes and grieve his heart.—iv. 1.

Consume thine eyes and grieve thine heart.—1 Sam. ii. 33.

Macbeth.—Lighted fools the way to dusty death.—V. 5.

Thou hast brought me into the dust of death.—Ps. xxii.

Othello.—I took him by the throat, the circumcised dog, and smote him.—V. 2.

I smote him, I caught him by his beard and smote him, and slew him.—1 Sam. xvii. 35.

Macbeth.—We will die with harness on our back.—V. 5.

Nicanor lay dead in his harness.—Maccabees xv. 28.

Curious Play Bill.

The following remarkable theatrical announcement is worthy of preservation for its effusion of vanity and poverty, in the shape of an appeal to the inhabitants of a town in Sussex:—

"At the old theatre in East Grimstead, on Saturday, May 5th, 1758, will be represented (by particular desire, and for the benefit of Mrs. P.) the deep and affecting tragedy of Theodosius; or, the Force of Love, with magnificent dresses, scenery, &c.

"Varanes, by Mr. P., who will strive, as far as possible, to support the character of this fiery Persian Prince, in which he was so much admired and applauded at Hastings, Arundel, Petworth, Lewes, &c.

"Theodosius, by a young gentleman from the University of Oxford, who never appeared on any stage.

"Athenais, by Mrs. P. Though her present condition will not permit her to wait on gentlemen and ladies out of the town with tickets, she hopes, as upon former occasions, for their liberality and support.

"Nothing in Italy can exceed the altar, in the first scene of the play. Nevertheless, should any of the nobility or gentry wish to see it ornamented with flowers, the bearer will bring away as many as they choose to favour him with.

"As the coronation of Athenias, to be introduced in the fifth act, contains a number of personages, more than sufficient to fill all the dressing room, &c., it is to be hoped no gentlemen and ladies will be offended at being refused admission behind the scenes.

"N. B.—The great yard dog that made so much noise on Thursday night during the last act of King Richard the Third, will be sent to a neighbor's over the way; and on account of the prodigious demand for places, part of the stable will be laid into the boxes on one side, and the granary be open for the same purpose on the other. *Vivat Rex.*"

Boone's Spelling.

An old letter written by Daniel Boone, furnishes this specimen of original spelling:—

"I hope you Will Wright me By the Bearer, Mr. goe, how you Com on with my Horsis—I Hear the Indians have Killed Some pepel near Limstone."

Vagaries of Spelling.

Queen Elizabeth spelt the word sovereign in seven different ways. The Earl of Leicester, her favorite, spelt his own name in eight different ways.   Sir Walter Raleigh spelt his own name in more than eight different ways.   In the deeds of the Villars family their name is spelt in fourteen different ways.   In the family documents of the Percy family their name is spelt in fifteen different ways.

Singular Specimen of Orthography in the Sixteenth Century.

The following letter was written by the Duchess of Norfolk to Cromwell, Earl of Essex.   It exhibits a curious instance of the monstrous anomalies of our orthography in the infancy of our literature:—

"My ffary gode lord,—her I sand you in tokyn hoff the neweyer, a glasse hoff setyl set in sellfer gyld.   I pra you tak hit in wort.   An hy wer habel het showlde be bater.   I woll hit war wort a m crone."

Translated.—"My very good lord.   Here I send you, in token of the new year, a glass of setyll set in silver gilt.   I pray you take it in worth.   An I were able it should be better.   I would it were worth a thousand crowns."

High-Sounding Prologue.

In a medical work entitled "The Breviarie of Health," published in 1547, by Andrew Borde, a physician of that period, is a prologue to physicians, beginning thus—

"Egregious doctors and masters of the eximious and arcane science of physic, of your urbanity exasperate not yourselves against me for making this little volume."

Inducements to Subscribers.

For journals to offer inducements to subscribers is not a modern feature.   A book was published in 1764, entitled

"A New History of England, Manchester, printed by Joseph Harrop, opposite the Exchange."   At the end of this octavo volume, which consists of 778 pages, is the following:—

"To the PUBLIC.

"The History of England being now brought down to that period which was at first proposed, the Publisher takes this opportunity of returning his thanks to his friends and subscribers for the kind encouragement they have given his News Paper; and hopes that as he has steadily persevered in going through with, and given gratis, The History of England, at the Expence of upwards of One Hundred Pounds, they will still continue their Subscription to his paper, which he will spare neither pains nor assiduity to render worthy their perusal.   Jos. Harrop."

Composition During Sleep.

Condorcet is said to have attained the conclusion of some of his most abstruse, unfinished calculations in his dreams. Franklin makes a similar admission concerning some of his political projects which, in his waking moments, sorely puzzled him.   Sir J. Herschel is said to have composed the following lines in a dream:—

> "Throw thyself on thy God, nor mock Him with feeble denial;
>   Sure of His love, and, oh! sure of His mercy at last!
>   Bitter and deep though the draught, yet drain thou the cup of thy trial,
>   And in its healing effect, smile at the bitterness past."

Goethe says in his "Memoirs," "The objects which had occupied my attention during the day often reappeared at night in connected dreams.   On awakening, a new composition, or a portion of one I had already commenced, presented itself to my mind.   In the morning I was accustomed to record my ideas on paper." Coleridge composed his poem of the "Abyssinian Maid" during a dream. Something analogous to this is what Lord Cockburn says in his "Life of Lord Jeffrey." · "He had a fancy that though he went to bed with his head stuffed with the names, dates and other details of various causes, they were all in order in the morning; which he accounted for by saying that during sleep 'they all *crystallized round their proper centres.'*"

A Bill of Particulars.

A certain gentleman of Worcester (Mass.) sent a very fine French clock to a well-known jeweler to be repaired, saying that he wished each item of repairing specified. The following is a copy of the bill as rendered:—

To removing the alluvial deposit and oleaginous con-
glomerate from clock a la French, . . $0.50
To replacing in appropriate juxtaposition the constituent
components of said clock, ...50
To lubricating with oleaginous solution the apex of pin-
ions of said clock, ...50
To adjusting horologically the isochronal mechanism of
said clock, ...50
To equalizing the acoustic resultant of escape wheel per-
cussion upon the verge pallets of said clock, . .50
To adjusting the distance between the centre of gravity
of the pendulum and its point of suspension, so that
the vibrations of the pendulum shall cause the index
hand to indicate approximately the daily arrival of
the sun at its meridian height, . . .50

$3.00

Lilly's Predictions.

While Lilly is ridiculed for his absurdities, let him have credit for as lucky a guess as ever blessed the pages even of

"Francis Moore, Physician." In Lilly's "Astrological Predictions for 1648," there occurs the following passage, in which we must allow that he attained to "something like prophetic strain," when we call to mind that the Great Plague of London occurred in 1665, and the Great Fire in the year following:—

"In the year 1656, the aphelium of Mars, who is the general signification of England, will be in Virgo, which is assuredly the ascendant of the English monarchy, but Aries of the kingdom. When this absis, therefore, of Mars shall appear in Virgo, who shall expect less than a strange *catastrophe* of human affairs in the commonwealth, monarchy and kingdom of England? There will then, either in or about these times, or within ten years, more or less, of that time, appear in this kingdom so strange a revolution of fate, so *grand a catastrophe*, and great mutation unto this monarchy and government as never yet appeared; of which, as the times now stand, I have no liberty or encouragement to deliver any opinion. *Only, it will be ominous to London, unto her merchants at sea, to her traffique at land, to her poor, to her rich, to all sorts of peop'e inhabiting in her or her liberties*, BY REASON OF SUNDRY FIRES AND A PLAGUE."

This is the prediction which, in 1666, led to Lilly's being examined by a committee of the House of Commons; not, as has been supposed, that he might "discover by the stars who were the authors of the Fire of London," but because the precision with which he was thought to have foretold the events gave birth to a suspicion that he was already acquainted with them, and privy to the (supposed) machinations which had brought about the catastrophe. Curran says there are two kinds of prophets—those who are really inspired and those who prophecy events which they themselves intend to bring about. Upon this occasion poor Lilly had the ill-luck to be deemed of the latter class.

Puritan Surnames.

The following names are given in Lower's English sirnames, as specimens of the names of the old Puritans in England about the year 1658. They are taken from a jury list in Sussex county:—

Faint-not Hewett.	Accepted Trevor.
Redeemed Compton.	Stand-fast-on-high Stringer.
God-reward Smart.	Called Lower.
Earth Adams.	Be-courteous Cole.
Meek Brewer.	Search-the-Scriptures Morton.
Repentance Avis.	Return Spelman.
Kill-sin Pimple.	Fly-debate Roberts.
Be-faithful Joiner.	Hope-for Bending.
More-fruit Flower.	Weep-not Billing.
Grace-ful Harding.	Elected Mitchell.
Seek-wisdom Wood.	The-peace-of-God Knight.
Fight-the-good-fight of Faith.	Make-peace Heaton.

Curious Old Memorandum.

We have supposed that no record of our Saviour's life older than the New Testament was known to exist; but it seems that a venerable journal is carefully preserved in Nablous (ancient Samaria), in which the following item appears in the handwriting of one of the Samaritan high priests:—

"In the year from Adam 4281, in the nineteenth year of my pontificate, Jesus, the Son of Mary, was crucified at Jerusalem."

This curious and interesting record was shown by the present high priest, who keeps it among the archives of his church, to Dr. El Kary, a Protestant missionary of Jewish descent and a native of Nablous. The doctor learned that the old journals of the priests of the Samaritan synagogue are still in existence, dating back to fifty or sixty years before Christ was born. It was the custom, he says, of all the high priests to set down in their books any notable events that happened during their term of office. He also learned that the tenth Samaritan high priest was named Shaboth, who lived in the days of our Saviour, and it was this Shaboth who wrote the record quoted above.

It will be remembered that Jesus visited Samaria in the early part of His ministry, where He first talked with the woman at Jacob's well, and afterwards stayed two days in the city, where He attracted public attention to His preaching, and won many followers. During those days Shaboth may have become personally acquainted with Him, and, though far from being His disciple, he would naturally follow Jesus' after-history and movements with considerable interest.

We gather the above account from the letter of an Eastern correspondent to the *Advance* (Chicago), who spent some time in Nablous, and received the statements from Dr. El Kary.

Double-Entendre.

This double-entendre was originally published in a Philadelphia newspaper à hundred years ago. It may be read three different ways: First, let the whole be read in the order in which it is written; second, read the lines downward on the left of each comma in every line; third, in the same manner on the right of each comma. In the first reading the Revolutionary cause is condemned, and by the others it is encouraged and lauded—

Hark! Hark! the trumpet sounds, the din of war's alarms,
O'er seas and solid grounds, doth call us all to arms;
Who for King George doth stand, their honors soon shall shine;
Their ruin is at hand, who with the Congress join.
The acts of Parliament, in them I much delight,
I hate their cursed intent, who for the Congress fight;

The Tories of the day, they are my daily toast, .
They soon will sneak away, who independence boast;
Who non-resistance hold, they have my hand and heart,
May they for slaves be sold, who act a Whiggish part;
On Mansfield, North and Bute, may daily blessings pour,
Confusion and dispute, on Congress evermore;
To North and British lord, may honors still be done,
I wish a block or cord, to General Washington.

Changes of Signification.

The meaning of the word *wretch* is one not generally understood. It was originally, and is now, in some parts of England, used as a term of fondest tenderness. This is not the only instance in which words in their present general acceptation bear a very opposite meaning to what they did in other times. The word *wench*, formerly, was not used in the low and vulgar acceptation that it now is.

Don Quixote's Sheep.

Don Quixote's mistaking two flocks of sheep for two armies is not without parallel. In Ariosto's Orlando Furioso, written 1516, the hero, in his madness, falls foul of a flock of sheep.

Still more ancient is "Ajax Mad," a tragedy founded on the madness of Ajax, because of the armor of Hector being awarded to Ulysses instead of himself. In his insanity, Ajax fell upon a flock of sheep, driven at night into the camp, supposing it to be an army led by Ulysses and the sons of Atreus. On discovering his mistake he stabs himself.

The Oldest Ballad.

The earliest English ballad is supposed to be the "Cuckoo Song," which commences in the following style:—

> " Sumer is ıncumen in
> Lhude sing cuccu,
> Groweth sed, and bloweth med,
> And sprigth ye wede nu,
> Singe cuccu."

Two Certificates of Gretna-Green Marriages.

" This is to sartfay all persons that may be consern'd, that A. B., from the parish of C. in the county of D., and E. F., from the parish of G., in the county of H., and both comes before me and declares themselves both to be single persons, and now mayried by the form of the Kirk of Scotland, and agreible to the Church of England, and givine ondre my hand, this 18th day of March 1793."

"Kingdom of Scotland,
"County of Dumfries,
"Parish of Gretna:

"These are to certify, to all whom it may concern, that John N——, from the parish of Chatham, in the County of Kent, and Rosa H——, from the parish of St. Maries, in the County of Nottingham, being both here now present, and having declared to me that they are single persons, but having now been married conformable to the Laws of the Church of England, and agreeable to the Kirk of Scotland. As witness our hands at Springfield, this 4th day of October, 1822.

"Witness me,
David Lang.

" Witness,
Jane Rae.
John N——.

John Ainsle.
Rosa H——."

Swift's Latin Puns.

Among the nugæ of Dean Swift are his celebrated Latin puns. They consist entirely of Latin words, but, by allowing for false spelling, and running the words into each other, the sentences make good sense in English. The subjoined is one of his best—

Mollis abuti,	Moll is a beauty.
Has an acuti,	Has an acute eye.
No lasso finis,	No lass so fine is.
Molli divinis.	Molly divine is.
Omi de armis tres,	O my dear mistress.
Imi na dis tres,	I'm in distress.
Cantu disco ver	Can't you discover.
Meas alo ver?	Me as a lover?

Rhyming Charter.

The following grant of William the Conqueror may be found in Stowe's *Chronicle* and in Blount's *Ancient Tenures:*

HOPTON, IN THE COUNTY OF SALOP.

To the Heyrs Male of the Hopton, lawfully begotten.

From me and from myne, to thee and to thyne,
While the water runs, and the sun doth shine,
For lack of heyrs to the king againe,
I, William, King, the third year of my reign,
Give to the Norman hunter,
To me that art both line (*) and deare,
The Hop and the Hoptoune,
And all the bounds up and downe,
Under the earth to hell,
Above the earth to heaven,
From me and from myne,
To thee and to thyne;

As good and as faire
As ever they myne were.
To witness that this is sooth,†
I bite the white wax with my tooth,
Before Judd, Marode and Margery,
And my third son Henery,
For one bow, and one broad arrow,
When I come to hunt upon the Yarrow.

Accidental Rhymes.

In President Lincoln's last inaugural address occurs the following instance of involuntary rhyme:—

" Fondly do we hope,
Fervently do we pray,
That this mighty scourge of war
May speedily pass away;
Yet, if it be God's will
That it continue until—"

And here the rhyme ceases. Cicero's prose shows, in places, similar instances of involuntary rhyme.

Cæsar's Wife must be above Suspicion.

No doubt this proverb originated from a passage in Suetonius, which says that "the name of Pompeia, the wife of Julius Cæsar, having been mixed up with an accusation against P. Clodius, her husband divorced her; not, as he said, because he believed the charge against her, but because he would have those belonging to him as free from suspicion as from crime."

Oddly Addressed Letters.

On one occasion a letter arrived by post in London,

* Related, or by lineage.   † True.

directed to "Sromfridevi, Angleterre." No such person had ever been heard of; but, on a little consideration, and judging from the sound, it was obvious that the foreign writer of the letter meant Sir Humphrey Davy, and such proved to be the case. Some years since there was returned to the French Dead Letter Office a letter which had gone the round of every seaport in the Levant, and the ambiguity of whose superscription had baffled a legion of postmasters. It was addressed, "J. Dubois, Sultan Crete," and was intended for J. Dubois *Surle* Tancrede, a quartermaster on board of the ship *Tancrede*. The name and address had been written just as they had sounded to the ear. A letter addressed as follows arrived safely at its destination:—

Wood,
John,
Mass.

It was for John *Under*wood, *Andover*, Massachusetts.

Amusements of some Learned Men.

Tycho Brake polished glass for spectacles, and made mathematical instruments; D'Andilly delighted in forest trees; Balzac, in manufacturing crayons; Pieresc, in his medals and antiques; the Abbé de Marolles, in engravings. Rohault's greatest recreation was in watching different mechanics at their labor; Arnauld and Warburton read trashy novels for recreation; Montaigne fondled his cat; Cardinal Richelieu enjoyed leaping.

Kant's Eccentricity.

Kant was probably the profoundest of metaphysicians that the world has yet seen. It was his custom, when deeply

engaged upon some abstruse topic, to walk backward and forward, upon a moonlight evening, along the avenue (bordered
on each side with magnificent trees) approaching his house.
He was observed, on one occasion, as he slowly, in deep
meditation, moved backward and forward along the avenue,
to leap over the *shadows* of the trees as they cast themselves
before him in his meditative walk. The delusion was strong
upon him that these same shadows were *ditches*, and that it
was incumbent upon him that he should *clear* them, and that
precisely in the way he did. Such are the occasional abber-
rations of true genius.

Death Warrant of the Saviour.

Of the many interesting relics brought to light by the
researches of antiquarians, none could be more interesting to
Christians than the following, which is faithfully transcribed—
"Sentence by Pontius Pilate, acting
Governor of Lower Galilee, stating that
Jesus of Nazareth shall suffer death
On the cross.
In the year seventeen of the Emperor Tiberius Cæsar, and
the 27th day of March, the city of the holy Jerusalem—Annas
and Caiaphas being priests, sacrificators of the people of God—
Pontius Pilate, Governor of Lower Galilee, sitting in the
presidential chair of the prætory, condemns Jesus of Nazareth
to die on the cross between two thieves, the great and notorious evidence of the people saying—
1. Jesus is a seducer.
2. He is seditious.
3. He is the enemy of the law.
4. He calls himself falsely the Son of God.
5. He calls himself falsely the King of Israel.
6. He entered into the temple followed by a multitude
bearing palm branches in their hands.

Orders the first centurian, Quilius Cornelius, to lead him to the place of execution.

Forbids any person whatsoever, either poor or rich, to oppose the death of Jesus Christ.

The witnesses who signed the condemnation of Jesus are—

1. Daniel Robani, a Pharisee.
2. Joannus Robani.
3. Raphael Robani.
4. Capet, a citizen.

Jesus shall go out of the city of Jerusalem by the gate of Struenus."

The foregoing is engraved on a copper plate, on the reverse of which is written, "A similar plate is sent to each tribe." It was found in an antique marble vase, while excavating in the ancient city of Aquilla, in the kingdom of Naples, in 1810, and was discovered by the Commissioners of Arts of the French Army. At the expedition of Naples, it was enclosed in a box of ebony and preserved in the sacristy of the Carthusians. The French translation was made by the Commissioners of Arts. The original is in the Hebrew language.

Quaint Recipes.

The following recipes are taken from a work entitled "New Curiosities in Art and Nature, or a collection of the most valuable Secrets in all Arts and Sciences. Composed and Experimented by Sieur Lemery, Apothecary to the French King. London, 1711."

To Make one Wake or Sleep.—You must cut off, dexterously, the head of a toad alive, and at once, and let it dry, observing that one eye be shut and the other open; that which is found open makes one wake, and that shut causes sleep, by carrying it about one.

Preservative against the Plague.—Take three or four great toads, seven or eight spiders, and as many scorpions, put them into a pot well stopp'd, and let them lye some time; then add virgin-wax, make a good fire till all become a liquor; then mingle them all with a spatula, and make an ointment, and put it into a silver box well stopp'd, being well assured that while you carry it about you, you will never be infected with the plague.

These recipes indicate the delusion which prevailed with respect to certain nostrums as late as 1711.

Chronological Table of Remarkable Events.

The following curious table is taken from Arthur Hopton's "Concordancie of Years," 1615:—

1077—A blazing star on Palm Sunday, near the sun.

1100—The yard (measure) made by Henry I.

1116—The moone seemed turned into bloud.

1128—Men wore haire like women.

1180—Paris in France, and London in Englande, paued, and thatching in both left, because all Luberick was spoiled thereby with fire.

1189—Robin Hood and Little John lived. This yeare London obtained to be gouerned by Sheriffes and Maiors.

1205—By reason of a frost from January to March wheate was sold for a marke the quarter, which before was at twelve pence.—*Anno Regni* 6. John.

1209—London bridge builded with stone; and this yeare the citizens of London had a grant to choose them a maior.

1227—The citizens of London had libertie to hunt a certain distance about the citie, and to pass toll-free through England.

1231—Thunder lasted fifteen daies; beginning the morrow after St. Martin's day.

1233—Four sunnes appeared, beside the true sunne, of a red colour.

1235—The Jews of Norwich stole a boy and circumcised him, minding to have him crucified at Easter.

1247—The king farmed Queene-hiue for fifty pounds per annum, to the citizens.

1252—Great tempests upon the sea, and fearful; and this year the king (Henry III.) granted, that wheretofore the citizens of London were to present the maior before the king, wheresoeuer he were, that now barons of the exchequer should serue (serve).

1292—The Jews corrupting England with vsury, had first a badge giuen them to weare, that they might be knowne, and after were banished to the number of 150,000 persons.

1313—This yeare the king of France burned all his leporous and pocky people, as well men as women; for that he supposed they had poysoned the waters, which caused his leprosie. About this time, also, the Jews had a purpose to poyson all the Christians, by poysoning all their springs.

1361—Men and beasts perished in diuers places with thunder and lightning, and fiends were seene speake unto men as they trauelled.

1386—The making of gunnes found; and rebels in Kent and Essex, who entered London, beheaded all lawyers, and burnt houses and all bookes of law.

1388—Picked shoes, tyed to their knees with siluer chains, were vsed. And women with long gownes rode in side-saddles, like the queen, that brought side-saddles first to England; for before they rode astrid.

1401—Pride exceeding in monstrous apparrell.

1411—Guildhall in London begun.
1417—A decree for lantherne and candle-light in London.
1427—Rain from the 1st of Aprill to Hollontide.

Hymn in the Form of a Cross.

The following hymn was composed by a Christian monk during the middle ages:—

THE CROSS.

Blest they who seek
While in their youth,
With   spirit   meek,
The way of truth.
To them the sacred Scriptures now display
Christ as the only true and living way;
His precious blood on Calvary was given
To make them heirs of endless bliss in heaven.
And e'en on earth the child of God can trace
The glorious blessings of his Saviour's face.
For them He bore
His Father's frown,
For them He wore
The thorny crown;
Nailed to the cross,
Endured its   pain
That His life's loss
Might be their gain.
Then haste to choose
That better part,
Nor dare refuse
The Lord your heart,
Lest He declare—
"I know you not!"
And deep despair
Shall be your lot.
Now look to Jesus who on Calvary died,
And trust on Him alone who there was crucified.

Curious Piece of Antiquity, on the Crucifixion of our Saviour and the two Thieves.

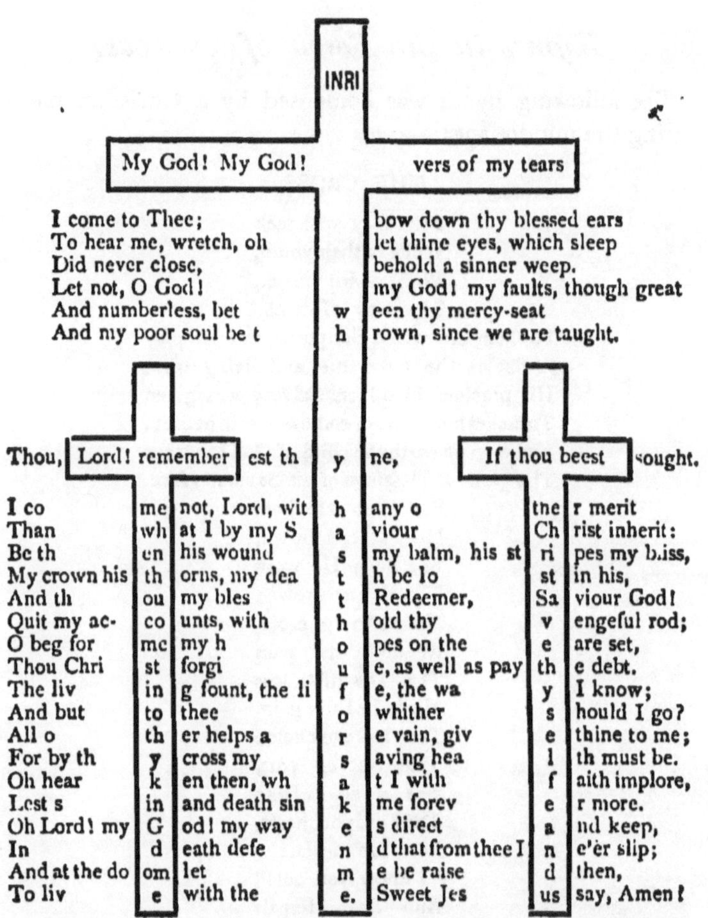

EXPLANATION.

The middle cross represents our Saviour; those on either side, the two thieves. On the top and down the middle cross are our Saviour's expression, "My God! My God! why hast thou forsaken me?" and on the top of the cross is the Latin inscription "INRI"—Jesus Nazarenus Rex Judæorum, *i. e.* Jesus of Nazareth, King of the Jews. Upon the cross on the right-hand is the prayer of one of the thieves:—"Lord! remember me when thou comest into thy kingdom." On the left-hand cross is the saying, or reproach, of the other: "If thou beest the Christ, save thyself and us." The whole, comprised together, makes a piece of excellent poetry, which is to be read across all the columns, and makes as many lines as there are letters in the alphabet. It is perhaps one of the most curious pieces of composition to be found on record.

Copy of a Letter written by Cardinal Richelieu to the French Ambassador at Rome.

First read the letter across, then double it in the middle, and read the first column.

SIR.—Mons. Compigne, a Savoyard by birth, is the man who will present to you this letter. He is one of the most meddling persons that I have ever known He has long earnestly solicited me to give him a suitable character, which I have accordingly granted to his importunity; for, believe me, Sir, I should be sorry that you should be misinformed of his real character; as some other gentlemen have been, and those among the best of my friends; I think it my duty to advertise you to have especial attention to all he does, nor venture to say any thing before him, in any sort; for I may truly say, there is none whom I should more regret to see received and trusted in decent society. And I well know, that as soon as you shall become acquainted with him you will thank me for this my advice. Courtesy obliges me to desist from saying any thing more on this subject. a Friar of the order of Saint Benedict, as his passport to your protection, discreet, the wisest and the least or have had the pleasure to converse with. to write to you in his favor, and together with a letter of credence; his real merit, rather I must say, than to his modesty is only exceeded by his worth, wanting in serving him on account of being I should be afflicted if you were misled on that score, who now esteem him, wherefore, and from no other motive that you are most particularly desired, to show him all the respect imaginable, that may either offend or displease him no man I love so much as M. Compigne, neglected, as no one can be more worthy to be Base, therefore, would it be to injure him. are made sensible of his virtues, and you will love him as I do; and then The assurance I entertain of your urging this matter to you further, or Believe me, Sir, &c., RICHELIEU.

Passage through the Isthmus of Panama,
Suggested Three Hundred Years Ago.

In the Town Library (*Stadt Bibliothek*) of Nuremberg is preserved an interesting globe, made by John Schoner, professor of mathematics in the gymnasium there, A. D. 1520. It is very remarkable that the passage through the Isthmus of Panama, so much sought after in later times, is, on this old globe, carefully delineated.

A False Conclusion.

Amongst the *deliramenta* of the learned, which have amused mankind, the following deserves a place:—

In 1815 a noted London professor occupied a window which overlooked the college garden. Amid the trees in the latter a number of rooks had taken up their abode. A young gentleman, who lodged in an attic opposite, frequently amused himself by shooting the rooks with a cross-bow. The professor noticed that the birds frequently dropped senseless from their perches, no sound being heard, no person being visible. It was a strange phenomenon, and he set his wits to work to account for the cause of it. At length he became fully satisfied that he had made a great ornithological discovery which would add vastly to his fame. He actually wrote a *learned treatise*, stating what he had seen, and declaring that it was a settled conviction in his mind that *rooks* were subject to *falling sickness.*

Posies from Wedding Rings.

Hamlet.—Is this a prologue, or a posy of a ring?
The following posies were transcribed by an indefatigable collector, from old wedding rings, chiefly of the seventeenth

and eighteenth centuries.   The orthography is, in most cases, altered :—

Death never parts Such loving hearts.	Joy day and night Be our delight.
'In thee, my choice, I do rejoice. 1677.	Endless as this, Shall be our bliss. 1719.
A heart content Need ne'er repent.	God alone Made us two one.
All I refuse, And thee I choose.	I change the life Of maid to wife.
In thee, dear wife, I find new life.	No gift can show The love I owe.
This ring doth bind Body and mind.	In love abide, Till death divide.

Private Expenses of Charles II.

Malone, the well-known editor of Shakespeare, possessed a curious volume—an account of the privy expenses of Charles II., kept by Baptist May.   A few extracts from Malone's transcripts are here subjoined :—

	£	s.	d.
My Lord St. Alban's bill, . . .	1,746	18	11
Lady Castlemaine's debts, . . .	1,116	1	0
For grinding cocoanuts, . . .	5	8	0
Paid Lady C., play-money, . . .	300	0	0
For a band of music, ...	50	0	0
For a receipt for chocolate . . .	227	0	0
Lady C., play-money, ...	300	0	0
Mr. Knight, for bleeding the king, . .	10	0	0
Mr. Price, for milking the asses, . .	10	0	0

Lady C., play-money, ...	300	0	0
To one that showed tumbler's tricks, .	5	7	6
For weighing the King, ...	1	0	0
The Queen's allowance, ...	1,250	0	0
Lost by the King at play on twelfth-night .	220	0	0
Nell Gwyn, ...	100	0	0
For 3,685 ribbons for healing, . . .	107	10	4
Lord Landerdale, for ballads, . . .	5	0	0
Paid what was borrowed for the Countess of Castlemaine, ...	1,650	0	0

First Brick House in Philadelphia.

The following editorial announcement is taken from the Philadelphia *Weekly Mercury* of November 30th, 1752, because it is a novelty in its way, and also affords an insight into the degree of communication which existed at the time between large towns and the provinces :—

"On Monday next the Northern Post sets out from New York, in order to perform his stage but once a fortnight, during the winter quarter; the Southern Post changes also, which will cause this paper to come out on Tuesdays during that time. The colds which have infested the Northern Colonies have also been troublesome here; few families have escaped the same, several have been carry'd off by the cold, among whom was David Brintnall, in the 77th year of his age; he was the first man that had a brick house in the city of Philadelphia, and was much esteem'd for his just and upright dealing. There goes a report here that the Lord Baltimore and his lady are arrived in Maryland, but the Southern Post being not yet come in, the said report wants confirmation."

The Pillory in Philadelphia.

Among the local items of news in the *Pennsylvania Gazette,* published in Philadelphia, and bearing date of November 4th, 1772, is recorded the following :—

"At the Mayor's Court, held in this city last week, John Underwood, for counterfeiting and passing counterfeit money, of this province, was ordered to be whipt, stand in the pillory, and have both his ears cut off and nailed to the post; others were ordered to be whipt and stand in the pillory for divers felonies, and five more to receive the discipline of the post, which was put in execution on Saturday last."

One Hundred Years too Soon.

The following appears in *Baker's Chronicle, sub anno* 1524:
"In this yeere, through bookes of prognostications, fore-showing much hurt by waters and floods, many persons withdrew themselves to high grounds for feare of drowning; specially one Bolton, prior of St. Bartholomew's, in Smithfield, builded him an house upon Harrow on the hill, and thither went and made provision for two moneths. These great waters should have fallen in February, but, no such thing happening, the astronomers excused themselves by saying, that, in the computation, they had miscounted in their number an hundred yeeres."

The Manner of Watchmen Imitating the Clock at Herrnhuth, in Germany.

VIII.—Past eight o'clock ! O, Herrnhuth, do thou ponder;
    . Eight souls in Noah's Ark were living yonder.
IX.—'Tis nine o'clock ! ye brethren, hear it striking ;
    Keep hearts and houses clean, to our Saviour's liking.
X.—Now, brethren, hear, the clock is ten and passing ;
    None rest but such as wait for Christ's embracing.

XI.—Eleven is past! Still at this hour eleven
    The Lord is calling us from earth to heaven.
XII.—Ye brethren, hear, the midnight clock is humming;
    At midnight our great Bridegroom will be coming.
I.—Past one o'clock ! The day breaks out of darkness;
    Great Morning Star appear, and break our hardness.
II.—' Tis two ! On Jesus wait this silent season,
    Ye two so near related, Will and Reason.
III.—The clock is three ! The blessed three doth merit
    The best of praise, from body, soul and spirit.
IV.—' Tis four o'clock! When three make supplication,
    The Lord will be the fourth on that occasion.
V.—Five is the clock ! Five virgins were discarded,
    While five with wedding garments were rewarded.
VI.—The clock is six, and I go off my station.
    Now, brethren, *watch yourselves for your salvation.*

Household Rules in the Sixteenth Century.

From Sir J. Harrington's (the translator of Ariosto) rules for servants, we obtain a very clear conception of the internal government of a country gentleman's house in 1566—

A servant who is absent from prayers to be fined.

For uttering an oath, 1*d.*; and the same sum for leaving a door open.

A fine of 2*d.* from Michaelmas to Lady Day, for all who are in bed after seven, or out after nine.

A fine of 1*d.* for any bed unmade, fire unlit, or candle-box uncleaned, after eight.

A fine of 4*d.* for a man detected teaching the children obscene words.

A fine of 1*d.* for any man waiting without a trencher, or who is absent at a meal.

For any one breaking any of the butler's glass, 12*d.*

A fine of 2*d*. for any one who has not laid the table for dinner by half-past ten, or the supper by six.

A fine of 4*d*. for any one absent without leave.

For any man striking another, a fine of 1*d*.

For any follower visiting the cook, 1*d*.

A fine of 1*d*. for any man appearing in a foul shirt, untied shoes, or torn doublet.

A fine of 1*d*. for any stranger's room left for four hours after he has dressed.

A fine of 1*d*. if the hall be not cleansed by eight in winter and seven in summer.

The porter to be fined 1*d*. if the court-gate be not shut during meals.

A fine of 3*d*. if the stairs be not cleaned every Friday after dinner.

All these fines were deducted by the steward at the quarterly payment of wages.

Hindoo Oaths.

The Hindoos regard the Ganges as a sacred river. It is a common practice in British Courts to "swear" Hindoo witnesses upon the waters of the Ganges, just as Christians are sworn upon the Bible.

Saturday a Fatal Day to the Royal Family of England.

Saturday has been a fatal day to the royal family of England during the last hundred and sixty years, as is shown by the following list :—

William III. died Saturday, March 18th, 1702.

Queen Anne died Saturday, August 1st, 1714.

George I. died Saturday, June 10th, 1727.
George II. died Saturday, October 25th, 1760.
George III. died Saturday, January 29th, 1820.
George IV. died Saturday, June 26th, 1830.
Duchess of Kent died Saturday, March 16th, 1861.
Prince Albert died Saturday, December 14th, 1861.
Princess Alice died Saturday, December 14th, 1878.

Edicts Against Fiddlers.

An idea may be formed of the strictness with which all popular amusements were prohibited when the Puritans had the ascendency, from the fact that in 1656–7 Oliver Cromwell prohibited all persons called fiddlers or minstrels from playing, fiddling or making music in any inn, ale-house or tavern, etc. If they proffered themselves, or offered to make music, they were adjudged to be rogues and vagabonds, and were to be proceeded against as such.

John O'Gaunt's Will.

Perhaps the shortest deed of land by a will in the world is the following:—

> "I, John of Gaunt,
>   Do give and do grant
>   To John of Burgoyne
>   And the heirs of his loin,
>   Both Sutton and Potton
>   Until the world's rotten."

It is by this tenure, it is said, that the estates of Sutton and Potton, in the county of Bedford, England, are now held by the house of Burgoyne.

Eccentric Will.

Mr. Tuke, of Wath, near Rotherham, England, who died in 1810, bequeathed one penny to every child that attended his funeral (there came from six to seven hundred); 1*s.* to every poor woman in Wath; 10*s.* 6*d.* to the ringers to ring one peal of grand bobs, which was to strike off while they were putting him into the grave. To his natural daughter, £4 4*s.* per annum. To his old and faithful servant, Joseph Pitt, £21 per annum. To an old woman who had for eleven years tucked him up in bed, £1 1*s.* only. Forty dozen penny loaves to be thrown from the church leads at twelve o'clock on Christmas day forever. Two handsome brass chandeliers for the church, and £20 for a set of new chimes.

Curious Custom at Strasbourg.

At Strasbourg they exhibit a large French horn, the history of which is as follows:—

About four hundred years ago the Jews formed a conspiracy to betray the city, and with this identical horn they intended to give the enemy notice when to attack. The plot, however, was discovered; many of the Jews were burnt alive; the rest were plundered of their money and effects, and banished the town. This horn is sounded twice every night from the battlements of the steeple in gratitude for the deliverance. The Jews deny the facts of this story, excepting the murdering and pillaging of their countrymen. They say the whole story is fabricated to furnish a pretext for the robberies and murders, and assert that the steeple of Strasbourg, as has been said of the monument of London,

"Like a tall bully lifts the head and lies."

Tooth-Picks.

In the fourteenth century it was the fashion to carry tooth-picks of silver suspended round the neck by a chain.

Phantom Menageries.

"The Magick of Kirami, King of Persia, and of Harpocration," printed in the year 1685, contains the following:—

"The hyena is a four-footed animal, savage and ambiguous; for this creature is born female, and, after a year, turns male, and then, for the next year, turns female again, and brings forth and gives suck; and the gall of this animal, being sweet, has efficacy for a miracle; and a great miracle is made of it; and this is the composition: Take the eyes of the fish glaucus, and the right eye of the said hyena, and all that is liquid of the said hyena; dissolve all together, and pot it up in a glass vessel, covering it well. If, therefore, you will show a great miracle, when you have set a light, mix the fat of any creeping thing, or four-footed beast you please, with a little of the foresaid composition; if you anoint the wick of the lamp or candle, they will think it is the beast of which it is the fat, whether of a lion, bull, serpent, or any other creature. If you put a little of the confection upon burning coals, in the middle of the house, the beast will appear whose fat you mixed with it. And you may do the same with birds. And if you mix a little sea-water with the composition, and sprinkle among the guests, they will all fly, thinking that the sea is in the midst of them."

Curious Law.

The following curious law was enacted during the reign of Richard I., for the government of those going by sea to the Holy Land: "He who kills a man on shipboard, shall be bound to the dead body and thrown into the sea; if the man is killed on shore, the slayer shall be bound to the dead body and buried with it. He who shall draw his knife to strike another, or who shall have drawn blood from him, to lose his hand; if he shall have only struck with the palm of the hand, without drawing blood, he shall be thrice ducked in the sea."

Curious Historical Coincidence.

The following curious historical coincidence has been remarked in the life of Thomas a-Becket, who was appointed Archbishop of Canterbury by Henry II:—

The dignity was conferred upon him on a Tuesday; Tuesday brought him face to face with the peers of Northampton; he was banished from England on a Tuesday; he had a celestial visit on a Tuesday, foretelling his "martyrdom;" he came home from exile on a Tuesday; he was slain at the altar on a Tuesday, and was canonized as a saint on a Tuesday.

Born within the Sound of Bow Bells.

One of the most celebrated peals of bells in London is that of St. Mary-le-bow, Cheapside, which forms the basis of a proverbial expression meant to mark emphatically a London nativity. Brand speaks of a substantial endowment by a citizen for the ringing of Bow-bells every morning to wake up the London apprentices.

Refreshments for the Pulpit.

In the books of Darlington parish church, the following items appear, which show that, in the olden time, provision was made for comforting the inner man:—

"Six quarts of sack to the minister who preached when he had no minister to assist, 9*s.*; for a quart of sack bestowed on Jillett, when he preached, 2*s.* 6*d.*; for pint of brandy when George Bell preached here, 1*s.* 4*d.*; for a stranger who preached, a dozen of ale. When the Dean of Durham preached here, spent in a treat in the house, 3*s.* 6*d.*"

Birthdays.

It is not generally known that the custom of keeping birthdays is many thousand years old. It is recorded in the fortieth chapter of Genesis, twentieth verse: "And it came to pass the third day, which was Pharaoh's birthday, that he made a feast unto all his servants."

Toppling Flower Pots.

An Act of Parliament was passed to "put down" the flower pots, "which were accustomed to topple on the *walkers'* heads, from the windows of houses wherein flower-fanciers dwelt."

Electioneering in 1640.

In Sir Henry Slingsby's diary is the following entry respecting the election at Knaresborough, in 1640: "There is an evil custom at such elections, to bestow wine on all the town, which cost me sixteen pounds at least."

Monks Ordered to Shave.

In the year 1200 the Council of Lateran ordered the monks to shave off their beards, "lest in the ceremony of receiving the sacrament, the beard might touch the bread and wine, or crumbs and drops fall and stick upon it."

Odd Bill for Repairs.

One meets with curious things in the old church registers of England. The subjoined, in the Record Office of Winchester Cathedral, dated 1182, is certainly unique. It is a bill for work done:—

	s.	d.
To soldering and repairing St. Joseph, . .	0	8
To cleaning and ornamenting the Holy Ghost, .	0	6
To repairing the Virgin Mary and cleaning the child,	4	8
To screwing a nose on the Devil, and putting in the hair on his head, and placing a new joint in his tail,	5	6

Antiquity of Riddles.

Riddles are of the highest antiquity. The oldest one on record is in the book of Judges, xiv. 14-18. We are told by Plutarch that the girls of his time worked at netting or sewing, and the most ingenius made riddles. The following riddle is attributed to Cleobolus, one of the seven wise men of Greece, who lived about 570 years before the birth of Christ:—

"There is a father with twice six sons; these sons have thirty daughters apiece, parti-colored, having one cheek white and the other black, who never see each other's faces, nor live more than twenty-four hours."

Cashing Lottery Prizes.

In the State Lottery of 1739, tickets, chances and shares were "bought and sold by Richard Shergold, printer, at his office at the Union Coffee-house over and against the Royal Exchange, Cornhill." He advertised that he kept numerical books during the drawing, and a book wherein buyers might register their numbers at sixpence each; that *fifteen per cent. was to be deducted* out of the prizes, which were to be paid at the bank in fifty days after the drawing. The heavy percentage demanded occasioned the following epigram :—

> "This lottery can never thrive,"
> Was broker heard to say,
> "For who but fools will ever give
> Fifteen per cent. to play?"
>
> A sage, with his accustomed grin,
> Replied, "I'll stake my doom,
> That if but half the fools come in
> The wise will find no room !"

Lottery for Women in India.

Advertisement.—BE IT KNOWN, that Six Fair Pretty Young Ladies, with two sweet and engaging young children, lately imported from Europe, having roses of health blooming on their cheeks and joy sparkling in their eyes, possessing amiable manners and highly accomplished, whom the most indifferent cannot behold without expressions of rapture, are to be RAFFLED FOR next door to the British gallery. Scheme: *Twelve tickets* at twelve rupees each; the highest of the three throws takes the most fascinating, &c., &c.—*Calcutta Newspaper of September 3rd,* 1818.

Ancient Lottery.

In 1612, King James I., "in special favour for the plantation of English colonies in Virginia, granted a Lottery to be held at the west end of St. Paul's; whereof one Thomas

Sharplys, a taylor of London, had the chief prize, which was four thousand crowns in fair plate."—*Baker's Chronicles*.

Child Played For.

In October, 1735, a child of James and Elizabeth Leesh, of Chester-le-street, in the county of Durham, was *played for at cards*, at the sign of the Salmon, one game, four shillings against the child, by Henry and John Trotter, Robert Thomson and Thomas Ellison, which was won by the latter two and delivered to them accordingly.—*Syke's Local Records*, page 79.

Lotteries.

The change in public opinion respecting lotteries is strikingly illustrated by the following entry in the day-book kept by the Rev. Samuel Seabury, father of the first Protestant Episcopal Bishop in the United States: "June, 1768. The ticket number 5866, by the blessing of God, in the Lighthouse and Public Lottery of New York, appointed by law, Anno Domini, 1763, drew in my favor £500 0s. 0d., of which I received £425, 0s. 0d., which, with the deduction of fifteen per cent., makes £500, for which I now record to my Posterity my thanks and praise to Almighty God the giver of all good gifts. Amen!"

Babes in the Wood.

This popular legend was a disguised recital of the reported murder of his young nephews by Richard III. Throughout the tale there is a marked resemblance to several leading facts connected with the king and his brother's children, as well as a correspondence with historical details. In an old black-letter copy of the ballad there is a rude representation of a stag, which is significant, because a stag was the badge of the unfortunate Edward V.

A Little Bird Told Me.

This expression comes from Ecclesiastes x. 20: "For a bird of the air shall carry the voice, and that which hath wings shall tell the matter."

Dead Drunk for Twopence.

From the "Gentleman's Magazine" (1736), we learn that at some of the taverns where the poorer classes drank to excess, the signs bore the following inscription: "*Drunk for a penny, dead drunk for twopence, clean straw for nothing.*" This record gives reality to the inscription in Hogarth's print of "Gin-lane."

How the Prophecy of the Destruction of Bath came About.

On the 30th of March, 1809, the destruction of the city of Bath was to have been effected by a convulsion of the earth, which should cause "Beaconhill to meet Beechen Cliff." This inauspicious juncture was said to have been foretold by an old woman who had derived her information from an angel. This reported prophecy rendered many of the inhabitants uneasy, and instigated crowds of visitors to quit the city. The portentous hour—twelve o'clock—passed, and the believers were ashamed of their credulity. The alarm is said to have originated with two noted cock-feeders, who lived near the before-mentioned hills; they had been at a public

house, and, after much boasting on both sides, made a match
to fight their favorite cocks on Good Friday; but fearing the
magistrates might interfere, if it became public, they named
the cocks after their respective walks, and in the agreement
it was specified that "Mount Beacon would meet Beechen
Cliff, precisely at 12 o'clock on Good Friday." The match
was mentioned with cautions of secresy to their sporting
friends, who repeated it in the same terms, and with the same
caution, until it came to the ears of some credulous beings,
who took the words in their plain sense; and, as stories seldom
lose by being repeated, each added what fear or fancy framed,
until the report became a marvellous prophecy, which in its
intended sense was fulfilled; for the cocks of Mount Beacon
and Beechen Cliff met and fought, and left their hills behind
them on their ancient sites, to the comfort and joy of multitudes who had been disturbed by the epidemical prediction.
—*Hone.*

Drop-Letter Retort.

An old gentleman by the name of Page, having found a
young lady's glove at a watering place, presented it to her
with the following couplet:—

> "If you from your glove take the letter G,
> Your glove leaves love, which I devote to thee."

To which the lady returned the following answer:—

> "If from your page you take the letter P,
> Your page is age, and that won't do for me."

Dean Swift's Marriage Ceremony.

Dean Swift was applied to, at a late hour on a stormy night,
after he had gone to bed, by a run-away couple, to be married.

He answered the call from his upper chamber window. He told them that as he was undressed, the weather very threatening, and they, he presumed, in a hurry, he would marry them as they stood. After asking the necessary questions, he said—

> " Under this window, in stormy weather,
> I marry this man and woman together;
> Let none but Him who rules the thunder
> Put this man and woman asunder."

Pious Guide-Posts.

In olden times the guide-posts not only pointed out the road, but furnished texts and maxims upon which to meditate. The following inscriptions were upon guide-posts in Devonshire, England:—

To Woodbury, Topsham, Exeter.—Her ways are ways of pleasantness, and all her paths are peace.

To Brixton, Ottery, Honiton.—O hold up our goings in thy paths, that our footsteps slip not.

To Otterton, Sidmouth, A. D. 1743.—O that our ways were made to direct, that we might keep thy statutes.

To Budleigh.—Make us to go in the paths of thy commandments, for therein is our desire.

A Bogus Dragon.

A curious anecdote of Jacob Bobart, keeper of the physic garden of Oxford, England, occurs in one of Grey's notes to *Hudibras:* "He made a dead rat resemble the common picture of a dragon, by altering its head and tail, and thrusting in taper sharp sticks, which distended the skin on each side till it resembled wings. He let it dry as hard as possible. The learned immediately pronounced it a dragon, and one of them sent an accurate description of it to Dr.

Magliabecchi, librarian to the Grand Duke of Tuscany; several fine copies of verses were written on so rare a subject. At last Mr. Bobart owned the cheat; however, it was looked upon as a master-piece of art, and, as such, was deposited in the museum.''

Donation to a Fair.

On one occasion Oliver Wendell Holmes sent a letter to the post-office of a ladies' fair at Pittsfield.   On the first page he wrote—

> '' Fair lady, whoso'er thou art,
>   Turn this poor leaf with tenderest care,
> And hush, Oh hush, thy breathing heart—
>   The *one* thou lovest will be there.''

On turning the ''poor leaf'' there was found a one dollar bill with the subjoined verse—

> '' Fair lady, lift thine eyes and tell
>   If this is not a truthful letter?
> This is the one (1) thou lovest well,
>   And nought (0) can make thee love it better.''

Confectionery Decorations.

Probably the ancients exceeded us in the art of decorating confectionery.   After each course in solemn feasts there was a ''subtilty.''   Subtilties were representations of castles, giants, saints, knights, ladies and beasts, all raised in pastry, upon which legends and coat-armor were painted in their proper colors.   At the festival, on the coronation of Henry VI., in 1429, there was a ''subtilty'' of St. Edward and St. Louis, ''armed, and upon either his coat-armor, holding between them a figure of King Henry, standing also in his coat-armor, and an inscription passing from both, saying,

'Beholde twoe perfecte kynges vnder one coate-armoure.' "—
Fabyan-Dallaway's Heraldic Inq.

Superscription to a Letter.

A letter upon which the following was written, passed through the Atlanta (Ga.) post-office:—

> "Steal not this for fear of shame—
> There is no money in the same;
> True, it does a check contain,
> But 't is for baggage on a train."

In Search of a Looking-Glass.

"When I was last in Lisbon, a nun made her escape from the nunnery. The first thing for which she inquired, when she reached the house in which she was to be secreted, was a looking-glass. She had entered the convent when only five years old, and from that time had never seen her own face."
—*Southey.*

Bleeding for Nothing.

"Whereas, the majority of Apothecaries in Boston have agreed to pull down the price of Bleeding to sixpence, let these certifie that Mr. Richard Clarke, Apothecary, will bleed any body at his shop, gratis."—*Stamford Mercury*, March 28th, 1716.

An Astonished Lawyer.

A curious instance occurred of a witness confounding a counsel, at Gloucester, England, some years ago. The witness, on being asked his name, gave it as Ottiwell Woodd.

The learned counsel did not seem to catch it, though it was several times pronounced. "Spell it, sir, if you please," he said, somewhat angrily. The witness complied as follows: "O-double t-i-double you-e-double l-double you-double o-double d." The spelling confounded the lawyer more than ever, and in his confusion, amid the laughter of the court, he took the witness aside to help him to spell it after him.

Duels Fought by Clergymen.

In England, in 1764, the Rev. Mr. Hill was killed in a duel by Cornet Gardener, of the carbineers. The Rev. Mr. Bates fought two duels, and was subsequently created a baronet, and preferred to a deanery after he had fought another duel. The Rev. Mr. Allen killed a Mr. Delany in a duel in Hyde Park, without incurring ecclesiastical censure, though the judge, on account of his extremely bad conduct, strongly charged his guilt upon the jury.

A Singular Coincidence.

On the 13th of February, 1746, as the records of the French criminal jurisprudence inform us, one Jean Marie Dunbarry was brought to the scaffold for murdering his father; and, strangely enough, on the 13th of February, 1846, precisely one hundred years later, another Jean Marie Dunbarry, a great-grandson of the first-mentioned criminal, paid the same penalty for the same crime.

Tavern Screens.

Centuries ago, the doors of taverns had an interior screen, similar to those in use at the present day. Lounging was just as much in vogue.   In Clare's "Shepherd's Calender," we read—

> "Now, musing o'er the changing scene,
> Farmers behind the tavern screen
> Collect; with elbow idly press'd
> On hob, reclines the corner's guest,
> Reading the news, to mark again
> The bankrupt lists, or price of grain,
> Puffing the while his red-tipt pipe,
> He dreams o'er troubles nearly ripe;
> Yet, winter's leisure to regale,
> Hopes better times, and sips his ale."

Ancient Antipathy to Red Hair.

Ages before the time of Judas, red hair was thought a mark of reprobation, both in the case of Typhon, who deprived his brother of the sceptre in Egypt, and Nebuchadnezzar, who acquired it in expiation of his atrocities.   Even the donkey tribe suffered from this ill-omened visitation, according to the proverb of "wicked as a red ass."   Asses of that color were held in such detestation among the Copths, that every year they sacrificed one by hurling it from a high wall.

Lightning-Prints.

Lightning-prints are appearances sometimes found on the skin of men or animals that are struck by lightning, and are currently believed to be photographic representations of surrounding objects or scenery.

At Candelaria, in Cuba, in 1828, a young man was struck dead by lightning near a house, on one of the windows of which was nailed a horse-shoe; and the image of the horse-shoe was said to be distinctly printed upon the neck of the young man. On the 14th of November, 1830, lightning struck the Chateau Benatonière, in Lavendèe. At the time a lady happened to be seated on a chair in the salon, and on the back of her dress were printed minutely the ornaments on the back of the chair. In September, 1857, a peasant-girl, while herding a cow in the department of Seine-et-Marne, was overtaken by a thunder-storm. She took refuge under a tree, and the tree, the cow and herself were struck with lightning. The cow was killed, but she recovered, and on loosening her dress for the sake of respiring freely, she saw a picture of the cow upon her breast.

No Buttons but Brass Buttons.

There is a curious law extant in England in regard to brass buttons. It is, by Acts of Parliament passed in three reigns, (William III., Anne and George I.), illegal for a tailor to make, or mortal to wear, clothes with any other buttons appended thereto but buttons of brass. The law was put in force for the benefit of the button-makers of Birmingham; and it further enacts, not only that he who makes or sells garments with any but brass buttons thereto affixed, shall pay a penalty of forty shillings for every dozen, but that he shall not be able to recover the price he claims, if the wearer thinks proper to resist payment. The Act is not a dead letter. Not more than thirty years ago a Mr. Shirley sued a Mr. King for nine pounds sterling due for a suit of clothes. King pleaded non-liability on the ground of an illegal transaction, the buttons on the garments supplied being made of cloth, or bone covered with cloth, instead of glittering brass, as the law directs. The judge allowed the plea; and the defendant having thus gained a double suit without cost, immediately proceeded against the plaintiff to recover his share of the forty shillings for every dozen buttons which the poor tailor had unwittingly supplied. A remarkable feature in the case was, that the judge who admitted the plea, the barrister who set it up, and the client who profited by it, were themselves all buttoned contrary to law!

Curious Signs in New York.

One may see in the shop-windows of a Fourth avenue confectioner, "Pies Open All Night." An undertaker in the same thoroughfare advertises, "Everything Requisite for a First-class Funeral." A Bowery placard reads, "Home-made Dining Rooms, Family Oysters." A West Broadway *restaurateur* sells "Home-made Pies, Pastry and 'Oysters." A Third avenue "dive" offers for sale "Coffee and Cakes off the Griddle," and an East Broadway caterer retails "Fresh Salt Oysters" and "Larger Beer." A Fulton street tobacconist calls himself a "Speculator in Smoke," and a purveyor of summer drinks has invented a new draught, which he calls by the colicky name of "Æolian Spray." A Sixth avenue barber hangs out a sign reading "Boots Polished Inside," and on Varick street, near Carmine, there are "Lessons Given on the Piano, with use for Practice." "Cloth Cutt and Bastd" is the cabalistic legend on the front of a millinery shop on Spring street; on another street the following catches the eye: "Washin Ironin and Goin Out by the Day Done Here."

Recipes from Albertus Magnus.

"If thou wylt see that other men cannot see: Take the gall of a male cat, and the fat of a hen all whyte, and mixe them together, and anoint thy eyes, and thou shalt see it that others cannot see.

"If the hart, eye or brayne of a lapwyng or blacke plover be hanged upon a man's neck, it is profitable agaynste forgetfulnesse, and sharpeth man's understanding."—*Black letter copy—very old.*

Infamous Nankeen.

The wearing of nankeen at one time was so popular among gentlemen in England, that it also became the fashion in France. English nankeen threatened to drive all French manufactured articles of summer wear out of the market. Louis XVI., however, was equal to the emergency. He ordered all the executioners and their assistants to perform their terrible office in no other dress but one made out of nankeen, which rendered the material so "infamous" that its use was discarded.

The Military Salute.

The military salute, which consists of the hand being brought to a horizontal position over the eyebrows, has a very old origin, dating, in fact, from the very commencement of the history of the English army. Its origin is founded on the tournaments of the Middle Ages, and was as follows: After the queen of beauty was enthroned, the knights who were to take part in the sports of the day, marched past the dais on which she sat, and as they passed they shielded their eyes from the rays of her beauty.

Book-keeping in Norway.

The process of keeping accounts among the Norway lumber-men is unique in style. The time-keeper, after comparing accounts with the workman, sends him to the cashier for his wages, with the amount due to him chalked on his back; and when the cashier has paid it, he takes his receipt by brushing off the chalk-marks.

Curious Post-Office.

The smallest post-office in the world is kept in a barrel, which swings from the outermost rock of the mountains overhanging the Straits of Magellan, opposite Terra del Fuego. Every passing ship opens it to place letters in or take them out. Every ship undertakes to forward all letters in it that it is possible for them to transmit. The barrel hangs by its iron chain, beaten and battered by the winds and storms, but no locked and barred office on land is more secure.

Inordinate Self-Esteem.

Some Frenchmen who landed on the coast of Guinea, found a negro prince seated under a tree on a block of wood for his throne, and three or four negroes, armed with wooden spears, for his guards. His sable majesty anxiously inquired: "Do they talk much of me in France?"

He's a Brick.

If this is slang, it is classical slang. Of the thousands who use the expression, very few know its origin or its primitive significance. Truly, it is a heroic thing to say of a man to call him a brick. The word so used, if not twisted from its original intent, implies all that is brave, patriotic and loyal. Plutarch, in his life of Agesilaus, King of Sparta, gives us the original of the quaint and familiar expression.

On a certain occasion an ambassador from Espirus, on a diplomatic mission, was shown by the king over his capital. The ambassador knew of the monarch's fame—knew that though only nominally king of Sparta, he was ruler of Greece —and he had looked to see massive walls rearing aloft their embattled towers for the defence of the town; but he found nothing of the kind.   He marvelled much at this, and spoke of it to the king.

"Sire," he said, "I have visited most of the principal towns, and I find no walls reared for defence.   Why is this?"

"Indeed, Sir Ambassador," replied Agesilaus; "thou canst not have looked carefully.   Come with me to-morrow morning, and I will show you the walls of Sparta."

Accordingly, on the following morning, the king led his guest out upon the plain where his army was drawn up in full array, and pointing proudly to the serried hosts, he said—

"There thou beholdest the walls of Sparta—ten thousand men, and EVERY MAN A BRICK!"

Punch and Judy in 1669.

Although Punch was not originally French, he has always been greatly esteemed in France.   The following entries are found in the registers of the royal treasury:—

"Paid to Brioché, the puppet-player, for sojourning at St. Germain-en-Laye, during September, October and November, 1669, to divert the royal children, 1365 livres."

"Paid to François Daitelin, puppet-player, for the fifty-six days he remained at St. Germain, to amuse Monseigneur le Dauphin (July and August, 1669), 820 livres."

Five successive months must almost have been enough of such amusement for the royal children of France.

Offending Barbers.

On the 20th of November, 1746, fifty-one barbers were convicted before the commissioners of excise, and fined twenty pounds each, for having in their custody hair-powder not made of starch, contrary to Act of Parliament.

Primitive Tavern Signs.

In Ireland, in the taverns by the road-side, in which illicit whiskey can be obtained, the traveler is informed of the fact by a piece of turf unobtrusively placed in the window. In the Middle Ages, road-side ale houses in England were indicated by a stake projecting from the front of the house, from which some object was suspended. Sometimes a garland was hung upon the stake, to which occasional reference is made in Chaucer's poems. The bush, however, was more common than the stake, and was often composed of ivy. The saying "Good wine needs no bush," no doubt originated from this custom.

Watch-Papers.

Years ago it was the custom for watch-makers to put their business cards inside of the case. These cards were sometimes enlivened with a couplet or a verse, of each of which we subjoin a sample—

He that wears a watch, two things must do;
Pocket his *watch* and *watch* his *pocket* too.

I labor here with all my might,
To tell the hours of day and night;
Therefore, example take by me,
And serve the Lord as I serve thee.

Echo Verse.

It was a sharp bit of echo verse that the *Sunday Times* of London threw off in 1831, when tickets to hear the great violinist were very high—

What are they who pay three guineas
To hear a tune of Paganini's?
Echo—Pack o' ninnies.

Signature of the Cross.

The mark which persons who are unable to write are required to make instead of their signatures, is in the form of a cross; and this practice having formerly been followed by kings and nobles, is constantly referred to as an instance of the deplorable ignorance of ancient times. This signature is not, however, invariably a proof of ignorance. Anciently, the use of the mark was not confined to illiterate persons; for among the Saxons the mark of the cross, as an attestation of the good faith of the persons signing, was required to be attached to the signature of those who *could* write, as well as to stand in the place of the signature of those who could not write.

Simply on Account of her Name.

Herrera, the Spanish historian, records an anecdote in which the choice of a queen entirely arose from her name. When two French ambassadors negotiated a marriage between one of the Spanish princesses and Louis VIII., the names of the royal females were *Urraca* and *Blanche*. The former was the elder and the more beautiful, and intended by the Spanish court for the French monarch; but they resolutely preferred Blanche, observing that the *name* of *Urraca* would never do! And for the sake of a more mellifluous sound, they carried off the happier-named but less beautiful princess.

Richelieu's Boast.

Richelieu one day boasted among his courtiers that out of any four indifferent words he could extract matter to send any one to a dungeon. One of his attendants immediately wrote upon a card: *"One and two make three."* *"Three* make only *One!*" exclaimed the cardinal. "To the Bastile with him. It is a blasphemy against our Holy Trinity."

Curious Parallel.

The story of Alnaschar, which is in the "Arabian Nights," tells how one Alnaschar had invested all his money in a basket of glassware, which he calculated to sell at a profit, and got into a day-dream of a splendid future.

Out of the profits of his glass he was to rise into the position of a merchant-prince, with the Grand Vizier's daughter for his wife. Offended, in this day-dream, with the lady, he fancied that he would spurn her before forgiving her, and kicked out his foot, which broke all his glass and left him beggared.

Rabelais makes Echepron, an old soldier, tell the advisers of King Picrochole, who wanted him to go to war, that a shoemaker bought a ha'p'orth of milk. This he intended to make into butter, and buy a cow with the money thus obtained. In due time the cow would have a calf; this calf would be sold, and so on money would pile up, until, having become a nabob, he should wed a princess. Only, just at this crisis, the jug fell, the milk was lost, and the dreamer sneaked, supperless, to bed.

Earliest Clocks.

The first clock which appeared in Europe was probably that which Eginhard (Secretary to Charlemagne) describes as sent to his royal master by Abdallah, King of Persia. "A horologe of brass, wonderfully constructed, for the course of the twelve hours, while as many little brazen balls dropped upon bells underneath, and sounded each other." The Venetians had clocks in 872, and sent a specimen of them that year to Constantinople.

Famous Astronomical Clock.

This clock, in the Strasburg Cathedral, was invented by Isaac Habrecht, a Jewish astrologer, in 1439. He called it the "Clock of the Three Sages," because once in every hour the figures of the Three Kings of Orient came out from a niche in its side, and made a reverential bow before an image of the Virgin Mary, seated just above the dial-plate, on the front of the clock. It is built of dark wood, gilded and carved, and is sixty feet high. In shape it is somewhat similar to a church, with a tower on either side of the entrance; and these towers of the clock are encircled by spiral staircases, which are used when repairs are necessary. When Isaac Habrecht invented this wonderful clock, he meant it to run forever, always displaying to the good people of Strasburg the days of the month, phases of the sun and moon, and other celestial phenomena; and while he lived it worked admirably, but when he had been dead awhile, the clock stopped; and as nobody else understood its machinery, it had quite a vacation, which lasted until 1681, when it was repaired and improved.

It will now not only give the time of Strasburg, but every principal city in the world; also the day of the week and month, the course of the sun and planets, and all the eclipses of the sun and moon, in their regular order. In an alcove above the dial is an image of the Saviour, and every day, at noon, figures of the twelve apostles march around it and bow, while the holy image, with uplifted hands, administers a silent blessing. A cock, on the highest point of the right-hand tower, flaps his wings and crows three times; and when he stops, a beautiful chime of bells rings out familiar and very musical tunes. A figure of Time, in a niche on one side, strikes the quarter hours from twelve to one, and four figures —Childhood, Youth, Manhood and Old Age—pass slowly before him.   In a niche on the other side is an angel turning an hour-glass.

Clock that Strikes Thirteen.

The Duke of Bridgewater was very fond of watching his men at work, especially when any enterprise was on foot.   When they were boring for coal at Worsley, the duke came every morning, and looked on for a long time.   The men did not like to leave off work while he remained there, and they became so dissatisfied at having to work so long beyond the hour at which the bell rang, that Brindley had difficulty in getting a sufficient number of hands to continue the boring. On inquiry, he found out the cause and communicated it to the duke, who from that time made a point of immediately walking off when the bell rang—returning when the men had resumed work, and remaining with them usually until six o'clock.   He observed, however, that though the men dropped work promptly as the bell rang, when he was not by, they were not nearly so punctual in resuming work—some straggling in many minutes after time.   He asked to know the reason, and the men's excuse was, that though they could always hear the clock when it struck twelve, they could not so readily hear it when it struck only one.   On hearing this, the duke had the mechanism of the clock altered so as to make it strike thirteen at one o'clock, which it continues to do to this day.

Westminster Clock.

The winding up of the going part of the great clock at Westminster, London, takes ten minutes, the weight of the pendulum being six hundred and eighty pounds; but the winding up of the striking parts—the quarter part and the hour part—takes five hours each, and this has to be done twice a week. The contract cost of winding up the clock is $500 a year. The error of the clock amounts to only about one second for eighty-three days in the year, and there is probably no other clock in the world of which the same can be said.

Wonderful Clock.

Toward the end of the last century a clock was constructed by a Geneva mechanic named Droz, capable of performing a variety of surprising movements, which were effected by the figures of a negro, a shepherd and a dog. When the clock struck, the shepherd played six tunes on his flute and the dog approached and fawned upon him. This clock was exhibited to the King of Spain, who was highly delighted with the ingenuity of the artist. The king, at the request of Droz, took an apple from the shepherd's basket, when the dog started up and barked so loud that the king's dog, which was in the same room, began to bark also. We are, moreover, informed that the negro, on being asked what hour it was, answered the question in French, so that he could be understood by those present.

Vocal Clock.

The subjoined description of a curious clock is given in the journal of the Rev. J. Wesley: "On Monday, April 27, 1762, being at Lurgan, in Ireland, I embraced the opportunity, which I had long desired, of talking to Mr. Miller, the contriver of that statue which was in Lurgan when I was there before. It was the figure of an old man standing in a case, with a curtain drawn before him, over against a clock which stood on the opposite side of the room. Every time the clock struck he opened the door with one hand, drew back the curtain with the other, turned his head, as if looking round on the company, and then said, with a clear, loud, articulate voice: 'Past 1,' or 2 or 3, and so on. But so many came to see this (the like of which all allowed was not to be seen in Europe), that Mr. Miller was in danger of being ruined, not having time to attend to his own business. So, as none offered to purchase it, or reward him for his pains, he took the whole machine to pieces.''

Harrison's Clock.

In 1735, John Harrison, a rural clock-maker, invented a time-piece which scarcely ever lost five seconds in six months. To him, in 1767, was paid $100,000, as the first prize for all but an infallible time-keeper.

A Cat-Clock.

The following curious incident is to be found in Hue's "Chinese Empire:''—

"One day when we went to pay a visit to some families of Chinese Christian peasants, we met, near a farm, a young lad who was taking a buffalo to graze along our path. We asked him carelessly, as we passed, whether it was yet noon. The child raised his head to look at the sun, but it was hidden behind thick clouds, and he could read no answer there. 'The sky is so cloudy,' said he; 'but wait a moment;' and with these words he ran toward the farm, and came back a few minutes afterward with a cat in his arms. 'Look here,' said he, 'it is not noon yet;' and he showed us the cat's eyes, by pushing up the lids with his hands. We looked at the child with surprise, but he was evidently in earnest. 'Very well,' said we; 'thank you;' and we continued on our way.

"To say the truth, we had not at all understood the proceeding, but we did not wish to question the little pagan, lest he should find out that we were Europeans by our ignorance. As soon as we reached the farm, however, we made haste to ask our Christian friends whether they could tell the clock by looking into a cat's eyes. They seemed surprised at the question; but as there was no danger in confessing to them our ignorance of the properties of a cat's eyes, we related what had just taken place. That was all that was necessary; our complaisant neophytes immediately gave chase to all the cats in the neighborhood. They brought us three or four, and explained in what manner they might be made use of for watches. They pointed out that the pupils of their eyes went on constantly growing narrower until twelve o'clock, when they became like a fine line, as thin as a hair, drawn perpendicularly across the eye, and that after twelve the dilation recommenced."

Curious Time-Piece.

About 1679 Nicholas Grallier de Servierre, an old soldier who had served in the Italian army, constructed a whimsical clock. A figure of a tortoise, dropped into a plate of water, having the hours marked on the rim, would float around and stop at the proper time, telling what o'clock it was. A lizard ascended a pillar, on which the hours were marked, and pointed to the time as it advanced. A mouse did the same thing by creeping along an hour-marked cornice.

Clock Presented to Charlemagne.

The French historians describe a clock sent to Charlemagne in the year 807, by the famous eastern caliph, Haroun-al-Raschid, which was evidently furnished with some kind of wheel-work, although the moving power appears to have been produced by the fall of water. In the dial of it were twelve small doors forming the divisions for the hours, each door opened at the hour marked by the index, and let out small brass balls which, falling on a bell, struck the hours—a great novelty at that time. The doors continued open until the hour of twelve, when twelve figures, representing knights on horseback, came out and paraded around the dial-plate.

Delicate Machinery.

Machines in a watch factory will cut screws with 589 threads to an inch. These threads are invisible to the naked eye, and it takes 144,000 of the screws to make a pound. A pound of them is worth six pounds of pure gold. Lay one of them upon a piece of white paper, and it looks like a tiny steel filing.

Ancient Dials.

The dial in use among the ancient Jews differed from that in use among us. Theirs was a kind of stairs; the time of the day was distinguished, not by lines, but by steps or degrees; the shade of the sun every hour moved forward to a new degree. On the dial of Ahaz, the sun went back *degrees* or *steps*, not *lines*.

Skull Watches.

Diana of Poictiers, the mistress of Henry II., being a widow, the courtiers of the period, to ingratiate themselves in her favor, used to present her with watches in such shapes as coffins, skulls, etc., and it became the fashion to have them made in this lugubrious style. Mary, Queen of Scots, is said to have had several, and she gave one to Mary Letown, in 1587, which is still in existence. It was made by Moyse, of Blois, France, and has been thus described:—

"The watch has a silver casing in the form of a skull, which separates at the jaws so as to expose the dial, which is also of silver, occupying about the position of the palate, and is fixed in a golden circle, with the hours in Roman letters. The movement appropriately occupies the place of the brains, but is enclosed in a bell, filling the hollow of the skull, which bell is struck by the hammer to sound the hours. The case is highly ornamented with fine engravings, showing on the front of the skull Death standing between a cottage and a palace; in the rear is Time devouring all things; on one side of the upper part of the skull are Adam and Eve in the Garden of Eden, with the serpent tempting Eve; on the opposite side is the Crucifixion. Inside, on the plate or lid, is the Holy Family in the stable, with the infant Saviour in the manger, and angels ministering to him. In the distance are the Shepherds with their flocks, etc." The works are said to be in good order and to perform astonishingly well.

Book-Shaped Watch.

One of the choicest rarities of the Bernal collection is a book-shaped watch. It was made for Bogislaus XIV., Duke of Pomerania, in the time of Gustavus Adolphus. On the dial-side there is an engraved inscription of the duke and his titles, with the date 1627, and the engraving of his armorial bearings; on the back of the case there are engraved two male portraits, buildings, &c. The watch has apparently two separate movements, and a large bell; at the back, over the bell, the metal is ornamentally pierced in a circle, with a dragon and other devices. It bears the maker's name, "Dionistus Hessichti."

Cruciform Watch

In the family of Lady Fitzgerald, of England, there is a cruciform watch made in 1770, and covered with elaborate drawings of a delicate character. The centre of the dial-plate has a representation of Christ's agony in the garden, the outer compartments being occupied by the emblems of the passion, and the lowermost by a figure of Faith.

Miniature Time-Piece.

The time-piece carried by Louis XIV. of France was so small that it was set in one of that luxurious monarch's finger-rings.

Resurrection Watch.

During the reign of Catherine II. of Russia, Kalutin, a peasant, made a musical repeating watch about the size of an egg, which had within it a representation of Christ's tomb, with sentinels on guard. On pressing a spring the stone would be rolled from the tomb, the angels appear, the holy women enter the sepulchre, and the same chant which is sung in the Greek Church on Easter eve accurately performed. The watch is now in the Academy of Sciences at St. Petersburg.

Borrowing Watches.

Watches were so rarely in use in the early time of James I. that it was deemed a cause of suspicion that one was found, in 1605, upon Guy Vaux. Jonson, in his "Alchemist," tells of the loan of one to wear on a particular occasion—

> And I had lent my watch last night to one
> 'That dines to-day at the sheriff's.

Striking Watches.

Hon. Mr. Barrington mentions that a thief was detected by watches called "strikers," which he says were introduced in the reign of Charles II.; but repeating watches were worn in the time of Ben Jonson.   In his "Staple of News," we read—

> —It strikes! one, two,
> Three, four, five, six.   Enough, enough, dear watch,
> Thy pulse hath beat enough.   Now stop and rest;
> Would thou couldst make the time to do so too;
> I'll wind thee up no more.

Too Many Watches.

Watches were very common in 1638.   It is complained in the "Antipodes," a comedy of that year, that

> —Every clerk can carry
> The time of day in his pocket.

On which account a projector in the same play proposes to diminish the grievance by a

> —Project against
> The multiplicity of pocket watches.

Wearing Two Watches.

About 1770 it became the fashion to wear two watches.   In a rhyming recipe of that date, " To Make a Modern Fop," appear the lines—

> "A lofty cane, a sword with silver hilt,
> A ring, *two watches* and a snuff-box gilt."

The ladies soon adopted the fashion, but as watches were still very expensive, mock watches were often substituted.

Minute Mechanisms.

There is a cherry stone at the Salem (Mass.) Museum which contains one dozen silver spoons. The stone itself is of the ordinary size, but the spoons are so small that their shape and finish can only be distinguished by the microscope. Dr. Oliver gives an account of a cherry stone on which were carved one hundred and twenty-four heads, so distinctly that the naked eye could distinguish those belonging to popes and kings by their mitres and crowns. It was bought in Prussia for fifteen thousand dollars, and thence conveyed to England, where it was considered an object of so much value that its possession was disputed, and it became the subject of a suit in chancery. One of the Nuremberg toy-makers enclosed in a cherry stone, which was exhibited at the French Crystal Palace, a plan of Sevastopol, a railway station, and the "Messiah" of Klopstock. In more remote times, an account is given of an ivory chariot, constructed by Mermecides, which was so small that a fly could cover it with its wing; also a ship of the same material, which could be hidden under the wing of a bee. Pliny tells us that Homer's Iliad, with its fifteen thousand verses, was written in so small a space as to be contained in a nutshell; while Elian mentions an artist who wrote a distich in letters of gold, which he enclosed in the rind of a kernel of corn. But the Harleian MS. mentions a greater curiosity than any of the former, it being nothing more nor less than the Bible, written by one Peter Bales, a chancery clerk, in so small a book that it could be enclosed within the shell of an English walnut. There is a drawing of the head of Charles II. in the library of St. John's College, Oxford, wholly composed of minutely written characters, which at a short distance resemble the lines of an ordinary engraving. The head and ruff are said to contain the book of Psalms, in Greek, and the Lord's Prayer.—*Bombaugh.*

Wonderful Lock.

Among the wonderful products of art in the French Crystal Palace was shown a lock which admitted of 3,674,385 combinations. Heuret spent one hundred and twenty nights in locking it; Fichet was four months in unlocking it; afterwards they could neither shut nor open it.

Roman Stamp.

This curiosity is preserved in the British Museum. It is the very earliest specimen of printing by means of ink or any similar substance. It is made of metal, a sort of Roman brass, the ground of which is covered with a green kind of verdigris rust with which antique medals are usually covered. The letters rise flush up to the elevation of the exterior rim which surrounds it. Its dimensions are about two inches long by one inch broad. At the back of it is a small ring for the finger, to make it more convenient to hold. As no person of the name which is inscribed upon it is mentioned in Roman history, he is, therefore, supposed to have been a functionary of some Roman officer, or private steward, who, perhaps, used this stamp to save himself the trouble of writing his name.

Talisman of Charlemagne.

The Emperor Napoleon III., when Prince Louis Napoleon, was stated to be in possession of the talisman of Charlemagne to which allusion is frequently made in traditional history. This curious object of vertu is mentioned in the Parisian journals as *la plus belle relique de l'Europe*, and it certainly has excited considerable interest in the archæological and religious circles on the continent. The talisman is of fine gold, of a round form, set with gems, and in the centre are two rough sapphires and a portion of the Holy Cross, besides other relics brought from the Holy Land. This was found round the neck of Charlemagne on the opening of his tomb, and given by the town of Aachen (Aix-la-Chapelle) to Bonaparte, and by him to his favorite Hortense, *ci-devant* Queen of Holland, at whose death it descended to her son Prince Louis, the late Emperor of the French.

The Black Stone at Mecca.

Near the entrance of the Kaaba, at 'Mecca, is the famous Black Stone, called by the Moslems *Hajra el Assouad*, or Heavenly Stone. It forms a part of the sharp angle of the building, and is inserted four or five feet above the ground. It is an irregular oval, and is about seven inches in diameter. Its color is now a deep reddish brown, approaching to black, and it is surrounded by a border of nearly the same color, resembling a cement of pitch and gravel, and from two to three inches in breadth. Both the border and the stone itself are encircled by a silver band, swelling to a considerable breadth below, where it is studded with nails of the same metal. The surface is undulated, and seems composed of about a dozen smaller stones, of different sizes and shapes, but perfectly smooth, and well joined with a small quantity of cement. It looks as if the whole had been dashed into many pieces by a severe concussion, and then re-united—an appearance that may perhaps be explained by the various disasters to which it has been exposed. During the fire that occurred in the time of Yezzid I. (A. D. 682), the violent heat split it into three pieces; and when the fragments were replaced, it was necessary to surround them with a rim of silver, which is said to have been renewed by Haroun-al-Raschid. It was in two pieces when the Karmathians carried it away, it having

been broken by a blow from a soldier during the plunder of
Mecca. Hakem, a mad Sultan of Egypt, in the eleventh
century, attempted, while on a pilgrimage, to destroy it with
an iron club which he had concealed under his clothes, but
was prevented and slain by the populace. After that accident
it remained unmolested until 1674, when it was found one
morning besmeared with dirt, so that every one who kissed
it returned with a sullied face. As for the quality of the
stone, it does not seem to be accurately determined. Burckhardt says it appeared to him like a lava containing several
small extraneous particles of a whitish and yellowish substance.
Ali Bey calls it a fragment of volcanic basalt, sprinkled with
small-pointed colored crystals, and varied with red feldspar.
The millions of kisses and touches impressed by the faithful
have worn the surface uneven, and to a considerable depth.
This miraculous block all orthodox Mussulmans believe to
have been originally a transparent hyacinth brought from
heaven to Abraham by the angel Gabriel; but that its substance, as well as its color, have long been changed by coming
in contact with the impurities of the human race.

The Portland Vase.

This was the name of a beautiful cinerary urn, of transparent dark blue glass, found about the middle of the sixteenth century in a marble sarcophagus near Rome. It was at
first deposited in the Barberini Palace at Rome, and hence is
often called the Barberini Vase. Next it became (in 1770) the
property, by purchase, of Sir William Hamilton, from whose
possession it passed into that of the Duchess of Portland. In
1810 the Duke of Portland, one of the trustees of the British
Museum, allowed it to be placed in that institution, retaining
his right over it as his own property. In 1845 a miscreant
named William Lloyd, apparently from an insane love of

mischief, or a diseased ambition for notoriety, dashed the valuable relic to pieces with a stone. Owing to the defective state of the law, only a slight punishment could be inflicted; but an act was immediately passed making such an offence punishable with imprisonment for two years. The pieces of the fractured vase were afterwards united in a very complete manner; and, thus repaired, it still exists in the Museum, but is not exhibited to the public.

Martin Luther's Tankard.

This interesting relic of the great reformer is of ivory, very richly carved, and mounted in silver-gilt. There are six medallions on its surface, which consist, however, of. a repetition of two subjects. The upper one represents the agony in the garden and the Saviour praying that the cup might pass from Him; the base represents the Lord's Supper, the centre dish being the incarnation of the bread. This tankard, now in the possession of Lord Londesborough, was formerly in the collection of Elkington, of Birmingham, who had some copies made of it. On the lid, in old characters, is the following: "C. M. L., MDXXIIII."

Brass Medal of the Saviour.

In 1702 Rev. H. Rowlands, author of *Mona Antiqua*, while superintending the removal of some stones near Aberfraw, Wales, for the purpose of making an antiquarian research, found a beautiful brass medal of the Saviour in a fine state of preservation, which he forwarded to his friend and countryman, the Rev. E. Lloyd, author of the *Archeologiæ Britannica*, and at that time-keeper of the Ashmolean Library at Oxford.

This medal has on one side the figure of a head exactly

answering the description given by Publius Lentulus of our Saviour, in a letter sent by him to the Emperor Tiberius and the Senate of Rome. On the reverse side it has the following legend or inscription in Hebrew characters: "This is Jesus Christ, the Mediator or Reconciler;" or, "Jesus the Great Messias, or Man Mediator." Being found among the ruins of the chief Druid's residence in Anglesea, it is not improbable that the curious relic belonged to some Christian connected with Brân the Blessed, who was one of Caractacus's hostages at Rome from A. D. 52 to 59, at which time the Apostle Paul was preaching the gospel at Rome. In two years afterwards, A. D. 61, the Roman General Suetonius extirpated all the Druids in the island. The following is a translation of the letter alluded to, a very antique copy of which is in the possession of the family of Lord Kellie, now represented by the Earl of Mar, a very ancient Scotch family, taken from the original at Rome :—

"There hath appeared in these our days a man of great virtue, named Jesus Christ, who is yet living among us, and of the Gentiles is accepted as a prophet, but his disciples call him The Son of God. He raiseth the dead, and cures all manner of diseases; a man of stature somewhat tall and comely, with very reverend countenance, such as the beholders both love and fear; his hair the color of chestnut, full ripe, plain to his ears, whence downward it is more orient, curling, and waving about his shoulders.

"In the midst of his head is a seam or a partition of his hair after the manner of the Nazarites; his forehead plain and very delicate; his face without a spot or wrinkle, beautified with the most lovely red; his mouth and nose so formed that nothing can be reprehended; his beard thickish, in color like his hair, not very long but forked; his look, innocent and mature; his eyes gray, clear and quick. In reproving, he is terrible; in admonishing, courteous and fair spoken; pleasant in conversation, mixed with gravity.   It cannot be remarked that any one saw him laugh, but many have seen him weep.   In proportion of body most excellent; his hands and arms most delicate to behold.   In speaking, very temperate, modest and wise.   A man, for his singular beauty, surpassing the children of men."

The representation of this sacred person which is in the Bodleian Library, somewhat resembles that of the print of this medal, when compared together.

Friar Bacon's Brazen Head.

The most famous of all the brazen heads was that of Roger Bacon, a monk of the thirteenth century.   According to the legend, he spent seven years in constructing the head, and he expected to be told by it how he could make a wall of brass around the island of Great Britain.   The head was warranted to speak within a month after it was finished, but no particular time was named for its doing so.   Bacon's man was therefore set to watch, with orders to call his master if the head should speak.   At the end of half an hour after the man was left alone with the head, he heard it say, "Time is," at the expiration of another half hour, "Time was," and at the end of a third half hour, "Time's past," when it fell down with a loud crash, and was shivered to pieces; but the stupid servant neglected to awaken his master, thinking that he would be very angry to be disturbed for such trifles; and so the wall of brass has never been built.

Crucifix of Columbus.

Mrs. General Hefferman, of Animas City, is the possessor of a very interesting and valuable relic, it being no less than the veritable crucifix which Columbus held in his hand when he

landed in America, of which she has ample documentary evidence, if one accept the witness, viz: the Catholic Church.
It has been in the possession of the missions and churches of
Mexico and California since a very early date; and even if
originally a fraud, it would nevertheless be almost as interesting, from its great age and as a work of art, as though what
is claimed for it were actually true. Mrs. Hefferman holds it
in trust for a religious order to which her mother belonged,
and sacredly believes it a genuine relic, as claimed. The
crucifix itself is of carved wood, of what kind no one is able
to determine. . The image of Christ upon it is of carved ivory.
The expression of agony depicted on the countenance and in
the drawn muscles and sunken flesh, as well as the delineation
of the anatomical structure, are triumphs of artistic skill which
could not be surpassed, if equalled, by the best artists of the
present day.—*Durango (Col.) Record.*

Scipio's Shield.

In 1656 a fisherman on the banks of the Rhone, in the
neighborhood of Avignon, drew to shore in his net a round
substance in the shape of a large plate, thickly encrusted with
a coat of hardened mud. A silversmith who happened to be
present bought it for a trifling sum. He took it home, and
upon cleaning and polishing it, found it to consist of pure
silver, perfectly round, more than two feet in diameter, and
weighing upwards of twenty pounds. Fearing that such a
massive and valuable piece of plate might awaken suspicion,
if offered for sale entire, he divided it into four equal parts,
each of which he disposed of at different times and places.

One of the pieces was sold at Lyons to Mr. Mey, a wealthy
and well-educated merchant, who at once saw its value and
who, after great effort, procured the other three sections. He
had them nicely rejoined, and the treasure was finally placed

in the cabinet of the King of France. This relic of antiquity, no less remarkable for the beauty of its workmanship than for having been buried at the bottom of the Rhone more than two thousand years, was a votive shield, presented to Scipio as a token of gratitude and affection by the inhabitants of Carthago Nova, now the city of Carthagena, for his generosity and self-denial in delivering one of his captives, a beautiful virgin, to her original lover. This act, so honorable to the Roman general, who was then in the prime vigor of manhood, is represented on the shield.

Horn of Oldenburg.

The story of the Horn of Oldenburg is a type of the legends which connect valuable plate, &c., belonging to old churches with underground fairies. The pictures of the horn represent it as a beautiful drinking vessel in the shape of a horn, exquisitely decorated with the finest fanciful silver-work, in the style contemporary with the richest Gothic architecture. The legend is, that one day, Otto of Oldenburg, being exhausted with hunting, and very thirsty, exclaimed: "O God, would that I had a cool drink!" Thereupon appeared before him, as if coming out of the rock, a lovely maiden, who offered him a drink in the fairy horn. He made off with it, and saved himself from evil consequences by bestowing it on the church.

Nebuchadnezzar's Golden Mask.

This interesting relic of remote antiquity is at present preserved in the Museum of the East India Company. It was found by Colonel Rawlinson while engaged in prosecuting the discoveries commenced by Layard and Botta, at Nineveh and Babylon, and is supposed to have belonged to King Nebuchadnezzar.   The body was discovered in a perfect state of preservation, and the face covered by the golden mask is described as handsome, the forehead high and commanding, the features marked and regular.   The mask is of thin gold, and, independent of its having once belonged to the great monarch, has immense 'value as a relic of an ancient and celebrated people.

Iron Crown of Lombardy.

When the Emperor Napoleon I. was crowned King of Italy, 1805, he placed the iron crown of the kings of Lombardy upon his head with his own hands, exclaiming, "God has given it to me—beware who touches," which was the haughty motto attached to it by its ancient owners.   The crown takes its name from the narrow iron band within it, which is about three-eighths of an inch broad and one-tenth of an inch in thickness.   It is traditionally said to have been made out of one of the nails used at the crucifixion, and given to Constantine by his mother, the Empress Helena, the discoverer of the Cross, to protect him in battle.   The crown is kept in the Cathedral of Monza.   The outer circlet is composed of six equal pieces of beaten gold, joined together by hinges, and set with large rubies, emeralds and sapphires, on a ground of blue-gold enamel.   Within the circlet is the iron crown, without a speck of rust, although it is more than fifteen hundred years old.

The Sacro Catino.

The celebrated Sacred Catino, part of the spoil taken by the Genoese at the storming of Cesarea, which was believed to be cut from a single emerald, and had, according to tradition, been presented·by the Queen of Sheba to Solomon, was for ages the pride and glory of Genoa, and an object of the greatest devotional reverence at the yearly exhibitions, which were attended with great pomp and ceremony. Such was the opinion of its intrinsic value, that on many occasions the republic borrowed half a million of ducats upon security of this precious relic. When the French armies, during the first revolution, plundered Italy of its treasures, it was sent, with other spoils, to Paris. Upon examination, it was, instead of emerald, proved to be composed of glass, similar to that found in Egyptian tombs, of which country it was, no doubt, the manufacture. At the Restoration the Sacro Catino was returned in a broken state, and now lies shorn of all its honors, a mere broken glass vessel, in the sacristy of the Church of San Lorenzo.

Curious Lantern.

In 1602 it is related that Sir John Harrington, of Bath, sent to James VI., of Scotland, as a new year's gift, a dark lantern. The top was a crown of pure gold, serving also to cover a perfume pan. Within it was a shield of silver, embossed, to reflect the light; on one side of the shield were the sun, moon and planets, and on the other side the story of the birth and passion of Christ, as it was engraved by David II., King of Scotland, who was a prisoner at Nottingham. The following words were inscribed in Latin on the present: "Lord, remember me when thou comest into thy kingdom."

Carrara's Toilet Box.

Francis Carrara, the last Lord of Padua, was famous for his cruelties. At Venice is exhibited a little box for the toilet, in which are six little guns, which were adjusted with springs in such a manner, that upon opening the box the guns were discharged, and killed the lady to whom Carrara had sent it for a present.

Executioner's Sword.

This weapon forms one of the curiosities in the superb collection of ancient armor which belonged to Sir Samuel R.
Meyrick, at Herefordshire. It bears the date of 1674. The
blade is thin and exceedingly sharp at both edges. Engraved
on it is a man impaled, above which are some words in German, of which the following is a translation:—

> Look every one that has eyes,
> Look here, and see that
> To erect power on wickedness
> Cannot last long.

A man holding a crucifix, his eyes bandaged, is on his
knees; the executioner, with his right hand on the hilt and
his left on the pommel, is about to strike the blow; above is
engraved—

> He who ambitiously exalts himself,
> And thinks only of evil,
> Has his neck already encompassed
> By punishment.

On the other side is a man broken on a wheel, over which
is—

> I live, I know not how long;
> I die, but I know not when.

Also a man suspended by the ribs from a gibbet, with the
inscription—

> I move, without knowing whither;
> I wonder I am so tranquil.

Luck of Eden-hall.

Hutchinson, in his "History of Cumberland," speaking of
Eden-hall, says: "In this house are some old-fashioned
apartments. An old painted drinking-glass, called the 'Luck

of Eden-hall,' is preserved with great care. In the garden, near to the house, is a well of excellent spring water, called St. Cuthbert's well. The glass is supposed to have been a sacred chalice, but the legendary tale is, that the butler, going to draw water, surprised a company of fairies who were amusing themselves upon the green near the well. He seized the glass which was standing upon its margin; they tried to get it from him, but, after an ineffectual struggle, flew away, singing—

> ' If that glass either break or fall,
> Farewell the luck of Eden-hall.' "

Bernini's Bust of Charles I.

Vandyck having drawn the king in three different faces, a profile, three-quarters and a full face, the picture was sent to Rome for Bernini to make a bust from it. Bernini was unaccountably dilatory in the work, and upon this being complained of, he said that he had set about it several times, but there was something so unfortunate in the features of the face that he was shocked every time that he examined it, and forced to leave off the work, observing, that if any stress was to be laid upon physiognomy, he was sure the person whom the picture represented was destined to a violent end. The bust was at last finished, and sent to England. As soon as the ship that brought it arrived in the Thames, the king, who was very impatient to see the bust, ordered it to be taken immediately to Chelsea. It was accordingly carried thither, and placed upon a table in the garden, whither the king went, with a train of nobility, to inspect the work. As they were viewing it, a hawk flew over their heads, with a partridge in his claws, which he had wounded to death. Some of the partridge's blood fell upon the neck of the bust, where it remained without being wiped off.

Burn's Snuff-box.

Burns and Mr. Bacon, the latter an inn-keeper near Dumfries, were very intimate, and, as a token of regard, the former gave to the latter his snuff-box, which for many years had been his pocket companion. On Mr. Bacon's death, in 1825, his effects were sold. The snuff-box was put up for sale among the other things, and some one bid a shilling. There was a general exclamation that it was not worth two-pence. The auctioneer, before knocking it down, opened the box. He saw engraved on the lid, and read aloud, the following inscription :—

" ROBT. BURNS,

OFFICER

OF

THE EXCISE."

The value of the box suddenly rose. Shilling after shilling was added, until it was finally knocked down for five pounds to a Mr. Munnell, of Closburn.—*Hone.*

Statue of Memnon.

This celebrated statue was situated at Thebes, and was either injured by Cambyses, to whom the Egyptian priests ascribed most of the mutilations of the Theban temples, or else thrown down by an earthquake. The peculiar characteristic of the statue was its giving out at various times a sound resembling the breaking of a harp-string or a metallic ring. Considerable difference has prevailed as to the reason of this sound, which has been heard in modern times, it being ascribed to the artifice of the priests, who struck the sonorous stone of which the statue is composed—to the passage of light draughts of air through the cracks, or the sudden expansion of aqueous particles, under the influence of the sun's rays. This remarkable quality of the statue is first mentioned by Strabo, who visited it about 18 B. C., and upwards of one hundred inscriptions of Greek and Roman visitors, incised upon its legs, record the visits of ancient travelers to witness the phenomenon, from the ninth year of Nero, 63 A. D., to the reign of the Emperor Severus, when it became silent.

The Head of Orpheus.

Whether the head of Orpheus spoke in the island of Lesbos, or, what is more probable, the answers were conveyed to it by the priests, as was the case with the tripod at Delphi, cannot with certainty be determined. That the imposter Alexander, however, caused his Æsculapius to speak in this manner, is expressly related by Lucian. He took, says that author, instead of a pipe, the gullet of a crane, and transmitted the voice through it to the mouth of the statue. In the fourth century, when Bishop Theophilus broke to pieces the statues at Alexandria, he found some which were hollow, and placed in such a manner against a wall that a priest could slip unperceived behind them and speak to the ignorant populace through their mouths.

Wonderful Automata.

Archytas, of Tarentum, is reported, so long ago as 400 B. C., to have made a pigeon that could fly. The most perfect automaton about which there is absolute certainty, was one constructed by M. Vaucanson, exhibited in Paris in 1738. It represented a flute-player, which placed its lips against the instrument, and produced the notes with its fingers in precisely the same manner as a human being does. In 1741 M. Vaucanson made a flageolet-player, which with one hand beat a tambourine, and in the same year he produced a duck. The latter was an ingenious contrivance ; it swam, dived, ate, drank, dressed its wings, etc., as naturally as its live companions ; and, most wonderful of all, by means of a solution in the stomach, it was actually made to digest its food. An automaton made by M. Droz drew likenesses of public characters. Some years ago a Mr. Faber contrived a figure which was able to articulate words and sentences very intelligibly, but the effect was not pleasant. The chess-player of Kempelen was long regarded as the most wonderful of automata. It represented a Turk of natural size, dressed in the national costume, and seated behind a box resembling a chest of drawers in shape. Before the game commenced, the artist opened several doors in the chest, which revealed a large number of pulleys, wheels, cylinders, springs, etc. The chessmen were produced from a long drawer, as was also a cushion for the figure to rest its arm upon. The automaton, not being able to speak, signified, when the queen of his antagonist was in danger, by two nods, and when the king was in check by three. It succeeded in beating most of the players with whom it engaged, but it turned out afterwards that a crippled Russian officer—a very celebrated chess-player—was concealed in the interior of the figure. The figure is said to have been constructed for the purpose of effecting the officer's escape out of Russia, where his life was forfeited. So far as the mental process was concerned, the chess-player was not, therefore, an automaton, but great ingenuity was evinced in its movement of the pieces.

Temple of the Sun.

The Temple of the Sun at Cuzco, called *Coricancha*, or "Place of Gold," was the most magnificent edifice in the Persian empire. On the western wall, and opposite the eastern portal, was a splendid representation of the Sun, the god of the nation. It consisted of a human face in gold, with innumerable golden rays emanating from it in every direction; and when the early beams of the morning sun fell upon this brilliant golden disc, they were reflected from it as from a mirror, and again reflected throughout the whole temple by the numberless plates, cornices, bands and images of gold, until the temple seemed to glow with a sunshine more intense than that of nature.

Tomb of Darius.

One of the most remarkable tombs of the ancients was that carved out of rock, by order of Darius, for the reception of his own remains, and which exists to this day at Persepolis, after a duration of twenty-three centuries.

The portico is supported by four columns twenty feet in height, and in the centre is the form of a doorway, seemingly the entrance to the interior, but it is solid; the entablature is of chaste design. Above the portico there is what may be termed an ark, supported by two rows of figures, about the size of life, bearing it on their uplifted hands, and at each angle a griffin—an ornament which is very frequent at Persepolis. On this stage stands the king, with a bent bow in his hand, worshipping the sun, the image of which is seen above the altar that stands before him, while above his head hovers his ferouher, or disembodied spirit. This is the good genius that in Persian and Ninevite sculpture accompanies the king when performing any important act. On each side of the ark are nine niches, each containing a statue in bas-relief. No other portion of the tomb was intended to be seen, excepting the sculptured front; and we must, therefore, conclude that the entrance was kept secret, and that the avenues were by subterranean passages, so constructed that none but the priviledged could find the way. We are told by Theophrastus that Darius was buried in a coffer of Egyptian alabaster; also that the early Persians preserved the bodies of their dead in honey or wax.

Temples the First Museums.

Natural objects of uncommon size or beauty were, in the earliest periods, consecrated to the gods, and conveyed to the temples, to awaken curiosity and to excite reverence. In the course of time the natural curiosities dedicated to the gods formed large collections. When Hanno returned from his distant voyages, he brought with him to Carthage two skins of the hairy women whom he found on the Gorgades Islands, and deposited them in the temple of Juno. The monstrous horns of the wild bulls which had occasioned so much devastation in Macedonia were, by order of King Philip, hung up in the temple of Hercules. The unnaturally formed shoulder-bones of Pelopos were deposited in the temple of Elis. The crocodile, found in attempting to discover the sources of the Nile, was preserved in the temple of Isis, at Cæsarea. The head of a basilisk was exhibited in one of the temples of Diana, and in the time of Pausanias the head of the celebrated Calydonian boar was to be seen in one of the temples of Greece.

Wesley's Plate.

An order was made in the House of Lords, in May, 1776, "that the commissioners of his majesty's excise do write circular letters to all such persons whom they have reason to suspect to have *plate*, as also to those who have not paid regularly the duty on the same." In consequence of this order, the accountant-general for household plate sent to the celebrated

John Wesley a copy of the order.   The reply was a laconic
one—

"SIR: I have *two* silver teaspoons in London and *two* at
Bristol.   This is all the plate which I have at present; and I
shall not buy any more while so many round me want bread.
   "I am, sir,
                    Your most humble servant,
                                        JOHN WESLEY."

Grace Knives.

There is in existence a curious class of knives, of the sixteenth century, the blades of which have on one side the musical notes to the benediction of the table, or grace before meat,
and on the other side the grace after meat.   The set of these
knives usually consisted of four.   They were kept in an upright
case of stamped leather, and were placed before the singer.

Religious Relics.

At the commencement of the seventeenth century there was
a crucifix belonging to the Augustine friars, at Burgos, in Spain,
which produced a revenue of nearly seven thousand crowns
per annum.   It was found upon the sea, not far from the coast,
with a scroll of parchment appended to it descriptive of the
various virtues it possessed.   The image was provided with a
false beard and a chestnut-colored periwig, which its holy
guardians declared were natural, and they also assured all
pious visitors that on every Friday it sweated blood and water
into a silver basin.   In the garden of this convent grew a
species of wheat, the grain of which was unusually large, and
which its possessors averred was brought by Adam out of Paradise. Cakes, for the cure of all diseases, were made out of
the wheat kneaded with the aforesaid blood and water, and

sold to the credulous multitude for a quartillo each. They also sold blue ribbons, of the exact length of the crucifix, for about a shilling each. The ribbons were a sovereign cure for headache, and had upon them, in silver letters, "La madi del santo crucifisco de Burgos."

Mammoth Bottle.

In January, 1751, a globular bottle was blown at Leith capable of holding two hogsheads. Its dimensions were forty inches by forty-two. This immense vessel was the largest ever produced at any glass-works.—*Hone*

A Drinking Glass a Yard Long.

"On the proclamation of James II., in the market place of Bromley, by the Sheriff of Kent, the commander of the Kentish troop, two of the king's trumpets, and other officers, they drank the king's health in a flint glass a yard long."—*Evelyn's Diary*, Feb. 10th, 1685.

Kneeling Statue of Atlas.

In the Museo Borbonico, at Naples, is a kneeling statue of Atlas sustaining the globe. It is a very interesting monument of Roman art, and one of great value to the student of ancient astronomy. Of the forty-seven constellations known to the ancients, forty-two may be distinctly recognized. The date of this curious sculpture is fixed as anterior to the time of Hadrian by the absence of the likeness of Antinous, which was inserted in the constellation Aquila by the astronomers of that period.

The Druid's Seat.

The "Druid's Judgment Seat" stands near the village of Killiney, not far from Drogheda, near the Martello tower. It was formerly enclosed with a circle of large stones and a ditch. The former has been destroyed, and the latter so altered that little of its ancient character remains. The "Seat" is composed of large, rough granite blocks, and if really of the period to which tradition credits it, an unusual degree of care must have been exercised in its preservation. The following are its measurements: Breadth at the base, eleven feet and a half; depth of the seat, one foot nine inches; extreme height, seven feet.

Curious Epitaphs.

> Praises on tombs are trifles vainly spent;
> A man's good name is his best monument.

From Childwald church-yard, England—

> Here lies me and my three daughters,
> Brought here by using seidlitz waters;
> If we had stuck to Epsom salts,
> We would n't have been in these here vaults

From Nettlebed church-yard, Oxfordshire—

> Here lies father, and mother, and sister, and I,
>   We all died within the space of one short year;
> They all be buried at Wimble, except I,
>   And I be buried here.

At Wolstanton—

> Mrs. Ann Jennings.
> Some have children, some have none:
> Here lies the mother of twenty-one.

In Norwich Cathedral—

> Here lies the body of honest Tom Page,
> Who died in the thirty-third year of his age.

At Torrington church-yard, Devon, England—

> She was—but words are wanting to say what:
> Think what a woman should be—she was that.

In the church-yard of Pewsey, Wiltshire—

Here lies the body of Lady O'Looney, great-niece of Burke, commonly called the Sublime. She was bland, passionate and deeply religious; also she painted in water-colors, and sent several pictures to the exhibition. She was first cousin to Lady Jones; and of such is the kingdom of heaven.

Shields (the Irish orator)—

> Here lie I at reckon, and my spirit at aise is,
>   With the tip of my nose, and the ends of my toes,
> Turned up 'gainst the roots of the daisies.

In Doncaster church-yard, 1816—

> Here lies 2 brothers by misfortin serounded,
> One dy'd of his wounds & the other was drownded.

On the monument of John of Doncaster—

> What I gave, I have;
> What I spent, I had;
> What I saved, I lost.

In a New England grave-yard—

> Here lies John Auricular,
> Who in the ways of the Lord walked perpendicular

Sternhold Oakes—

> Here lies the body of Sternhold Oakes,
> Who lived and died like other folks.

On a tombstone in New Jersey—

> Reader, pass on! don't waste your time
> On bad biography and bitter rhyme;
> For what I *am*, this crumbling clay insures,
> And what I *was*, is no affair of yours!

In East Hartford, Connecticut—

> Hark! she bids all her friends adieu;
> An angel calls her to the spheres;
> Our eyes the radiant saint pursue
> Through liquid telescopes of tears.

In Newington church-yard—

> Through Christ, I am not inferior
> To William the Conqueror.

In Bideford church-yard, Kent—

> The wedding-day appointed was,
> And wedding-clothes provided,
> But ere the day did come, alas!
> He sickened, and he die did.

Rebecca Rogers, Folkestone, 1688—

> A house she hath, 't is made of such good fashion,
> The tenant ne'er shall pay for reparation;
> Nor will her landlord ever raise her rent,
> Or turn her out of doors for non-payment.
> From chimney-tax this cell's forever free—
> To such a house who would not tenant be?

At Augusta, Maine—

> — After life's *scarlet fever*,
> I sleep well.

John Mound—

> Here lies the body of John Mound,
> Lost at sea and never found.

POETRY, PIETY AND POLITENESS.

The following epitaph was copied from a stone in a country church-yard—

> " You who stand around my grave,
> And say, 'His life is gone;'
> You are mistaken—*pardon me*—
> My life is but begun."

At Loch Rausa—

> Here lies Donald and his wife,
> Janet MacFee:
> Aged 40 hee,
> And 30 shee.

On Mr. Bywater—

> Here lie the remains of his relatives' pride,
> Bywater he lived and by water he died;
> Though by water he fell, yet by water he'll rise,
> By water baptismal attaining the skies.

At Staverton, England—

> Here lieth the body of Betty Bowden,
> Who would live longer but she couden;
> Sorrow and grief made her decay,
> Till her bad leg carr'd her away.

At Penryn—

> Here lies William Smith; and, what is somewhat rarish,
> He was born, bred and hanged in this here parish.

From St. Agnes', London—

> Qu an tris di c vul stra
> Os guis ti ro um nere vit.
> H san Chris mi t mu la.

In Linton church-yard, 1825—

> Remember man, that passeth by,
> As thou is now so once was I ;
> And as I is so must thou be :
> Prepare thyself to follow me.

Under this inscription some one wrote—

> To follow you's not my intent,
> Unless I knew which way you went.

At Queenborough—

> Henry Knight, master of a shipp to Greenland, and
> Herpooner 24 voyages.
> In Greenland I whales, sea-horses, bears did slay,
> Though now my body is intombe in clay.

At Minster—

> Here interr'd George Anderson doth lye,
> By fallen on an anchor he did dye,
> In Sheerness Yard, on Good Friday,
> Ye 6th of April, I do say,
> All you that read my allegy : Be alwaies
> Ready for to dye—aged 42 years.

At Hadley church-yard, Suffolk—

> The charnel mounted on the w
> Sets to be seen in funer
> A matron plain domestic
> In care and pain continu
> Not slow, not gay, not prodig
> Yet neighborly and hospit   **ALL.**
> Her children seven, yet living
> Her sixty-seventh year hence did ^c
> To rest her body natur
> In hopes to rise spiritu

The middle line furnishes the terminal letters or syllables of the words in the upper and lower lines, and when added they read thus—

> Quos anguis tristi diro cum vulnere stravit,
> Hos sanguis Christi miro tum munere lavit.
> [Those who have felt the serpent's venomed wound,
> In Christ's miraculous blood have healing found.]

In a Paris cemetery—

I' attends ma femme.	I await my wife.
1820.	1820.
Me voilá.	I am here.
1830.	1830.

Shakespeare's tomb—

The inscription on Shakespeare's tomb forbids the removal of the body.   Subjoined is the prohibition—

> " Good Friend, for Jesvs sake forbeare
> To digg Y-E dvst EncloAsed HERE.
> Blest be Y-E Man T-Y spares T-hs Stones
> And cvrst be He T-Y moves my bones."

In consequence of this inscription, the people of Stratford-on-Avon are afraid to put their feet on the stones above the grave, and the body of the greatest English poet has not been placed with other geniuses in Westminster Abbey.

Stone tablet puzzle—

The following letters are inscribed on a stone tablet placed immediately over the Ten Commandments in a church in England, and are deciphered with only one letter—

> PRSVR Y PRFCT MN!
> VR KP THS PRCPTS TN.

Grimmingham church-yard, Norfolk, England—

To the memory of Thomas Jackson, Comedian, who was *engaged*, 21st of Dec., 1741, to *play a comic cast of characters, in this great theatre*—the World: for many of which he was *prompted* by nature to excel.

The *season* being ended, his *benefit* over, the charges all paid, and his account closed, he made his *exit* in the *tragedy* of Death, on the 17th of March, 1798, in full assurance of being called once more to *rehearsal;* where he hopes to find his *forfeits* all cleared, his *cast of parts* bettered, and his situation made agreeable by Him who paid the great stock-debt, for the love which he bore to *performers* in general.

An inculpatory epitaph—

The following epitaph at West Allington, Devon, England, is not only a memorial of the deceased, but reproves the parson of the parish—

Here lyeth the Body of
Daniel Jeffery the son of Micb
ael Jeffery and Joan his wife he
was buried ye 22 day of September
1746 and in ye 18th year of his age.
This Youth When In his sickness lay
did for the minister Send+that he would
Come and with bim Pray+But he would not atend
But when this Young Man Buried was
The minister did him admit+he should be
Caried into Church+that he might money geet
By this you see what man will dwo+to geet
money if he can+who did refuse to come
pray+by the Foresaid young man.

At St. Benedict Fink—

"1673, April 23rd, was buried Mr Thomas Sharrow, Cloth-worker, late Churchwarden of this parish, killed by an accidental fall into a vault, in London Wall, men Corner, by Paternoster Row, and was supposed had lain there eleven days and nights before any one could tell where he was. *Let all that read this take heed of drink.*"

At Clophill, Bedfordshire—

DEATH DO NOT KICK AT MEE
FOR CHRIST HATH TAKEN
THY STING AWAY.
1623.

In the same—

HEAR
LIES THE
BODEY OF
THOMAS
DEARMAN T
HAT GAVE 6 *P*
OVND   A YEAR
TO TH   E LABE
RERS O   F CLOPH
ILL   1631.

A watchmaker's epitaph—

Among the curious epitaphs to be seen in the graveyards of England, this one in the old church-yard of Lidford, Devon, is worthy of insertion—

Here lies, in a horizontal position,
The outside case of
George Rougleigh, watchmaker,
Whose abilities in that line were an honor
To his profession.
Integrity was the mainspring
And prudence the regulator
Of all the actions of his life.
Humane, generous and liberal,
His hand never stopped
Till he had relieved distress;

So nicely were all his actions regulated
That he never went wrong
Except when set a-going
By people
Who did not know his key;
Even then he was easily set aright again.
He had the art of disposing his time so well
That his hours glided away
In one continual round
Of pleasure and delight,
Till an unlucky minute put a period to
his existence.
He departed this life November 14, 1802,
Aged 57;
Wound up
In hopes of being taken in hand
By his Maker,
And of being thoroughly cleaned and repaired
And set a-going
In the world to come.

Grave of Robin Hood—

At Kirklees, in Yorkshire, formerly a Benedictine nunnery,
is a gravestone, near the park, under which it is said Robin
Hood lies buried. Mr. Ralph Thoresby, in his "Ducatus
·Leodiensis," gives the following as the epitaph—

Here undernead dis laith stean
Laiz Robert Earl of Huntington,
Nea arcir ver az hie sa geude:
An piple kaud im Robin Heud
Sic utlawz as hi, an iz men,
Wil England never sigh agen.

Obiit 24 kal. Dekembris, 1247.

Great Tom of Lincoln.

The finest bell in England was the Great Tom of Lincoln,
considerably older than St. Paul's. Its elevation gave it an

horizon of fifty miles in every direction. Its note was like the chord of A upon a full organ. It fell from its support and was destroyed.

Mammoth Bell of Buddah.

Klaprath states that in an edifice before the great temple of Buddah, at Jeddo, is the largest bell in the world. It weighs 1,700,000 pounds, four times greater than the great bell of Moscow, and fifty-six times larger than the great bell of Westminister, England.

Great Bell of Rouen.

The grand entrance to the cathedral of Rouen is flanked by two towers; the one was erected by St. Romain; the expense of constructing the other, which bears the whimsical name of *Tour-de-beurre*, was raised by the sum received for granting the more wealthy and epicurean inhabitants of the city permission to eat butter during Lent. It was in this tower that the celebrated bell was erected; it was named George D'Amboise, after its founder, who died from joy upon seeing it completed. It weighed 40,000 pounds, and was melted into cannon in the year 1793.

St. Fillan's Bell.

In Sinclair's "Statistical Account of Scotland," the Rev. Mr. Patrick Stuart, minister of Killin parish, Perthshire, says: "There is a bell belonging to the chapel of St. Fillan that was in high reputation among the votaries of that saint in old times. It is a foot high, oblong in form, and made of mixed metal. It usually lay on a grave-stone in the church-yard. When mad people were brought to be dipped in the saint's pool, it was necessary to perform certain ceremonies in which. there was a mixture of druidism and popery. After remaining all night in the chapel, bound with ropes, the bell was set upon their head with great solemnity. It was also the popular opinion that if the bell was ever stolen, it would extricate itself out of the thief's hands and return home, ringing all the way."

The Bells of Jersey.

The following is the bell-legend connected with Jersey: "Many years ago the twelve parish churches in that island possessed each a valuable peal of bells; but during a long civil war the government determined to sell the bells to defray the expenses of the troops. The bells were accordingly collected and sent to France for that purpose; but on the passage, the ship foundered, and everything was lost, to show the wrath of Heaven at such a sacrilege. Since then, during a storm, these bells always ring from the deep, and to this day the fishermen of St. Owen's Bay always go to the edge of the water before embarking, to listen if they can hear the bells upon the wind. If so, nothing will induce them to leave the shore; if all is quiet, they fearlessly set sail."

Subterranean Christmas Bells.

Near Raleigh, in Nottinghamshire, there is a valley, said to have been caused by an earthquake several hundred years ago, which swallowed up a whole village, together with the church. Formerly, it was a custom for people to assemble in this valley on Christmas morning, to listen to the ringing of the bells of the church beneath them. This it was positively asserted might be heard by putting the ear to the ground and harkening attentively. Even now, it is usual on Christmas morning for

. old men and women to tell the children to go to the valley, stoop down, and hear the bells ringing merrily.—*Hone*, 1827.

St. Sepulchre's Bell.

It has been a very ancient practice, on the night preceding the execution of condemned criminals, for the bellman of the parish of St. Sepulchre to go under Newgate, and, ringing his bell, to repeat the following, as a piece of friendly advice to the unhappy wretches under sentence of death:—

> All you that in the condemn'd hold do lie,
> Prepare you, for to-morrow you shall die;
> Watch all, and pray, the hour is drawing near,
> That you before the Almighty must appear;
> Examine well yourselves, in time repent,
> That you may not to eternal flames be sent.
> And when St. Sepulchre's bell to-morrow tolls.
> The Lord above have mercy on your souls!
> Past twelve o'clock'

The Passing Bell.

The Passing Bell was so named from being tolled when any one was passing from life. Hence it was sometimes called the *Soul Bell*, and was rung that those who heard it might pray for the person dying, and who was not yet dead. We have a remarkable mention of the practice in the narrative of the last moments of the Lady Katherine Grey (sister of Lady Jane Grey), who died a prisoner in the Tower of London, in 1567. Sir Owen Hopton, constable of the tower, "perceiving her to draw toward her end, said to Mr. Bockeham, 'Were it not best to send to the church, that the bell may be rung?' and she herself, hearing him, said: 'Good Sir Owen, be it so;' and almost immediately died."—*Ellis's Original Letters.*

Bell-ringing in Holland.

The Hollanders exhibit the most enthusiastic fondness for bells. Every church and public building is hung round with them in endless variety. In Amsterdam not less than a thousand bells are kept constantly ringing, which creates a din that is almost intolerable to strangers.

Babes of Bethlehem.

It is an ancient custom at Norton, Worcestershire, England, on the 28th of December (Innocents' Day) to ring a muffled peal in token of sorrow for the slaughter of the hapless "babes of Bethlehem," and, immediately afterwards, an un-muffled peal, in manifestation of joy for the deliverance and escape of the infant Saviour.

Ringing the Changes.

It is curious to note the number of changes which may be rung on different peals. The changes on seven bells are 5040; on twelve, 479,001,600, which it would take ninety-one years to ring, at the rate of two strokes in a second. The changes on fourteen bells could not be rung through at the same rate in less than 16,575 years, and upon four-and-twenty they would require more than 117,000 billions of years.—*E. F. King.*

Bell Inscriptions.

Epigraphs or legends on bells were quite common in England. We subjoin specimens—

On the Six Bells of the Ancient Abbey of Hexham.

Even at our earliest sound,
The light of God is spread around.

At the echo of my voice,
Ocean, earth and air rejoice.

Blend thy mellow tones with mine,
Silver voice of Catherine !

Till time on ruin's lap shall nod,
John shall sound the praise of God.

With John in heavenly harmony,
Andrew, pour thy melody.

Be mine to chant Jehovah's fame,
While Maria is my name.

A not uncommon epigraph is—

Come when I call,
To serve God all.

At Aldbourne, on the first bell, we read : " The gift of Jos. Pizzie and Wm. Gwynn.

Music and ringing we like so well,
And for that reason we gave this bell."

On the fourth bell is—

Humphry Symsin gave xx pounds to buy this bell,
And the parish gave xx more to make this ring go well.

At Broadchalk—

I in this place am second bell,
I'll surely do my part as well.

At Coln, on the third bell—

Robert Forman collected the money for casting this bell
Of well-disposed people, as I do you tell.

At Devizes, St. Mary—

> I am the first, altho' but small,
> I will be heard above you all.
>
> I am the second in this ring;
> Therefore next to thee I will sing.

Amesbury, on the fifth bell—

> Be strong in faith, praise God well,
> Frances Countess Hertford's bell.

Amesbury, on the tenor bell—

> Altho' it be unto my loss,
> I hope you will consider my cost.

At Bath Abbey—

> All you of Bath that hear my sound,
> Thank Lady Hopton's hundred pound.

At Stowe, Northamptonshire—

> Be it known to all that doth me see,
> That Newcombe, of Leicester, made me.

At St. Michael's, Coventry—

> I ring at six to let men know
> When to and from their work to go.

On the seventh bell is—

> I ring to sermon with lusty bome,
> That all may come, and none can stay at home.

At St. Peter-le-Bailey, Oxford, in expectation of other bells which were never purchased—

> With seven more I hope soon to be
> For ages joined in harmony.

On the eighth bell is—

I am and have been called the common bell,
To ring when fire breaks out to tell.

St. Helen's church, at Worcester, England, has a set of
bells cast in the time of Queen Anne, with names and inscriptions recording victories gained in that reign—

1. BLENHEIM.

First is my note, and Blenheim is my name;
For Blenheim's story will be first in fame.

2. BARCELONA.

Let me relate how Louis did bemoan
His grandson Philip's flight from Barcelon.

3. RAMILIES.

Deluged in blood, I, Ramilies, advance
Britannia's glory on the fall of France.

4. MENIN.

Let Menin on my sides engraven be,
And Flanders freed from Gallic slavery.

5. TURIN.

When in harmonious peal I roundly go,
Think on Turin, and triumphs on the Po.

6. EUGENE.

With joy I bear illustrious Eugene's name;
Fav'rite of fortune and the boast of fame.

7. MARLBOROUGH.

But I for pride the greater Marlborough bear;
Terror of tyrants and the soul of war.

8. QUEEN ANNE.

The immortal praise of Queen Anne I sound,
With union blest, and all these glories crowned.

On the famous alarm-bell called Roland, in a belfry-tower in the once powerful city of Ghent, is engraved the subjoined inscription, in the old Walloon or Flemish dialect—

"My name is Roland; when I toll there is fire,
And when I ring there is victory in the land."

The following inscription, remarkable for bad taste, is on one of eight bells in the church tower of Tilton, Devon—

"Recast by John Taylor and Son,
Who the best prize for church bells won
At the Great Ex-hi-bi-ti-on
In London, 1-8-5 and 1."

Articles of Ringing.

The following "Articles of Ringing" are upon the walls of the belfry in Dunster, Somersetshire, England:—

1. You that in ringing take delight,
    Be pleased to draw near;
    These articles you must observe.
    If you mean to ring here.

2. And first, if any overturn
    A bell, as that he may,
    He forthwith for that only fault
    In beer shall sixpence pay.

3. If any one shall curse or swear
    When come within the door,
    He then shall forfeit for that fault
    As mentioned before.

4. If any one shall wear his hat
    When he is ringing here,
    He straightway then shall sixpence pay
    In cyder or in beer.

5. If any one these articles
    Refuseth to obey,
  Let him have nine strokes of the rope,
  And so depart away.

Old Weather Rhymes.

If New Year's eve night-wind blow south,
It betokeneth warmth and growth;
If west, much milk, and fish in the sea;
If north, much cold, and storms there will be;
If east, the trees will bear much fruit;
If north-east, flee it, man and brute.

If St. Paul's day be fair and clear,
It does betide a happy year;
But if it chance to snow or rain,
Then will be dear all kinds of grain;
If clouds or mists do dark the skie,
Great store of birds and beasts shall die;
And if the winds do fly aloft,
Then wars shall vex the kingdome oft.

A swarm of bees in May
Is worth a load of hay;
A swarm of bees in June
Is worth a silver spune;
A swarm of bees in July
Is not worth a fly.

The hind had as lief see his wife on the bier,
As that Candlemas-day should be pleasant and clear.

If Candlemas-day be fair and bright,
Winter will have another flight;
But if Candlemas-day be clouds and rain,
Winter is gone, and will not come again.

When Candlemas-day is come and gone,
The snow lies on a hot stone.

If Candlemas is fair and clear,
There 'll be twa winters in the year.

February fill dike, be it black or be it white;
But if it be white, it's the better to like.

When the cuckoo comes to the bare thorn,
Sell your cow and buy your corn;
But when she comes to the full bit,
Sell your corn and buy your sheep.

If the cock moult before the hen,
We shall have weather thick and thin;
But if the hen moult before the cock,
We shall have weather hard as a block.

When the wind's in the south,
It blows the bait into the fishes' mouth.

As the days lengthen
So the colds strengthen.

If there be a rainbow in the eve,
It will rain and leave;
But if there be a rainbow in the morrow,
It will neither lend nor borrow.

A rainbow in the morning
Is the shepherd's warning;
But a rainbow at night
Is the shepherd's delight.

No tempest, good July,
Lest corn come off blue by.

When the wind's in the east,
It's neither good for man nor beast;
When the wind's in the south,
It's in the rain's mouth.

When the sloe-tree is as white as a sheet,
Sow your barley, whether it be dry or wet.

No weather is ill
If the wind be still.

A snow year,
A rich year.

Winter's thunder
Is summer's wonder.

St. Swithin's day, if thou dost rain,
For forty days it will remain;
St. Swithin's day, if thou be fair,
For forty days 't will rain na mair.

The bat begins with giddy wing
  His circuit round the shed and tree;
And clouds of dancing gnats to sing
  A summer night's serenity.

At New Year's tide,
The days are lengthened a cock's stride.

If the red sun begins his race,
Expect that rain will fall apace.

The evening red, the morning gray,
Are certain signs of a fair day.

If woolly fleeces spread the heavenly way,
No rain, be sure, disturbs the summer's day.

In the waning of the moon,
A cloudy morn—fair afternoon.

When clouds appear like rocks and towers,
The earth 's refresh'd by frequent showers.

As the days grow longer
The storms grow stronger.

Blessed is the corpse that the rain falls on.
Blessed is the bride that the sun shines on.

He that goes to see his wheat in May,
 Comes weeping away.

Signs of Foul Weather.

The soot falls down, the spaniels sleep,
And spiders from their cobwebs peep.
Loud quack the ducks, the sea-fowl cry,
The distant hills are looking nigh.

Puss on the hearth, with velvet paws,
Sits wiping o'er her whisker'd jaws.

The smoke from chimneys right ascends,
Then spreading, back to earth it bends.

The walls are damp, the ditches smell,
Clos'd is the pink-ey'd pimpernel.

Quite restless are the snorting swine,
The busy flies disturb the kine.

The wind unsteady veers around,
Or settling in the south is found.

The glow-worms, numerous and bright,
Illumed the dewy hill last night.

Through the clear stream the fishes rise
And nimbly catch the incautious flies.

First Meerschaum Pipe.

In 1723 there lived in Pesth, the capital of Hungary, Karol Kowates, a shoemaker, whose ingenuity in cutting and carving on wood, etc., brought him in contact with Count Andrassy, ancestor to the present prime minister of Austria, with whom he became a favorite. The count, on his return from a mission to Turkey, brought with him a large piece of whitish clay, which had been presented to him as a curiosity on account of its extraordinary light specific gravity. It struck the shoemaker that, being porous, it must naturally be well adapted for pipes, as it would absorb the nicotine. The experiment was tried, and Karol cut a pipe for the count and one for himself. But in the pursuit of his trade he could not keep his hands clean, and many a piece of wax became attached to the pipe. The clay, however, instead of assuming a dirty appearance, as was naturally to be expected, when Karol wiped it off, received, wherever the wax had touched, a clear brown polish, instead of the dull white it previously had. Attributing this change in the tint to the proper source, he waxed the whole surface, and, polishing the pipe, again smoked it, and noticed how admirably and beautifully it colored; also, how much more sweet the pipe smoked after being waxed. Karol had struck the smoking philosopher's stone; and other noblemen, hearing of the wonderful properties of this singular species of clay, imported it in considerable quantities for the manufacture of pipes. The natural scarcity of this much esteemed article, and the great cost of transportation in those days of limited facilities for transportation, rendered its use exclusively confined to the richest European noblemen until 1830, when it became a more general article of trade. The first meerschaum pipe made by Karol Kowates has been preserved in the museum at Pesth.

The First Oval Lathe.

William Murdock, the inventor of the oval lathe, was a poor millwright. He was a good workman, but rather shiftless, until he came into the employ of Boulton & Watt, the English manufacturers of steam-engines in the last century. The way in which the millwright first attracted the attention of these great machinists is thus told:—

Somewhere about the year 1780, a traveling millwright, weary and foot-sore, and with the broadest of Northern Doric accent, stopped at a factory in England and asked for work. His aspect indicated beggary, and the proprietor, Mr. Boulton, had bidden him seek some other workshop, when, as the man was turning sorrowfully away, he suddenly called him back, saying—

"What kind of hat's yon ye have on your head, my man?"

"It's just timmer, sir," replied the man.

"Timmer, my man!" ejaculated the manufacturer. "Just let me look at it. Where on earth did you get it?"

"I just turned it in the lathe," said the mechanic, with a flush of pride.

"But it's oval, not round, my man," said Mr. Boulton, in surprise; "and lathes turn things round."

"A-weel, I just gar'd the lathe gang anither gait to please me; and I'd a long journey before me, and I thocht I'd have a hat to keep out water; and I had na muckle to spare, so I just make ane."

The man was a born inventor, but he didn't know it. By his ingenuity he had invented the oval lathe, one of the most useful of machines. He had made his hat with it, and the hat made his fortune. Great events often result from seeming trifles. Mr. Boulton was a sharp man of business. He saw that the man who could turn out of a block of wood an oval hat, was too valuable a workman for the firm of Boulton & Watt to lose sight of. William Murdock was then and there employed. In 1784 he made the first wheeled vehicle impelled by steam in England,—made it with his own hands and brains. He gained fame and fortune, but the "timmer" hat, made for a long journey and to keep out water, was the corner-stone of both.

Porcelain.

An alchemist, while seeking to discover a mixture of earths that would make the most durable crucibles, one day found that he had made porcelain.

Origin of Blue-tinted Paper.

The origin of blue-tinted paper came about by a mere slip of the hand. The wife of William East, an English paper-maker, accidentally let a blue bag fall into one of the vats of pulp. The workmen were astonished when they· saw the peculiar color of the paper, while Mr. East was highly incensed over what he considered a grave pecuniary loss. His wife was so much frightened that she would not confess her agency in the matter. After storing the damaged paper for four years, Mr. East sent it to his agent at London, with instructions to sell it for what it would bring. The paper was accepted as a "purposed novelty," and was disposed of at quite an advance over the market price. Mr. East was astonished at receiving an order from his agent for another large invoice of the paper. He was without the secret, and found himself in a dilemma. Upon mentioning it to his wife, she told him about the accident. He kept the secret, and the demand for the novel tint far exceeded his ability to supply it.

Following His Nose.

While Marshall Jewell was Minister to Russia, he found out, by the use of his nose, the secret of making Russia leather. Instead of using tallow and grease in the dressings of skins, the Russians employed birch-bark tar. By careful inquiry, and literally following his nose, during a visit to one of their large tanneries, he found the compound in a mammoth kettle, ready for use. He reported his discovery, and the result is that genuine Russian leather goods are now made in America.

Discovery of Composition for Printing Rollers.

The composition of which printing-rollers are made was discovered by a Salopian printer. Not being able to find the pelt-ball, he inked the type with a piece of soft glue which had fallen out of a glue pot. It was such an excellent substitute that, after mixing molasses with the glue, to give the mass proper consistency, the old pelt-ball was entirely discarded.

Mezzotinting.

This art was suggested by the simple accident of the gun-barrel of a sentry becoming rusted with dew.

Whitening Sugar.

The process of whitening sugar was discovered in a curious way. A hen that had gone through a clay puddle went with her muddy feet into a sugar house, leaving her tracks on a pile of sugar. It was noticed that wherever her tracks were the sugar was whitened. Experiments were instituted, and the result was that wet clay came to be used in refining sugar.

Discovery of Glass.

Pliny informs us that the art of making glass was accidentally discovered by some merchants who were traveling with nitre, and stopped near a river issuing from Mount Carmel. Not readily finding stones to rest their kettles on, they employed some pieces of their nitre for that purpose. The nitre, gradually dissolving by the heat of the fire, mixed with the sand, and a transparent matter flowed, which was, in fact, glass.

Essence of Pearl.

A French bead-maker named Jaquin discovered the manner of preparing the glass pearls used at present, which approach as near to nature as possible, without being too expensive.

He once noticed, at his estate near Passy, that when the small fish called *ables* or *ablettes* were washed, the water was filled with fine silver-colored particles.   He suffered the water. to stand for some time, and obtained from it a sediment which had the lustre of the most beautiful pearls, which suggested to him the idea of making pearls from it.   He scraped off the scales of the fish, and called the soft shining powder which was diffused in the water essence of pearl, or *essence d'orient.* He succeeded in coating the interior of glass beads with the pearly liquid, and amassed a large fortune.   This was during the reign of Henry IV. (according to some authors), and Jaquin's heirs continued the business down to a late period, and had a considerable manufactory at Rue de Petit Lion, at Paris.   It required from eighteen to twenty thousand fish (which were not more than four inches in length) to make a pound of the essence of pearl.   These pearls were frequently taken for genuine ones.   Mercure Galant (1686), tells us in that year of a poor marquis, who, being in love with a lady, gained her affections by presenting her with a string of artificial pearls.   They cost him not more than three louis, while she, believing them to be genuine pearls, valued them at 2,000 francs.   Jewelers and pawnbrokers were frequently deceived by them.

Diminutive Note Paper.

A Brighton stationer took a fancy for dressing his show-window with piles of writing paper, rising gradually from the largest to the smallest size in use; and to finish his pyramids off nicely, he cut cards to bring them to a point.   Taking these cards for diminutive note paper, lady customers were continually wanting some of " that lovely little paper," and the stationer found it advantageous to cut paper to the desired pattern.   As there was no space for addressing the notelets after they were folded, he, after much thought, invented the envelope, which he cut by the aid of metal plates made for the purpose. The sale increased so rapidly that he was unable to produce the envelopes fast enough, so he commissioned a dozen houses to make them for him, and thus set going an important branch of the manufacturing stationery trade.

Etching upon Glass.

This process was discovered by accident about the year 1670, by an artist named Schwanhard. We are told that some aqua-fortis having fallen by accident upon his spectacles, the glass was corroded by it. He thence learned to make a liquid by which he could etch writing and figures upon glass.

Lundyfoot's Luck.

The shop of a Dublin tobacconist by the name of Lundy-foot was destroyed by fire. While he was gazing dolefully into the smouldering ruins, he noticed that his poorer neighbors were gathering the snuff from the canisters. He tested the snuff for himself, and discovered that the fire had largely improved its pungency and aroma. It was a hint worth profiting by. He secured another shop, built a lot of ovens, subjected the snuff to a heating process, gave the brand a particular name, and in a few years became rich through an accident which he at first thought had completely ruined him.

Citric Acid.

A London chemist was the inventor of citric acid, and, having his own prices as long as the way of making the acid was a secret, realized a large fortune.

This chemist trusted nobody, but worked entirely alone. He thought his secret very safe. It was necessary, however, to have a chimney to his laboratory, and chimneys sometimes want sweeping.

A rival, disguising himself as a chimney-sweep, got into the sanctum. He had all his eyes about him, as the saying is, and, when the chimney was swept, knew how to make citric acid, and thus a monopoly was ended.

A Half-Starved Tramp.

Mr. Huntsman, who had devised some important processes in the manufacture of cast steel, built his factory, to be out of observation, in the middle of a bleak moor, and "No Admission for Strangers" was painted on the outer gate.

One terribly snowy night, however, a poor, belated, half-frozen traveler, who said he had lost his way on the moor, craved shelter, was charitably admitted, and was placed near the furnace, to be thawed. He watched what was done, and, being an expert, took it all away in his mind. Next morning he walked away, and took the secret with him. So perished Huntsman's El Dorado.

Fiddling to some Purpose.

Stourbridge, a smoky town in Worcestershire, England, has long been famous for its iron, glass and fire-brick works, and also for its *nails*, as long as they were produced by hand-work. For the Crystal Palace, of 1851, a Stourbridge "hand" received an order to make a thousand gold and a thousand silver and a thousand iron *tacks*—the whole three thousand not to weigh more than *three* grains.

Nailmaking by machinery, which was accomplished in Sweden before it was perfected in New England, was drawing the trade away from England, and a Stourbridge man, one Richard Foley, resolved to get into the heart of the mystery. The case is curious, as showing the danger that has always beset successful inventors, and has often converted the golden hills into mere rocks of talc, and reduced many a secret El Dorado into commonplace little workshops.

Foley, who was a very good violinist, took his fiddle, fiddled his way to the Swedish splitting mills, and then fiddled his way into them. As often happens with musicians, he presently conceived the idea that there was "a great deal of brains *outside* of his head."

At any rate, he could look and speak foolishly, but his fiddling was wonderfully good. No one suspected that "soft" fellow, who lounged about with an idiotic want of expression in his face, but was ready to play whenever asked to do so.

He ingratiated himself so thoroughly with the workmen that they gave him a shakedown inside the mill or factory. He quietly exercised his faculty of observation, saw all the processes of manipulation, and one day was missing. He carried home their secrets of work, and fame and fortune became his own.

German Silver.

German silver derives its name from the fact that its first introduction in the arts, to any great extent, was made in Germany. It is, however, nothing more than the white copper long known in China. It does not contain a particle of real silver, but is an alloy of copper, nickel and zinc.

Isabella Color.

The Archduke Albert married the infanta Isabella, daughter of Philip II., King of Spain, with whom he had the Low Countries in dowry. In the year 1602 he laid siege to Ostend, then in the possession of the heretics, and his pious princess, who attended him in that expedition, made a vow that she would not change her clothes until the city was taken. Contrary to expectation, it was three years before the place was reduced, in which time the linen of her highness had acquired a hue which, from the superstition of the princess and the times, was much admired, and was adopted by the court fashionables under the name of the "Isabella color." It is a whitish yellow, or soiled buff—better imagined than described.

Parisian Scarlet.

The tincture of cochineal alone yields a purple color, which may be changed to a most beautiful scarlet by adding a solution of tin in aqua-regia, or muriatic acid, a discovery which was made by accident. Cornelius Drebbel, who died in London in 1634, having placed in his window an extract of cochineal, made with boiling water, for the purpose of filling a thermometer, some aqua-regia dropped into it from a phial, broken by accident, which stood above it, and converted the purple dye into a most beautiful scarlet. After some conjectures and experiments, he discovered that the tin by which the window frame was divided into squares had been dissolved by the aqua-regia, and was the cause of the change. Giles Gobelin, a dyer at Paris, used it for dyeing cloth. It became known as Parisian scarlet dye, and rose into such great repute that the populace declared that Gobelin had acquired his art from the devil.

Tyrian Purple.

The purple dye of Tyre was discovered about fifteen centuries before the Christian era, and the art of using it did not become lost until the eleventh century after Christ. It was obtained from two genera of one species of shell-fish, the smaller of which was called *buccinum*, the larger *purpura*, and to both the common name mure was applied. The dye-stuff was procured by puncturing a vessel in the throat of the larger genus, and by pounding the smaller entire. The tints capable of being imparted by this material were various—representing numerous shades between purple and crimson, but the imperial tint was that resembling coagulated blood. That it was known to the Egyptians, in the time of Moses, is sufficiently obvious from the testimony of more than one Scriptural passage. Ultimately, in later ages, a restrictive policy of the eastern emperors caused the art to be practised by only a few individuals, and at last, about the commencement of the tweifth century, when Byzantium was suffering from attacks without and dissensions within, the secret of imparting the purple dye of Tyre was lost.

The rediscovery of Tyrian purple, as it occurred in England, was made by Mr. Cole, of Bristol. About the latter end of the year 1683, this gentleman heard from two ladies residing at Minehead, that a person living somewhere on the coast of Ireland supported himself by marking with a delicate crimson color the fine linen of ladies and gentlemen sent him for that purpose, which color was the product of a shell-fish. This recital at once brought to the recollection of Mr. Cole the tradition of Tyrian purple. He, without delay, went in search of the shell-fish, and, after trying various kinds without success, his efforts were at length successful. He found considerable quantities of the buccinum on the sea-coast of Somersetshire and the opposite coast of South Wales. The fish being found, the next difficulty was to extract the dye, which in its natural state is not purple but white, the purple being the result of exposure to the air. At length our acute investigator found the dye-stuff in a white vein lying transversely in a little furrow or cleft next to the head of the fish.

Odor of Patchouli.

The odor of patchouli was known in Europe before the material itself was introduced, in consequence of its use in cashmere to scent the shawls with a view of keeping out moths, which are averse to it; hence the genuine cashmere shawls were known by their scent, until the French found out the secret and imported the herb for use in the same way.

Veneered Diamonds.

Quite a notable industry is carried on in Paris, namely, the manufacture of what are termed veneered diamonds. The body of the gem is of quartz or crystal. After being cut into a proper shape, it is put into a galvanic battery, which coats it with a liquid, the latter being made of diamonds which are too small to be cut and of the clippings taken from diamonds during the process of shapening them. In this way all the small particles of diamonds that heretofore have been regarded as comparatively worthless, can, by means of this ingenious process, be made of service to the jeweler.

Hungary Water.

This is a spirit of wine distilled upon rosemary, and con-tains a powerful aroma of the plant. For many years it was mainly manufactured at Beaucaire and Montpellier, in France, where the plant grows in abundance. The name seems to signify that this water, so celebrated for its medicinal virtues, is an Hungarian invention; and we read in various books that the recipe for preparing it was given to a queen of Hungary by a hermit, or, as others say, by an angel, who appeared to her in a garden, all entrance to which was shut, in the form of a hermit or youth. Others affirm that Elizabeth, wife of

Charles Robert, king of Hungary, who died in 1380, was the inventor. By often washing with this spirit of rosemary, when in the seventieth year of her age, she was cured, as we are told, of the gout and an universal lameness; so that she not only lived to pass eighty, but became so lively and beautiful that she was courted by the king of Poland, who was then a widower, and who wished to make her his second wife. Hoyer says that the recipe for preparing this water, written by Queen Elizabeth's own hand, in golden characters, is still preserved in the Imperial Library at Vienna. Beckmann says such is not the case.

Cork Jackets.

The use of cork for making jackets, as an aid to swimming, is very old. We are informed that the Roman whom Camillus sent to the Capitol, when besieged by the Gauls, put on a light dress, and took cork with him under it, because, to avoid being taken by the enemy, it was necessary for him to swim across the Tiber.

Nothing New under the Sun.

The Romans used movable types to mark their pottery and indorse their books. Mr. Layard found, in Nineveh, a magnificent lens of rock-crystal, which Sir D. Brewster considers a true optical lens, and the origin of the microscope. The principle of the stereoscope, invented by Professor Wheatstone, was known to Euclid, described by Galen fifteen hundred years ago, and more fully in 1599, A. D., in the works of Baptista Porta. The Thames tunnel, though such a novelty, was anticipated by that under the Euphrates at Babylon, and the ancient Egyptians had a Suez canal. Such examples might be indefinitely multiplied; but we turn to Photography.

M. Jobarb, in his "Neuvelles Inventions aux Expositions Universelles," 1856, says a translation from German was discovered in Russia, three hundred years old, which contains a clear explanation of Photography.   The old alchemists understood the properties of chloride of silver in relation to light, and its photographic action is explained by Fabricius in "De Rubus Metallicis," 1566.   The daguerreotype process was anticipated by De La Roche, in his "Giphantic," 1760, though it was only the statement of a dreamer.

How the Ancients Rewarded Inventors.

A Roman architect discovered the means of so far altering the nature of glass as to render it malleable; but the Emperor Tiberius caused the architect to be beheaded.   A similar discovery was made in France during the reign of Louis XIII. The inventor presented a bust, formed of malleable glass, to Cardinal Richelieu, and was rewarded for his ingenuity by perpetual imprisonment, lest the French glass manufacturers should be injured by the discovery of it.

Deutsche Luft.

A German newspaper tells an amusing story of the famous scientist, Alexander von Humboldt, who took advantage of the exemption from duty of the covering of articles free from duty, formerly the rule in France.   In the year 1805 he and Gay-Lussac were in Paris, engaged in their experiments on the compression of air.   The two scientists found themselves in need of a large number of glass tubes, and since this article was exceedingly dear in France at that time, and the duty on imported glass tubes was something alarming, Humboldt sent an order to Germany for the needed articles, giving directions that the manufacturer should seal the tubes at both ends, and put a label upon each with the words *"Deutsche Luft"* (German air).   The air of Germany was an article upon which there was no duty, and the tubes were passed by the custom officers without any demand, arriving free of duty in the hands of the two experimenters.

The Great Hero of the Bretons.

Merlin, the enchanter, is the great hero of the Bretons as he is of the Welsh, the same legends being common to both people.   Among other lays respecting him is the following, which is of high antiquity:—

> "Merlin! Merlin! whither bound
> With your black dog by your side?" (1)
> "I seek until the prize be found,
> Where the red egg loves to hide.
>
> "The red egg of the sea-snake's nest, (2)
> Where the ocean caves are seen,
> And the cress that grows the best,
> In the valley fresh and green.
>
> "I must find the golden herb, (3)
> And the oak's high bough must have, (4)
> Where no sound the trees disturb
> Near the fountain as they wave."
>
> "Merlin! Merlin! turn again—
> Leave the oak-branch where it grew;
> Seek no more the cress to gain,
> Nor the herb of gold pursue.
>
> "Nor the red egg of the snake,
> Where amid the foam it lies,
> In the cave where billows break:
> Leave these fearful mysteries.
>
> "Merlin, turn! to God alone
> Are such fatal secrets known!"

(1.) At the foot of Mont St. Michel extends a wide marsh. If the mountaineer sees in the dusk of the evening a tall man, thin and pale, followed by a black dog, whose steps are directed toward the marsh, he hurries home, shuts and locks the door of his cottage, and throws himself on his knees to pray, for he knows that the tempest is approaching. Soon after, the winds begin to howl, the thunder bursts forth in tremendous peals, and the mountain trembles to its base. It is the moment when Merlin, the enchanter, evokes the souls of the dead.

(2.) The red egg of the sea-snake was a powerful talisman, whose virtue nothing could equal; it was to be worn around the neck.

(3.) The golden herb is a medicinal plant. The peasants of Bretàgne hold it in great esteem, and say that it shines at a distance like gold. If any one tread it under foot he falls asleep, and can understand the language of dogs, wolves and birds. This simple is supposed to be rarely met with, and only at daybreak. In order to gather it (a privilege only granted to the devout), it is necessary to be *en chemise* and with bare feet. It must be torn up, not cut. Another way is to go with naked feet, in a white robe, fasting, and, without using a knife, gather the herb by slipping the right hand under the left arm and letting it fall into a cloth, which can only be used once.

(4.) The high oak bough is probably the mistletoe. The voice which warns Merlin in the poem may be intended for that of Saint Colombar, who is said to have converted Merlin.

The Wandering Jew.

Brought to Europe from the East, after the first crusade under Peter the Hermit, late in the eleventh century, was the legend of the Wandering Jew. This appellation was given

by the popular voice to almost every mendicant with a long
white beard and scanty clothing, who, supported by a long
staff, trudged along the roads with eyes downcast, and without
opening his lips.

In the year 1228 this legend was told for the first time by
an Armenian bishop, then lately arrived from the Holy Land,
to the monks of St. Alban, in England. According to his
narrative, Joseph Cartaphilus was door-keeper at the prætorium of Pontius Pilate when Jesus was led away to be crucified.
As Jesus halted upon the threshold of the prætorium, Cartaphilus struck him in the loins and said : "Move faster! Why
do you stop here?" Jesus, the legend continues, turned
round to him and said, with a severe look : "I go, but you
will await my coming."

Cartaphilus, who was then thirty years old, and who since
then has always returned to that age when he had completed
a hundred years, has ever since been awaiting the coming of
our Lord and the end of the world. He was said to suffer
under the peculiar doom of ceaselessly traversing the earth on
foot. The general belief was that he was a man of great
piety, of sad and gentle manners, of few words, often weeping,
seldom smiling, and content with the scantiest and simplest
food and the most poverty-stricken garments. Such was the
tradition which poets and romancists in various lands and
many languages have introduced into song and story.

As the ages rolled on new circumstances were added to
this tale. Paul of Eitzen, a German bishop, wrote in a letter
to a friend that he had met the Wandering Jew at Hamburg,
in 1564, and had a long conversation with him. He appeared
to be fifty years of age. His hair was long, and he went
barefoot. His dress consisted of very full breeches, a short
petticoat or kilt reaching to the knees, and a cloak so long
that it descended to his heels. Instead of Joseph Cartaphilus,
he then was called Ahasuerus. He attended Christian wor-

ship, prostrating himself with sighs, tears and beating of the breast whenever the name of Jesus was spoken. The bishop further stated that this man's speech was very edifying. He could not hear an oath without bursting into tears, and when offered money would accept only a few sous.

According to the bishop's version of the affair, Cartaphilus was standing in front of his house, in Jerusalem, with his wife and children, when he roughly accosted Jesus, who had halted to take breath while carrying his cross to Calvary. "I shall stop and be at rest," was all that the Lord said; "but you will ever be on foot." After this sentence Cartaphilus quitted home and family to do perpetual penance by wandering on foot over the whole world. He did not know, the bishop said, what God intended to do with him, in compelling him so long to lead such a miserable life, but had hope and faith in His mercy. There was scarcely a town or village in Europe, in the sixteenth century, but what claimed to have given hospitality to this unfortunate witness of the Passion of our Lord.

The Pyed Piper.

Verstegan, in his "Restitution of Decayed Intelligence," 1634, relates the following strange story: "Hulberstadt, in Germany, was extremely infested with rats, which a certain musician, called, from his habit, the Pyed Piper, agreed for a large sum of money to destroy. He tuned his pipes, and the rats immediately followed him to the next river, where they were all drowned. But when the piper demanded his pay he was refused with scorn and contempt, upon which he began another tune, and was followed by all the children of the town to a neighboring hill called Hamelen, which opened and swallowed them up, then closed again. One boy, being lame, came after the rest, but seeing what had happened, he returned and related the strange circumstance. The story was believed, for the parents never after heard of their lost children. This incident is stated to have happened on the 22d of July, in the year 1376, and since that time the people of Hulberstadt permit not any drum, pipe or other instrument to be sounded in that street which leads to the gate through which the children passed. They also established a decree that in all writings of contract or bargain, after the date of our Saviour's nativity, the date also of the year of the children's going forth should be added, in perpetual remembrance of this surprising event."

Thomas, the Rhymer.

This character was one of the earliest poets of Scotland. His life and writings are involved in much obscurity, though he is supposed to have been Thomas Learmount, of Ercildonne. The time of his birth is unknown, but he appears to have reached the height of his reputation in 1283, when he is said to have predicted the death of Alexander III., king of Scotland. One day the Rhymer, when visiting at the Castle of Dunbar, was interrogated by the Earl of March in a jocular manner as to what the morrow would bring forth. "Alas for to-morrow! a day of calamity and misery!" replied the Rhymer. "Before the twelfth hour shall be heard a blast so vehement that it shall exceed all those which have yet been heard in Scotland—a blast which shall strike the nations with amazement; shall confound those who hear it; shall humble what is lofty, and what is unbending shall level with the ground." On the following day the earl, who had been unable to discover any unusual appearance in the weather, when seating himself at table, observed the hand of the dial to point to the hour of noon, while, at the same moment, a messenger appeared, bringing the mournful tidings of the accidental death of the king.   The legend says that the Rhymer was carried off at an early age to Fairyland, where he acquired all the knowledge which made him so famous.   After seven years' residence there, he was permitted to return to the earth to enlighten and astonish his countrymen by his prophetic powers, but bound to return to the Fairy Queen, his royal mistress, whenever she should intimate her pleasure.   Accordingly, while the Rhymer was making merry with his friends at his tower at Ercildonne, a person came running in and told, with marks of alarm and astonishment, that a hart and hind had left the neighboring forest, and were slowly and composedly parading the street of the village.   The Rhymer instantly rose, left his habitation, and followed the animals to the forest, whence he was never seen to return.

Pontius Pilate at Vienne.

There is a tradition at Vienne, in Provence, that in the reign of the Emperor Tiberius, Pontius Pilate was exiled to that city, where he died not long after of grief and despair for not having prevented the crucifixion of the Saviour, and his body was thrown into the Rhone.   There it remained, neither carried away by the force of the current nor consumed by decay, for five hundred years, until the town, being afflicted with the plague, it was revealed to the then archbishop, in a vision, that the calamity was occasioned by Pilate's body, which, unknown to the good people of Vienne, was lying at the foot of a certain tower.   The place was accordingly searched, and the body drawn up entire, but nothing could equal its intolerable odor.   It was carried to a marsh two leagues from the town and there interred, but for many years after strange noises were reported to issue continually from the place.   The sounds were believed to be the groans of Pontius Pilate, and the cries of the devils tormenting him.   It was imagined that it was the presence of his body which caused the violent thunder-storms which are so frequent at Vienne; and as the tower where the body was found has been several times struck by lightning, it is called the tower of *Mauconseil.*

The Sea-woman of Haarlem.

In the "History of the Netherlands" there is the following strange account of the Sea-woman of Haarlem :—

"At that time there was a great tempest at sea, with exceeding high tides, the which did drowne many villages in Friseland and Holland ; by which tempest there came a seawoman swimming in the Zuyderzee betwixt the towns of Campen and Edam, the which passing by the Purmerie, entered into the straight of a broken dyke in the Purmermer, where she remained a long time, and could not find the hole by which she entered, for that the breach had been stopped after that the tempest had ceased. Some country women and their servants who did dayly pass the Pourmery to milk their kine in the next pastures, did often see this woman swimming on the water, whereof at first they were much afraid ; but in the end, being accustomed to see it very often, they viewed it neerer, and at last they resolved to take it if they could. Having discovered it, they rowed towards it, and drew it out of the water by force, carrying it into the town of Edam.

"When she had been well washed and cleansed from the sea-moss which was grown about her, she was like unto another woman. She was appareled, and began to accustome herself to ordinary meats like unto any other, yet she sought still means to escape and to get into the water, but she was straightly guarded. They came from farre to see her. Those of Haarlem made great sute to them of Edam to have this woman, by reason of the strangenesse thereof. In the end they obtained her, where she did learn to spin, and lived many years (some say fifteen), and for the reverance which she bore unto the signe of the crosse whereunto she had been accustomed, she was buried in the church-yarde. Many persons worthy of credit have justified in their writings that they had seene her in the said towne of Haarlem.''

Legends of Judas Iscariot.

It was believed in Pier della Valle's time that the descendants of Judas Iscariot still existed at Corfu, though the persons who suffered under the imputation stoutly denied it.

When the ceremony of washing the feet is performed in the Greek Church at Smyrna, the bishop represents Christ, and the twelve apostles are acted by as many priests. He who personates Judas must be paid for it, and such is the feeling of the people, that whoever accepts this odious part commonly retains the name of Judas for life.—*Hasselquiet*, p. 43.

Judas serves in Brazil for a Guy Faux to be carried about by the boys. The Spanish sailors hang him at the yard-arm. The Armenians, who believe hell and limbo to be the same place, say that Judas, after having betrayed the Lord, resolved to hang himself, because he knew Christ was to go to limbo and deliver all the souls which he found there, and therefore he thought to get there in time. But the devil was more cunning than he, and knowing his intention, held him over limbo till the Lord had passed through, and then let him fall plum into hell.—*Thevenot.*

Blue Beard.

Perrault, the author of "Blue Beard," founded the story, popular belief assures us, on the history of a real person. The original was Giles de Retz, Lord of Laval, who was made Marshal of France in 1429. He was born in 1406, and fought under the command of Joan of Arc. He lived like a king in his castle, with two hundred horsemen for his guard of honor, besides fifty choristers, chaplains and musicians. He was wild and profligate, lavish with his own money and of other people's, and lived at the costliest rate.

When he had squandered his property, he took to the study of sorcery and magic, having an especial fancy for murdering young children. From the villages within a circuit of twenty miles, little boys and girls were seduced into his castle and there immolated according to some wild Pagan rites. Among his papers, history says, was found a list of two hundred children whom he had thus sacrificed.

On the 26th of October, 1440, then being thirty-four years old, he was burned in the city of Nantes, having been previously strangled in view of a vast multitude. The records of his trial, which lasted a whole month, are preserved among the manuscripts of the public library in Paris. In one of his castles the bones of forty-six, and in another of eighty children, were discovered. Marshal de Retz was certainly the type of Perrault's story. It appears that in his lifetime he was known by the *sobriquet* of Barbe Bleu.

African Rain-Doctors.

How a belief in *imaginary* virtues of things may grow out of the evidence of their *real* virtues, is indicated by Dr. Livingstone, when speaking of the belief in rain-making among the tribes in the heart of South Africa. The African priest and the medicine-man is one and the same, and his chief function is to make the clouds to give out rain. The preparations for this purpose are various: charcoal made of burned bats; lion's hearts, and hairy calculi from the bowels of old cows; serpent skins and and vertebræ, and every kind of tuber, bulb, root and plant to be found in the country.

"Although you disbelieve their efficacy in charming the clouds to pour out their refreshing treasures, yet, conscious that civility is useful everywhere, you kindly state that you think they are mistaken as to their power. The rain-doctor selects a particular bulbous root, pounds it, and administers a cold infusion of it to a sheep, which in five minutes afterwards expires in convulsions. Part of the same bulb is converted into smoke and ascends towards the sky: rain follows in a day or two. The inference is obvious."

Whittington and his Cat.

This fable of the cat is borrowed from the East. Sir William Gore Ousely, speaking of the origin of the name of an island in the Persian Gulf, says that in the tenth century, one Keis, the son of a poor widow in Siraf, embarked for India with his sole property, a cat. "He fortunately arrived there at a time when the palace was so infested by mice or rats that they invaded the king's food, and persons were employed to drive them away from the royal banquet. Keis produced his cat; the noxious animals disappeared; Keis was magnificently rewarded, sent for his mother and brother, and settled on the island, which was subsequently called after him."

Head of James IV. of Scotland.

The king was slain in the battle at Flodden Field. At the close of the bloody arbitrament his body was found among a heap of the fallen. The discoverers made a prize of the corpse, wrapped it up in lead, and transmitted it as a thanksgiving offering to the monastery of Sheen, in Surrey. It was well taken care of by the honest people there as long as the monastery stood; but when the dissolution of those religious establishments took place, and the edifice was converted into a mansion for the Duke of Suffolk, the king's body was put into a fresh wrapping of lead and carried into an upper lumber-room. Some workmen engaged in the house cut off the head out of sheer wantonness. Their master, a glazier from Cheapside, carried the head with him to the city. There, on his sideboard, the dried remnant of a crowned king, with its red hair and beard, was long the admiration of the glazier's evening parties and a subject of conversation for his guests. John Stow saw it there, expostulated, purchased the anointed skull, and gave it quiet and decent burial within the old church of St. Michael's.

Discovery of the Body of Canute the Great.

In June, 1776, some workmen who were repairing Winchester Cathedral discovered a monument which contained the body of King Canute. It was remarkably fresh, had a wreath round the head and several ornaments of gold and silver bands. On his finger was a ring, in which was set a large and remarkably fine stone, and in one of his hands a silver coin. The coin found in the hand is a singular instance of a continuance of the Pagan custom of always providing the dead with money to pay Charon.

Martyrdom of Isaiah.

There is a tradition that the prophet Isaiah suffered martyrdom by a saw. The ancient book entitled, "The Ascension of Isaiah the Prophet," accords with the tradition. It says: "Then they seized Isaiah the son of Amos and sawed him with a wooden saw. And Manasseh, Melakira, the false prophets, the princess and the people, all stood looking on.

But he said to the prophets who were with him before he was sawn, 'Go ye to the country of Tyre and Sidon, for the Lord hath mixed the cup for me alone.' Neither while they were sawing him did he cry out nor weep, but he continued addressing himself to the Holy Spirit until he was sawn asunder."

Courtship of William the Conqueror

The following extract from the life of the wife of the Conqueror is exceedingly curious as characteristic of the manners of a semi-civilized age and nation :—

"After some years of delay, William appears to have become desperate, and, if we may trust to the evidence of the 'Chronicle of Ingerbe,' he waylaid Matilda in the streets of Bruges as she was returning from mass, seized her, rolled her in the dirt, spoiled her rich array ; and, not content with these outrages, struck her repeatedly, then rode off at full speed. This Teutonic method of courtship, according to our author, brought the affair to a crisis ; for Matilda, either convinced of the strength of William's passion by the violence of his behaviour, or afraid of encountering a second beating, consented to become his wife. How he ever presumed to enter her presence again after such enormities the chronicler sayeth not, and we are at a loss to imagine."

Court Fools.

From very ancient times there existed a class of persons whose business it was to amuse the rich and noble, particularly at table, by jests and witty sayings. It was, however, during the Middle Ages that this singular vocation became fully developed. The symbols of the court fool were : the shaven crown, the fool's cap of gay colors with asses' ears and cock's

comb and bells, the fool's sceptre, and a wide collar. Some
of these professional fools obtained an historical reputation, as
Triboulet, jester to Francis I. of France ; Klaus Narr, at the
Court of the Elector Frederic, the Wise of Prussia, and Sco-
gan, court-fool to Edward IV. of England. Besides the
regular fools, dressed and recognized as such, there was a
higher class called merry counsellors, generally men of talent,
who availed themselves of the privilege of free speech to ridicule in the most merciless manner the follies and vices of
their contemporaries. At a later period, imbecile or weak-
minded persons were kept for the entertainment of company.
Even ordinary noblemen considered such an attendant indispensable, and thus the system reached its last stage, and
toward the end of the seventeenth century it was abolished.
It survived longest in Russia, where Peter the Great had so
many fools that he divided them into distinct classes.

A Cunning Astrologer.

An astrologer in the reign of Louis XI. of France, having
foretold something disagreeable to the king, his majesty, in
revenge, resolved to have him killed. The next day he sent
for the astrologer and ordered the people about him, at a
given signal, to throw him out of the window. The king
said to him : " You pretend to be such a wise man, and know
so perfectly the fate of others, inform me a little what will be
your own, and how long you have to live." The astrologer,
who now began to apprehend some danger, promptly answered,
with great presence of mind, " I know my destiny, and am
sure I shall die three days before your majesty." The king,
on this, was so far from having him thrown out of the window,
that, on the contrary, he took particular care not to have him
want for anything, and did all that was possible to retard the
death of one whom he was likely soon to follow.

Stone Barometer.

A Finland newspaper mentions a stone in the northern part of Finland which serves the inhabitants instead of a barometer. This stone, which they call Tlmakiur, turns black, or blackish gray, when it is going to rain; but on the approach of fine weather it is covered with white spots. Probably it is a fossil mixed with clay, and containing rock-salt, nitre or ammonia, which, according to the degree of dampness in the atmosphere, attracts it, or otherwise. In the latter case the salt appears, forming the white spots.

Crinoline in 1744.

Addison, who wrote a good deal about female fashions in the "Spectator," very much ridiculed the hoop-petticoat, which was so large, about the year 1744, that a woman wearing one occupied the space of six men.

Pagoda-shaped Head-dresses.

The head-dresses of the ladies in 1776 were remarkable for their enormous height. Fashion ruled its votaries then as arbitrarily as in our day. The *coiffure* of a belle of fashion was described as "a mountain of wool, hair, powder, lawn, muslin, net, lace, gauze, ribbon, flowers, feathers and wire." Sometimes these varied materials were built up tier upon tier, like the stages of a pagoda!

Preserved in Salt.

We are told that Pharnaces caused the body of his father, Mithridates, to be deposited in salt brine, in order that he might transmit it to Pompey. Sigebert, who died in 1113, informs us that a like process was employed upon the body of St. Guibert, that it might be kept during a journey in summer. The priests preserved in salt the sow which afforded a happy omen to Æneas by having brought forth a litter of thirty pigs, as we are told by Varro, in whose time the animal was still shown at Lavinium. The hippopotamus described by Columna was sent to him from Egypt preserved in salt.

Luxury in 1562.

The luxury of the present time does not equal, in one article at least, that of the sixteenth century. Sir Nicholas Throckmorton, the queen's ambassador at Paris, in a letter to Sir Thomas Chaloner, the ambassador at Madrid, in June 1562, says—

" I pray you good my Lord Ambassador sende me two paire of perfumed gloves, perfumed with orrange flowers and jacemin, th' one for my wives hand, the other for mine owne ; and wherin soever I can pleasure you with anything in this countrey, you shall have it in recompence thereof, or els so moche money as they shall coste you, provided alwaies that they be of the best choise, wherin your judgment is inferior to none."

Trains in the Fourteenth Century.

In Mr. Wright's collection of Latin stories, there is one of the fourteenth century—a monkish satire upon dresses with long trains—

Of a Proud Woman.—I have heard of a proud woman who wore a white dress with a long train, which, trailing behind her, raised a dust as far as the altar and the crucifix. But, as she left the church, and lifted up her train on account of the dirt, a certain holy man saw a devil laughing ; and

having adjured him to tell why he laughed, the devil said:
"A companion of mine was just now sitting on the train of
that woman, using it as if it were his chariot, but when she
lifted her train up, my companion was shaken off into the
dirt, and that is why I was laughing."

Foppery in Eminent Men.

"Peculiarities of dress, even amounting to foppery, so common among eminent men, are carried off from ridicule by
ease in some or stateliness in others. We may smile at Chatham, scrupulously crowned in his best wig, if intending to
speak; at Erskine, drawing on his bright yellow gloves
before he rose to plead; at Horace Walpole, in a cravat of
Gibbon's carvings; at Raleigh, loading his shoes with jewels
so heavy that he could scarcely walk; at Petrarch, pinching
his feet till he crippled them; at the rings which covered the
philosophical fingers of Aristotle; at the bare throat of Byron;
the American dress of Rousseau; the scarlet and gold coat of
Voltaire; or the prudent carefulness with which Cæsar
scratched his head so as not to disturb the locks arranged
over the bald place. But most of these men, we apprehend,
found it easy to enforce respect and curb impertinence.—
Edinburgh Review.

The Turban in Arabia.

A fashionable Arab will wear fiftcen caps one above the
other, some of which are linen, but the greater part of which
are thick cloth or cotton. That which covers the whole is
richly embroidered with gold, and inwrought with texts or
passages from the Koran. Over all there is wrapped a sash
or large piece of muslin, with the ends hanging down, and
ornamented with silk or gold fringe. This useless encum-

brance is considered a mark of respect towards superiors. It is also used, as the beard was formerly in Europe, to indicate literary merit; and those who affect to be thought men of learning, discover their pretensions by the size of their turbans. No part of oriental costume is so variable as this covering for the head. Niebuhr has given illustrations of forty-eight different ways of wearing it.—*King*.

Queen Elizabeth's Dresses.

The list of the queen's wardrobe, in 1600, shows us that she had then *only* 99 robes, 126 kirtles, 269 gowns (round, loose and French), 136 fore parts, 125 petticoats, 27 fans, 96 cloaks, 83 safe guards, 85 doublets, 18 lap mantles.

Absurdities of the Toilet.

The ladies of Japan gild their teeth; those of the Indies paint them red; while in Guzerat the test of beauty is to render them sable. In Greenland the women used to color their faces blue and yellow. The Chinese torture their feet into the smallest possible dimensions. The ancient Peruvians used to flatten their heads; among other nations, the mothers, in a similar way, maltreat the nose of their offspring.

Gambling for Fingers.

Such is the passion among the Chinese for gambling, that when they have lost all their money they will stake houses, lands, their wives, the clothes on their backs. Those who have nothing more to lose will collect around a table and actually play for *their fingers*, which they will cut off reciprocally with frightful stoicism.—*Hue's Chinese Empire*.

Pigmies.

"Among vulgar errors is set down this, that there is a nation of pigmies, not above two or three feet high, and that they solemnly set themselves in battle to fight against the cranes."—*Strabo.*

"Strabo thought this a fiction ; and our age, which has fully discovered all the wonders of the world, as fully declares it to be one."—*Brand.*

This refers to accounts of the Pechinians of Ethiopia, who are represented of small stature, and as being accustomed every year to drive away the cranes which flocked to their country in the winter.   They are portrayed on ancient gems as mounted on cocks or partridges, to fight the cranes ; or carrying grasshoppers, and leaning on staves to support the burden.

The Letter "M" and the Napoleons.

The "Frankforter Journal," of September 21st, 1870, remarked, that among other superstitions peculiar to the Napoleons, is that of regarding the letter M as ominous, either of good or of evil, and it took the pains to make the following catalogue of men, things and events, the names of which begin with M, with the view of showing that the two emperors of France had cause for considering the letter a red or a black one, according to circumstances.

It says, "Marbœuf was the first to recognize the genius of Napoleon I. at the military college.   Marengo was the first great battle won by General Bonaparte, and Melas made room for him in Italy.   Mortier was one of his best generals, Moreau betrayed him, and Marat was the first martyr to his cause.   Marie Louise shared his highest fortunes ; Moscow was the abyss of ruin into which he fell.   Metternich vanquished him in the field of diplomacy.   Six marshals (Massena, Mortie, Marmont, Macdonald, Murat, Moncey) and twenty-six generals of division under Napoleon I. had the letter M for their initial. Marat, Duke of Bassano, was his most trusted counsellor. His first battle was that of Montenotte; his last, Mont St. Jean, as the French term Waterloo. He won the battles of Millesimo, Mondovi, Montmirail and Montereau; then came the storming of Montmartre. Milan was the first enemy's capital, and Moscow the last, into which he entered victorious. He lost Egypt through Menou, and employed Miellis to take Pius VIII. prisoner. Mallet conspired against him; Murat was the first to desert him, then Marmont. Three of his ministers were Maret, Montalivet and Mallieu; his first chamberlaind was Montesquien. His last halting place in France was Malmaison. He surrendered to Captain Maitland, and his companions at St. Helena were Montholon and his valet Marchand."

If we turn to the career of his nephew, Napoleon III., we find the same letter no less prominent, and it is said that he attached even greater importance to its mystic influence than did his uncle.

The Physician's Symbol.

De Paris tells us that the Physician of the present day continues to prefix to his prescriptions the letter R, which is generally supposed to mean *Recipe*, but which is, in truth, a relic of the astrological symbol of Jupiter, formerly used as a species of superstitious invocation.

Chinese Giants.

The Chinese pretend to have men among them so prodigious as fifteen feet high. Melchior Nunnez, in his letters from India, speaks of porters who guarded the gates of Pekin, who were of that immense height ; and in a letter dated in 1555, he avers that the emperor of that country entertained and fed five hundred of such men for archers of his guard. Hakewill, in his "Apologie," 1627, repeats this story. Purchas, in his "Pilgrimes," 1625, refers to a man in China who "was cloathed with a tyger's skin, the hayre outward, his arms, head and legges bare, with a rude pole in his hand ; well-shaped, seeming ten palmes or spans long ; his hayre hanging on his shoulders."

Trying Land Titles in Hindostan.

According to the "Asiatic Researches," a very curious mode of trying the titles of land is practised in Hindostan : Two holes are dug in the disputed spot, in each of which the lawyer for the plaintiff and the lawyer for the defendant put one of their legs, and remain there until one of them is tired or complains of being stung by the insects, in which case his client is defeated. In this country it is the *client*, and not the lawyer, who *puts his foot into it.*

An Asylum for Destitute Cats.

Of all the curious charitable institutions in the world, the most curious, probably, is the Cat Asylum at Aleppo, which is attached to one of the mosques there, and was founded by a misanthropic old Turk, who, being possessed of large granaries, was much annoyed by rats and mice, to rid himself of which he employed a legion of cats, who so effectually rendered him service, that in return he left them a sum in the Turkish funds, with strict injunctions that all destitute and sickly cats should be provided for till such time as they took themselves off again. In 1845, when a famine was raging in all North Syria, when scores of poor people were dropping down in the streets and dying there, from sheer exhaustion and want, men might daily be encountered carrying away sack loads of cats to be well fed on the proceeds of the last will and testament of that vagabond old Turk.

Treasure Digging.

A patent passed the great seal in the fifteenth year of James I. "to allow to Mary Middlemore, one of the maydes of honor to our dearest consort Queen Anne (of Denmark), and her deputies, power and authority to enter into the abbies of St. Albans, St. Edmunsbury, Glassenbury and Ramsay, and into all lands, houses and places, within a mile belonging to said abbies, there to dig and search after treasure supposed to be hidden in such places."

House of Hen's Feathers.

There exists at Pekin a phalanstery which surpasses in eccentrictity all that the fertile imagination of Fourier could have conceived. It is called Ki-mao-fan ; that is, " House of Hen's Feathers." This marvellous establishment is simply composed of one great hall, the floor of which is covered over its whole extent with one vast, thick layer of feathers. Mendicants and vagabonds who have no other domicile come to pass the night in this immense dormitoy. Men, women and children, old and young, are admitted without exception. Every one settles himself, and makes his nest as well as he can for the night in this ocean of feathers. When day dawns he must quit the premises, and an officer of the company stands at the door to receive the rent of one sapeck (one-fifth of a farthing) each for the night's lodging. In deference, no doubt, to the principle of equality, half places are not allowed, and a child must pay the same as a grown person.

On the first establishment of this eminently philanthropic institution, the managers of it furnished each of the guests with a covering ; but it was found necessary to modify this regulation, for the communist company got into the habit of carrying off their coverlets to sell them, or to supply an additional garment during the cold weather. It was necessary, therefore, to devise some method of reconciling the interests of the establishment with the comfort of the guests, and the way in which the problem was solved was this—

An immense coverlet, of such gigantic dimensions as to cover the whole dormitory, was made, and in the day-time suspended from the ceiling like a great canopy. When everybody had gone to bed—that is to say, had lain down upon the feathers—the counterpane was let down by pulleys, the precaution having been previously taken to make a number of holes in it for the sleepers to put their heads through in order to escape the danger of suffocation. As soon as it is daylight the phalansterian coverlet is hoisted up again, after a signal has been made on the tam-tam to awaken those who are asleep, and invite them to draw their heads back into the feathers in order not to be caught by the neck.

St. George's Cavern.

Near the town of Moldavia, on the Danube, is shown the cavern where St. George slew the dragon, from which, at certain periods, issue myriads of small flies, which tradition reports to proceed from the carcass of the dragon. It is thought when the Danube rises, as it does in the early part of the summer, the caverns are flooded, and the water which remains in them becomes putrid, and produces the noxious fly. But this supposition appears to be at fault, for the people closed up the caverns, and still they were annoyed with the flies. The latter resemble mosquitoes, and appear in such swarms as to look like a volume of smoke, sometimes covering a space of six to seven miles. Covered with these insects, horses not unfrequently gallop about until death puts an end to their sufferings. Shepherds anoint their hands with a decoction of wormwood, and keep large fires burning to ptotect themselves from them.

Remarkable Echoes.

In the gardens of Les Rochas, which was the residence of Madame de Sevigne, is a remarkable echo which finely illu trates the conducting and reverberating powers of a flat su face. The chateau is situated near the old town of Vitre. A broad gravel walk on a dead flat conducts through the garden to the house. In the centre of this, on a particular spot, the listener is placed at the distance of about ten or twelve yards from another person, who, similarly placed addresses him in a low and, in the common acceptation of the term, inaudible whisper, when, "Lo ! what myriads rise !" for immediately, from thousands and tens of thousands of invisible tongues, starting from the earth beneath, or as if every pebble was gifted with powers of speech, the sentence is repeated with a slight hissing sound, not unlike the whirling of small shot through the air. On removing from this spot, however trifling the distance, the intensity of the repetition is sensibly diminished, and within a few feet ceases to be heard. Under the idea that the ground was hollow beneath, the soil has been dug up to a considerable depth, but without discovering any clue to the solution of the mystery.

An echo in Woodstock Park, Oxfordshire, repeats seventeen syllables by day and twenty by night. One on the bank of the Lago del Lupo, above the fall of Terni, repeats fifteen.

The most remarkable echo known is one on the north side of Shipley church, in Sussex, which distinctly repeats twenty-one syllables. In the Abbey church at St. Albans is a curious echo. The tick of a watch may be heard from one end of the church to the other. In Gloucester Cathedral a gallery of an octagonal form conveys a whisper seventy-five feet across the nave.

In the Cathedral of Girgenti, in Sicily, the slightest whisper is borne with perfect distinctness from the great door to the cornice behind the high altar, a distance of two hundred and fifty feet. In the whispering gallery of St. Paul's, London, the faintest sound is faithfully conveyed from one side of the dome to another, but is not heard at any intermediate point.

In the Manfroni Palace at Venice is a square room, about twenty-five feet high, with a concave roof, in which a person standing in the centre and stamping gently with his foot on the floor, hears the sound repeated a great many times ; but as his position deviates from the centre, the reflected sounds grow fainter, and at a short distance wholly cease. The same phenomenon occurs in a large room of the library of the Museum at Naples.

Moving Gods.

The Italian temples were celebrated tor their moving gods. In the fane of the two fortunes at Antium, the goddess moved her arms and head when that solemnity was required. So at Præneste, the figures of the youthful Jupiter and Juno, lying in the lap of Fortune, moved, and thereby excited awe. The marble Servius Tullius is said to have shaded his eyes with his hand whenever that remarkably strong-minded woman, his daughter and murderess, passed before him. When the Athenians were tardy in deserting their capital, and taking to the ships for flight, it is said that the sacred wooden dragon of

Minerva rolled himself out of the temple and down into the sea, as though to indicate to the people the direction in which safety was to be secured.—*Dr. Doran.*

Roving Tinkers.

In the Irish county of Donegal there is a tradition antago‑ nistic to the race of tinkers. The alleged cause of this is the belief that, when the blacksmith was ordered to make nails for the Cross, he refused, but that the tinker consented. Hence he and his race had cast on them the doom of being perpetual wanderers, without any roof to cover them.

The Freischutz.

The free-shooters is the name given in the legend to a hunter or marksman who, by entering into a compact with the devil, procured balls, six of which infallibly hit, however great the distance, while the seventh, or, according to some, one of the seven, belonged to the devil, who directed it at his pleasure. Legends of this nature were rife among the troop- ers of Germany of the fourteenth and fifteenth centuries, and during the thirty years' war. The story was adapted, in 1843, to the opera composed by Weber in 1821, which has made it known in all civilized countries.

Moon-struck.

In the 121st Psalm it is written of those who put their trust in God's protection, "The sun shall not smite thee by day, nor the moon by night." The allusion to the moon is ex- plained by the common belief in the East that exposure to the moon's rays while sleeping is injurious. Travelers in oriental countries have noticed that when the natives slept out of doors they invariably, if the moon was shining, covered their faces.

Curious Locality for Saying Prayers.

Francis Atkins was porter at the palace gate at Salisbury from the time of Bishop Burnet to the period of his death, in 1761, at the age of 104 years. It was his office every night to wind up the clock, which he was capable of performing regularly till within a year of his decease, though on the summit of the palace. In ascending the lofty flight of stairs, he usually made a halt at a particular place and said his evening prayers. He lived a regular and temperate life, and took a great deal of exercise ; he walked well, and carried his frame upright and well-balanced to the last.

Egyptian Physicians.

Montaigne says it was an Egyptian law that the physician, for the first three days, should take charge of a patient at the patient's peril, but afterwards at his own. He mentions that, in his time, physicians gave their pills in odd numbers, appointed remarkable days in the year for taking medicine, gathered their simples at certain hours, assumed austere and even severe looks, and prescribed, among their choice drugs, the left foot of a tortoise, the liver of a mole, and blood drawn from under the wing of a white pigeon.

Not Divine until Smeared with Red Paint.

The inhabitants of the village of Balonda, in Africa, manufacture their idols by rudely carving a head upon a crooked stick. There is nothing divine about the idol, however, until it is dotted over with a mixture of medicine and red ochre.—*Livingstone.*

Gipsy Reticence.

A gipsy will never give a history of himself nor of his race. " My father is a crow, and my mother a magpie," is frequently the only answer obtained.

Carrying Coals to Newcastle.

The old North of England phrase, "To carry coals to Newcastle," finds its parallel in the Persian taunt of "carrying pepper to Hindostan," and in the Hebrew, "To carry oil to the City of Olives."

Mammoth Pawnbroker's Shop.

The *Monte de piété*, in Paris, established by royal command in 1717, often has in its possession forty casks filled with gold watches that have been pledged.

Half-Penny and Farthing.

In 1060, when William the Conqueror began to reign, the penny was cast with a deep cross, so that it might be broken in half, as a half-penny, or in quarters, for *four*-things or *far*-things, as we now call them.

An Egg Mistaken for a Pearl.

Linnæus announced to the king and council, in 1761, that he had discovered an art by which mussels might be made to produce pearls.   In the year 1763 it was said, in the German newspapers that Linnæus was ennobled on account of his discovery, and that he bore a pearl in his coat-of-arms.   Both statements were false.   His patent of nobility makes no mention of the pearl discovery, and what in his arms has been taken for a pearl is an egg, which is meant to represent all nature, after the manner of the ancient Egyptians.

Spacious Halls.

The old English halls were sometimes so spacious as to admit of a knight riding up to the high table, as the champion of England was accustomed to do at the coronation.   Chaucer says—

> " In at the hall door all suddenly
> There came a knight upon a steed,
> And up he rideth to the high board."

Medallions only for the Royal.

Medallions, prior to the time of Hadrian, are rare and of great value, one of the most beautiful and most famous being a gold medallion of Augustus Cæsar.   Of the Roman medallions, some were struck by order of the emperors—some by order of the senate.   No portrait of a person not princely occurs on any ancient medal—a remarkable circumstance, considering the numerous contemporary poets, historians and philosophers.

The Queen's Vow.

Catherine de Medicis made a vow, that if some enterprises which she had undertaken terminated successfully, she would send a pilgrim on foot to Jerusalem, and that at every three steps he advanced he should go one step back. A citizen of Verberic offered to accomplish the queen's vow most scrupulously, and her majesty promised him an adequate recompense. She was well assured, by constant inquiries, that he fulfilled his engagement with exactness, and on his return he received a considerable sum of money and was ennobled.

Swearing on the Book.

In testimony, oaths have always been associated with something to be touched or kissed. In England people used to kiss their thumbs instead of the Bible, and so supposed that they had saved their consciences. A rustic, in one of Mr. Meredith's novels says, "I swore, but not upon oath," meaning that he had kissed his thumb, not the book. Arthur Orton, in the Bush, laid his hand on a copy of Sheridan's plays, "which, though not a Bible, bore a cross." So Zeus lays his hand on the earth, in Homer, when he swears by that planetary body. People had to touch relics when they swore in the Middle Ages, as in the famous oath of Harold. The Danes, when they invaded England, were ready to take any oath with impunity, save that of touching a certain sacred ring or armlet. Hamlet made his comrades lay their hands on the blade of his sword.

Chinese Oath.

At the Thames public office, in London, some years ago, two Chinese sailors were examined on a charge of assaulting another Chinese sailor. The complainant was examined according to the custom of their country. A Chinese saucer being given to him, and another to the interpreter, they both advanced toward the window, directed their eyes to heaven, and repeated in their own tongue the following : "In the face of God I break this saucer ; if it comes together again, Chinaman has told a lie, and expects not to live five days ; if it remains asunder, Chinaman has told the truth, and escapes the vengeance of the Almighty." They then smashed the saucers in pieces on the floor, and returned to their places to be examined.

Color of the Hat for Cardinals.

Innocent IV. first made the hat the symbol or cognizance of the cardinals, enjoining them to wear a *red* hat at the ceremonies and processions, in token of their being ready to spill their blood for the Saviour.

Cat-Concert.

Some years ago there was a cat-concert held in Paris. It was called "Concert Miaulant," from the mewing of the animals. They were trained by having their tails pulled every time a certain note was struck, and the unpleasant remembrance caused them to mew each time they heard the sound again.

Mob Wisdom.

A singular instance of a mob cheating themselves by their own headlong impetuosity is to be found in the life of Woodward, the comedian. On one occasion, when he was in Dublin, and lodged opposite the Parliament House, a mob, who were making the members swear to oppose an unpopular bill, called out to his family to throw them a Bible out of the window. Mr. Woodward was frightened, for they had no such book in the house, but he threw them out a volume of Shakespeare, telling the mob they were welcome to it. They gave him three cheers, swore the members upon the book, and afterwards returned it without having discovered its character.

Queer Arctic Music.

One of the greatest curiosities in the arctic regions is the music which the traveler has with him wherever he goes. The moisture exhaled from his body is at once condensed and frozen, and falls to the ground in the form of hard spikes of crystals, which keep up a constant and not unpleasing clatter.

Fineness of Indian Muslins.

At the time of the Great Exhibition of 1851, the local committee of Dacca, in India, gave notice that they would award prizes for the best piece of muslin that could be woven in time for the Exhibition. The piece which received the first prize was ten yards long and one yard wide, weighed only three ozs. two dwts., and could be passed through a very small ring.—*Prof. Royle.*

Mummies Converted into Paint.

Few persons are aware that veritable Egyptian mummies are ground into paint. In Europe mummies are used for this purpose—the asphaltum with which they are impregnated being of a quality far superior to that which can elsewhere be obtained, and producing a peculiar brownish tint when made into paint, which is highly prized by distinguished artists. The ancient Egyptians, when they put away their dead, wrapped them in clothes saturated with asphaltum, and could never have realized the fact that ages after they had been laid in the tombs and pyramids along the Nile. their dust would be used in painting pictures in a country then undiscovered, and by artists whose languages were unknown to them.

Swallowed by an Earthquake and Thrown out Again.

A tombstone in the island of Jamaica has the following inscription : "Here lieth the body of Lewis Galdy, Esq., who died on the 22d of September, 1737, aged 80. He was born at Montpellier, in France, which place he left for his religion, and settled on this island, where, in the great earthquake, 1672, he was swallowed up, and by the wonderful providence of God, by a second shock was thrown out into the sea, where he continued swimming until he was taken up by a boat, and thus miraculously preserved. He afterwards lived in great reputation, and died universally lamented."

Scripture Prices.

Abraham paid 400 shekels of silver ($200) for a piece of land for a burying-place. In Solomon's time (1 Kings x. 29) it is mentioned that the price of a chariot from Egypt was 600 shekels of silver ($250). The price of a horse was 150 shekels (about $72).—*Wells.*

Manufacturing Feat.

In 1811 a gentleman made a bet of one thousand guineas that he would have a coat made in a single day, from the first process of shearing the sheep till its completion by the tailor. The wager was decided at Newbury, England, on the 25th of June in that year, by Mr. John Coxeter, of Greenham mills, near that town. At five o'clock that morning Sir John

Throckmorton presented two Southdown sheep to Mr. Coxeter, and the sheep were shorn, the wool spun, the yarn spooled, warped, loomed and wove, the cloth burred, milled, rowed, dried, 'sheared and pressed, and put into the hands of the tailors by four o'clock that afternoon. At twenty minutes past six the coat, entirely finished, was handed by Mr. Coxeter to Sir John Throckmorton, who appeared with it before more than five thousand spectators, who rent the air with acclamations at this remarkable instance of despatch.

Wall Paper Pattern.

In the Great Exhibition at London, in 1851, a single pattern of wall paper, representing a chase in a forest, attracted much attention. To produce the pattern, twelve thousand blocks had been used.

Feathers for the Ladies.

Statistics of a late feather sale in England show that to furnish material for that one sale, at least 9,700 herons or egrets and 15,574 humming birds must have been killed.

A Man Carries his House on his Head.

Simeon Ellerton, of Craike, Durham, died in 1799, aged 104. This man, in his day, was a noted pedestrian, and before the establishment of regular "Posts," was frequently employed in walking commissions, from the northern counties to London and other places, which he executed with fidelity and despatch. He lived in a neat stone cottage of his own erecting, and, what is remarkable, he had literally carried his house on his head. It was his constant practice to bring back with him from every journey which he undertook, some suitable stone, or other material for his purpose, and which, not unfrequently, he carried 40 or 50 miles on his head.

Queen Anne's Farthings.

The farthings of Queen Anne have attained a celebrity from the large prices sometimes given for them by collectors. Their rarity, however, has been much overrated; it was, indeed, long a popular notion that only three farthings were struck in her reign, of which two were in public keeping, while a third was still going about, and, if recovered, would bring a fabulous price. The Queen Anne farthings were designed by a German name Crocker or Croker, principal engraver to the mint. They were only patterns of an intended coin, and, though never put into circulation, are by no means exceedingly rare.

No Lead in Lead Pencils.

Lead pencils contain no lead. Lead pencil is as much a misnomer as it would be to call a horse a cow. Red lead is an oxide of lead, and white lead is a carbonate of lead, but the black lead used in pencils is neither a metal nor a compound of metal. It is plumbago or graphite, one of the forms of carbon.

Whalebone.

This substance is improperly named, since it has none of the properties of bone; its correct name is baleen. It is found attached to the upper jaw, and serves to strain the water which the whale takes into its mouth, and to retain the small animals upon which it subsists. For this purpose the baleen is abundant, sometimes eight hundred pieces in one whale, placed across each other at regular distances, with the fringed edge towards the mouth.

Light from Potatoes.

The emission of light from the common potato, when in a state of decomposition, is sometimes very striking. Dr. Phipson, in his work on "Phosphorescence," mentions a case in which the light thus emitted from a cellarful of these vegetables was so strong as to lead an officer on guard at Strasburg to believe that the barracks were on fire.

A Very Long Word.

The longest Nipmuck word in Eliot's Indian Bible is in St. Mark i. 40, *Wutteppesittukgussunnoowehtunkquoh*, and signifies "kneeling down to him."

Cobblers' Stalls in Rome.

The streets of Rome in the time of Domitian were so blocked up with cobblers' stalls that he caused them to be removed.

Luminous Human Bodies.

Bartholin, in his treatise "De Luce Hominumet Brutorum" (1647), gives an account of an Italian lady whom he designates as "mulier splendens," whose body shone with phosphoric radiations when gently rubbed with dry linen; and Dr. Kane, in his last voyage to the polar regions, witnessed almost as remarkable a case of phosphorescence. A few cases are recorded by Sir H. Marsh, Professor Donovan and other undoubted authorities, in which the human body, shortly before death, has presented a pale, luminous appearance.

Sacred Anchors.

The ancient Greek vessels carried several anchors, one of which, called the "sacred anchor," was never let go until the ship was in dire distress.

Anne Boleyn's Gloves.

Anne Boleyn was remarkably dainty about her gloves. She had a nail which turned up at the sides, and it was the delight of Queen Catherine to make her play at cards without her gloves, in order that the deformity might disgust King Hal.

Adding Insult to Injury.

This expression has reached us from a fable by Phædrus, a Roman author who lived in the reign of Augustus Cæsar, and whose writings were first discovered to modern literature in 1596, at Rheims, in France. The fable is called "The Bald Man and the Fly," and reads as follows:—

"A fly bit the bare pate of a bald man, who, endeavoring to crush it, gave himself a heavy blow. Then said the fly, jeeringly, 'You wanted to avenge the sting of a tiny insect with death. What will you do to yourself, who have added insult to injury?'"

St. Anthony's Fire.

St. Anthony's fire is an inflammatory disease which, in the eleventh century, raged violently in various parts. According to the legend, the intercession of St. Anthony was prayed for, when it miraculously ceased; and, therefore, from that time, the complaint has been called St. Anthony's fire.

Before Houses were Numbered.

Before houses were numbered it was a common practice with tradesmen not much known, when they advertised, to mention the color of their next neighbor's door, balcony or lamp, of which custom the following copy of a hand-bill presents a curious instance:—

"Next to the *Golden Door*, opposite Great Suffolk street, near Pall Mall, at the Barber's Pole, liveth a certain person, Robert Barker, who has found out an excellent method for sweating or fluxing of wiggs; his prices are 2*s.* 6*d.* for each bob, and 3*s.* for every tye wigg and pig-tail, ready money."

Monkish Prayers.

The monks used to say their prayers no less than seven times in twenty-four hours—

1st. Nocturnal, at cock-crowing (2 o'clock in the morning).

2d. Matins, at 6 o'clock in the morning.

3d. Tierce, at 9 o'clock in the morning.

4th. Sext, at 12 o'clock noon.

5th. None, at 3 o'clock in the afternoon.

6th. Vespers, at 6 o'clock in the afternoon.

7th. Compline, soon after 7.

Quarles wrote a neat epigram on the subject—

> "For all our prayers the Almighty does regard
> The judgment of the *balance*, not the *yard;*
> He loves not words, but matter; 't is His pleasure
> To buy His wares by *weight*, and not by *measure*."

A Mammoth Feast.

Leland mentions a feast given by the Archbishop of York, at his installation, in the reign of Edward IV. There were disposed of—300 quarters of wheat, 300 tuns of ale, 100 tuns of wine, 1000 sheep, 104 oxen, 304 calves, 304 swine, 2000 geese, 1000 capons, 400 swans, 104 peacocks, 1500 hot vension pasties, 4000 cold ones, 5000 custards, hot and cold.

Gluttony of the Monks.

The monks of St. Swithin made formal complaint to Henry II. because the Abbot deprived them of three dishes out of thirteen at every meal. The monks of Canterbury had seventeen rich and savory dishes every day.

Ancient Smokers.

When the ancient tower of Kukstatt Abbey fell, in 1779, Whitaker, a few days afterwards, discovered, embedded in the mortar of the fallen fragments, several little smoking pipes, such as were used in the reign of James I., for tobacco, a proof of the fact, which has not been generally recorded, that long prior to the introduction of that plant from America, the practice of inhaling the smoke of some indigenous vegetable prevailed in England.

Gipsy Dance.

The gipsy women of Spain especially and exclusively dance the Romalis, imported from the Orient. It is said to be the voluptuous dance which the daughter of Herodias danced before Herod and his court.

Chinese Medical Prescriptions.

The Chinese divide their prescriptions into seven classes:
1. The great prescription; 2. The little prescription; 3. The
slow prescription; 4. The prompt prescription; 5. The odd
prescription; 6. The even prescription; 7. The double prescription. Each of these recipes apply to particular cases,
and the ingredients are weighed with scrupulous accuracy.

Queer Evidence of Divinity.

Among the ancients the voluntary motion of inanimate
objects was considered an evidence of their divinity. When
Juno paid her celebrated visit to Vulcan, she found him
engaged in the manufacture of tripods, which moved about
and performed their office with a bustling air of zealous
activity—

> "Full twenty tripods for his hall be framed,
> That, placed on living wheels of massive gold,
> Wondrous to tell, instinct with spirit, roll'd
> From place to place around the blest abodes,
> Self-moved, obedient to the beck of gods."

Picnics Centuries Ago.

Mainwaring, in a letter to the Earl of Arundel, dated November 22d, 1618, says: "The prince his birthday has been
solemnized here by the few marquises and lords which found
themselves here; and (to supply the want of lords) knights
and squires were added to a consultation, wherein it was resolved that such a number should meet at Gamiges, *and bring
every man his dish of meat.* It was left to their own choice
what to bring; some chose to be substantial, some curious,
some extravagant. Sir George Young's invention bore away

the bell, and that was four huge brawny pigs, piping hot, bitted and harnessed with ropes of sarsiges, all tied to a monstrous bag-pudding.''

Skeletons at Feasts.

In old times the guests at an Egyptian feast, when they grew hilarious, were called back to sober propriety by the exhibition of a little skeleton, and the admonition to reflect upon the lesson it conveyed.

Hair Cutting in Russia.

Among the lower classes in Russia, the barber, a primitive artist, claps an earthen pot over the head and ears, and trims off whatever hair protrudes from the pot.

Antiquity of Tarring and Feathering.

Tarring and feathering, it seems, is an European invention. One of Richard Cœur de Leon's ordinances for seamen was, "that if any man were taken with theft and pickery, and thereof convicted, he should have his head polled, and hot pitch poured upon his pate, and upon that the feathers of some pillow or cushion shaken aloft, that he might thereby be known as a thief, and at the next arrival of the ships to any land be put forth of the company to seek his adventures without all hope of return unto his fellows."—*Holinshed*.

Grinning for a Wager.

In 1796, at Hendon, England, on Whit-Tuesday, a burlesque imitation of the Olympic Games was held. One prize was a gold-laced hat, to be grinned for by six candidates, who were placed on a platform with horse-collars to exhibit through. Over their heads was printed in capitals—

Detur Tetriori ; or,
The ugliest grinner
Shall be the winner.

Each party grinned five minutes *solus*, and then all united in a grand *chorus* of distortion. The prize was carried off by a porter to a *vinegar* merchant, though he was accused by his competitors of foul play for rinsing his mouth with *verjuice*.

Eating for a Wager.

The hand-bill, of which the subjoined is a copy, was circulated by the keeper of the public house at which the gluttony was to happen, as an attraction for all the neighborhood to witness— .

"*Bromley in Kent*, July 14th, 1726.—A strange eating worthy is to preform a Tryal of Skill on St. James's Day, which is the day of our *Fair*, for a wager of Five Guineas, viz: he is to eat four pounds of bacon, a bushel of French beans, with two pounds of butter, a quartern loaf, and to drink a gallon of strong beer." .

Curious Wagers.

Mr. Whalley, an Irish gentleman, for a wager of twenty thousand pounds, set out on Monday, the 22d of September, 1788, to walk to Constantinople and back in one year. Some years ago Sir Henry Liddel, a rich baronet, laid a considerable wager that he would go to Lapland, bring home two females of that country, and two reindeer, in a given time. He performed the journey, and effected his purpose in every respect. The Lapland women lived with him about a **year,** but, desiring to go back to their own country, the baronet furnished them with the means.

The Jumping Jack.

This toy is of quite antiquated parentage. In the tombs of ancient Egypt figures have been found whose limbs were made movable, for the delight of children, before Moses was born.

Love-handkerchiefs.

At one time it was the custom in England to present love-handkerchiefs. They were not more than three or four inches square, wrought with embroidery, a tassel at each corner and a small button in the centre. The finest of these favors were edged with narrow gold lace or twist, and then, being folded up in four cross-folds, so that the middle might be seen, they were worn by the accepted lovers in their hats or on the breast. These tokens of love became at last so much in vogue that they were sold ready-made in the shops in Elizabeth's time at from sixpence to sixteen-pence apiece. Tokens were also given by the gentlemen, and accepted by the ladies, as is indicated in an old comedy of the time—

> "Given earrings we will wear,
> Bracelets of our lover's hair;
> Which they on our arms shall twist,
> (With our names carved) on our wrists."

Umbrellas.

Umbrellas are an older invention than some writers would have us suppose. Even the usually entertained notion that

Jonas Hanway introduced the umbrella into England, in the year 1752, is proved to be false by evidence that can be cited. Ben Jonson refers to it by name in a comedy produced in 1616; and so do Beaumont and Fletcher in "Rule a Wife and Have a Wife." Swift, in the "Tatler" of October 17th, 1710, says, in "The City Shower"—

> "The tucked-up seamstress walks with hasty strides,
> While streams run down her oiled umbrella's sides."

The following couplet also occurs in a poem written by Gay in 1712—

> "Housewives underneath th' umbrella's oily shed
> Safe through the wet in clinking pattens tread."

It is probable that Hanway was the first *man* seen carrying an umbrella in London.

At Persepolis, in Persia, are some sculptures supposed to be as old as the time of Alexander the Great, and on one of these is represented a chief or king, over whose head some servants are holding an umbrella. At Takht-i-Bostan are other sculptures, one of which is a king witnessing a boar hunt attended by an umbrella-bearer. Recent discoveries at Nineveh show that the umbrella was in use there, it being common to the sculpturings, but always represented open. The same is to be seen upon the celebrated Hamilton vases preserved in the British Museum. In many Chinese drawings ladies are attended by servants holding umbrellas over their heads.

Loubère, who went to Siam as envoy from the king of France, describes the use of umbrellas as being governed by curious regulations. Those umbrellas resembling ours are used principally by the officers of state; while those several tiers in height, as if two or more umbrellas were fixed on one stick, are reserved for the king alone. In Ava, a country adjacent to Siam, the king designates himself, among other titles, as "Lord of the Ebbing and Flowing Tide, King of the White Elephant, and Lord of the Twenty-four Umbrellas." This last title, although ridiculous to us, is supposed to relate to twenty-four states or provinces combined under the rule of the king, the umbrella being especially a royal emblem in Ava. The umbrella is also the distinguishing sign of sovereignty in Morocco.

Fashionable Disfigurement.

The custom of dotting the face with black patches, of different patterns, was introduced into England and France from Arabia, and was at its height during the reign of Charles I. The ladies, old and young, covered their faces with black spots shaped like suns, moons, stars, hearts, crosses and lozenges, and some even carried the mode to the extravagant extent of shapening the patches to represent a carriage and horses.

Fine for Insulting a King.

The use of gold and silver was not unknown to the Welsh in 842, when their laws were collected. The man who dared to insult the king of Aberfraw was to pay (besides certain cows and a silver rod) a cup which would hold as much wine as his majesty could swallow at a draught. It was to be made of gold; its cover was to be as broad as the king's face, and the whole as thick as a goose's egg or a ploughman's thumb-nail.

True-Lovers' Knots.

Among the ancient Northern nations a knot was the symbol of indissoluble love, faith and friendship. Hence the ancient runic inscriptions are in the form of a knot, and hence, among the Northern English and Scots, who still retain, in a great measure, the language and manners of the ancient Danes, that curious kind of knot exists which is a mutual present between the lover and his mistress, and which, being considered as the emblem of plighted fidelity, is therefore called "a true-love knot." The name is not derived, however, as would be naturally supposed, from the words "true" and "love," but is formed from the Danish verb "trulofa," *fidem do*, I plight my troth or faith. In Davidson's "Poetical Rhapsody," published in 1611, the following is the opening verse of a poem entitled "The True-Love's Knot"—

> "Love is the linke, the knot, the band of unity,
> And all that love do love with their beloved to be;
> Love only did decree
> To change this kind in me."

Hundred Families' Lock.

A common Chinese talisman is the "hundred families' lock," to procure which a father goes round among his friends, and, having obtained from an hundred different parties a few of the copper coins of the country, he himself adds the balance to purchase an ornament or appendage fashioned like a lock, which he hangs on his child's neck for the purpose of figuratively locking him to life and causing the hundred persons to be concerned in his attaining old age.

The King's Cock-crower.

A singular custom of matchless absurdity formerly existed in the English court. During Lent an ancient officer of the crown, called the King's Cock-crower, crowed the hour each night within the precincts of the palace. On Ash Wednesday, after the accession of the House of Hanover, as the Prince of

Wales (afterwards George II.) sat down to supper, this officer abruptly entered the apartment, and in a sound resembling the shrill pipe of a cock, crowed past ten o'clock. The astonished prince, at first conceiving it to be a premeditated insult, rose to resent the affront, but upon the nature of the ceremony being explained to him, he was satisfied.

Mourning Robes.

Under the empire male Romans wore black, and Roman women wore white mourning. In Turkey, at the present day, it is violet; in China, white; in Egypt, yellow; in Ethiopia, brown; in Europe and America, black; it was white in Spain until the year 1498. The mourning worn by sovereigns and their families is purple.

Mole-skin Eyebrows.

Some of the ladies of the Court of Louis XV., in connection with the patches, rouge and paint with which they disfigured their faces, were so whimsical as to wear eyebrows made out of mole-skin.

Praying for Revenge.

In North Wales, when a person supposes himself highly injured, it is not uncommon for him to go to some church dedicated to a celebrated saint, as Llan Elian, in Anglesea, and Clynog, in Carnarvonshire, and there to offer up his enemy. He kneels down on his bare knees, and offering a piece of money to the saint, calls down curses and misfortunes upon the offender and his family for generations to come, in the most firm belief that the imprecations will be fulfilled. Sometimes they repair to a sacred well instead of to a church.

Selling Snails.

The sale of snails in the town of Tivoli, near Rome, is a source of much profit to the inhabitants of that district in rainy weather, when this curious edible is abundant in the olive groves. The flavor is pronounced delicious, and when artistically cooked, the foreigner does not long decline this much despised crustacea. The cooked snail is said to restore tone to the coating of the stomach when badly injured by strong drink.

Coral and Bells.

A superstitious belief exists that the color of coral is affected by the state of health of the wearer, it becoming paler in disease. Paracelsus recommended it to be worn around the necks of infants as an admirable preservative against fits, charms and poison. "In addition to the supposed virtues of coral usually suspended around the necks of children, it may be remarked that silver bells are generally attached to it, which are regarded as mere accompaniments to amuse children by their jingle ; but the fact is, they have a very different origin, having been designed to frighten away evil spirits."—*Dr. Paris.*

Bagging his Rival.

Two gentlemen, one a Spaniard, the other a German, asked of Maximilian II. the hand of his daughter, the fair Helene Scharfequinn, in marriage. After a long delay, the emperor one day informed them that, esteeming them equally, and not being able to bestow a preference, he should leave it to the force and address of the claimants to decide the question. He did not mean, however, to risk the life of one or the other, or perhaps of both. He could not, therefore, permit them to encounter with offensive weapons, but had ordered a large bag to be produced. It was his decree that whichever succeeded in putting his rival into the bag should have the hand of his daughter. The singular encounter between the two gentlemen took place in the presence of the whole court. The contest lasted for more than an hour. At length the Spaniard yielded, and the German, Ehberhard, Baron de Talbert, having planted his rival in the bag, took it upon his back and gallantly laid it at the feet of his mistress, whom he espoused the next day. This incident is gravely vouched for by M. de St. Foix.

Deepened Damnation.

In his " History of all the Heresies," Bernino records an instance of diabolical superstition. Pope Theodorus wrote the sentence of deposition against the Monothelite secretary Pyrrhus with ink in which had been mingled the blood from the sacramental cup, in order that the fulmination of the pope might possess the greater potency of damnation.

Ancient Bit of Waggery.

We find the following in a book printed in 1607, entitled, "Pleasant Conceits of old Hobson, the merry Londoner; full of Humourous Discourses and Merry Merriments:"—

"When the order of hanging out lanterne first of all was brought about, the bedell of the warde where Maister Hobson dwelt, in a darke evening, crieing up and down, 'Hang out your lanternes! Hang out your lanternes!' using no other words, Maister Hobson tooke an emptie lanterne, and, according to the bedell's call, hung it out. This flout, by the lord mayor, was taken in ill part, and for the offence Hobson was sent to the Counter, but being released the next night following, thinking to amende his call, the bedell cryed out, with a loud voice, 'Hang out your lanternes and candle!' Maister Hobson hereupon hung out a lanterne and candle unlighted, as the bedell again commanded ; whereupon he was sent again to the Counter ; but the next night, the bedell being better advised, cryed 'Hang out your lanterne and candle-light!' which Maister Hobson at last did, to his great commendations, which cry of lanterne and candle-light is in right manner used to this day."

A Walking Apothecary Shop.

Mr. Samuel Jessup, an opulent grazier, of pill-taking memory, died at Heckington, England, on the 17th of June, 1817. In twenty-one years the deceased took 226,934 pills, supplied by a respectable apothecary at Bottesford, which was at the rate of 10,806 pills a year, or twenty-nine pills each day ; but as the patient began with a more moderate appetite, and increased it as he proceeded, in the last five years he took the pills at the rate of seventy-eight a day, and in the year 1814 he swallowed not less than 51,590. Notwithstanding this, and the addition of 40,000 bottles of mixture and juleps and electuaries, extending altogether to fifty-five closely written columns of an apothecary's bill, the deceased lived to attain the age of sixty-five years.—*Hone.*

To Disappoint his Wife.

On the 20th of May, 1736, the body of Samuel Baldwin, Esq , was, in compliance with a request in his will, buried, *sans ceremonie*, in the sea at Lymington, Hants. His motive for this extraordinary mode and place of interment was to prevent his wife from "dancing over his grave," which she had frequently threatened to do in case she survived him.

Boots an Object of Honor.

Among the Chinese no relics are more valuable than the boots which have been worn by an upright magistrate. In Davis's interesting description of the Empire of China we are informed that whenever a judge of unusual integrity resigns his situation, the people congregate to do him honor. If he leaves the city where he has resided, the crowd accompany him from his residence to the gates, where his boots are drawn off with great ceremony, to be preserved in the hall of justice. Their place is immediately supplied by a new pair, which, in turn, are drawn off to make room for others before he has worn them five minutes, it being considered sufficient to consecrate them that he should have merely drawn them on.

St. Cuthbert's Beads.

These beads were made from the single joints of the articulated stems of Encrinites. The central perforation permitted them to be strung. From the fancied resemblance of this perforation to a cross, they were formerly used as rosaries, and associated with the name of St. Cuthbert—

> "On a rock by Lindisfarm
> St. Cuthbert sits and toils to frame
> The sea-born beads that bear his name."

Eating Animals that have Died a Natural Death.

The gypsies in Europe are very peculiar in their eating, and are, perhaps, the only race who will eat animals that have died a natural death. "Dead pig" is their favorite delicacy; and one of the most typical and most amusing of the Rom-

many ballads which Borrow has collected, celebrates the
trick formerly so common among them of poisoning a pig
in order the next day to beg its carcass for food.

Embalmed in Honey.

The ancients put dead bodies into honey to preserve them
from putrefaction. The body of Agesipolis, King of Sparta,
who died in Macedonia, was sent home in honey. The faith-
less Cleomenes caused the head of Archonides to be put in
honey, and had it always placed near him when he was
deliberating upon any affair of great importance, in order to
fulfil the oath he had made to undertake nothing without
consulting the head. The body of the Emperor Justin II.
wasembalmed in honey. The wish of Democritus to be
buried in honey is a confirmation of the practice.

Perfumed Butter.

We are told by Plutarch that a Spartan lady paid a visit to
Berenice, the wife of Dejotarus, and that the one smelled so
much of sweet ointment and the other of butter that neither
of them could endure the other. Was it customary, therefore, at that period, for the ladies to perfume themselves with
butter?

Wine at Two Millions a Bottle.

Some years ago wine graced the table of the King of Wurtem-
burg, which had been deposited in a cellar at Bremen two
centuries and a half before. One large case of the wine, containing five oxhoft of two hundred and forty bottles, cost five
hundred rix-dollars in 1624. Including the expenses of keeping up the cellar, and of the contributions, interest of the

amount, and interest upon interest, an oxhoft costs at the present time 555,657,640 rix dollars, and consequently a bottle is worth 2,723,812 rix-dollars. The fact illustrates the operation of interest, if it does not show the cost of the luxury.—*Bombaugh.*

Opal of Nonius.

The ancients valued opals very highly. The Roman senator, Nonius, preferred exile to giving up an opal to Mark Antony. This opal was still to be seen in the days of Pliny, who ascribed to it a value of more than $500,000.

Children's Day in Japan.

There is a children's day in Japan on the fifth day of the fifth month, when a flag of gay colors is hung from every house where there are children. The family and friends have a feast, and, among the articles of food are long, narrow rice cakes, upon each of which a sweet-flavored rush-leaf is fastened by straws. Where there are no children there may be a family party, but no flag can be exhibited. On this day ornaments made of paper, of five different colors, are bound into balls and hung up in the house as a charm against sickness.

Cock-Fighting among the Ancient Greeks.

Æschines reproaches Timarchus for spending the whole day in gaming and cock-fighting. Cock-fights were represented by the Greeks on coins and cut stones. Mr. Pegge caused engravings to be made of two gems in the collection of Sir William Hamilton, on one of which is seen a cock in the humble attitude of defeat, with its head hanging down, and another in the attitude of victory, with an ear of corn in its bill as the object of contest. On the other stone two cocks are fighting, while a mouse carries away the ear of corn, for the possession of which they had quarreled—a caricature of law-suits, in which the greater part of the property in dispute falls to the lawyers. Two cocks in the attitude of fighting are represented also on a lamp found in Herculaneum.

Colors Most Frequently Hit in Battle.

It would appear, from numerous observations, that soldiers are hit during battle according to the color of their dress in the following order : Red is the most fatal color ; Austrian gray is the least fatal. The proportions are—red, twelve ; rifle green, seven ; brown, six ; Austrian bluish-gray, five.

Immense Value Placed upon Gems by the Ancients.

The immense value placed by the ancients on their gems can be estimated by the scabbard of Mithridates, valued at 400 talents, or £7,572 ; the pearl given by Julius Cæsar to Servillia was worth £4,800 ; that swallowed by Cleopatra valued at £5,000 ; and the pearls and emeralds worn by Lollia Paulina, wife of Caligula, valued at £320,000.

Candlel Cock.

Alfred the Great noted the time by the gradual burning down of candles colored in rings. He had six tapers made, each twelve inches long, and each divided into twelve parts or inches. Three of these would burn for one hour, and the six tapers, lighted one after the other, would burn for twenty-four hours.

Twins in Africa.

Among some of the tribes in Africa if two babies come to a family at the same time they think it a dreadful thing. Nobody except the family can go into the hut where they were born, nor even use any of the things in it. The twins cannot play with other children, and the mother cannot talk to anyone outside of the family. This is kept up for six years. If the babies live to be six years old, the restrictions are removed, and they are treated like other children.

Right and Left Hand.

Dr. Zinchinelli, of Padua, in an essay on the "Reasons why People use the Right Hand in preference to the Left," will not allow custom or imitation to be the cause. He affirms that the left arm cannot be in violent and continued motion without causing pain in the left side, because there is the seat of the heart and of the arterial system ; and that, therefore, nature herself compels man to make use of the right hand.

Earliest Traders.

The earliest record we have of nations trading with each other occurs in the Book of Genesis, when Joseph's brethren sold him to a caravan of Ishmaelites who were carrying spices, balm and myrrh into Egypt. The balm was from Gilead and the myrrh from Arabia. Thus commerce is of great antiquity.

The First Hermits.

The first hermit was Paul, of Thebes, in Egypt. who lived about the year 260 ; the second was Anthony, also of Egypt, who died in 345, at the age of 105.

The First Opera.

The first composer who tried his hand at setting an opera to music was Francisco Bamirino, an Italian artist. The piece to which he affixed the charms of a melodious accompaniment was "The Conversion of St. Paul," which was brought out at Rome in 1460.

The First Artificial Limb.

The first artificial limb on record is the iron hand of the German knight, Gotz Von Berlichingen, who flourished in the early part of the sixteenth century (1513), and who was named *The Iron-Handed.* The hand weighed three pounds, was so constructed as to grasp a sword or lance, and was invented by a mechanic at Nuremberg. It is preserved at Jaxthausen, near Heilbronn, and a duplicate of it is in the Castle of Erbach, in the Odenwald.

Kircher's Speaking-Trumpet.

"The Musurgia," printed in 1650, gives an account of a speaking-trumpet invented by Kircher. From a convent situated on the top of a mountain, he assembled twelve hundred persons to divine service, and read the litany to them through the trumpet, at a distance of from two to five Italian miles. Soon after a tube was made, according to Kircher's directions, by which words, without elevating the voice, could be understood from Ebersdorf to Neugeben.

Fish Market at Scarborough.

The fish market is held on the sands by the sides of the boats, which, at low water, are run upon wheels with a sail set, and are conducted by the fishermen, who dispose of their cargoes in the following manner :

One of the female fishmongers inquires the price, and bids a groat; the fishermen ask a sum in the opposite extreme; the one bids up, and the other reduces the demand, till they meet at a reasonable point, when the bidder suddenly exclaims : "Het !" The purchase is afterwards retailed among the regular or occasional purchasers.

Few Fish Found at Sea.

Paradoxical as the fact may appear, there is no class of persons who eat so few fish as the sailors; and the reason is, they seldom obtain them. With the exception of flying-fish and dolphins, and perhaps a few others, fish are not found on the high seas at a great distance from land. They abound most along coasts, in straights and bays, and are seldom caught in water more than forty or fifty fathoms in depth.—*Wells.*

Musical Stones.

A correspondent of *Nature* writes that, in roaming over the hills and rocks in the neighborhood of Kendal, near Lancaster, England, which are composed chiefly of limestone, he had often found what are called "musical stones." They are generally thin, flat, weather-beaten stones, of different sizes and peculiar shapes, which, when struck with a piece of iron or another stone, produce a musical tone, instead of the dull, heavy, leaden sound of an ordinary stone. The sound of these stones is, in general, very much alike, but sets of eight stones have been collected which produce, when struck, a distinct octave.

The new French scientific weekly, *La Nature,* copies the communication from its English namesake, and brings forward some additional instances of the same phenomenon. We are also informed of the accidental discovery of musical properties in a stone fountain at the French Institute. Its musical sound, when struck, corresponds with extreme pre cision to the perfect accord major of *fa* natural. The fountain in question is in the grand court of the institute.

Musical Sand.

A singular phenomenon is the "musical sand" of Jebel Nagus, a sandy hill lying to the west of the mountain usually called Sinai. According to Captain Palmer, an English traveler, the sand of this hill possesses the marvellous property of giving out musical sounds whenever it is set in motion. The sandy slope is two hundred feet in height, the sand being very much the same as that in the desert around. When any considerable quantity of this sand is set in motion, it is seen to move in undulations, and, simultaneously, a singnlar sound is heard, which is first feeble, but may be heard at some distance when it has attained its maximum intensity.

The sound is not easily described. It is neither metallic nor vibratory. It might be compared to the sharpest notes of the Æolian harp, or the sound produced by forcibly drawing a cork over wet glass. The phenomenon attains its greatest intensity during the day in summer, when the sun is hottest, and while the wind blows from the northwest. Captain Palmer has observed it on all sides of the hill, and the only difference he has found are such as depend on the direction of the wind.

A River of Ink.

In Algeria there is a river of genuine ink. It is formed by the union of two streams, one coming from a region of ferruginous soil, the other draining a peat swamp. The water of the former is strongly impregnated with iron, that of the latter with gallic acid. When the two waters mingle, the acid of the one unites with the iron of the other, forming a true ink. We are familiar with a stream called Black Brook, in the northern part of New York, the inky color of whose water is evidently due to like conditions.—*Scientific American.*

A Warlike Bantam.

In the "Life of Rodney" it is related that in the famous victory of the 12th of April, 1782, a bantam cock perched himself upon the poop of Rodney's ship, and at every broadside that was poured into the *Ville-de-Paris*, clapped his wings and crew. Rodney gave special orders that this cock should be taken care of as long as he lived.

Oyster-dredging Chaunt.

During the oyster-dredging the fishermen keep up a wild monotonous song, or rather chaunt, which they assert charm the oysters into the dredge—

> "The herring loves the merry moonlight,
> The mackeral loves the wind.
> But the oyster loves the dredger's song,
> For he comes of a gentle kind."

Normandy Treasures.

At Bayeux, Normandy, a strong belief exists among the people of some hidden treasure in the ground beneath the ruined churches and castles so abundant in the neighborhood; but they are supposed to be guarded by supernatural means. Even so late as 1827 persons were found credulous enough to follow the directions of a Douster-swivel and employ much time and labor uselessly in searching after imaginary riches beneath the stones in front of the Cathedral. This belief that the hidden or lost treasure is guarded by a spiritual attendant is very generally diffused. On this point Southey, in the "Doctor," observes: "The popular belief that places are haunted where money has been concealed, or where some great and undiscovered crime has been committed, shows how consistent this is with our natural sense of likelihood and fitness."

Tenacity of Odors.

Dr. Carpenter states, in his "Comparative Physiology," that a grain of musk has been kept freely exposed to the air of a room, of which the door and window were constantly open, for ten years, during all which time the air, though constantly changed, was completely impregnated with the odor of musk, and yet at the end of that time the particle was found not to have sensibly diminished in weight.

Antiquity of Acrobatic Figures.

Modern toys of acrobats are made to perform evolutions by the use of quicksilver. Dædalus, the famous Greek figure-maker, who is said to have lived about a thousand years before Christ, introduced quicksilver into a wooden image of Venus, thereby lending to it a sort of Chinese tumbling motion.—*Dr. Doran.*

Saffron as a Perfume.

It seems a little odd to us that the ancients used saffron as a perfume. Not only were halls, theatres and courts strewn with the plant, but it entered into the composition of many spirituous extracts, which retained the scent. These costly smelling waters were often made to flow in small streams, which spread abroad their much admired odor. Luxurious people even moistened with them all those things with which they were desirous of surprising their guests in an agreeable manner, or with which they ornamented their appartment. From saffron, with the addition of wax and other ingredients, the Greeks and Romans prepared scented salves.

Spontaneous Combustion.

In Levoux's "Journal de Medicine" is an account of a very fat woman, twenty-eight years of age, who was found on fire in her chamber, where nothing else was burning. The neighbors heard a noise of something like frying, and when the body was removed it left a layer of black grease. The doctor conceived that the combustion began in the internal parts, and that the clothes were burned secondarily.

Egyptian Perfumes.

So perfect were the Eyptians in the manufacture of perfumes, that some of their ancient ointment, preserved in an alabaster vase in the museum at Alnwick, still retains a very powerful odor, though it must be almost three thousand years old.

Magic Rain Stone.

The Indian magi, who are to invoke Yo He Wah, and meditate with the supreme holy fire that he may give seasonable rains, have a transparent stone of supposed great power in assisting to bring down the rain when it is put in a basin of water. It is reputed to possess divine virtue ; it would suffer decay, they assert, were it even seen by their own laity ; but if by foreigners, it would be utterly despoiled of its divine communicative power.

Decapitation by the Guillotine.

A reliable gentleman who witnessed an execution, wrote as follows : "It appears to be the best of all modes of inflicting the punishment of death, combining the greatest impression on the spectator with the least possible suffering to the victim. It is so rapid that I should doubt whether there was any suffering ; but from the expression of the countenance, when the executioner held up the head, I am inclined to believe that sense and consciousness may remain for a few seconds after the head is off. The eyes seemed to retain speculation for a moment or, two, and there was a look in the ghastly stare with which they stared upon the crowd, which implied that the head was aware of its ignominious situation."

Chateaubrun's Escape from the Guillotine.

During the Reign of Terror, M. de Chateaubrun was sentenced to death and sent to execution with twenty other prisoners; but after the fifteenth head had fallen, the guillotine got out of order, and a workman was required to repair it. The six remaining victims were left standing in front of the machine with their hands tied behind them. A French crowd is very curious, and the people kept pressing forward to see the man who was arranging the guillotine. By degrees M. de Chateaubrun, who was to the rear of his companions, found himself in the front line of the spectators, then in the second, and finally well behind those who had come to see his head cut off. Before the man could get the guillotine in working order night began to fall, and M. de Chateaubrun slipped away. When in the Champs Elysees he told a man that a wag had tied his hands and stole his hat, and this simple individual cut him free. A few days later M. de Chateaubrun escaped from France.

A Lucky Find.

During the month of April, 1733, Sir Simon Stuart, of Hartley, England, while looking over some old writings, found on the back of one of them a memorandum noting that 1500 broad pieces were buried in a certain spot in an adjoining field. After a little digging the treasure was found in a pot, hidden there in the time of the civil wars by his grandfather, Sir Nicholas Stuart.

Paradise of Old Hats.

The group of islands known as the Nicobars, situated about one hundred and fifty miles south of the Andamans, have been but little explored, though the manners and customs of the inhabitants of these islands offer interesting peculiarities. One of the most noticeable, and one which seriously affects the trade of the islands, is the passion for old hats which pervades the whole frame-work of society. No one is exempt, and young and old endeavor to outvie each other in the singularity of shape no less than in the number of the old hats they can acquire during a lifetime. On a fine morning at the Nicobars it is not unusual to see the surface of the ocean in the vicinity of the islands dotted over with canoes, in each of which the noble savage, with nothing whatever on but the conventional slip of cloth and a tall white hat with a black band, may be watched standing up and catching fish for his daily meal. Second-hand hats are more in request, new hats being looked upon with suspicion and disfavor. The passion is so well known that traders from Calcutta make annual excursions to the Nicobars with cargoes of old hats, which they barter for cocoanuts, the only product of the island, a good, tall white hat with a black band bringing from fifty-five to sixty-five good cocoanuts. Intense excitement pervades the is'and while the trade is going on. When the hats or the cocoanuts have come to an end, the trader generally lands a flask or two of rum, and the whole population, in their hats, get drunk without intermission until the rum also comes to an end.

Wedding-Rings.

The wedding-ring, symbolical of the perpetuity of the conjugal relation, has ever been the accepted accompaniment of marriage. Its being put on the fourth finger of the left hand has been continued from long-established usage, because of the fanciful conceit that from this finger a nerve went direct to the heart.

The Prince of Charlatans.

Paracelsus was the prince of charlatans; indeed he styled himself the "King of Physic." Although he professed to have discovered the "Elixir of Life," it did not seem to have been available in his own case, for he died at the early age of forty-eight years.

One Meal a Day.

Dr. Fordyce contented that as one meal a day was enough for a lion, it ought to suffice for a man. Accordingly, for more than twenty years, the doctor used to eat only a dinner in the whole course of a day. A pound and a half of rump steak, half a broiled chicken, a plate of fish, a bottle of port, a tankard of strong ale, and a quarter of a pint of brandy satisfied his moderate wants. Dinner over, occupying an hour and a half, he returned home from the chop house to deliver his six o'clock lecture on anatomy and chemistry.

Gold-headed Canes for Physicians.

In the times of the renowned Radcliffe, the gold-headed cane was the sceptre of authority among the medical profession. Dignity dwelt in the mysterious symbol. It also protected the owner against contagious diseases, being filled with disinfecting herbs, which he applied to his nose when visiting patients.

> He pursed his brows, then wink'd his eyes,
> Put his cane to his nose and look'd wise.

Yearly Food of one Man.

From the army and navy diet scales of France and England, which, of course, are based upon the recognized necessities of large numbers of men in active life, it is inferred that about two and one-fourth pounds avordupois of dry food per day are required for each individual; of this amount three-fourths are vegetable and the rest animal. At the close of an entire year, the amount is upwards of eight hundred pounds. Enumerating under the title of water all the various drinks—coffee, tea, alcohol, wine, etc.—its estimated quantity is about fifteen hundred pounds per annum; that for the air received by breathing may be taken at eight hundred pounds. The food, water and air which a man consumes amount in the aggregate to more than three thousand pounds a year; that is, about a ton and a half, or more than twenty times his own weight.—*Wells.*

Eating Tea.

It was not until the end of the seventeenth century that tea was indulged in as a beverage. The first brewers of tea were often sorely perplexed with the preparation of the new mystery; after boiling the tea, "they sat down to eat the leaves with butter and salt." The Dutch were the first to discover the utility and value of the herb, and when, in 1666, it was first introduced into England, it sold at about three guineas per pound.—*Salad for the Solitary.*

Human Hair.

It has been estimated that a single square inch of the scalp —the skin of the head—contains about seven hundred and forty-four hairs. This number, multiplied by one hundred and twenty square inches—the surface of the head—gives us eighty-nine thousand two hundred and eighty as the number of the hairs of the head. If a lady's hair is a half-yard in length, she will have one hundred and thirty-three thousand nine hundred and twenty feet of hair. A man who has arrived at the age of fifty years will have lost, by hair cutting, about thirteen feet, which, multiplied by the number of hairs (eighty-nine thousand two hundred and eighty), will amount to one million one hundred and sixty thousand six hundred and forty feet of hair tubing, or about two hundred and twenty miles.

Durability of Bricks.

The bricks of Nineveh and Babylon, in the museums, show that they were selected by the ancients as the most lasting material. Plutarch thinks them superior to stone, if properly prepared; and it is admitted that the baths of Caracalla, those of Titus, and the Thermæ of Dioclesian, have withstood the effects of time and fire better than the stone of the Colisseum or the marble of the Forum Trajan.

Origin of Long-toed Shoes.

Long-toed shoes were invented by Fulk, Count of Anjou. to hide an excrescence on one of his feet. These toes were so long as to be fastened to the knees with gold chains, and carved at the extreme point with the representation of a church-window, a bird or some fantastic device.

A Good Tenant.

In the "Gentleman's Magazine" for September, 1775, Mr. Clayton, a wealthy farmer of Berkshire, is related to have died at the extraordinary age of one hundred and fifteen years, during which time he rented the same farm for ninety years. An occupancy of so great duration, by one individual, is perhaps uneqalled in the history of landlord and tenant.

Three Borrowed Days.

There is an old proverb still used by the English and Scotch rustics, which represent March as borrowing three days from April. In the "Complaynt of Scotland" they are thus described—

> " The first it shall be wind and weet ;
> The next it shall be snaw and sleet ;
> The third it shall be sic a freeze
> Shall gar the birds stick to the trees."

But it is disputed whether these " borrowed days " are the last three of March or the first three of April.

Luncheon.

This word is said to have been originally *noon-shun*, a meal partaken of by laborers in the fields at *noon*, when they retire to the shade to *shun* the noontide heat.

Value of a Long Psalm.

In old times a culprit, when at the gallows, was allowed to select a Psalm, which was then sung, thereby lengthening the chances for the arrival of a reprieve. It is reported of one of the chaplains to the famous Montrose, that being condemned in Scotland to die for attending his master in some of his exploits, he selected the 119th Psalm. It was well for him that he did so, for they had sung it half through before the reprieve came. A shorter Psalm, and he would have been hung.

Barbers' Basins.

Anciently, one of the utensils of the barber was a brass basin with a semi-circular gap in one side, to encompass a man's throat, by means of which, in applying the lather to the face, the clothes were not soiled. It will be recollected that Don Quixote crazily assumed a barber's basin as a helmet.

Strained Politeness.

On the 30th of April, 1745, the battle of Fontenoy was fought between the allied armies of England, Holland and Austria, under the command of the Duke of Cumberland, and the French army under Marshal Count De Saxe. The battle was commenced with the formal politeness of a court minu t Captain Lord Charles Hay, of the English guards, advanced

from the ranks with his hat off; at the same moment Lieuten-
ant Count D'Auteroche, of the French guards, advanced also,
uncovered, to meet him.   Lord Charles bowed, and said:
"Gentlemen of the French guards, fire !" The Count bowed
to Lord Charles.   "No, my lord," he answered, "we never
fire first."   They again bowed ; each resumed his place in
his own ranks, and after these testimonies of "high consideration," the bloody conflict commenced, ending with a
loss of twelve thousand men on each side.

Can a Clergyman Marry Himself?

This question was officially decided in the affirmative in
the Court of Queen's Bench, Dublin, on November 16th,
1855, in the case of Beamish vs. Beamish, where the point
came into direct issue.

Novel Way of Curing Vicious Horses.

Burckhardt tells us of the strange mode of curing a vicious
horse.   He has seen, he says, vicious horses in Egypt cured
of the habit of biting by presenting to them, while in the act
of doing so, a leg of mutton just taken from the fire.   The
pain which the horse feels in biting through the hot meat
causes it to abandon the practice.

Pope's Skull.

William Howitt says that, by one of those acts, which
neither science nor curiosity can excuse, the skull of Pope is
now in the private collection made by a phrenologist.   On
some occasion of alteration in the church, or burial of some
one in the same spot, the coffin of Pope was disinterred and

opened to see the state of the remains. By a bribe to the sexton at the time, possession of the skull was obtained for a night, and another skull was returned instead of it, in the morning. Fifty pounds were paid to manage and carry out the transaction. Be that as it may, the skull of Pope figures in a private museum.

Pawning Bibles and Waterloo Medals.

Among a list comprising the articles found in a pawn-broker's establishment in Glasgow, in 1836, were one hundred and two Bibles and forty-eight Waterloo medals.

A Drum made of Human Skin.

John Zisca, general of the insurgents who took up arms in 1419 against the Emperor Sigismund, to revenge the deaths of John Huss and Jerome of Prague, who had been cruelly burned at the stake for their religious tenets, defeated the emperor in several pitched battles. He gave orders that, after his death, they should make a drum out of his skin. The order was most religiously obeyed, and those very remains of the enthusiastic Zisca proved, for many years, fatal to the emperor, who, with difficulty, in the space of sixteen years, recovered Bohemia, assisted by the forces of Germany. The insurgents were 40,000 in number, and well disciplined.

Groaning Boards.

Groaning boards were the wonder in London in 1682. An elm plank was exhibited to the king, which, being touched by a hot iron, invariably produced a sound resembling deep groans. At the Bowman tavern, in Drury Lane, the mantel-

piece gave forth like sounds, and was supposed to be part of
the same elm tree.   The dresser at the Queen's Arm Tavern,
St. Martin le Grand, was found to possess the same quality.
Strange times, when such things were deemed wonderful—
so much so as to merit exhibition before the monarch.

Abyssinian Tradition.

A curious tradition exists among the Abyssinians concerning the origin of burial.   They say that when Adam found
the body of the murdered Abel he carried it about upon his
shoulders for twenty days, not knowing how to dispose of it.
The Almighty took pity on him and sent forth a crow with a
dead young one on its back.   The crow flew before Adam
until it came to a tract of sandy ground, in which it dug a
hole with its feet, and there buried its young one.   When
Adam saw this, he dug a grave in the sand and buried his
dead boy in it.

Cutting Timber by the Moon.

Columella, Cato, Vitruvius and Pliny all had their notions
of the advantage of cutting timber at certain ages of the
moon—a piece of mummery which was long preserved in the
royal ordonnances of France to the conservators of the
forests, who were directed to fell oaks only "in the wane of
the moon" and "when the wind was in the north."

An Artist Tradition.

There is a tradition that Poussin, the French painter,
unable to depict the foam on a horse's mouth in a picture he
was finishing, angrily threw his sponge at the canvas, and
thus accidentally produced the desired effect.   It is a pity

to spoil such an effective story, but it was told of Apelles, the Greek painter, nearly two thousand years before Poussin was born.

Born of a Peri.

A Peri, according to the mythical lore of the East, is a being begotten by fallen spirits, which spends its life in all imaginable delights.   It is immortal, but is forever excluded from the joys of Paradise.   It takes an intermediate place between angels and demons, and is either male or female.   One of the finest compliments to be paid to a Persian lady is to speak of her as *Perizadeh*—born of a Peri.

A Regal Hunting Party.

The following is an account of the destruction of game in Bohemia, by a hunting party of which the Emperor Francis made one, in 1755.   There were twenty-three persons in the party, three of whom were ladies, among the latter the Princess Charlotte of Lorraine.   The chase lasted eighteen days, and during that time they killed 47,950 head of game. 19 stags, 77 roebucks, 10 foxes, 18,243 hares, 19,545 partridges, 9499 pheasants, 114 larks, 353 quails, 454 other birds.   The emperor fired 9798 shots, and the princess 9010; in all there were 116,209 shots fired.

Care of the Beard.

The Mahometans are very superstitious touching the beard. They bury the hairs which come off in combing it, and break them first, because they believe that angels have charge of every hair, and that they gain them their dismissal by breaking it. They used to wear pasteboard covers over their beards at night, lest they should turn upon them and rumple them in their sleep. The famous Raskolniki Schismatics had a similar superstition about the beard. They believed that the divine image of man resided in it.

A Royal Sportsman.

When the King of Naples (the greatest sportsman of Europe) was in Germany, about the year 1792, it was said in the German papers that he had killed, in Austria, Bohemia and Moravia, 5 bears, 1,820 wild boars, 1,968 stags, 13 wolves, 354 foxes, 15,350 pheasants, 1,121 rabbits, 16,354 hares, 1,625 she-goats, 1,625 roebucks and 12,435 partridges.

Origin of Attar of Roses.

In the "Histoire Generale de l'Empire du Mogol," compiled by Catrou the Jesuit, this perfume is said to have been discovered by accident. "Nur-Jahan, the favorite wife of the Mogul Jahan-Ghur, among her other luxuries, had a small canal of rose water. As she was walking with the Mogul upon its banks, they perceived a thin film upon the water, which was an essential oil made by the heat of the sun. They were delighted with its exquisite odor, and means were immediately taken for preparing by art a substance like that which had been thus fortuitously produced."

Effect of a New Nose.

Van Helmont tells a story of a person who applied to Taliacotius to have his nose restored. This person, having a dread of an incision being made in his own arm, for the purpose of removing enough skin therefrom for a nose, induced a laborer, for a remuneration, to allow the skin for the nose to be taken from his arm. About thirteen months after the adscititious nose suddenly became cold, and, after a few days, dropped off, in a state of putrefaction. The cause of this unexpected occurrence was investigated, when it was discovered that, at the same moment in which the nose grew cold, the laborer at Bologna expired.

Cader Idris Couch.

On the very summit of Cader Idris there is an excavation in the solid rock, resembling a couch; and the residents of the vicinity say that whoever rests for the night in the couch, will be found in the morning dead, or raving mad, or endued with supernatural genius.

Rights and Lefts.

Centuries ago shoes were made, as now, "rights and lefts." The shoes found in the tomb of Bernard, King of Italy, were "rights and lefts." Shakespeare describes his smith as—

> "Standing on slippers, which his nimble haste,
> Had falsely *thrust upon contrary feet.*"

Scott, in his "Discoverie of Witchcraft," observes, "that he who receiveth a mischance will consider whether he put not on his shirt wrong side outwards, or his *left* shoe on his *right* foot."

Efficacy in a Mutilated Saint.

There is a church connected with the convent at Chartreux, Provence. It was dedicated to St. John, and over the portico were colossal statues of the four evangelists, which have been

thrown down, and the fragments lie scattered about. When
Miss Plumptre and her party visited the spot, they observed
a woman upon her knees over a fragment of stone, muttering
to herself. When asked whether there was any particular
virtue in the stone, she replied, in French : "Ah, yes ? 'Tis
a piece of St. John." She seemed to think that the saint's
intercession in her behalf, mutilated as he was, might still
avail her.

Feasts at Coronations.

The quantity of provisions consumed at the coronations
of some of the English kings was extraordinary. For that of
King Edward I., February 10th, 1274, the different sheriffs
of twelve of the counties were ordered to deliver, at Windsor,
a total of 440 oxen, 743 swine, 430 sheep and 22,560 fowls.

A Baker's Dozen.

The "baker's dozen" is an old saying. In "The Witch,"
written by Thomas Middleton, about 1620, we find the following :—

Firestone.—"May you not have one o'clock into the
dozen, mother ?"

Witch.—"No."

Firestone.—"Your spirits are the more unconscionable
than *baker's.* "

Wonderful Exhibition with Bees.

On the 14th day of October, 1766, Mr. Wildman, of Ply-
mouth, who had made himself famous throughout the west of
England for his command over bees, was sent for to wait
on Lord Spencer, at his seat at Wimbledon, in Surrey, and

he attended accordingly.   Several of the nobility and persons of fashion were assembled, and the countess had provided three stocks of bees.   The first of his performances was with one hive of bees hanging on his hat, which he carried in his hand, and the hive they came out of in his other hand ; this was to show that he could take honey and wax without destroying the bees.   Then he returned to his room, and came out with them hanging on his chin with a very venerable beard.   After showing them to the company, he took them out upon the grass walk facing the windows, where, a table and a table-cloth being provided, he set the hive upon the table and made the bees hive therein.   Then he made them come out again and swarm in the air, the ladies and nobility standing amongst them, and no person stung by them. He made them go on the table and took them up by handfuls, and tossed them up and down like so many peas ; he then made them go into the hive at the word of command.

At five o'clock in the afternoon he exhibited again with the three swarms of bees, one on his head, one on his breast, and the other on his arm, and waited on Lord Spencer in his room, who had been too much indisposed to see the former experiment; the hives which the bees had been taken from were carried by one of the servants.   After this exhibition he withdrew, but returned once more to the room with the bees all over his head, face and eyes, and was led blind before his lordship's window.   One of his lordship's horses being brought out in his body clothes, Mr. Wildman mounted the horse, with the bees all over his head and face (except his eyes) ; they likewise covered his breast and left arm : he held a whip in his right hand, and a groom led the horse backwards and forwards before his lordship's window for some time.   Mr. W. afterwards took the reins in his hand, rode round the house, dismounted, and at his word of command the bees sought their hives.   The performance surprised and gratified the earl and countess and all the spectators who assembled to witness the bee-master's extraordinary exhibition.—*Annual Register*, 1766.

A Treacherous Talisman.

Gübner mentions that a Jew once presented himself before Duke Albrecht, of Saxony, and offered him a charm, engraved with rare signs and characters, which should render him invulnerable. The duke, determined to try it, had the Jew led out in the field, with his charm round his neck; he then drew his sword, and at the first thrust ran the Jew through.

The Cavern Chapel.

Waldron, in his "Description of the Isle of Man" (1731), speaking of a crypt or subterranean chapel near Peel Castle, says: "Within are thirteen pillars, on which the whole chapel is supported. They have a superstition that whatsoever stranger goes to see this cavern out of curiosity, and omits to count the pillars, shall do something to occasion his being confined there."

Glastonbury Thorn.

This famous hawthorn, which grew on a hill in the churchyard of Glastonbury Abbey, was said to have sprung from the staff of Joseph of Arimathea, who, having fixed it in the ground with his own hand on Christmas day, the staff took root immediately, put forth leaves, and the *next* day was covered with milk-white blossoms. It was declared that this thorn continued to blow every Christmas day during a long series of years, and that slips from the original plant are still preserved, and continue to blow every Christmas day to the present time.

There certainly was in the abbey church-yard a hawthorne-tree which blossomed in winter, and was cut down in the time of the civil wars; but that it always blossomed on Christmas day was a mere tale of the monks, calculated to inspire the vulgar with notions of the sanctity of the place.

Buying and Selling.

There was a singular custom at Rome in connection with the purchase of provisions. Purchaser and vendor simultaneously closed, and then suddenly opened, one of their hands or some of their fingers. If the number of fingers on both sides was even, the vendor obtained the price which he had previously asked : but if the number was uneven, the buyer received the goods for the sum he had just tendered.

Fairy Treasure.

In the Leverian Museum were deposited "Orbicular sparry bodies, commonly called fairies' money, from the banks of the Tyne, Northumberland." Ramon, a character in the play of "The Fatal Dowry," 1632, says—

> But not a word of it, 't is fairies' treasure ;
> Which but reveal'd, brings on the babbler's ruine.

Hour Glasses in Coffins.

A writer in the "Gentleman's Magazine," 1746, says : "In June, 1718, as I was walking in the fields, I stopt in Clerkenwell church-yard to see a grave digger at work. He had dug pretty deep, and was come to a coffin which had lain so long that it was quite rotten, and the plate eaten so with rust that he could not read anything of the inscription. In cleaning away the rotten pieces of wood, the grave-digger found an hour-glass close to the left side of the skull, with sand in it, the wood of which was so rotten that it broke where he took hold of it. Being a lover of antiquity, I bought it of him, and made a drawing of it as it then appeared. Some time after, mentioning this affair in company of some antiquarians, they told me that it was an ancient custom to put an hour-glass into the coffin as an emblem of the sand of life being run out; others conjectured that little hour-glasses were anciently given at funerals, like rosemary, and by the friends of the dead put in the coffin or thrown into the grave."

Macduff's Cross.

The law of Clan Macduff was a privilege of immunity for homicide anciently enjoyed by those who could claim kindred with Macduff, Earl of Fife, within the ninth degree. Macduff's cross stood on the march or boundary between Fife and Strathearn, above Newburg. Any homicide possessed of the right of clanship who could reach it, and who gave nine kye (cows) and a clopindash (a young cow) was free of the slaughter committed by him.

Woman's Cleverness.

It is a singular fact that on one occasion the lives of thousands of the Irish Protestants were saved by a clever device of a woman.

At the latter end of Queen Mary's reign a commission was signed for the purpose of punishing the heretics in that kingdom, and Dr. Cole, Dean of St. Paul's, was honored with the appointment, to execute which he set off with great alacrity. On his arrival at Chester, he sent for the mayor to sup with him, and, in the course of conversation, related his business. Going to his cloak bag, he took out the box containing the commission, and, having shown it, with great joy exclaimed : "This will lash the heretics of Ireland." Mrs. Edmonds, the landlady, overheard this discourse, and having several relations in Ireland who were Protestant, as well as herself, resolved to play a trick upon the doctor, and while he went to attend the magistrate to the door, took the commission out of the box, and in its room placed a pack of cards, with the knave of clubs uppermost. The zealous doctor, suspecting nothing of the matter, put up his box, took shipping and arriving safe in Dublin, went immediately to the viceroy. A council was called, and, after a speech, the doctor delivered his box, which being opened by the secretary, the first thing that presented itself was the knave of clubs. The sight surprised the viceroy and the council, but much more the doctor, who assured them that he had received a commission from the queen, but what had become of it he could not tell. "Well, well," replied the viceroy, "you must go back for another, and we will shuffle the cards in the meantime." The doctor hastened across the channel, but at Holyhead he received the intelligence of the queen's death, and the accession of Elizabeth, who settled on Mrs. Edmonds a pension of forty pounds a year for saving her Protestant subjects in Ireland.

Queer Place to Secrete a Diamond.

An old gentleman recently died at Brussels who has solved in his will a problem which his friends could never quite unravel. He came home after a few years absence abroad, some time ago, with plenty of pecuniary means, though when he left Brussels he went literally to seek his fortune, since he had none on starting. In his will, before he specifies his bequests, of which there are several very liberal ones to friends, relatives, and also to charitable institutions, he tells for the first time how he became possessed of his wealth. He went to Asia and engaged himself as a day laborer in the mines, and while working there found a diamond of large size and great value. He at once made a deep cut in the calf of his leg, where he secreted the gem. Of course, the limb became very sore and lame, and led to his being permitted to leave the mine unsuspected. Having reached a safe locality, he removed the stone and the sore healed up. He worked his way to Amsterdam, where he sold the diamond for \$80,000. This money, put at interest, not only afforded him a good living, but enabled him to go on accumulating. The precious stone is now one of the crown diamonds of Russia.

Incredible Liars.

The French papers, in the autumn of 1821, mention that a man named Desjardins was tried, on his own confession, as an accomplice with Louvel, the assassin of the Duke de Berri. But on his defense, Desjardins contended that his confession ought not to be believed because he was so notorious for falsehood that nobody would give credit to a word he said. In support of this, he produced a host of witnesses, his friend and relatives, who all swore that the excessively bad character which he had given of himself was true, and he was declared not guilty.

Before that a similar instance occurred in Ireland. A man was charged with highway robbery. In the course of the trial the prisoner roared out from the dock that he was guilty, but the jury, in their verdict, pronounced him "not guilty." "Good heavens, gentlemen!" exclaimed the astonished judge, "did you not hear the man himself declare that he was guilty?" The foreman answered: "We did, my lord, and that was the very reason we acquitted him, for we *knew* the fellow to be such a notorious liar that he never told a word of truth in his life."

Force of Imagination.

A peasant saw his dog attacked by a strange and ferocious mastiff. He tried to separate the animals, and received a bite from his own dog, which instantly ran off through the fields. The wound was healed in a few days, and the dog was not to be found, and the peasant after some time began to feel symptoms of nervous agitation. He conceived that the dog, from disappearing, was mad, and within a day or two after this idea had struck him, he began to feel symptoms of hydrophobia. They grew hourly more violent; he raved, and had all the evidence of a violent distemper.

As he was lying with the door open to let in the last air he was to breathe, he heard his dog bark. The animal ran up to the bedside and frolicked about the room; it was clear that he at least was in perfect health. The peasant's mind was relieved at the instant; he got up with renewed strength, dressed himself, plunged is head into a basin of water, and thus refreshed walked into the room to his astonished family.—*Prof. Barrantini.*

A Wife Returned.

The annexed story is gravely recorded in "Dodsley's Annual Register :" "The following extraordinary affair happened at Ferrybridge, in 1767. The wife of one Thomas Benson, being suddenly taken ill, she, to all appearances, expired, and continued without any symptoms of life the whole day, and every proper requisite was ordered for her burial; but the husband, hoping for consolation in his distress, by some money which he had reason to believe she had secreted from him in her lifetime, began a rummage for it, and found seven pounds ten shillings in crown pieces concealed in an old box; but, upon his attempting to take it away, he was surprised by his wife, who was just then recovered, and met him and terribly frightened him by appearing as if nothing had happened."

Life in Death.

The wife of the consul of Cologne, Retchmuth, apparently died of the plague, in 1571. A ring of great value, buried with her, tempted the cupidity of the grave-digger, and was the cause of many future years of happiness. At night the purloiner marched to his plunder, and she revived. She lived to be the mother of three children, and, when really dead, she was reburied in the same church, where a monument was erected, upon which the above particulars are recited in German verse.—*Edmund Fillingham King.*

Remedy for Bad Dreams.

When a man has dreamed a bad dream in China he need not despair, for an interpreter of dreams is ready to supply him with a mystic scroll, which will avert the impending calamity. It is written on red or yellow paper, and the interpreter rolls it up in the form of a triangle and attaches it to the dress of his client. The dreamer is then made to look toward the east, with a sword in his right hand and his mouth full of spring water. In this position he ejects the water from his mouth, and beats the air with the sword, repeating in an imperative tone certain words, of which the following is an interpretation: "As quickly and with as much strength as rises the sun in the east, do thou, charm or mystic scroll, avert

all the evil influences which are likely to result from my bad dream. As quickly as lightning passes through the air, O charm, cause impending evils to disappear."—*Credulities Past and Present.*

The Letiche.

At Bayeux, in Normandy, one of the superstitions still current relates to a being called a letiche. It is an animal whose form is scarcely defined—of dazzling whiteness—which is only seen in the night time, and disappears the moment any one attempts to touch it. The letiches are believed to be the souls of infants who died without baptism. Most probably this pretty little spirit was no other than the agile and timid ermine of Normandy and Brittany.—*Summer Among the Bocages.*

Hell-stones.

These were vast stones formerly used for covering graves, *helicin* being the Saxon for " to cover " or conceal. In Dorsetshire is one of these stones ; and the tradition is, that the devil flung it from Portland Pike to its present position, as he was playing at quoits.

The Golden Tooth.

In 1593 it was reported that a Silesian child, seven years old, had lost all its teeth, and that a golden tooth had grown in the place of a natural double one. In 1595 Horstius, professor of medicine in the University of Helmstadt, wrote the history of this golden tooth. He said it was partly a natural event and partly miraculous, and that God had sent it to the child to console the Christians for their persecution by the Turks. In the same year Rullandus drew up another account of the golden tooth. Two years afterwards, Ingosteterus, another learned man, wrote against the opinion which Rullandus had given on this golden tooth. Rullandus immediately replied in a most elegant and erudite dissertation. Libavius, a very learned man, compiled all that had been said relative to this tooth, and subjoined his remarks upon it. Nothing was wanting to recommend these erudite writings to posterity but proof that the tooth was gold. A goldsmith examined it, and found it a natural tooth artificially gilt.

The Devil Regarded as a Benefactor of the Human Race.

The Ophites were a sect who, like most Gnostics, regarded the Jehovah of the Old Testament with great abhorrence. Regarding the emancipation of man from the power and control of Jehovah as the most important end, they considered the serpent who tempted Eve and introduced "knowledge" and "revolt" into the world, to have been the great benefactor of the human race. They worshipped the serpent, and sought to engraft Ophism upon Christianity by causing the bread designed for the Eucharistic sacrifice to be licked by a serpent which was kept in a cave for the purpose, and which the communicants kissed after receiving the Eucharist.

Curse of Scotland.

This is a term applied to the nine of diamonds in a pack of playing cards. Much uncertainty prevails respecting the origin of the phrase. The most probable explanation is that it refers to the detestation entertained in Scotland toward John Dalrymple, first Earl of Stair, on account of his connection with the Massacre of Glencoe, for which he had to resign office in 1695. The heraldic bearing of this person consisted of nine lozenges on a field of azure. These nine lozenges resembled the nine of diamonds, and hence the popular phrase, the " Curse of Scotland."

Curse of Innocent Blood.

Southey, in his "Common-place Book," has traced the outlines of what might be worked up into a very effective story of "citation" for those who unjustly and cruelly put others to death. "The Philipsons of Colgarth coveted a field, like Ahab, and had the possessor hung for an offence which he had not committed. The night before his execution the old man (for he was very old) read the 109th Psalm as his solemn and dying commination, verses 2, 3, 8, 9, 10, 12, 13, 14, 15, 16." The verses contain a prayer for vengeance upon the "wicked and deceitful," who "have spoken with a lying tongue," and whose days are to be few, their children to be fatherless and continually vagabonds and beggars, and their posterity to be cut off. "The curse," Southey adds, "was fully accomplished; the family were cut off, and the only daughter who remained sold laces and bobbins about the country."

Legend of an Inventor.

A story is told of an inventor whose skill was the occasion of his own death. An immense bell, with the twelve hours carved upon it, had been hung in a high tower. A female figure was so arranged as to glide from her hiding place and strike each hour on the bell with a huge hammer. Everything was in its place, and it had been previously arranged with the concourse below, who had assembled to hear the bell strike, that it should sound the hour of one. Forgetful that the hour approached, the artist was still at work upon the carving of the bell, with his head near it, when the female figure, true to the machinery that moved it, glided from its place, and, hammer in hand, struck a fatal blow upon the head of the workman.

A Strange Legend.

We are told that when St. Helena had discovered the true cross of Christ, she permitted various fragments to be taken from it, which were encased, some in gold and some in gems, and conveyed to Europe, leaving the main part of the wood in the charge of the Bishop of Jerusalem, who exhibited it annually at Easter, until Chosroes, King of Persia, plundered Jerusalem in the reign of Phocas, and took away the holy relic. Before this fatal event we are taught to believe, by Rigordus, an historian of the thirteenth century, that the mouths of Christians used to be supplied with thirty teeth, and in some instances, no doubt according to their faith, with thirty-two teeth; but that *after* the cross was stolen by the infidels no mortal has ever been allowed more than twenty-three!

Abraham and Sarah.

The Talmudists relate that Abraham, in traveling to Egypt, brought with him a chest. At the custom house the officers exacted the duties. Abraham would have readily paid them, but desired they would not open the chest. They first insisted on the duties for clothes, which Abraham consented to pay; but then they thought, by his ready acquiescence, that it might be gold; he consented to pay for gold. They then began to suspect it might contain silk, whereupon Abraham was willing to pay for silk or costly pearls; in short, he consented to pay as if the chest contained the most valuable of things. It was then resolved to open and examine the chest; and. behold! as soon as the chest was opened, that great lustre of human beauty broke out which made such a noise in the land of Egypt,—it was Sarah herself! The jealous Abraham, to conceal her beauty, had locked her up in the chest.

Tradition of the Temple.

There is a beautiful tradition connected with the site on which the temple of Solomon was erected. It is said to have been occupied in common by two brothers, one of whom had a family and the other none. On the spot was a field of wheat. On the evening succeeding the harvest, the wheat having been gathered in shocks, the elder brother said to his wife, "My younger brother is unable to bear the burden and heat of the day; I will arise, take of my shocks, and place them with his, without his knowledge." The other brother, actuated by the same benevolent motives, said within himself, "My elder brother has a family, and I have none; I will contribute to their support; I will arise, take of my shocks, and place them with his, without his knowledge."

Judge of their mutual astonishment when, on the following morning, they found their respective shocks undiminished. This course of events transpired for several nights, when each resolved in his mind to stand guard and solve the mystery. They did so, and on the following night met each other half-way between the respective shocks, with their arms full.

Magnetic Cures.

The use of the magnet for the cure of diseases was known to the ancients. It was known to Aëtius, who lived as early as the year 500. He says: "We are assured that those who are troubled with the gout in their hands or their feet, or with convulsions, find relief when they hold a magnet in their hands." Paracelsus recommended the magnet in a number of diseases, while Kircher tells us that it was worn around the neck as a preventive against convulsions and affections of the nerves. About the end of the seventeenth century magnetic tooth-picks were made, and extolled as a secret preventive against pains in the teeth, eyes and ears.

May Dew a Cure for Freckles.

The "Morning Post," (England,) issued for the 2d day of May, 1791, states that the day before, "being the first of May, according to annual and superstitious custom, a number of persons went into the fields and bathed their faces with the dew on the grass, under the idea that it would render them beautiful."

Singular Hindoo Vow.

The following extraordinary vow is performed by some of the Hindoos at their festival of *Charak Puja :* Stretching himself on the ground on his back, the devotee takes a handful of moist earth, and placing it on his under lip, he plants in it some mustard seed, and exposes himself to the dews of the night and the heat of the day until the seeds germinate. In this posture the man must remain in a fixed, motionless condition, without food or drink, until the vegetable process liberates him, which will generally be about the fourth day.

Satanic Superstitions.

That the devil has a "cloven foot," which he cannot hide if it be looked for, is a common belief with the vulgar. There is a popular superstition in England relative to goats, that they are never to be seen for twenty-four hours together, and that once in that space they pay a visit to the devil in order to have their beards combed.

Healing by the King.

On the 18th of May, 1664, the following public advertisement was issued for the healing of the people by King Charles II.:—

NOTICE.

His sacred majesty having declared it to be his royal will and purpose to continue the healing of his people for the evil during the month of May, and then give over till Michalmas next, I am commanded to give notice thereof, that the people may not come up to the town in the interim and lose their labour. NEWES, 1664.

Hallow E'en Customs.

Burns says that "burning the nuts is a favorite charm. They name the lad and lass to each particular nut, as they lay them in the fire; and accordingly, as they burn quietly together or start from beside one another, the course and issue of the courtship will be." In Ireland, when the young women would know if their lovers are faithful, they put three nuts upon the bars of the grates, naming the nuts after the lovers. If a nut cracks or jumps, the lover will prove unfaithful; if it begins to blaze or burn, he has a regard for the person making the trial. If the nuts, named after the girl and her lover, burn together, they will be married. This sort of divination is also practiced in England. Gay mentions it in his " Spell "—

> "Two hazel nuts I threw into the flame,
> And to each nut I gave a sweetheart's name;
> This with *the loudest bounce* me sore amaz'd,
> That in a *flame of brightest colour* blaz'd;
> As *blaz'd the nut*, so *may thy passion grow*,
> For 'twas thy nut that did so brightly glow."

Another charm consisted in eating an apple. "Take a candle and go alone to a looking-glass; eat an apple before it, and some traditions say you should comb your hair all the time; the face of your conjugal companion *to be* will be seen in the glass, as if peeping over your shoulder."

A third is, "to dip your left shirt-sleeve in a burn where three lairds' lands meet." "You go out, one or more—for this is a social spell—to a south-running spring or rivulet, where three lairds' lands meet, and dip your left shirt-sleeve. Go to bed in sight of a fire, and hang your wet sleeve before it to dry. Lie awake; and some time near midnight an apparition, having the exact figure of the party in question, will come and turn the sleeve, as if to dry the other side of it."

A fourth is performed as follows: "Take three dishes; put clean water in one, foul water in another, and leave the third empty; blindfold a person and lead him to the hearth where the dishes are ranged; he (or she) dips the left hand; if by chance in the clean water, the future husband or wife will come to the bar of matrimony a maid; if in the foul, a widow; if in the empty dish, it foretells with equal certainty no marriage at all. It is repeated three times, and every time the arrangement of the dishes is altered."

Pennant says that the young women in Scotland determine the figure and size of their prospective husbands by *drawing cabbages blindfolded*. "They must go out, hand in hand, with eyes shut, and pull the first they meet with. Its being little, straight or crooked, is prophetic of the size and shape

of the grand object of all their spells—the husband or wife.
Earth sticking to the roots indicates a fortune."

St. Agnes' Eve.

Formerly this was a night of great import to maidens who
desired to know whom they were to marry. Of such it was
required that they should not eat on this day, and those who
conformed to the rule called it fasting St. Agnes' fast. Ben
Jonson says—

> And on sweet St. Agnes' night,
> Please you with the promis'd sight,
> Some of husbands, some of lovers,
> Which an empty dream discovers.

Old Aubrey gives a form whereby a lad or lass was to
attain a sight of the fortunate lover. "Upon St. Agnes'
night you take a row of pins, and pull out every one, one
after another, saying a Pater Noster, sticking a pin in your
sleeve, and you will dream of him or her you shall marry."

> —Her vespers done
> Of all its wreathed pearls her hair she frees;
> Unclasps her warmed jewels one by one;
> Loosens her fragrant boddice; by degrees
> Her rich attire creeps rustling to her knees.
> Half hidden, like a mermaid in sea-weed,
> Pensive awhile she dreams awake, and sees,
> In fancy, fair St. Agnes in her bed,
> But dares not look behind, or all the charm is fled.—*Keates.*

St. Patrick's Birth-day.

Saint Patrick, according to ancient lore, having been born
at Kilpatrick, Scotland, landed near Wicklow, in the year of
grace 433. Originally there was a dispute, according to

Lover, as to the true anniversary of this renowned saint, some supposing the eighth and others the ninth to be the correct day. The humorist represents a priest as settling the difficulty as follows :—

> Says he, "Boys, don't be fighting for eight or for nine;
> Don't be always dividing—but sometimes combine;
> Combine eight with nine, and seventeen is the mark,
> So let that be his birthday." "Amen," says the clerk.
> So they all got blind drunk—which completed their bliss,
> And we keep up the practice from that day to this!

Wassailing the Orchards.

In Devonshire, according to Brand, on the eve of the Epiphany, the farmer and his men, with a large pitcher of cider, visit the orchard, and, encircling one of the best bearing trees, they drink the following toast three several times :—

> "Here's to thee, old apple tree,
> Whence thou may'st bud, and whence thou may'st blow,
> And whence thou may'st bear apples enow!
> Hats full! caps full!
> Bushel—bushel—sacks full!
> And my pockets full too!   Huzza!"

This done, they return to the house, to find the doors bolted by the ladies, who will not open until some one guesses what is on the spit, and which is the reward of him who names it. Some are so superstitious as to believe that if they neglect this ceremony, the trees will bear no apples that year. In allusion to a similar ceremony practiced in Sussex and Essex on New Year's eve, Herrick, in his "Hesperides," says—

> "Wassail the trees, that they may bear
> You many a plum, and many a pear;
> For more or less fruits they will bring,
> As you do give them wassailing."

Cutting Off the Fiddler's Head.

A very singular merriment in the Isle of Man is mentioned by Waldron, in his history of that place. He says that "during the whole twelve days of Christmas there is not a barn unoccupied, and that every parish hires fiddlers at the public charge. On twelfth-day the fiddler lays his head in some one of the girls' laps, and a third person asks who such a maid, or such a maid shall marry, naming the girls then present one after another; to which the fiddler answers, according to his own whim, or agreeably to the intimacies he has taken notice of during this time of merriment. But whatever he says is as absolutely depended upon as an oracle; and if he happens to couple two people who have an aversion to each other, tears and vexation succeed the mirth. This they call cutting off the fiddler's head; for after this he is dead for the whole year."

Striking with Nettles.

A painful and mischievous custom prevailed on May eve in the south of Ireland so late as the year 1825. "It was a common practice for school boys, on that day, to consider themselves privileged to run wildly about with a bunch of nettles, striking at the face and hands of their companions, or any other person whom they felt they could assault with impunity."

Singular Burial Customs.

In the department of the Hautes Alpes, of France, in and around the village of Andrieux, the dead are wrapped in a winding sheet, but are not inclosed in a coffin. In the valleys of Queyras and Grave, the dead are suspended in a barn during five months in the winter, until the earth is softened by the sun's rays, when the corpse is consigned to its native element. On the return to the home of the deceased, it becomes a scene of bacchanalian revelry, in which the groans and sighs of the mourners mingle with the songs and jests of the inebriated guests. At Argentiere, after the burial, the tables are set out round the church-yard; that of the curate and the mourning family over the grave itself.

Treatment of Lepers in England.

According to the tenor of various old civil codes and local enactments, when a person became affected with leprosy he was looked upon as legally and politically dead, and lost the privileges of citizenship. He was classed with idiots, madmen and outlaws, and was not allowed to inherit. The church performed the solemn ceremonies of the burial of the dead over him on the day on which he was separated from his fellow-men, and confined to a lazar-house. A priest, with surplice, stole and crucifix, conducted the leper from his residence to the church, and thence to the lazar-house. As the priest left the latter place he threw upon the body of the poor outcast a shovelful of earth, in imitation of the closing of a grave.

Kissed while Asleep.

There exists an old social custom of claiming a pair of gloves, from man or woman, by a kiss given when asleep. Allusion to this occurs in Scott's "Fair Maid of Perth." Catherine Glover, on St. Valentine's day, found Henry of the Wynd asleep in a chair in her father's house. She stole a kiss from him, thereby choosing him as her valentine, and winning a pair of gloves. Her father, who was a glove-maker, says: "Thou knowest the maiden who ventures to kiss a sleeping man wins of him a pair of gloves. Come to my booth. Thou shalt have a pair of delicate kid-skin that will exactly suit her hand and arm.''

How the Chinese Secure a Pastor.

The fourth of February, says the Nevada *Transcript*, is the day on which the Chinese select one of their number to preside over their Joss house. The manner of proceeding is as follows: The two companies here are permitted to have each a certain number of representatives, and the fleetest and strongest men are generally chosen. These delegates repair to a vacant lot at the rear of the Joss house. A stipulated number of bombs, each one containing a metallic ring, are placed in charge of a committee, whose duty it is to fire off the bombs, one at a time. When the explosion takes place, the ring contained in the bomb is sent flying into the air. It is the desire of the two factions to have their respective delegates to secure as many of the rings as possible. Of course, a general scramble ensues. At the close, the side which has secured the most rings is entitled to select a Joss (equivalent to a minister of the gospel with us) from among their number.

Easter-Box.

A custom was instituted in the city of Toulouse by Charlemagne, that at Easter any Christian might give a box on the ear to a Jew wherever he chanced to meet him, as a mark of contempt for the nation which had, at that season, crucified the Saviour of mankind. This usage, scandalous in itself, was sometimes, through zeal, practiced with great violence. It is stated that the eye of a poor Jew was forced out on the side of the head whereon the blow was given. In the course of centuries this cruel custom was commuted for a tax, and the money appropriated to the use of the church of St. Saturnin.

Antipathies.

Amatus Lusitanus relates the case of a monk who fainted whenever he saw a rose, and never quitted his cell when that flower was blooming. Scaliger mentions one of his relatives who experienced a similar horror when seeing a lily. Montaigne stated that there were men who dreaded an apple more than they did a musket ball. Zimmerman tells us of a lady who could not endure the touch of silk and satin, and shuddered when placing her hand upon the velvet skin of a peach. Boyle records the case of a man who felt a natural abhorrence to honey. Without his knowledge, some honey was mixed with a plaster applied to his foot, and his agony compelled his attendants to withdraw it. A young man was known to faint whenever he heard the servant sweeping. Hippocrates mentions one Nicanor who swooned whenever he heard a flute. Erasmus experienced febrile symptoms when smelling fish. The Duke d'Epernon swooned on beholding a leveret, although a hare did not produce the same effect. Henry III. of France fainted at the sight of a cat, and Marshal d'Albert at the sight of a pig.

Superstitions Respecting Bees.

The lower order of people in some parts of England have curious superstitions respecting the bee. A poor old widow once complained to me that all her stocks of bees had died, and on inquiring the cause, she informed me that on the death of her husband, a short time before, she had neglected to *tap* at each of the hives, to inform the bees of the circumstance;

that, in consequence of this omission, they had been gradually getting weaker and weaker, and that now she had not one left. Mr. Loudon mentions, that when he was in Bedfordshire, he was informed of an old man who sang a psalm in front of some hives which were not doing well, but which he said would thrive in consequence of that ceremony. In Norfolk, at places where bees are kept, it is an indispensable ceremony, in case of the death of any of the family, to put the bees in mourning, or the consequence would be that all of them would die. The method of putting them in mourning is to attach a piece of black cloth to each of the hives. In the neighborhood of Coventry, in the event of the death of any of the family, it is considered necessary to inform the bees of the circumstance, otherwise they will dwindle and die. The manner of communicating the intelligence to the little community, is, with due form and ceremony, to take the key of the house, and knock with it three times against the hive, informing the inmates, at the same time, of the bereavement. A similar custom prevails in Kent.—*Mr. Jesse.*

Welcoming the New Moon.

In Scotland, especially among the Highlanders, the women make a courtesy to the new moon. In some parts of England the women exclaim, upon seeing the new moon: "A fine moon, God bless her!"

The Bodach Glas.

Among the warnings or notices of death to be found in the dark chronicle of superstitions, the omens peculiar to certain families are not the least striking. Pennant tells us that many of the great families in Scotland had their demon, or genius, who gave them monitions of future events. Thus the family of Rothmurchan had the Bodac an Dun, or Ghost of the Hill; and the Kincardines, the Spectre of the Bloody Hand. The Bodach Glas is introduced in the novel of "Waverley," as the family superstition of the MacIvors, the truth of which had been proved by an experience of three hundred years. Bodach is from the Saxon, Bode, a messenger, a tidings-bringer; Glas, the Gælic for gray, the "Gray Messenger." The appearance of a tall figure in a gray plaid was always regarded as an omen of an early death in the family.

Strange Instance of Sympathy.

The Duke de Saint Simon mentions in his "Memoirs" a singular instance of constitutional sympathy between two brothers. These were twins—the President de Banquemore and the Governor de Bergues, who were surprisingly alike, not only in their persons, but in their feelings. One morning, he tells us, when the president was at his royal audience, he was suddenly attacked by an intense pain in the thigh; at the same instant, as it was discovered afterwards, his brother, who was with the army, received a severe wound from a sword on the same leg, and precisely the same part of the leg.

Double Apparition.

In a letter of Philip, the second Earl of Chesterfield, it is related, that "on a morning in 1652, the earl saw an object in white, like a standing sheet, within a yard of his bedside. He attempted to catch it, but it slid to the foot of the bed, and he saw it no more. His thoughts turned to his lady, who was then at Networth, with her father, the Earl of Northumber-land. On his arrival at Networth, a footman met him on the stairs, with a packet directed to him from his wife, whom he found with Lady Essex, her sister, and Mr. Ramsey. He was asked why he had returned so suddenly. He told his motive; and on perusing the letters in the packet, he found that his lady had written to him, requesting his return, for she had seen an object in white, with a black face, by her bedside. These apparitions were seen by the earl and countess *at the same moment*, when they were forty miles asunder."

Spirit of Dundee.

At the time Viscount Dundee fell in the battle of Killie-crankie, in 1689, his friend, the Lord Balcarras, was a prisoner in the Castle of Edinburg, upon a strong suspicion of attachment to the unfortunate house of Stuart. The captive earl was in bed, when a hand drew aside the curtain, and the figure of his friend was revealed to him, armed as for battle. The spectre gazed mournfully on Lord Balcarras, passed to the other end of the chamber, leaned some time on the mantle-piece, and then slowly passed out of the door. The earl, not for a moment supposing that he was looking at an apparition, called out "Stop!" but the figure heeded him not. Immediately afterwards, the news was conveyed to his lordship of the battle, and that the gallant Dundee was slain; or, as the song says, that

"Low lay the bonnet of bonny Dundee."

Captain Kidd's Vision.

Lord Byron used to mention a strange story which the commander of a packet related to him. This officer stated, that being asleep one night in his berth, he was awakened by the pressure of something heavy on his limbs; and, there being a faint light in his room, could see, as he thought distinctly, the figure of his brother, who was at that time in the same service in the East Indies, dressed in his uniform, and stretched across the bed.   Concluding it to be an illusion of the senses, he shut his eyes and made an effort to sleep.   But still the same pressure continued, and still, as often as he ventured to look, he saw the figure lying across in the same position.   To add to his wonder, on putting forth his hand to touch the figure, he found the uniform in which it appeared to be dressed *dripping wet.*   On the entrance of one of his brother officers, to whom he called out in alarm, the apparition vanished.   A few months later Captain Kidd received intelligence that on that very night his brother had been drowned in the Indian seas.—*Moore's Life of Byron.*

Sir Henry Wotton's Strange Dream.

Honest Isaac Walton makes Sir Henry Wotton a dreamer in the family line ; for, just before his death, he dreamed that the University treasury was robbed by townsmen and poor scholars, and that the number was five.   He then wrote to his son Henry at Oxford, inquiring about it, and the letter reached him the morning after the night of the robbery. "Henry," says the account, "shows his father's letter about, which causes great wonderment, especially as the number of thieves was exactly correct."

Supernatural Appearance at Holland House.

Aubrey tells us, in his "Miscellanies," that "the beautiful Lady Diana Rich, daughter of the Earl of Holland, as she was walking in her father's garden, at Kensington, to take the fresh air before dinner, about eleven o'clock, being then very well, met with her own apparition—habit and everything—as in a looking-glass. About a month after she died of small-pox. It is said that her sister, the Lady Elizabeth Thynne, saw the like of herself also, before she died. This account I had from a person of honor."

Old Grimaldi's Death.

Grimaldi, the father of "Joe," the celebrated clown, had a vague yet profound dread of the 14th day of the month. At its approach he was always nervous, disquieted, anxious; directly it had passed, he was another man again, and invariably exclaimed, in his broken English, "Ah! now I am safe for anoder month." If this circumstance were unaccompanied by any singular coincidence, it would be scarcely worth mentioning; but it is remarkable that Grimaldi actually died on the 14th of March, and that he was born, christened and married on the 14th of the month.—*Dickens' Life of Grimaldi.*

Twelfth-night Omens.

In Normandy, if any of the family are absent when the cake is cut on Twelfth-night, his share is carefully put by. If he remains well, it is believed that the cake continues fresh; if ill, it begins to be moist; if he dies, the cake spoils.

Twofold Apparition.

Mrs. Mathews relates, in the memoirs of her husband, the celebrated comedian, that he was one night in bed and unable to sleep from the excitement that continues some time after acting; when, hearing a rustling by the side of his bed, he looked out and saw his first wife, who was then dead, standing by the bedside, dressed as when alive. She smiled and bent forward, as if to take his hand; but in his alarm he threw himself out on the floor to avoid the contact, and was found by the landlord in a fit. On the same night, and at the same hour, the second Mrs. Mathews, who was far away from her husband, received a similar visit from her predecessor, whom she had known when alive. She was quite awake, and in her terror seized the bell-rope to summon assistance; the rope gave way, and she fell with it in her hand to the floor.

Dr. Donne's Apparition.

Isaac Walton gives an account of this apparition in the life of Dr. Donne. The doctor left his wife unwell in London, and went with Sir Robert Drury to Paris. Two days after arriving there he stated to Drury that he had had a vision of his wife walking through his room, with her hair hanging over her shoulders, and a dead child in her arms. So impressed were they by the incident that they immediately sent a messenger to London to inquire regarding Mrs. Donne's health. The intelligence procured by the man was, that she had been brought to bed of a dead child at the very hour in which her husband thought he had seen her in Paris.

Picture Omens.

Archbishop Laud, not long before the disastrous circumstance happened which hastened his tragical end, on entering his study one day, found his picture at full length on the floor, the string which held it to the wall having snapped. The sight of this struck the prelate with such a sense of the probability of his fate, that from that time he did not enjoy a moment's peace. The Duke of Buckingham was struck by an occurrence of a similar kind; he found his picture in the Council Chamber fallen out of its frame. This accident, in that age of omens, was looked upon with a considerable degree of awe.

Felling Oaks.

In the "Magna Britannia," the author, in his "Account of the Hundred of Croydon," says: "Our historians take notice of two things in this parish which may not be convenient to us to omit, viz: A great wood called Norwood, belonging to the archbishops, wherein was anciently a tree called the Vicar's Oak, where four parishes met, as it were, in a point. It is said to have consisted wholly of oaks, and among them was one that bore a mistletoe, which some persons were so hardy as to cut for the gain of selling it to the apothecaries of London, leaving a branch of it to sprout out; but they proved unfortunate after it, for one of them fell lame and others lost an eye. At length, in the year 1678, a certain man, notwithstanding that he was warned against it, upon the account of what the others had suffered, ventured to cut the tree down, and he soon after broke his leg.

"To fell oaks has long been counted fatal, and such as believe it produce the instance of the Earl of Winchilsea, who, having felled a curious grove of oaks, soon after found his countess dead in her bed suddenly, and his eldest son, the Lord Maidstone, was killed at sea by a cannon ball."

Lord Bacon's Dream.

When Lord Bacon, as he himself records, dreamt in Paris that he saw "his father's house in the country plastered all over with black mortar," his feelings were highly wrought upon; the emotions under which he labored were of a very apprehensive kind, and he had no doubt that the next intelligence from England would apprise him of the death of his father. The sequel proved that his apprehensions were well grounded, for his father actually died the same night in which he had his remarkable dream.

Reckless Disregard of Omens.

P. Claudius, in the First Punic War, caused the sacred chickens, who would not leave their cage, to be pitched into the sea, saying: "If they will not eat, they must drink."

Sailors' Whistling.

Zoraster imagined there was an evil spirit that could excite violent storms of wind. The sailors are tinctured with a superstition of the kind, which is the reason why they so seldom whistle on ship-board; when becalmed, their whistling is an invocation.

The Hinder Well-spout Unlucky.

A curious instance of popular superstition, in defiance of plain facts to the contrary, is related in a letter written in the year 1808, published in Dr. Aikin's "Athenæum." The writer says that in the year 1801, he visited Glasgow, and, passing one of the principal streets in the neighborhood of the Iron Church, observed about thirty people, chiefly women and girls, gathered round a large public pump, waiting their turn to draw water. The pump had two spouts, behind and before; but he noticed that the hinder one was carefully plugged up, no one attempting to fill her vessel from that source, although she had to wait so long till her turn came at the other spout.

On inquiry, the visitor was informed that, though the same handle brought the same water from the same well through either and both of the spouts, yet the populace, and even some better informed people, had for a number of years conceived an idea, which had become hereditary and fixed, that the water passing through the hindermost spout would be *unlucky and poisonous*. This prejudice received from time to time a certain sanction; for in the spout, through long disuse, a kind of dusty fur collected, and this, if at any time the water was allowed to pass through, made it at first run foul—thus confirming the superstitious prejudice of the people, who told the traveler that it was certain death to drink of the water drawn from the hindermost spout. The magistrates had sought to dispel the ignorant terror of the populace, by cleaning out the well repeatedly in their presence, and explaining to them the internal mechanism of the pump, but all was in vain.

Assuming the Form of a Bird.

That the soul quits the dead body in the form of a bird, is a wide-spread belief, and has been the subject of superstitious fancies from the earliest times. In the Egyptian hieroglyphics, a bird signifies the soul of man.

In the legend of St. Polycarp, who was burned alive, his blood extinguished the flames, and from his ashes arose a white dove which flew towards heaven. It was said that a dove was seen to issue from the funeral pyre of Joan of Arc.

In the Breton ballad of "Lord Nann and the Korrigan" there is an allusion to spirit-bearing doves—

> "It was a marvel to see, men say,
> The night that followed the day,
> The lady in earth by her lord lay,
> To see two oak-trees themselves rear
> From the new-made grave into the air;

> • "And on their branches two doves white,
> Who were there hopping gay and light;
> Which sang when rose the morning ray,
> And then toward heaven sped away."

A wild song, sung by the boatmen of the Mola, in Venice, declares that the spirit of Daniel Manin, the patriot, is flying about the lagoons to this day in the shape of a beautiful dove.

In the Paris *Figaro* (October, 1872), is an account of the death of a gipsy belonging to a tribe encamped in the Rue Duhesme. Among other ceremonies, a live bird was held close to the lips of the dying girl, with the view of introducing her soul into the bird.

In certain districts of Russia bread-crumbs are placed in a piece of white linen, outside of the window, for six weeks, under the belief that the soul of the recent inmate will come, in the shape of a bird, to feed upon the crumbs. When Deacon Theodore and his three schismatic brethren were burnt in 1681, the souls of the martyrs, as the "Old Believers" affirm, appeared in the air as pigeons.

Talismanic Stones in Birds.

Among the curiosities of ancient credulity was the belief that certain birds possessed stones of remarkable talismanic virtue. One of these was supposed to be found in the brain of the vulture, which gave health to the finder and successful results when soliciting favors. Dioscorides gives an account of the use of an eagle-stone in detecting larceny. The *Alectorius*, a stone worn by the wrestler Milo, was so called from being taken out of the gizzard of a fowl. A stone like a crystal, as large as a bean, extracted from a cock, was considered by the Romans to make the wearer invisible. *Corvia* was the name of a stone obtained from the nest of a crow. The swallow-stone was a Norman superstition, according to which the bird knows how to find on the seashore a stone that restores sight to the blind. Longfellow, in "Evangeline," says—

"Seeking with eager eyes that wondrous stone which the swallow
Brings from the shore of the sea, to restore the sight of her fledglings."

Birds Prognosticating Death.

In old times it was believed that certain birds prognosticated death. In Lloyd's "Stratagems of Jerusalem" (1602), he says: "By swallows lighting upon Pirrhus' tents, and lighting upon the mast of Mar. Antonius' ship, sayling after Cleopatra to Egypt, the soothsayers did prognosticate that Pirrhus should be slaine at Argos, in Greece, and Mar. Antonius in Egypt." He alludes to swallows following Cyrus from Persia to Scythia, from which the magi foretold his death. Ravens followed Alexander the Great in returning from India, and going to Babylon, which was a sure presage of his end.

Among the Danish peasantry the appearance of a raven in the village is considered an indication that the parish priest is to die. "There is a common feeling in Cornwall," observes Mr. Hunt, "that the croaking of a raven over the house bodes evil to some of the family." Marlowe, in his "Rich Jew of Malta," described the "sad-presaging raven"—

"That tolls
The sick man's passport in her hollow beak,
And in the shadow of the silent night
Doth shake contagion from her sable wings."

Gay, in "The Dirge," notices the presage—

"The boding raven on her cottage sat
And with hoarse croakings warn'd us of our fate."

A number of crows are said to have fluttered about Cicero's head on the very day he was murdered.

An evil prognostic attends the bittern in its flight. Bishop Hall, alluding to a superstitious man, says: "If a bittern flies over his head by night, he makes his will."

Homer has immortalized the crane as foreboding disaster—

> "That when inclement winters vex the plain
> With piercing frosts, or thick descending rain,
> To warmer seas the cranes embodied fly,
> With noise and order, through the midway sky;
> To pigmy nations wounds and death they bring,
> And all the war descends upon the wing."

Here is a saying that includes the magpie as a presager of death—

> "One's joy, two's a greet [crying],
> Three's a wedding, four's a sheet [winding sheet]."

The *burree churree*, an Indian night bird, preys upon dead bodies. The Mohammedans say that should a drop of the blood of a corpse, or any part of it, fall from this bird's beak on a human being, he will die at the end of forty days.

The Crossbill.

There is an odd superstition connected with the crossbill, in Thuringia, which makes the wood-cutters very careful of the nests. This bird in captivity is subject to many diseases, such as weak eyes, swelled and ulcerated feet, etc., arising probably from the heat and accumulated vapors of the stove-heated rooms where they are kept. The Thuringian mountaineer believes that these wretched birds can take upon themselves any diseases to which he is subject, and always keeps some near him. He is satisfied that a bird whose upper mandible bends to the right, has the power of transferring colds and rheumatisms from man to itself; and if the mandible

turns to the left, he is equally certain that the bird can render
the same service to the women.   The crossbill is often attacked
with epilepsy, and the Thuringians drink every day the water
left by the bird, as a specific against that disease.

The Ostrich.

The ancient myth about the ostrich was that she did not
hatch her eggs by setting upon them, but by the rays of light
and warmth from her eyes.   Southey alludes to this in
"Thalaba"—

> With such a look as fables say
> The mother ostrich fixes on her eggs,
> Till that intense affection
> Kindle its light of life.

Honoring the Lark.

In Russia, on the 9th of March, the day on which the larks
are supposed to arrive, the rustics make clay images of those
birds, smear them with honey, tip their heads with tinsel, and
then carry them about, singing songs to spring, or to Lada,
their vernal goddess.

The Nightingale.

Milton's exquisite sonnet to the nightingale makes pointed
reference to the fancy that her song portended success in love.
Faber, in the "Cherwell Water Lily," gives an angelic character to the strains of the nightingale.   The classical fable of
the unhappy Philomela may have given origin to the conception that the nightingale sings with its breast impaled upon a
thorn.   The earliest notice of this myth by an English poet

is, probably, that in the "Passionate Pilgrim" of Shakespeare—

> "Everything doth banish moan,
> Save the nightingale alone.
> She, poor bird, as all forlorn,
> *Lean'd her breast up till a thorn,*
> And there sung the dolefull'st ditty,
> That to hear it was great pity."

The Blackbird originally White.

There is a curious story of the blackbird that its original color was white, but it became black because one year three of the days were so cold that it had to take refuge in a chimney. Mr. Swainson says that "these three days (January 30th, 31st and February 1st) are called in the neighborhood of Brescia, "I giorni della merla," the blackbird's days.

The Dove.

The dove amongst birds, from its gentle and loving nature in the first place, and in the second from the purity of its plumage, has been preferably selected as the image of the Holy Ghost.

According to an apocryphal gospel, the Holy Ghost, under the form of a dove, designated Joseph as the spouse of the Virgin Mary by alighting on his head; and in the same manner, says Eusebius, was Fabian indicated as the divinely-appointed Bishop of Rome. According to a singular legend, the Holy Spirit, in the form of a dove, was present at the Council of Nice, and *signed the creed* that was there framed! There are many legends of a similar character.

At the consecration of Clovis the divine dove is said actually to have presided over the Christian destinies of France.

Clovis and the Bishop of Rheims, St. Remi, proceeded in procession to the baptistry, where the chief of the Franks was to be consecrated king and made a Christian. When they arrived there, the priest, bearing the holy chrism, was stopped by the crowd, and could not reach the font. But a dove, whiter than snow, brought thither in her beak the "ampoule" (a phial of white glass) filled with chrism sent from heaven. St. Remi took the vessel and perfumed with chrism the baptismal water.

In a painted window at Lincoln College, Oxford, Elisha the prophet is represented with a double-headed dove seated on his shoulder. This becomes intelligent on referring to his petition to Elijah, when he entreated that "a double portion" of his spirit might rest upon him.

The dove, as a harbinger of good news, is alluded to in one of Martial's epigrams—

> " A dove soft glided through the air
> On Aretulla's bosom bare.
> This might seem chance, did she not stay,
> Nor would, permissive, wing her way.
> But, if a pious sister's vows
> The Master of mankind allows,
> This envoy of Sardoan skies
> From the returning exile flies."

Killing a Robin.

In old times ill-luck attended the killing of a robin. If one died in the hand, it was believed that the hand would always tremble. In "Six Pastorals," by George Smith, 1770, the following occurs :—

> "I found a robin's nest within our shed
> And in the barn a wren has young one's bred;
> I never take away their nest, nor try
> To catch the old ones, lest a friend should die.

Dick took a robin's nest from the cottage side,
And ere a twelvemonth pass'd his mother died."

In Derbyshire, among many other places, it is believed that the catching and killing of a robin, or taking the eggs from the nest, is sure to be followed by misfortune, such as the death of cattle, blight of corn, etc.   The folks say—

"Robins and wrens
  Are God's best cocks and hens.
  Martins and swallows
  Are God's best scholars."

In Yorkshire, if a robin is killed, it is believed that the family cow will give bloody milk.

The Cuckoo.

A superstition prevails in Ireland, and in some parts of England, that any young person, on first hearing the cuckoo, will find a hair of the color of their sweetheart's adhering to their stocking, if they will at once take off their left shoe and examine it carefully.   Gay, in his "Shepherd's Week," says—

"Upon a rising bank I sat adown,
  Then doff'd my shoe, and, by my troth, I swear
  Therein I spied this yellow frizzled hair,
  As like to Lubberkin's in curl and hue
  As if upon his comely pate it grew."

In Norfolk there is a belief that an unmarried person will remain single as many years as the cuckoo utters its call, when first heard in the spring.   Subjoined is an old English invocation—

"Cuckoo, cherry-tree,
  Good bird, tell me,
  How many years I have to live?"

At the first call of the cuckoo the German peasant does the same thing as when he hears thunder for the first time in the year. He rolls himself two or three times on the grass, thinking himself thereby insured against pains in the back throughout the rest of the year, and all the more so if the bird continues its cry whilst he is on the ground.

If the first note of the cuckoo comes upon you when you have no money in your pocket, it is held, both in Germany and England, to portend want of money throughout the year.

A valuable virtue is attributed to cuckoos in keeping off fleas. In Hill's "Naturall and Artificiall Conclusions," (1650), we find: "A very easie and merry conceit to keep off fleas from your beds or chambers. Pliny reporteth that if, when you first hear the cuckow, you mark well where your first foot standeth, and take up that earth, the fleas will by no means breed where any of the same earth is thrown or scattered." This belief still exists in some parts of France.

Why the Cuckoo Builds no Nest.

"If you wish to know," says Horace Marryat, in his "Jutland and the Danish Isles," "why the cuckoo builds no nest of its own, I can easily explain it, according to the belief in Denmark. When in early spring-time the voice of the cuckoo is first heard in the woods, every village girl kisses her hand, and asks the question: 'Cuckoo! cuckoo! when shall I be married?' And the old folks, borne down with age and rheumatism, inquire: 'Cuckoo! when shall I be relieved from this world's cares?' The bird, in answer, continues singing 'Cuckoo!' as many times as years will elapse before the object of their desires will come to pass. But as many old people live to an advanced age, and many girls die old maids, the poor bird has so much to do in answering the questions put to her, that the building season goes by; she has no time to make her nest, but lays her eggs in the nest of the hedge-sparrow."

The Magpie.

The magpie has always had many superstitions connected with it. *One* magpie foretells misfortune, which can be obviated, however, by pulling off the hat and making a polite bow to the bird. In Lancashire the saying is—

> "One for anger, two for mirth,
> Three for a wedding, four for a birth,
> Five for rich, six for poor,
> Seven for a witch, I can tell you no more."

To meet a magpie portends misfortune in a journey, and it is thought best to return. It is the usual habit of the peasants to cross themselves when they meet a single chattering magpie. In the north of England the bird is thus addressed—

> "Magpie, magpie, chatter and flee,
> Turn up thy tail, and good luck fall me."

Of all living creatures in Russia, magpies are those whose shapes witches like best to take. The wife of the false Demetrius, according to popular poetry, escaped from Moscow in the guise of a magpie.

Why the Magpie Builds but Half a Nest.

The half-nest of the magpie is accounted for by a rural ornithological legend. Once on a time, when the world was very young, the magpie, by some accident or other, although she was quite as cunning as she is at present, was the only bird that was unable to build a nest. In this perplexity she applied to the other members of the feathered race, who kindly undertook to instruct her. So, on a day appointed, they assembled for the purpose, and, the materials having been collected, the blackbird said, "Place that stick there," suiting the action to the word, as she commenced the work. "Ah!" said the magpie, "I knew that before." The other birds followed with their suggestions, but to every piece of advice the magpie kept saying, "Ah! I knew that before." At length, when the nest was half finished, the patience of the company was fairly exhausted by the pertinacious conceit of the magpie; so all left her, with the united exclamation, "Well, Mistress Mag, as you seem to know all about it, you may finish the nest yourself." Their resolution was obdurate and final, and to this day the magpie exhibits the effects of partial instruction by her incomplete abode.

A Swallow Drinks the King's Health.

Aubrey, in his "Miscellanies," relates that "At Stretton, in Hertfordshire, 1648, when Charles I. was prisoner, the tenant of the manor-house there sold excellent cyder to gentlemen of the neighborhood. Among others that met there was old Mr. Hill, B. D., parson of the parish, *quondam* Fellow of Brazennose College at Oxford. This venerable good old man one day (after his accustomed fashion), standing up, with his head uncovered, to drink his Majesty's health, saying, 'God bless our gracious sovereign,' as he was going to put the cup to his lips, a swallow flew in at the window, and pitched on the brim of the little earthen cup (not half a pint) and sipt, and so flew out again. This was in the presence of the aforesaid Parson Hill, Major Gwillim, and two or three more that I knew very well then, my neighbors, and whose joint testimony of it I have more than once had in that very room. It was in the bay-window of the parlor, and Mr. Hill's back was next to the window. The cup is preserved there still as a rarity."

Birds of Paradise.

These birds have been the subject of many a fable. Old naturalists describe them as being destitute of feet, dwelling in the air, without an abiding place, nourished by dews and the odor of flowers. Tavernier relates, "that they come in flocks during the nutmeg season to the south cities of India. The strength of the nutmeg intoxicates them, and while they lie in this state on the earth, the ants eat off their legs!" Moore says, in his "Lalla Rookh—"

> "Those golden birds that in the spice-time drop
>   About the gardens, drunk with that sweet fruit
>   Whose scent hath lur'd them o'er the summer flood."

The natives of New Guinea and the neighboring islands looked upon the skins of these birds as sacred, and as charms against the dangers of war. In preparing them, the legs of the bird were cut off in a manner that gave rise to the idea, when the skins were exported from the islands, that the birds were legless.

> "But thou art still that Bird of Paradise,
>   Which hath no feet, and ever nobly flies."

The Owl.

The owl, "the fatal bellman which gives the sternest good night," was the dread of the superstitious from the earliest times. Virgil introduces the owl among the prodigies and horrors that foreran the suicide of Dido. It was said that two large owls would perch upon the battlements of Wardour Castle whenever an Arundel's last hour had come. The cry of the owl is heard by Lady Macbeth, during the murder. Hogarth introduces the owl in the murder scene of his "Four Stages of Cruelty."

The Ethiopians, wnen they wished to pronounce sentence of death upon any person, carried to him a table upon which an owl was painted. When the guilty man saw it, he was expected to destroy himself with his own hand. To the peasants, the cry of the owl foretells hail and rain, accompanied by lightning. The practice of nailing the bird to a barn-door, to avert evil consequences, is common throughout Europe, and is mentioned by Palladius in his "Treatise on Agriculture." Pliny wrote: "If an owl be seen either within cities or otherwise abroad in any place, it is not for good, but prognosticates some fearful misfortune."

The Phœnix.

The Rabbins tell us "that all the birds having complied with the first woman, and, with her, having eaten of the forbidden fruit, except the phœnix, as a reward it obtained a sort of immortality. It lived five hundred years in the wilderness; then making a nest of spices, it lighted it by the wafting of its wings, and the body was consumed. From the ashes arose a worm which grew up to be a phœnix." Moore, in "Paradise and the Peri," alludes to

> The enchanted pile of that lonely bird
> Who sings at the last his own death-lay,
> And in music and perfumes dies away.

"The myth of the phœnix," says George Stephens, in Archæologia, "is one of the most ancient in the world. Originally a temple type of the immortality of the soul, its birthplace appears to have been the sunny clime of the fanciful and gorgeous East. Even in the days of Job and David it was already a popular tradition in Palestine and Arabia."

Herodotus describes the phœnix in the following words: "The plumage is partly red, partly golden, while the general make and size are almost exactly that of the eagle. They tell a story in Egypt of what this bird does, which appears incredible,—that he comes all the way from Arabia, and brings the parent bird, all plastered over with myrrh, to the Temple of the Sun, and there buries the body. In order to bring him, they say, he first forms a ball of myrrh as big as he finds that he can carry; then he hollows out the ball and puts his parent inside, after which he covers over the opening with fresh myrrh, and the ball is then exactly of the same weight as at first. So he brings it to Egypt, as I have said, and deposits it in the Temple of the Sun." Ariosto alludes to this fable in the voyage of Astolfo—

> "Arabia, named the Happy, now he gains;
>   Incense and myrrh perfume her grateful plains;
>   The virgin phœnix there, in need of rest,
>   Selects from all the world her balmy nest."

The phœnix, as a sign over chemists' shops, was adopted from the association of this fabulous bird with alchemy.

The Wren.

The story of the contest for the crown, in which the wren outwitted the eagle, is traditional in Germany, France, Ireland and other countries. It seems that the birds all met together one day, and settled among themselves that which ever of them could fly the highest was to be king of them all. As they were starting, the wren, unknown to the eagle, perched himself on his tail. Away flew the birds, and the eagle soared far above the others, until, tired, he perched himself on a rock, and declared that he had gained the victory. "Not so fast," cried the wren, getting off the tail and springing above the eagle; "you have lost your chance, and I am king of the birds." The eagle, angry at the trick played upon him, gave the wren, as he came down, a smart stroke with his wing, from which time the wren has never been able to fly higher than a hawthorn bush.

The story is told with a different conclusion in Germany. According to the German version, the tricky wren was imprisoned in a mouse-hole, and the owl was set to watch before it, whilst the other birds were deliberating upon the punishment to be inflicted upon the offender. The owl fell asleep, and the prisoner escaped. The owl was so ashamed that he has never ventured to show himself by daylight.

In the Ojibua legend the gray linnet is the tricky bird, and the verdict was rendered in favor of the eagle, for he not only flew nearest to the sun, but carried the linnet with him.

In France the wren is called *roitelet* (little king), and also *poulette au bon Dieu*, "God's little hen." To kill it or to rob its nest would bring down lightning on the culprit's head. Robert Chambers, in "Popular Rhymes," says—

> "Malisons, malisons, mair than ten
> That harry the Ladye of Heaven's hen."

At Carcasonne the wren was carried about on a staff adorned with a garland of olive, oak and mistletoe. In the Isle of Man the wren is believed to be a transformed fairy.

White-breasted Birds.

In Devonshire the appearance of a white-breasted bird has long been considered an omen of death. This belief has been traced to a circumstance which happened to the Oxenham family in that county, and related by Howell, in his "Familiar Letters," wherein is the following monumental inscription: "Here lies John Oxenham, a goodly young man, in whose chamber, as he was struggling with the pangs of death, a bird with a white breast was seen fluttering about his bed, and so vanished." The same circumstance is related of his sister Mary, and two or three others of the family.

The Penguin's Solitary Egg.

The female penguin of Patagonia does not commit her offspring to any kind of nest. She constantly carries her solitary egg in a pouch formed by a fold in the skin of the abdomen, and it is held so fast in this that she leaps or sometimes rolls from rock to rock without letting it fall. It is well for her she does so, for should such a mishap befall her the male bird chastises her without pity.

The Crocodile Plover.

One of the best friends of the crocodile is a little bird of the plover species. The mouth of the reptile is infested with painful parasites, and the bird fearlessly flies into the open jaws and picks out the insects. The crocodile appears to be conscious of this kindly office, for it never offers to hurt its little feathered friend.

Peacocks' Crests.

In ancient times peacocks' crests were among the ornaments of the kings of England. Ernald de Aclent (Acland) "paid a fine to King John in a hundred and forty palfries, with sackbuts, gilt spurs and peacocks' crests, such as would be for his credit."

Worshipful Cranes.

Tame cranes, kept in the Middle Ages, are said to have stood before the table at dinner, and kneeled and bowed the.

head when a bishop pronounced the benediction. But how they knelt is as fairly open to inquiry as how Dives could take his seat in torment, as he did, according to an old carol, "all on a serpent's knee."

The Great Auk.

Pennant says that this bird never wanders beyond soundings, by which sailors are assured that land is not very remote. Aristophanes tells us that the Greek mariners, more than two thousand years ago, made note of the habits and movements of birds.

> "From birds, in sailing, men instructions take,
> Now lie in port, now sail and profit make."

The Kingfisher.

Sir Thomas Brown, in his "Vulgar Errors," says: "A kingfisher hanged by the bill sheweth what quarter the wind is, by an occult and secret property, converting the breast to that part of the horizon from whence the wind doth blow. This is a received opinion, and very strange, introducing natural weathercocks and extending magnetical positions as far as animal natures, a conceit supported chiefly by present practice, yet not made out by reason nor experience." The ancients believed that so long as the female kingfishers sat on their eggs, no storm or tempest disturbed the ocean. In Wild's "Iter Boreale," we read—

> "The peaceful kingfishers are met together
> About the decks, and prophesy calm weather."

Gmelin, in his "Voyage en Sibérie," says that "the Tartars believe that if they touch a woman, or even her clothes, with a feather from a kingfisher. she must fall in love with them. The Ostiacs take the skin, the bill and the claws of this bird, shut them up in a purse, and so long as they preserve this sort of amulet they believe they have no ill to fear. The person who told me of this means of living happily could not forbear shedding tears, for the loss of a kingfisher's skin had caused him to lose both his wife and his goods."

The Albatross.

The albatross is remarkable for its migrations; indeed, it may almost be said to pass from pole to pole, and is seen at a greater distance from land than any other bird. Hence sailors regard this companion of their voyage with superstitious fondness. Coleridge speaks of the albatross in his "Ancient Mariner"—

> And all averr'd I had killed the bird
> That made the breezes to blow;
> "A wretch," said they, "the bird to slay,
> That made the breezes to blow."

The Stork.

A feeling of attachment, not devoid of superstition, procures the stork an unmolested life in all Moslem countries. The Dutch regard them as birds of good omen, and a wagon-wheel is often laid upon the house-top for the stork to build his nest on, during which time the house is safe from fire. It is sometimes called by them the "fire-fowl" and "baby-bringer."

In North Germany, the first time in the year that a girl hears the stork, if it clatter with its bill, she will break something; if it be flying, she will be a bride before the year is out; if it be standing, she will be asked to stand godmother.

Storks are "fabled" to be very attentive to their aged

parents, carrying them from place to place and feeding them if they are blind.   Aristophanes says—

> " 'T is an ancient law
> Among the birds, on the storks' tables writ,
> Soon as the father stork hath nourished all
> His brood, and made them fit for flight, in turn
> The younglings should support their aged sire."

Cocks and Hens.

Schweinfurth, in his "Heart of Africa," gives the following curious auguries from cocks and hens, common to various negro tribes: "An oily fluid, concocted from a red wood called 'Bengye,' is administered to a hen.   If the bird dies, there will be misfortune in war; if it survives, there will be victory.   Another mode of trying their fortune consists in seizing a cock and ducking its head repeatedly under water, until the creature is stiff and senseless.   They then leave it to itself.   If it should rally, they draw an omen that is favorable to their design; if it should succumb, they look for an adverse issue."

A curious notion respecting fowls existed in various parts of England.   On the morning of St. Valentine's day, the girls, before opening the outer door, would look into the yard through the key-hole.   If they saw a cock and hen in company, it was taken for granted that the person most interested would be married before the year was out.

In Hooker's "Tour in Morocco," recently published, he mentions that in a storm in the heights of the Atlas, one of his attendants cut the throat of a cock he carried, to appease the wrath of the demons of the mountains.

Mr. Dalyell, in his "Darker Superstitions of Scotland," observes that during the prevalence of infectious diseases in the East, a cock was killed over the bed of the invalid, sprinkling him with the blood. A red cock was dedicated by sick persons in Ceylon to a malignant divinity, and afterwards offered as a sacrifice in the event of recovery.

In "Credulities Past and Present," it is stated that "in Durham there is a superstition that if any person was bewitched, the author of the evil might be discovered by the following means: To *steal* a black hen, take out the heart, stick it full of pins, and roast it at midnight. The 'double' of the witch would come and nearly pull the door down. If the 'double' was not seen, any one of the neighbors who had passed a remarkably bad night was fixed upon!"

Led by a Gander.

In Germany an aged blind woman was led to church every Sunday by a gander, which dragged her along, holding her gown in his beak. As soon as the old woman was seated in her pew the gander retired to the church-yard to feed upon the grass, and when the service was ended he conducted his mistress to her home.—*Menault.*

Crows Lost in a Fog.

The Hartford Times tells a curious story of a flock of crows in that vicinity who recently lost their way in a fog. They lost their bearings at a point directly above the South Green, in Hartford. For a good while they hovered there, coming low down, circling and diving aimlessly about, like a blindfolded person in "blind man's buff," and keeping up a hoarse cawing and general racket beyond description. It was plain enough that of the entire company each individual crow was not only puzzled and bothered, but highly indignant, and inclined to utter "cuss words" in his frantic attempts to be heard above the general din, and tell the others which way to go. Once or twice the whole flock swept down to a distance of not more than one hundred feet above the street. Finally, after going around for many times, they sailed away in a southerly direction, evidently having got some clue to the way out of the fog, or desperately resolved to go *somewhere* till they could see daylight.

The Peacock at Home.

Peacocks are found in almost all parts of India and Siam, and the multitudes in which they occur in some districts is wonderful. Colonel Williamson, in his "Oriental Field Sports," says: "About the passes in the Jungletery district whole woods were covered with the beautiful plumage, to which a rising sun imparted additional brilliancy. I speak within bounds when I assert that there could not have been less than 1200 or 1500 pea-fowls, of various sizes, within sight of the spot where I stood." Sir James Emerson Tennent says, in his work on Ceylon, "that in some of the unfrequented portions of the eastern province, to which Europeans rarely resort, and where the pea-fowl are unmolested by the natives, their number is so extraordinary that, regarded as game, it ceased to be sport to destroy them; and their cries at early morning are so tumultuous and incessant as to banish sleep, and amount to an actual inconvenience."

Story of the Dodo.

This extinct bird was a native of Mauritius, in the Indo-African Ocean, and was first described by Van Neck, a Dutchman, in 1598, in which year a living specimen was embarked for Holland, but died on its way. This specimen is supposed to have been preserved at Leyden; and one of the feet is believed to be that in the British Museum. Several successive voyagers mention the bird, down to Canche, in 1638, in which year a living dodo was brought to England by Sir Hamon l'Estrange, who describes the back as of "dunn or deare colour." It was exhibited for money in London, in a house which bore a figure of the bird represented on canvas. This specimen has been traced to Tradescant's Museum at Lambeth, whence it was conveyed, in 1682, to Oxford by Ashmole. The body and a leg were destroyed by vermin before 1775, but the other leg and the head are preserved to this day in the Ashmolean Museum, in which place there also is a large drawing of a dodo, taken from nature, by John Savery. It was not related to the ostrich or the vulture, as many have supposed, but was closely allied to the pigeons and the solitaire bird seen by Leguat in the Island of Rodrigeux in 1691.—*Wells.*

An Old Gander.

Willoughby states, in his work on Ornithology, that a friend of his possessed a gander eighty years of age, which in the end became so ferocious that they were forced to kill it, in consequence of the havoc it committed in the barn-yard. He also mentions a swan three centuries old and several parrots that attained the age of one hundred and fifty years.

Chaffinch Contest.

At the town of Armentières, in France, there is a *fete du pays*, in which the chaffinch and its fellows are the chief actors and objects of attraction. Numbers of these birds are trained with the greatest care and no small share of cruelty, for they are frequently blinded by their owners, that their song may not be interrupted by the sight of any external object. The point upon which the amusement, the honor and the emolument rests is the number of times a bird will repeat his song in a given time.

A day being fixed, the amateurs repair to the appointed place, each with his bird in a cage. The prize is then displayed, and the birds are placed in a row. A bird-fancier notes how many times each bird sings, and another verifies his notes. In the year 1812, a chaffinch repeated his song seven hundred times in one hour. Emulated by the songs of each other, they strain their little plumed throats, as if conscious that honor was to result from their exertions.

The Fabulous Roc.

The roc, the huge bird that gave Sindbad the sailor his ride through the air, is not to be compared with some of those mentioned in the Talmud. Some mariners saw one of those large birds standing up to the lower joint of the leg in a river, and thinking the water could not be deep, they were hastening to bathe, when a voice from heaven said: "Step not in there; seven years ago a carpenter dropped his axe there, and it hath not yet reached the bottom."

Fable of the Pelican.

The pelicans are said to carry water to their young, as well as food, in their pouch. During the night the pelican sits with its bill resting on its breast. The nail or hook which terminates the bill is red, and Mr. Broderip supposes that the ancient fable of the pelican feeding its young with blood from its own breast originated from its habit of pressing the bill upon the breast in order the more easily to empty the pouch, when the red tip might be mistaken for blood.

Night Owls.

It is worthy of remark that in all owls that fly by night the exterior edges and sides of the wing-quills are slightly recurved, and end in fine hairs or points, by means of which the bird can pass through the air with the greatest silence—a provision necessary to enable it the better to surprise its prey.—*Adam White.*

Imprisoned During Incubation.

In his work on "The Birds of India," M. Jerdon details the curious domestic arrangements of some species of the genus Homrain of French naturalists, the males of which, at the time of laying, imprison the female in her nest. They close the entrance to it by means of a thick wall of mud, leaving only a small hole by which the hen breathes and through which she protrudes her beak to receive food, which is brought by her spouse. Though barbarous enough to imprison her, he is not cruel enough to starve her. This forced retirement only ceases with the termination of the hatching, when the pair break the prison door.

Love-Birds.

These birds receive their name from the affection which they manifest towards one another. Anatomically, this genus is remarkable in the parrot tribe for having no furcula, or merry-thought bone.

Penguin Breeding Grounds.

These birds often occupy acres for their breeding ground, which is laid out and leveled and divided into squares, as nicely as if done by a surveyor. They march between the compartments as accurately as soldiers on parade, and somewhat resembling them from a distance, or, according to another similitude which has been used, looking like bands of little children in white aprons. Bennett describes one breeding ground on Macquarie Island as covering thirty or forty acres, and, to give some notion of the multitudes, speaks of 30,000 or 40,000 birds as continually landing, and as many putting to sea.

The Ear of Birds not to be Deceived.

A bird-catcher, wishing to increase his stock of bullfinches, took out his caged bird and his limed twigs and placed them in such a situation of hedge and bush as he judged favorable to his success. It so happened that his own bird was an educated one, such as is usually termed a piping bullfinch. In the first instance a few accidentally thrown out natural notes or calls had attracted three or four of his kindred feather, which had taken their station not far distant from the cage. There they stood in doubt and curiosity, and, presently, moving inch by inch and hop by hop toward him and the fatal twigs, they again became stationary and attentive. It was in this eager and suspended moment that the piping bullfinch set up the old country dance-tune of ''Nancy Dawson.'' Away flew every astonished bullfinch as fast as wings could move, in confusion and alarm.

A Bird Hammock.

In his voyage to India, Sonnerat speaks of a Cape titmouse, the nest of which is made of cotton and is shaped like a bottle. While the female is hatching inside, the male, a most watchful sentinel, remains outside in a pouch or hammock, fixed to one side of the neck of the nest. When his mate moves off and he wishes to follow her, he beats the opening of the nest violently with his wing until he closes it, in order to protect the young from enemies.

Sagacity of a Bird.

In the museum of Brown University, Providence, R. I., is a curiosity in the shape of a bird's nest. Aside from its ingenious construction as a swinging nest, partly suspended by strings and cords carefully woven into it and around the slender branch which holds it, another evidence of the builder's sagacity is given. As the young birds grew, and the nest daily became heavier, the mother saw that the slender twig, about the thickness of a pipe-stem, to which it was attached, could not support it much longer, so she made it secure by fastening a stout cord about it and passing the end around a strong limb above, which steadied it and made it safe.

Change of Sight in Birds.

Birds destined to move in the medium of a very rare atmosphere and which has but little tendency to refract the rays of the sun, have a great quantity of aqueous humor, in order that the light, strongly refracted in entering their eyes, may bring distinct images. Thus birds at heights where they appear to us only as points, perceive the smallest reptile concealed in the grass. But, as presbyte birds do not distinguish objects when brought near, nature has provided for this difficulty, which occurs when they descend from the heights of the air to seize their prey. To provide for this emergency, they have a membrane, by means of which they remove the crystalline lens from the retina; and thus changing the power of the eye by changing the focal distance of objects, as we do with spectacles, they never lose sight of their prey, whether in the air or on the ground.

Nest of the Flamingo.

The flamingo arranges its nest in a peculiar way, as its long legs would not adapt themselves to the ordinary style of nest-building. The nests are placed upon the ground, are built solely of coarsely-tempered mud, and are very curiously shaped, being like narrow, lengthened cones. They are twenty inches in height, and their truncated summit presents a concavity, at the bottom of which the female deposits her eggs. In order to hatch them she places her abdomen over them, and allows her legs to hang down on both sides of the raised nest.

Barking of Dogs.

The Australian dog never barks; indeed, Gardiner, in his "Music of Nature," states "that dogs in a state of nature never bark; they simply whine, howl and growl; the explosive noise is only heard among those which are domesticated." Sonnini speaks of the shepherd dogs in the wilds of Egypt as not having this faculty; and Columbus found the dogs which he had previously carried to America to have lost their propensity for barking.

Superstitions about Eggs.

Thiers, in his "Traité des Superstitions," observes that he has known people who preserved all the year such eggs as are laid on Good Friday, as they think them good to extinguish fires when thrown on them.

People in the northern parts of Germany, remarks William Jones, say that to cross one's face with the first new-laid egg of a chicken that has been hatched in spring and begins to lay shortly before Christmas of the same year, is considered the means of improving and beautifying the complexion.

Camden, in his "Ancient and Modern Manners of the Irish," says that if the owners of horses eat eggs, they must take care to eat an even number, otherwise some mischief will betide the horses. Grooms are not allowed eggs, and the riders are obliged to wash their hands after eating eggs.

In Derbyshire it is considered a bad omen to gather eggs and bring them into the house after dark. Eggs ought not to be brought in on Sunday, and no hen must be set on that day. The number of eggs for a setting must be either eleven or thirteen; the number must be odd, and if twelve eggs are sat upon, the hen will scarcely succeed in hatching them; or, if hatched, the chickens will do no good.

In some parts of England it is believed that the first egg laid by a white pullet, placed under the pillow at night, will bring dreams of those you wish to marry.

In some parts of Java, at a wedding, the bride, as a sign of her subjection, kneels and washes the feet of the bridegroom, after he has trodden upon raw eggs.

In Ireland, at Hallow E'en, among other curious customs, the women take the yolks from some eggs boiled hard, fill the cavity with salt, and eat egg, shell and salt. They are careful not to quench their thirst until morning. If at night they dream that their lovers are at hand with water, they believe they will be jilted.

The Camel as a Scape-Goat.

A very singular account of the use to which a camel is sometimes put is given by the traveler Bruce. He tells us that he saw one employed to appease a quarrel between two parties, somewhat in the same way as the scape-goat was used in the religious sacrifices of the Jewish people. The camel being brought out, was accused of all the injuries, real or fancied, which belonged to each. All the mischief that had

been done they accused this camel of doing. They upbraided
it with being the cause of all the trouble that had separated
friends, called it by every opprobious epithet, finally killed it,
and then declared themselves reconciled over its body.

The Mark of the Cross on the Ass.

It is a common superstition that the dark marks across the
shoulders of the ass, and which bear some resemblance to a
cross, were given as memorials of our Saviour having entered
Jerusalem riding on one of that humble species. In the north
of England, however, a tradition prevails that the dark streaks
are a memento of Balaam's having thrice smitten one of the
family, which carried him, and, as the Bible states, reproved
him for wilful disobedience of the Divine command.

White Elephants.

White elephants are reverenced throughout the East, and
the Chinese pay them a certain kind of worship. The Burmese monarch is called "The King of the White Elephants,"
and is regarded under that title with more than ordinary ven-
eration, which oriental despotism extracts from its abject
dependants.

Tenacity of Life in an Elephant.

In March, 1826, it became necessary to kill an infuriated
elephant at Exeter Change, in London. One hundred and
fifty-two bullets were fired into him at short range, and
directed toward vital parts, before he fell dead. It was found
necessary to kill an elephant at Geneva, May 31st, 1820.
Three ounces of prussic acid and three ounces of arsenic were

administered, but produced no effect. He was shot by a cannon thrust through a breach in the wall, the muzzle almost touching him. The ball entered near the ear, behind the right eye, went through a thick partition on the opposite side of the enclosure, and spent itself against a wall. The animal stood still two or three seconds, then tottered, and fell without any convulsive movement.

Ears of the Elephant.

The ears of the African elephant are said to be much larger, in proportion to the size of the animal, than those of the Indian species. Baker, the African traveler, says that he has frequently cut off an ear of one of these animals to form a mat, on which he has slept comfortably.

A Shaved Bear.

"At Bristol I saw a shaved monkey shown for a fairy, and a shaved bear, in a check waistcoat and trousers, sitting in a great chair as an Ethiopian savage. This was the most cruel fraud I ever saw. The unnatural position of the beast and the brutality of the woman keeper, who sat upon his knee, put her arm around his neck, called him husband and sweetheart, and kissed him, made it the most disgusting spectacle I ever witnessed. Cottle was with me.—*Southey.*

Retailing a Lion.

A lion in a Cincinnati menagerie recently lost a part of his tail. A vicious hyena, confined in an adjoining cage, nipped it off, for want of something better or worse to do. The *Enquirer* of that city tells the sequel of the story—

"The noble king of the woods was much mortified in consequence, and it was feared would worry himself to death. He kept continually biting his tail and playing all kinds of mysterious pranks in his cage. Two men were kept continually employed, at an expense of $21 a week each, to watch the lion and prevent him from further injury upon himself.

"Mr. John Carney, the new superintendent of the Zoological Gardens, devised a plan for the pacification of the king of the forest, which has succeeded beyond the most sanguine expectations. He had a small box-cage constructed adjoining the lion's cell, and coaxed the wounded beast therein. The cage was so constructed that the lion could not turn about in it. Once in, his tail was treated medically, and covered with a black snake's skin. The lion now seems perfectly satisfied with the amendment to his tail, and holds his head as erect and is as proud as ever. Mr. Carney is a genius."

Magpie Stoning a Toad.

There is a story told of a tame magpie which was seen busily employed in a garden gathering pebbles, and with much solemnity and a studied air dropping them into a hole about eighteen inches deep, made to receive a post. After dropping each stone it cried "Currack" triumphantly, and set off for another. On examining the spot, a poor toad was found in the hole, which the magpie was stoning for his amusement.

Cynocephalic Apes.

A correspondent in the "Transvaal Republic" writes that a species of large cynocephalic apes are in the habit of ravaging the coffee plantations there, which therefore have to be guarded. Among the coffee trees there grows a shrub whose fruit the apes particularly enjoy. But a species of wasp had fastened their nests to these shrubs, and the apes were kept from their tempting food by their fear of being stung. One morning fearful cries were heard from the apes, and the following scene was witnessed: A large baboon, the leader of the band, was throwing some young apes down into the shrubs, that they might break off the wasp nests with the shock of their fall. The poor victims, stung by the infuriated insects, were crying piteously, but the old baboon paid no heed to their miserable condition. While they were down below, suffering from the anger of the wasps, he quietly proceeded to regale himself with the fruit, now safely within his reach, and occasionally threw a handful to some females and young a little way off.

Monkeys Demanding their Dead.

Mr. Forbes tells a story of a female monkey who was shot by a friend of his and carried to his tent. Forty or fifty of her tribe advanced with menacing gestures, but stood still when the gentleman pointed his gun at them. One, however, who appeared to be the chief of the tribe, came forward, chattering and threatening in a furious manner. Nothing short of firing at him seemed likely to drive him away. At length he approached the door of the tent with every sign of grief and supplication, as if he were begging for the body. It was given to him; he took it in his arms and carried it to his companions with actions expressive of affection, after which they all disappeared.

Can Dogs Count?

A gentleman on a visit to Scotland came across some men who were washing sheep. Close to the water where the operation was being carried on was a small pen, in which a detatchment of ten sheep were placed handy to the men for washing. While watching the performance his attention was called to a sheep-dog lying down close by. This animal, on the pen becoming nearly empty, without a word from any one, started off to the main body of the flock, and brought back ten of their number, and drove them into the empty washing-pens. The fact of his bringing exactly the same number of sheep as had vacated it he looked upon at first as a strange coincidence—a mere chance. But he continued looking on, and, much to his surprise, as soon as the men had reduced the number to three sheep, the dog started off again, and brought back ten more, and so he continued throughout the afternoon, never bringing one more nor one less, and always going for a fresh lot when only three were left in the pen, evidently being aware that during the time the last three were washing he would be able to bring up a fresh detachment.

Can Hens Count?

On one occasion the author found a hen disposed to set in a horse-trough. She had but eight eggs under her, and he added five more. The next morning he noticed that she had discarded five of the eggs; they were replaced, and were again hustled to the other end of the trough. He next marked the eggs, in order to discover whether she objected to the five eggs with which he had supplied her. At his next visit he found that she had once more rejected five eggs, two of which were marked and three not marked. She would accept but eight eggs, and was left to incubate in peace.

How Rats and Mice use their Tails.

To test the correctness of the popular belief that rats and mice use their tails for feeding purposes, when the food to be eaten is contained in vessels too narrow to admit the entire body of the animal, a writer in "Nature" made the following experiments: Into a couple of preserve bottles with narrow necks he put as much semi-liquid fruit jelly as filled them within three inches of the top. The bottles were then covered with bladder and set in a place frequented by rats. Next morning the covering of each bottle had a small hole gnawed in it, and the level of the jelly was lowered to an extent about equal to the length of a rat's tail, if inserted in the hole. The next experiment was still more decisive. The bottles were refilled to the extent of half an inch above the level left by the rats, a disk of moist paper laid upon the surface, and the bottles covered as before. The bottles were now laid aside in a place unfrequented by rats, until a good crop of mould had grown upon one of the moistened disks of paper. This bottle was then transferred to the place infested by the rats. Next morning the bladder had again been eaten through at one edge, and upon the mould were numerous and distinct tracings of the rats' tails, evidently caused by the animals sweeping their tails about in the endeavor to find a hole in the paper.

Kicked by a Camel.

The camel's kick is a study. As it stands demurely chew-ing the cud, and gazing abstractedly at some totally different far-away object, up goes a hind leg, drawn close in to the body, with the foot pointing out; a short pause, and out it flies with an action like the piston and connecting-rod of a steam-engine, showing a judgment of distance and direction that would lead you to suppose the leg gifted with perceptions of its own, independent of the animal's proper senses. I have seen a heavy man fired several yards into a dense crowd by the kick of a camel, and picked up insensible.—*Keane.*

Crocodiles of the Nile.

The crocodile of the Nile is one of the most celebrated of the eastern species. Among the ancient Egyptians it was a sacred animal, and to destroy it was a crime. The priests kept crocodiles in tanks in the temple grounds; they ornamented them with jewels and fed them with the choicest food. After death the bodies were carefully embalmed and buried with great ceremony, and it is not uncommon at this date to find crocodile mummies in their tombs.

Alligators Swallowing Stones.

The alligators on the banks of the Oronoko, previous to going in search of prey, swallow large stones, that they may acquire additional weight to aid them in diving and dragging their victims under water. Bolivar shot several with his rifle, and in all of them were found stones varying in weight according to the size of the animal. The largest killed was about seventeen feet in length, and had within him a stone which weighed sixty or seventy pounds.

Animals Forecasting Danger.

That animals forebode the approach of an earthquake is a fact which frequently has been demonstrated. When no sign announces to unthinking man the coming terror, these creatures indicate it by their agitation and their cries. Every animal, without exception, feels this singular presentiment, but it has been more particularly observed among the poultry in the barn-yard. Dogs howl distressingly, and great restlessness is shown by horses and oxen in the open country.

Humboldt relates that, in the earthquakes so frequent in South America, oxen and other domesticated animals will stand with their legs placed wide apart, as if they hoped by that device to lessen the danger of being precipitated into a crevasse which might suddenly open under their feet. It is for this reason that men in the same regions are advised, on the occurrence of an earthquake, to extend their arms from their bodies in the shape of a cross. The precaution is one which tradition and experience have impressed on the inhabitants.

Singular Provision against Famine.

The synapta is a marine animal closely allied to the sea-cucumber. If one of them is preserved in sea-water for a short time, and subjected to a forced fast, a very strange thing will be observed. The animal, being unable to feed itself, successively detaches various parts of its body, which it amputates spontaneously. "It would appear," says M. Quatrefages, "that the animal, feeling that it had not sufficient food to support its whole body, is able successively to abridge its dimensions by suppressing the parts it would be most difficult to support, just as we should dismiss the most useless mouths from a besieged city." This singular mode of meeting a famine is employed by the synapta up to the last moment. In order to preserve life in the head, all the other parts of the . body are sacrificed.

Looking for the Head of the Bed.

Every one has observed that dogs, before they lie down, turn themselves round and round, which has been facetiously called "looking for the head of the bed." Those who have had an opportunity of witnessing the actions of animals in a wild state, know that they seek long grass for their beds, which they beat down and render more commodious by turning around in it several times. It would appear, therefore, that the habit of our domesticated dogs in this respect is derived from the nature of the same species in the wild state.—*Mr. Jesse.*

Getting Himself Outside of his Dinner.

The intelligence of a toad is remarkable. When an insect is too large to swallow, it thrusts the creature against a stone to push it down its throat. On one occasion, when a toad was attempting to swallow a locust, the head was down the former's throat, the hinder part protruding. The toad then sought a stone or clod, but as none were to be found, he lowered his head and crept along, pushing the locust against the ground. But the ground was too smooth (a rolled path), and the angle at which the locust lay to the ground too small, and thus no progress was made. To increase the angle, he straightened up his hind legs, but in vain. At length he threw up his hind quarters, and actually stood on his head, or, rather, on the locust sticking out of his mouth; and, after repeating this several times, succeeded in getting himself outside of his dinner.

Superstition about the Camel.

The Orientals declare that, at the time of the rising of the Pleiades, the camel sees the constellation before it is visible to the human eye, and will not lie down in any other direction than with its head toward the east.

Pedigree of Arabian Horses.

The Arabs claim that their finest horses are direct descendants of the stud of Solomon. The pedigree of an Arabian horse is hung around his neck soon after his birth, properly witnessed and attested. The following is the pedigree of a horse purchased by a French officer in Arabia:—

"In the name of God, the merciful and compassionate, and of Saed Mahomed, agent of the high God, and of the companions of Mahomed, and of Jerusalem. Praised be the Lord, the omnipotent Creator. This is a high-bred horse, and its colt's tooth is here in a bag about his neck, with his pedigree, and of undoubted authority, such as no infidel can refuse to believe. He is the son of Rabbamy, out of the dam Labadah, and equal in power to his sire of the tribe of Zazhalah; he is finely moulded, and made for running like an ostrich. In the honors of relationship he reckons Zuluah, sire of Mahat, sire of Kallac, and the unique Alket, sire of Manasseh, sire of Alsheh, father of the race down to the famous horse, the sire of Lahalala. And to him be ever abundance of green meat and corn, and water of life, as a reward from the tribe of Zazhalaha; and may a thousand branches shade his carcass from the hyæna of the tomb, from the howling wolf of the desert; and let the tribe of Zazhalah present him with a festival within an enclosure of walls; and let thousands assemble at the rising of the sun in troops hastily, where the tribe holds up, under a canopy of celestial signs within the walls, the saddle with the name and family of the possessor. Then let them strike the bands with a loud noise incessantly, and pray to God for immunity for the tribe of Zoab, the inspired tribe."

Voracity of the Mole.

A naturalist has calculated that a mole devours annually 20,000 grubs. It is so voracious that it must eat every six hours. No animal is so favored in its carnivorous instincts as the mole; forty-four teeth studded with points never cease working from morning to night. It requires nourishment to such an extent, that if deprived of food for a day it dies of inanition. It is a complete eating machine, gulping down every day a proportionately enormous quantity of food, so that M. de la Blanchére was right in saying that "if we could magnify the mole to the size of an elephant, we should be face to face with the most terrific brute the world ever brought forth."

Cat Worship.

In the Middle Ages animals formed as prominent a part in the worship of the time as they did in the old religion of Egypt. The cat was a very important personage in religious festivals. At Aix, in Provence, on the festival of Corpus Christi, the finest tom cat of the country, wrapt in swaddling clothes like a child, was exhibited in a magnificent shrine to public admiration. Every knee was bent, every hand strewed flowers or poured incense, and the cat was treated in all respects as the god of the day.

Horses Feeding one Another.

M. de Bossanelle, captain of cavalry in the regiment of Beauvilliers, relates in his "Military Observations," printed in Paris in 1760, "that in the year 1757 an old horse of his company, that was very fine and full of mettle, had his teeth suddenly so worn down that he could not chew his hay and corn, and that he was fed for two months, and would still have been so fed had he been kept, by two horses on each side of him that ate in the same manger. These two horses drew hay from the rack, which they chewed, and afterward threw before the old horse; that they did the same with the oats, which they ground very small and also put before him. This was observed and witnessed by a whole company of cavalry, officers and men."

Odd Mode of Revenge.

Monkeys in India are more or less objects of superstitious reverence, and are, consequently, seldom destroyed. In some places they are fed, encouraged and allowed to live on the roofs of the houses. If a man wishes to revenge himself for any injury done him, he has only to sprinkle some rice or corn upon the top of his enemy's house or granary, just before the rains set in, and the monkeys will assemble upon it, eat all they can find outside, and then pull off the tiles to get at that which falls through the crevices. This, of course, gives access to the torrents which fall in such countries, and house, furniture and stores are all ruined.

Cats with Knotted Tails.

We extract the following paragraph from the narrative of a voyager in the Indian Ocean, because it contains an account of a rarity in natural history with which few, we suspect, are acquainted:—

 "The steward is again pillowed on his beloved saltfish, and our only companion is a Malacca cat, who has also an attachment for the steward's pillow. Puss is a tame little creature and rubs herself mildly against our shoes, looking up in our faces and mewing her thoughts. Doubtless she is surprised that you have been so long looking at her without noticing the peculiarity in her tail, which so much distinguishes her from the rest of the female race in other quarters of the globe. Did you ever observe such a singular knot? so regular, too, in its formation? Some cruel monster must have tied it in a knot while puss was yet a kitten, and she has outlived both the pain and the inconvenience. But here comes a kitten, all full of gambols and fun, and we find that the tail is in precisely the same condition. So, then, this is a remarkable feature amongst the whole race of Malayan cats, but for which no one we meet with is able to give us a satisfactory explanation."

Tortoises Afraid of Heat and Rain.

Tortoises seem, by their thick shells, to be protected against all changes of the weather. But one of immense size, imported from the Galapagos Islands to England, was actually afraid of rain. Its owner says: "No part of its behaviour ever struck me more than the extreme timidity it always expresses with regard to rain; and though it has a shell that would secure it against a loaded cart, yet it exhibits as much solicitude about rain as a lady dressed in her best attire, shuffling away on the first sprinklings and running its head into a corner. If attended to, it becomes an excellent weather glass; for as sure as it walks elate, and as it were on tip-toe, feeding with great earnestness in the morning, so sure will it rain before night." The same tortoise was careful to keep out of the hot sun, and always sought a shady nook at mid-day in summer.

Pea Crabs.

The fact that these small crabs take up their abode within the shells of mollusks was well known to the ancients, and gave rise to many curious fables. A species is very common in the *pinnæ* (mollusks) of the Mediterranean, and was imagined to render important services to its host in return for its lodging, keeping a lookout for approaching dangers, against which the blind pinna itself could not guard, and particularly apprising it, that it might close its shell when the cuttle-fish came near. It is curious to find this repeated by Hasselquist, in the middle of the last century, as a piece of genuine natural history. Whether the pea crab lives at the expense of the mollusk, and sucks its juices, is uncertain. It is certain, however, that the flesh of such mollusks is palatable to pea crabs, as they eat it greedily in the aquarium.

Extraordinary Muscular Strength of the Bat.

When bats bring forth their young they are obliged to carry them on their backs, as they do not build nests like the birds, the little things hanging fast to their fur during flight. The extrordinary strength of muscle possessed by the bat is shown in the fact that two of the young, which are often born at a birth, weigh two-thirds as much as the parent. Thus, flying at nearly double its ordinary weight, we can fancy the power of this animal, surpassing in proportion the strength of the eagle or condor.

Great Digestive Powers.

In certain caterpillars the digestive power is so great that they swallow every day three or four times their own weight in food. If the elephant and rhinoceros were to feed on this scale, and were as numerous as the caterpillars, they would require but a short time to devour all the vegetation on the globe.

The Earwig.

This insect is supposed to have a "fondness" for getting into the human ear, the effect of which, it has been believed, is to penetrate the brain and cause madness. The earwig is not more likely than any other insect to enter the ear. The wings of the earwig, when fully expanded, are in shape precisely like the human ear, from which fact it is highly probable that the original name of the insect was *ear-wing* and not ear-*wig*, which appears to be entirely without meaning. The name is also traced to the Saxon *ear-wigca*, from its destroying ears of grain and fruit.

Eyes of the Cuttle-Fish.

The eyes of the cuttle-fish are so solid as to be almost calcareous. They are exceedingly beautiful, and reflect light with a splendid play of color, like an opal. They are used for necklace beads in Italy, and are highly valued objects for the jeweler's art.

Innate Appetite

McKenzie mentions the following fact as having been witnessed by Sir James Hall: He had been engaged in making experiments in hatching eggs by artificial heat, and on one occasion observed in one of his boxes a chicken in the act of breaking from its confinement. It happened that just as the creature was getting out of the shell a spider ran along the box, when the chicken darted forward, seized and swallowed it.

Leaf-Butterfly of Java.

This butterfly, as a defense against the birds of the tropics, almost exactly imitates, in its color and appearance, the leaves of the trees among which it lives. The upper surface of the wings, when outspread, of a rich orange blue, is very marked, but the lower side consists of some shade of ash or brown or ochre, such as are found among dead and decaying leaves. When the insect is at rest on a tree, it resembles so closely a leaf that the most acute observation fails to note the difference. It sits on a twig, the wings closely fitted back to back, con-

cealing the antennæ and head, which are drawn up beneath
their basis.   The little tails of the hind wing touch the branch
and form a perfect stalk to the seeming leaf.   The irregular
outline of the wings gives exactly the perspective effect of the
outline of a shriveled leaf.

The Jump of a Flea.

M. de Fonvielle, in his interesting work on the "Invisible
World," maintains that a flea can raise itself from the ground
to a height equal to two hundred times its stature.   At this
rate, he says, a man would only make a joke of jumping over
the towers of Notre-Dame or the heights of Montmartre.   A
prison yard would be useless unless the walls were more than
a quarter of a mile in height.

Book-Worms.

An instance is recorded of twenty-seven folio volumes being
perforated, in a straight line, by the same worm, in such a
manner that, by passing a cord through the round hole made
by it, the twenty-seven volumes could be raised at once.

Spider Barometers.

If the weather is likely to become rainy, windy or in other
respects disagreeable, spiders fix the terminating filaments, on
which the whole web is sustained, unusually short.   If the
terminating filaments are made uncommonly long, the weather
will be serene, and continue so, at least for ten or twelve days.
If spiders be totally indolent, rain generally succeeds; their
activity during rain is certain proof that it will be of short
duration, and followed by fair and constant weather.   Spiders

usually make some alteration in their webs every twenty-four hours; if these changes take place between the hours of six and seven in the evening, they indicate a clear and pleasant night.

> "The clouds grow heavier over head—
> The spider strengtheneth his web."

Muscles of the Caterpillar.

Our varied movements are executed by the aid of fleshy muscles attached to the skeleton. In these, insects possess a numerical and dynamical superiority over the human race. Anatomists calculate that there are only 370 of these muscles in a man, whilst the patient Lyonet discovered more than 4000 in a single caterpillar.

A Persistent Fly.

Linnæus saw one of the flies which attack cattle follow a reindeer an entire day, though dragging its sled at a gallop over the snow. The fly flew almost continuously by its side, watching for the moment when it might introduce one of its eggs beneath the skin.

Phosphorescent Insects.

In tropical America there are phosphorescent insects of remarkable splendor. In Cuba the women often inclose several of the luminous beetles in little cages of glass, which they hang up in their rooms, and this living lustre throws out sufficient light for them to work by. Travelers, in a difficult road, light their path in the middle of the night by attaching one of these beetles to each of their feet. The creoles sometimes set them in the curls of their hair, where, like resplendent jewels, they give a fairy-like aspect to their heads. The negresses, at their nocturnal dances, scatter these brilliant insects over their robes of lace which nature provides for them, all woven from the bark of the Lagetto.

Eating Clouds.

Dr. Livingstone, relating his adventures on Lake Nyassa, says: "During a portion of the year the northern dwellers on the lake have a harvest which furnishes a singular kind of food. As we approached our limit in that direction, clouds as of smoke arising from miles of burning grass were observed tending in a southeasterly direction, and we thought that the unseen land on the opposite side was closing in, and that we were near the end of the lake. But next morning we sailed through one of the clouds on our own side, and discovered that it was neither smoke nor haze, but countless millions of midges, called "kungo," (a cloud or fog.) They filled the air to an immense height and swarmed upon the water, too light to sink in it. Eyes and mouth had to be kept closed while passing through this living cloud—they struck upon the face like fine drifting snow. The people gathered these insects by night, and boiled them into thick cakes to be used as a relish—millions of midges in a cake. A kungo cake an inch thick, and as large as the blue bonnet of a Scotch plowman, was offered to us. It was very dark in color, and tasted not unlike caviare or salted locust."

A Hundred Stomachs.

Some of the animalcules have in the interior of the body large cavities, which incessantly empty and fill themselves with colored fluid. These cavities represent the heart of large animals and their fluid the blood; and this circulating system is relatively so large that it may be stated, without exaggeration, that some microscopic beings have hearts fully fifty times as large and as strong, in proportion, as that of the horse or ox. A man has only one stomach, whilst invisible microzoa have sometimes a hundred.

Motherly Sacrifice by the Gall Insect.

Some kinds of gall insects immolate themselves in order to protect their offspring. As the enormously distended insect gradually expels its eggs, it heaps them up in a little pile, and when its body is quite cleared out, and only resembles a hollow bladder, the female straightway covers its progeny with it, attaches the edges round them, and dies directly after. It thus forms for them a convex, solid roof, the impermeability of which protects its eggs against the injurious agency of the air and storms. The mother pays for her childbirth with her life, and her young are born under the shelter of her mummified corpse.

Wonderful Spider's Web.

Across the sunny paths of Ceylon, where the forest meets the open country, and which constitute the bridle-roads of the island, an enormous spider stretches its web at the height of from four to eight feet from the ground. The cordage of these webs is fastened on either side to projecting shoots of trees or shrubs, and is so strong as to hurt the traveler's face, and even lift off his hat, if he happened not to see the line. The nest in the centre is sometimes as large as a man's head, and is continually growing larger, as it is formed of successive layers of the old webs rolled over each other, sheet after sheet, into a ball. These successive envelopes contain the limbs and wings of insects of all descriptions, which have been the prey of the spider and his family, who occupy the den formed in the midst. There seems to be no doubt that the spider casts the web loose and rolls it around the nucleus in the centre when it becomes overcharged with carcasses, and then proceeds to construct a fresh one, which in its turn is destined to be folded up with the rest.

Horrible Mode of Assassination.

Before English law and custom had subdued the barbarism of Hindostan, the following mode of assassination was not uncommon: The murderer would kill one of a pair of cobras, and drag the body of the snake along the ground into the bungalow, over the floor, and into the very bed of the victim. After a few moments, the dead snake, having accomplished the purpose of leaving an odorous trail to the sleeping couch of the victim, would be thrown away. The dead cobra's living mate would infallibly follow the trail to the bed, where it would coil itself at rest, waiting to strike the sleeper.

Fighting Fish.

It is a favorite amusement among the natives of the East Indian islands to secure a number of these fish, and pit them one against the other, just as English "gentlemen" of days gone by used to match game-cocks to fight each other. Mons. Carbonnier has never placed two together in the same vessel, but if two are put into separate glasses and placed near to each other, it is very amusing to watch their attempts at combat. At first they will closely scan each other from a distance; then, changing color and becoming almost black, the gill-covers are opened out and form a sort of collarette round the head, giving the fish a most curious appearance. The tail and fins become phosphorescent in color, as well as the eyes, and are tinted with the most beautiful hues. Then they attempt to get at each other, but are prevented by the intervening glass. When their anger is sufficiently aroused, they are turned into the same vessel, when they fight vigorously with rapid strokes of the tails and fins, till one of them seeks safety in flight, and turns a sort of grayish-white color, often jumping out of the water to escape his conqueror.

A Snake's Attachment for Home.

Lord Monboddo relates the following anecdote of a serpent: "I am well informed of a tame serpent in the East Indies, which belonged to the late Dr. Vigot, once kept by him in the suburbs of Madras. This serpent was taken by the French when they invested Madras, and was carried to Pondicherry in a close carriage. But from thence he found his way back to his old quarters, though Madras was above one hundred miles distant from Pondicherry."

Queer Legend about Fish.

Most of the flat-fish, such as the flounder, plaice, sole, &c., are white or colorless on one side and dark colored on the other. Naturalists account for this by saying that these fish live at the bottom of the sea, dark side uppermost, to prevent their being easily seen by the ocean monsters that devour them. The Egyptians give another explanation. They tell that Moses was once cooking a flat-fish, and when it had been broiled on one side, the fire or the oil gave out, and Moses angrily threw the fish into the sea, where, though half broiled, it became as lively as ever, and its descendants have retained its parti-colored appearance to the present day, being white on one side and brown or black on the other.

An Old Pike.

In the year 1497 a pike was captured in the vicinity of Manheim, Germany, with the following announcement, in Greek, appended to his muzzle :—

"I am the first fish that was put into this pond by the hands of the Emperor Frederic the Second, on this third day of October, 1262."

The age of the pike, therefore, if the notice spoke the truth (and the enormous dimensions of his body left little doubt on that point), was more than two hundred and thirty-five years. Already he had been the survivor of many important changes in the political and social world around him, and would have survived perhaps as many more, had it not been for his capture. His carcass, which weighed three hundred and fifty pounds, and measured nineteen feet, was sent to the museum at Manheim, where it now hangs, a light, desicated skeleton, which a child might move.

Colossal Shells.

One of these in particular has acquired a certain celebrity on account of its size and the peculiar use to which it has been put. It is the gigantic Tridacna, commonly known as the "font," because it is sometimes employed in churches to contain the sacred water. The great Tridacnæ, which are only detached from the rocks by cutting their cable with an axe, sometimes weigh more than five hundred pounds. The natives of the Molucca Islands eat them like we do oysters, to which they are analogous, and the flesh of one is a sufficient meal for twenty people. Their thick valves, which are sometimes five feet long, serve as troughs for the inhabitants, which nature offers ready cut and polished, and which they often use for feeding pigs, or convert into bath-tubs for their children. Buffon speaks of a shell, the diameter of which was equal to that of a carriage-wheel, and which was used for a mill-stone.

Changing Colors in a Dying Mullet.

The mullet is a fish that was much esteemed by the ancients. The Italians have a proverb which says: "He who catches a mullet is a fool if he eats it and does not sell it"—owing to the high price which the fish commanded. When it is dying, it changes its colors in a very singular manner until it is lifeless. This spectacle was so gratifying to the Romans that they used to show the fish dying in a glass vessel to their guests before dinner.

An Immense Zoological Cabinet.

Schleiden maintains that a single visiting card, when it is covered with a white layer of chalk, represents a zoological cabinet containing nearly 100,000 shells of animals. These shells are formed of carbonate of lime, and are so extremely small that it has been calculated that it would require 10,000,-000 of them to make a pound of chalk.

Chank-Shell.

This name is given to a shell of several species of *Turbinella*, a genus of mollusks found in the East Indian seas. They are much used as ornaments by Hindoo women, the arms and legs being encircled with them. Many of them are buried with opulent persons.   A chank-shell opening to the right is **rare,** and highly prized in Calcutta, one' hundred pounds being sometimes paid for one.

Edifices of the Polypi.

The prodigious surface over which the combined and cease-less toil of these little architects extends, must be taken into consideration in order to understand the important part they play in nature.   They have built a barrier of reefs 400 miles long round New Caledonia, and another which extends along the northeast coast of Australia 1000 miles in length.   This represents a mass in comparison with which the walls of Baby-lon and the Pyramids of Egypt are as children's toys.   And these edifices of the Polypi have been reared in the midst of the ocean waves, and in defiance of tempests which so rapidly annihilate the strongest works constructed by man.   They build their reefs and islands with remarkable rapidity.   One of the straits in the approaches to Australia, which a few years ago only possessed twenty-six madrepore islands, at present displays one hundred and fifty.

Showers of Blood.

In the old chronicles we often read of drops of blood scat-tered here and there being regarded as a sinister omen, or even of regular showers of blood which carried terror into the minds of our superstitious ancestors.   Now-a-days we know that the phenomenon is connected with the metamorphosis of insects.   Gregory of Tours speaks of a shower of blood which fell in the reign of Childebert and spread alarm among the Franks.   But the most celebrated is that which took place at Aix during the summer of 1608.   It struck the inhabitants of the country with terror. The walls of the church-yard and those of the houses for half a league round were spotted with great drops of blood. A careful examination of them convinced a savant of that day, M. de Peirese, that all that was told about the subject was only a fable. He could not at first explain the extraordinary phenomenon, but chance revealed the cause. Having inclosed in a box the chrysalis of one of the butterflies which were then showing themselves in great numbers, he was astonished to see a stain of scarlet red at the spot where the metamorphosis had taken place. He had discovered the cause of the wondrous rain which had alarmed the people. A prodigious swarm of butterflies had appeared at the time, and his conjectures were confirmed by the fact that no drops of blood had been found on the roofs of the houses, but only on the lower stories, the places which the butterflies had chosen for their metamorphoses.

Shirts Growing on Trees.

"We saw on the slope of the Cerra Dnida," says Humboldt, "shirt trees fifty feet high. The Indians cut off cylindrical pieces two feet in diameter, from which they peel the red and fibrous bark without making any longitudinal incision. This bark affords them a sort of garment which resembles a sack of very coarse texture, and without a seam. The upper opening serves for the head, and two lateral holes are cut to admit the arms. The natives wear these shirts of Marina in the rainy season; they have the form of the ponchos and manos of cotton which are so common in New Grenada, at Quito and in Peru. As in this climate the riches and beneficence of nature are regarded as the primary cause of the indolence of the inhabitants, the missionaries do not fail to say, in showing the shirts of Marina,   in the forests of Oroonoka garments are found ready made upon the trees." '

Whistling Trees.

Schweinfurth, in his "Heart of Africa," describes what may be termed an insect organ-builder. In the country of the Shillooks, he says, the acacia groves extend over an area of a hundred miles square and stretch along the right bank of the stream. From the attacks of larvæ of insects, which have worked to the inside, their ivory white shoots are often distorted in form and swollen out at their base with globular bladders measuring about an inch in diameter. After the mysterious insect has unaccountably managed to glide out of its circular hole, this thorn-like shoot becomes a sort of musical instrument, upon which the wind, as it plays, produces the regular sound of a flute. On this account the natives of the Soudan have named it the whistling tree.

Aconite.

This plant was regarded by the ancients as the most violent of poisons. They said that it was the invention of Hecate, and that it sprung from the foam of Cerberus.

Oysters Growing on Trees.

Mr. C. H. Williams, of the Geographical Society of England, tells us how oysters inhabit the Mangrove woods in Cuba: "For several years I resided in that island, and have several times come across scenes and objects which many people would consider great curiosities—one in particular. Oysters grow on trees, in immense quantities, especially in the southern part of the island. I have seen miles of trees, the lower stems and branches of which were literally covered with them, and many a good meal have I enjoyed with very little trouble in procuring it. I simply placed the branches over the fire, and, when opened, I picked out the oysters with a fork or a pointed stick.   These peculiar shell-fish are indigenous in lagoons and swamps on the coast, and as far as the tide will rise and the spray fly so will they cling to the lower parts of the Mangrove trees, sometimes four or five deep, the Mangrove being one of the very few trees that flourish in salt water.''

The Shaking Aspen.

The aspen is popularly said to have been the tree which formed the cross upon which the Saviour was crucified, and since then its boughs have been filled with horror and tremble ceaselessly.   Unfortunately for the probability of this story, the shivering of the aspen in the breeze may be traced to other than a supernatural cause.   The construction of its foliage is particularly adapted for motion; a broad leaf is placed upon a long footstalk so flexible as scarcely to be able to support the leaf in an upright posture.   The upper part of this stalk, on which the play or action seems mainly to depend, is contrary to the nature of footstalks in general, being perfectly flattened, and, as an eminent botanist has acutely observed, is placed at a right-angle with the leaf, being thus particularly fitted to receive the impulse of every wind that blows.

Tree Planting in Java.

In Java a fruit tree is planted on the birth of each child, and is carefully tended as the record of his or her age.

Turkish Superstition about the Geranium.

The Turks believe that the geranium was originally a swallow, and that its existence was changed by a touch from the robe of Mahomet.

Four-leaved Clover.

For centuries it has been considered lucky to find a four-leaved clover. Melton, in his "Astrologaster," says: "That if a man, walking in the fields, find any foure-leaved grasse, he shall in a small while after find some good thing."

Bitterness of Strychnia.

Strychnia, the active principle of the nux vomica bean, which has become so famous in the annals of criminal poisoning, is so intensely bitter that it will impart a sensibly bitter taste to six hundred thousand times its weight of water.

Copied from Nature.

The remarkably pleasing patterns which adorn the Cashmere shawls from the foot of the Himalaya mountains are copied from the leaves of the begonia.

Rose of Jericho.

Under this trivial name is known one of the most singular forms of plant-life.   It is an annual, and is found in northern Africa, Syria and Arabia.   It presents nothing strange during the growing season, but, as the pods begin to ripen on the approach of dry weather, the branches drop their leaves and curl inward, appearing like dead twigs. When completely ripe the whole plant presents the aspect of a ball of curious wicker-work at the top of a short stem. The roots die away, and the wind carries the plant to great distances. When the apparently dead, worthless ball reaches the sea or other water, or becomes wedged somewhere till a rain comes, then the curled and dried ball, under the influence of water, unbends, and the branches resume their proper places. The pods open and discharge their seeds perhaps hundreds of miles from the place of original growth.

The monks of Palestine call it "Mary's Flower," from the belief that it expands each year on the day and hour of the birth of the Saviour. It is also known as the resurrection plant, and women in Palestine, about to undergo the pangs of childbirth, place it in water at the beginning of their pains in the hope that the blooming may be the signal of their deliverance.

Curious Oranges.

There are many oranges, of curious shape and flavor, which we seldom or never see in this country. Such are the pear-shaped kind grown in the far East; the orange of the Philippines, which is no larger than a good-sized cherry; the double orange, in which two perfect oranges appear, one within the other; and the "fingered citron" of China, which is very large, and is placed on the table by the Celestials rather for its exquisite fragrance than for its flavor.

Trifoliated Plants considered Sacred.

Many trifoliated plants have been held sacred from a remote antiquity. The trefoil was eaten by the horses of Jupiter, and a golden, three-leaved, immortal plant, affording riches and protection, is noticed in Homer's Hymn *in Mercurium*. In the palaces of Nineveh, and on the medals of Rome, representations of triple branches, triple leaves and triple fruit are to be found. On the temples and pyramids of Gibel-el-Birkel, considered to be much older than those of Egypt, there are representations of a tri-leaved plant, which, in the illustrations of Hoskin's "Travels in Ethiopia," seem to be nothing else than the shamrock. The triad is still a favorite figure in national and heraldic emblems.

The Belladonna Lily.

This flower (the *Amaryllis formosissima*), in a strong light, has a yellow lustre like gold. It was originally named *flos Jacobæbus*, because some imagined that they discovered in it a likeness to the badge of the knights of the order of St. James, founded in Spain in the fourteenth century.

Thirty Years in Blossoming.

The bamboo tree does not blossom until it attains its thirtieth year, when it produces seed profusely and then dies. It is said that a famine was prevented in India, in 1812, by the sudden flowering of the bamboo trees, where fifty thousand people resorted to the jungles to gather the seed for food.

Mouse-Ear.

Lupton, in his third "Book of Notable Things," 1660, says: "Mousear, any manner of way administered to horses, brings this help unto them, that they cannot be hurt while the smith is shoeing of them; therefore it is called of many, herba clavorum, the herb of nails."

Mugwort.

Coles, in his "Art of Simpling," says: "If a footman take mugwort and put into his shoes in the morning, he may goe forty miles before noon, and not be weary."

The Shoe-black Plant.

There is a species of hibiscus growing in New South Wales, the showy flowers of which contain a large proportion of mucilaginous juice of a glossy, varnish-like appearance. Chinese ladies use the juice for dyeing their hair and eyebrows. In Java the flowers are used for blacking shoes.

St. John's Wort.

The common people in France and Germany gather this plant with great ceremony on St. John's day, and hang it in their windows as a charm against thunder and evil spirits. In Scotland it is carried about as a charm against witchcraft and enchantment, and the people fancy it cures ropy milk, which they suppose to be under some malignant influence. As the flowers, when rubbed between the fingers, yield a red juice, it has obtained the name of *Sanguis hominis* (human blood) among some fanciful medical writers.

> The young maid stole through the cottage door,
> And blushed as she sought the plant of pow'r—
> "Thou silver glow-worm, O lend me thy light,
> I must gather the mystic St. John's wort to-night."

Vegetable Fungus.

At the beginning of the present century Sir Joseph Banks, of London, had a cask of wine which was too sweet for immediate use, and it was placed in the cellar to become mellowed by age. At the end of three years he directed his butler to ascertain the condition of the wine, when, on attempting to open the cellar door, he could not effect it in consequence of some powerful resistance. The door was cut down, and the cellar was found completely filled with a firm fungus vegeta-

ble production—so firm that it was necessary to use an ax for
its removal. This had grown from and had been nourished
by the decomposed particles of the wine. The cask was
empty and touched the ceiling, where it was supported by the
surface of the fungus.—*Hone.*

The Rose at Midsummer.

The gathering of a rose on midsummer eve was once superstitiously associated with the choice of a husband. The custom is stated to be a relic of Druidical times, and is thus mentioned in the *Connoisseur*, No. 50:—

"Our maid Betty tells me, that if I go backward, without
speaking a word, into the garden, upon midsummer eve, and
gather a rose, and keep it in a clean sheet of paper without
looking at it until Christmas day, it will be as fresh as in
June; and if I then stick it in my bosom, he that is to be my
husband will come and take it out."

Another custom was to gather the rose and seal it up while
the clock was striking twelve at mid-day.

The House Leek.

A superstition used to exist that the house leek preserved a
house from lightning. It is still common in many parts of
England to plant it on top of the houses.

Ordeal of the Cross.

When a person accused of crime had declared his innocence
upon oath, and appealed to the cross for its judgment in his
favor, he was brought into church before the altar. The
priest previously prepared two sticks exactly alike, upon one

of which was carved the figure of a cross. They were both wrapped up with great care and much ceremony in a quantity of wool, and laid upon the altar, or upon the relics of the saints. A solemn prayer was then offered up to God, that he would be pleased to discover, by the judgment of his holy cross, whether the accused person was innocent or guilty. A priest then approached the altar and took up one of the sticks, and the assistants reverently unswathed it. If it was marked with the cross, the accused person was innocent; if unmarked, he was guilty. It would be unjust to assert that the judgments delivered were in all cases erroneous, and it would be absurd to believe that they were left altogether to chance.

Ordeal of the Eucharist.

This ordeal was in use among the clergy. The accused party took the sacrament in attestation of innocence, it being believed that, if guilty, he would be immediately visited with divine punishment for the sacrilege. A somewhat similar ordeal was that of the *corsned*, or consecrated bread and cheese. If the accused swallowed it freely, he was pronounced innocent; if it stuck in his throat, he was presumed to be guilty. Godwin, Earl of Kent, in the reign of Edward the Confessor, when accused of the murder of the king's brother, is said to have appealed to the ordeal of the corsned, and was choked by it.

Ordeals in Africa.

Ordeals seem to be prevalent in Africa. "When a man," says Dr. Livingstone, "suspects that any of his wives have bewitched him, he sends for the witch-doctor, and all the wives go forth into the field, and remain fasting till that person has made an infusion of a plant called goho. They all drink it, each one holding up her hand to heaven in attestation of her innocence. Those who vomit it are considered innocent, while those whom it purges are pronounced guilty, and put to death by burning. The innocent return to their homes, and slaughter a cock as a thank-offering to their guardian spirits. The Barotse pour the medicine down the throat of a cock or dog, and judge of the innocence or guilt of the person accused by the vomiting or purging of the animal.''

Ordeal of Cold Water.

The suspected person was flung into the river. If he floated, without any appearance of swimming, he was judged guilty; while if he sank he was acquitted.

Ordeal of Chewing Rice.

It is a common practice, in many parts of India, to oblige persons suspected of crimes to chew dry rice in the presence of the officers of the law. Curious as it may appear, such is the intense influence of fear on the salivary glands, that, if they are actually guilty, there is no secretion of saliva in the mouth, and chewing is impossible. Such culprits generally confess without any further efforts. On the contrary, a consciousness of innocence allows of a proper flow of fluid for softening the rice.

Ordeal by Fire.

This ordeal was allowed only to persons of high rank. The accused had to carry a piece of red-hot iron for some distance in his hand, or to walk nine feet, blindfolded and barefooted, over red-hot ploughshares. The hand or foot was bound up and inspected three days afterwards; if the accused had escaped unhurt, he was pronounced innocent; if otherwise, guilty.

Ordeal of Touch.

At one time a superstition prevailed that if a murderer, at the inquest, or when on trial, touched the dead body of his victim, it would commence to bleed. On the trial, in Edinburgh, of Philip Standsfield, for the murder of his father, the following deposition was made by Mr. Humphrey Spurway:—

"When the chirurgeons had caused the body of Sir James to be, by their servants, sewen up again, and his grave-clothes put on, a speech was made to this purpose: 'It is requisite, now, that those of Sir James Standsfield's relations and nearest friends should take him off from the place where he now lies, and lift him into his coffin.' So I saw Mr. James Rowe at the left side of Sir James' head and shoulder, and Mr. Philip Standsfield at the right side of his head and shoulder; and, going to lift off the body, I saw Mr. Philip drop the head of his father upon the form, and much blood in hand, and himself flying off from the body, crying, 'Lord, have mercy upon me,' or 'upon us,' wiping off the blood on his clothes, and so laying himself over a seat in the church; some, supposing that he would swaiff or swoon away, called for a bottle of water for him."

Sir George McKenzie takes this notice of the above evidence, in his speech to the inquest:—

"But they, fully persuaded that Sir James was murdered by his own son, sent out some chirurgeons and friends, who, having raised the body, did see it bleed miraculously upon his touching it. In which God Almighty himself was pleased to bear a share in the testimonies which we produce: that Divine Power which makes the blood circulate during life, has ofttimes, in all nations, opened a passage to it after death upon such occasions, but most in this case."

Chinese Veneration for the Lily.

Among the Chinese, should the lily blossom on New Year's day, it is regarded as a most happy omen, presaging the best of luck to the fortunate owner of the plant.

The Passion Flower.

This genus of plants received its name from some fanciful persons among the first Spanish settlers in America, who imagined that they saw in its flowers a representation of our Lord's Passion—the filamentous processes being taken to represent the crown of thorns, the nail-shaped styles the nails of the cross, and the five anthers the marks of the wounds.

Burned Wastes Replenished.

Mr. Veitch, the well-known author on "Coniferæ," recently stated that the cones of many of the species on the Pacific coast never open and permit the seed to escape unless opened by a forest fire, when they fall out and replenish the burned waste.   They hang on the trees for many generations —even for thirty years.

Unlucky Stumbling.

When Mungo Park took his leave of Sir Walter Scott, prior to his second and fatal expedition to Africa, his horse stumbled on crossing a ditch which separated the moor from the road.   "I am afraid," said Scott, "this is a bad omen." Park smilingly answered: "Omens follow them who look to them," and, striking spur into his horse, he galloped off. Scott never saw him again.

Patagonian Superstitions.

To the Patagonians the cry of the nightjar on the Cordillera betokens sickness, a certain toad-like lizzard mysteriously lames horses, a fabulous two-headed guanaco is a sure forerunner of epidemic disease, &c. To counteract the influence of these, charms and talismans are liberally employed.

Superstition about the Caul.

One of the superstitions that still clings to seafaring life, is the confidence in the virtues of a child's caul, as a preservative against drowning. The caul is a thin membrane found encompassing the head of some chiidren when born; it was considered a good omen for the child itself, and productive of good fortune and security from danger to the purchaser. The superstition was so common in the primitive church that St. Crysostom felt it his duty to inveigh against it in many of his homilies. In later times midwives sold the caul at enormous prices to advocates, "as an especial means of making them eloquent," and to seamen as "an infallible preservative against drowning." In Ben Jonson's "Alchemist" Face says to Dapper—

> "Ye were born with a caul o' your head."

In Digby's "Elvira" (Act V.), Don Sancho says—

> "Were we not born with cauls upon our heads?
> Think'st thou, chicken, to come off twice arow
> Thus rarely from such dangerous adventures?"

The caul is alluded to in a *rondeau* by Claude de Malleville, born 1597. "*Il est né coiffé*" is a well-known expression, describing a lucky man, and indicating that he was born with a caul. Weston, in his "Moral Aphorisms from the Arabic"

(1801), says that the superstition came from the East, and that there are several Arabic words for it.

The Will-with-a-Wisp.

This phenomenon, known also as "Jack-with-a-Lantern" and "Ignis fatuus," has terrified many a simple-minded rustic, whereas it is simply the phosphuretted hydrogen gas which rises from stagnant waters and marshy grounds. Its origin is believed to be in the decomposition of animal substances. Collins has left us some fine lines upon this phenomenon, beginning—

> "Ah, homely swains! your homeward steps ne'er lose;
>   Let not dank Will mislead you to the heath;
> Dancing in murky night o'er fen and lake,
>   IIe glows to draw you downward to your death,
> In his bewitch'd, low, marshy willow brake."

At Bologna, in 1843, the painter Onofrio Zanotti saw this phenomenon in the form of globes of fire, issuing from between the paving-stones in the street, and even about his feet. They rose into the air and disappeared; he even felt their heat when they passed near him.

Cramp Rings.

These rings were supposed to cure cramp and the "falling sickness." They are said to have originated as far back as the middle of the eleventh century, in a ring presented by a pilgrim to Edward the Confessor, which, after that ruler's death, was preserved as a relic in Westminster Abbey, and was applied for the cure of epilepsy and cramp. Hence appears to have arisen the belief that rings blessed by English sovereigns were efficacious in such cases, and the custom of

blessing for distribution large numbers of cramp rings on **Good
Friday**, which continued in existence down to the time of
Queen Mary. The accomplished Lord Berners, ambassador
to Spain in the time of Henry VIII., wrote from Saragossa to
Cardinal Wolsey: "If your grace remember me with some
cramp rings ye shall doo a thing muche looked for; and I
trust to bestow thaym with Goddes grace."

Horseshoes.

An ancient superstition existed that horseshoes kept witches
out of the house. It was a common practice to nail them to
the threshold, stipulated, however, that the shoe was to be
one that had been found. In Gay's fable of "The Old
Woman and her Cats," the supposed witch makes the following complaint:—

> "—Crowds of boys
> Worry me with eternal noise;
> Straws laid across, my pace retard;
> The horseshoe 's nailed (each threshold's guard);
> The stunted brooms the wenches hide,
> For fear that I should up and ride."

Breaking a Piece of Money.

It was an ancient custom to break a piece of gold or silver
in token of a verbal contract of marriage and promises of love;
one half of the coin was kept by the woman, the other half
was retained by the man.

Love Charms.

Theocritus and Virgil both introduce women into their
pastorals, using charms and incantations to recover the affec-

tions of their sweethearts. Shakespeare represents Othello as accused of winning Desdemona "by conjuration and mighty magic." In Gay's "Shepherd's Week," these are represented as country practices—

> "Strait to the 'pothecary's shop I went,
>   And in love-powder all my money spent,
>   Behap what will, next Sunday, after prayers,
>   When to the ale-house Lubberkin repairs,
>   These golden flies into his mug I'll throw,
>   And soon the swain with fervent love shall glow."

Throwing bay leaves into the fire, or bruising poppy flowers in the hands, was believed to influence the love of others. In Herrick's "Hesperides" is given "a charm or an allay for love"—

> "If so a toad be laid
>   In a sheep-skin newly flay'd,
>   And that ty'd to a man, 't will sever
>   Him and his affections ever."

Spellbound.

It was a popular belief in Scotland that the Duke of Monmouth was spellbound to Lady Henrietta Wentworth, the charm being lodged in the gold toothpick case which he sent to her from the scaffold.—*William Jones, F.S.A.*

Amulets Inserted under the Skin.

Devices to procure invulnerability are common in the Indo-Chinese countries. The Burmese sometimes insert pellets of gold under the skin with this view. At a meeting of the Asiatic Society of Bengal, in 1868, gold and silver coins were shown which had been extracted from under the skin of a Burmese convict, at the Andaman Islands. Friar Odoric speaks of the practice in one of the Indian Islands (apparently Borneo), and the stones possessing such virtue were, according to him, found in the bamboo, presumably the silicious concretions called *Tabashir*. Conti also describes the practice in Java of inserting amulets under the skin.

Divining Rods.

Divination by the rod or wand is an imposition of the highest antiquity. Hosea reproaches the Jews for believing in it: "My people ask counsel at their stocks, and their *staff* declareth it unto them." (IV. 12.) It was a custom in vogue among the Chaldeans, among almost every nation with any pretence to scientific knowledge, and also among the wilder or ruder races, as the Alani and the ancient Germans. Dr. Henry states that after the Saxons and Danes had embraced Christianity, the priests were commanded by their ecclesiastical superiors to preach very frequently against *diviners*, sorcerers, augurers, and "all the filth of the wicked and the dotages of the Gentiles." The divining rod, *virgula divina*, or *baculus divinatorius*, was a forked branch of hazel, cut in the form of a Y, and was supposed to reveal not only the hidden spring, but mines of gold and silver, and any other concealed treasure.

The "Quarterly Review," in an early number, relates that a certain Lady Noel possessed the divining faculty: "She took a thin forked hazel twig, about sixteen inches long, and held it by the ends, the joint pointing downwards. When she came to the place where water was under the ground, the twig immediately bent, and the motion was more or less rapid as she approached or withdrew from the spring. When just over it, the *twig turned so quick as to snap, breaking near the fingers,* which, by pressing it, were indented and heated and *almost blistered;* a degree of agitation was also visible in her face. The exercise of the faculty is independent of any volition."

Washing but Once in a Lifetime.

No devout Spanish woman dares to bathe without the permission of her confessor. A female Bulgarian is permitted to wash only once in her life—on the day before her wedding; and in most South Sclavonian families the girls are rarely allowed to bathe—the women never.

Looking Back.

The superstition of the ill-luck of looking back, or returning, is nearly as old as the world itself, having no doubt originated in Lot's wife "having looked back from behind him," when he was leaving the doomed city of the Plain. Whether walking or riding, the wife was behind the husband, according to a usage still prevalent in the East. In Robert's "Oriental Illustrations" it is stated to be "considered exceedingly unfortunate in Hindostan for men or women to look back when they leave their house. Accordingly, if a man goes out and leaves something behind him which his wife knows he will want, she does not call him to turn or look back, but takes or sends it after him; and if some emergency obliges him to look back, he will not then proceed on the business he was about to transact."

Toad-Stone Rings.

During the fifteenth and sixteenth centuries a curious superstition was prevalent in England in connection with what was known as the toad-stone ring. The setting was of silver, and

the stone was popularly believed to have been formed in the
heads of very old toads. It was eagerly coveted by sovereigns,
and by all persons in office, because it was supposed to have
the power of indicating to the person who wore it the prox-
imity of poison, by perspiring and changing color. Fenton,
who wrote in 1569, says: "There is to be found in the heads
of old and great toads a stone they call borax or stelon;" and
he adds, "They, being used as rings, give forewarning
against venom." Their composition is not actually known;
by some they are thought to be a stone—by others, a shell;
but of whatever they may be formed there is to be seen in
them a figure resembling that of a toad, but whether produced
accidentally or by artificial means, is not known, though,
according to Albertus Magnus, the stone always bore the
figure on its surface when it was taken out of the toad's head.
Lupton, in his "One Thousand Notable Things," says: "A
toad-stone, called crepaudina, touching any part envenomed,
hurt or stung with rat, spider, wasp or any other venomous
beast, ceases the pain or swelling thereof." The well known
lines in Shakespeare are doubtless in allusion to the virtue
which Lupton says it possesses—

> "Sweet are the uses of adversity,
> Which, like a toad, ugly and venomous,
> Wears yet a precious jewel in his head."

And Lyly, in his Euphues, says—

> "The foule toad hath a faire stone in his head."

Royal Dinner Time.

The Khan of the Tartars, who had not a house to dwell in,
who subsisted by rapine, and lived on mare's milk and horse
flesh, every day after his repast caused a herald to proclaim,

"That the Khan having dined, all other potentates, princes and great men of the earth might go to dinner."

Throwing an Old Shoe.

The custom of throwing an old shoe after a person is still, in many rural districts, believed to propitiate success, as in servants seeking or entering upon situations, or about to be married. In Scripture, "the receiving of a shoe was an evidence and symbol of asserting or accepting dominion or ownership; the giving back the shoe was the symbol of rejecting or resigning it." Hence the throwing of a shoe after a bride was a symbol of renunciation of dominion over her by her father or guardian; and the receipt of the shoe by the bridegroom, even if accidental, was an omen that the authority was transferred to him.

Cock-crowing an Omen of Victory.

Cicero quotes an instance where a Bœotian soothsayer promised victory to the Thebans from the crowing of a cock. The same circumstance once served the Bœotians as an omen of victory over the Lacedæmonians.

The Unicorn's Horn.

The unicorn's horn was considered an amulet of singular efficacy. It is now known that the object shown as such in various museums is the horn of the rhinoceros. They were sold at six thousand ducats, and were thought infallible tests of poison, just as Venitian glass and some sorts of jewels were. The Dukes of Burgundy kept pieces of the horn in their wine jugs, and used others to touch all the meat they tasted.

Drinking-cups of this kind were greatly esteemed in former times. In the inventory of jewels and plate in the Tower (1649), with cups and beakers of unicorn's horn, is entered, "A rinoceras cupp, graven with figures, with a golden foot," valued at £12. Decker, in "Gul's Hornbook," speaks of "the unicorn whose horn is worth a city."

The Evil Eye in Spain.

In the Gitano language casting the evil eye is called *querelar nasula*, which simply means "making sick," and which, according to the common superstition, is accomplished by casting an evil look at people, especially at children, who, from the tenderness of their constitution, are supposed to be more easily blighted than those of a more mature age. After receiving the evil glance, they fall sick and die in a few hours. The Spaniards have very little to say about the evil eye, though the belief in it is very prevalent, especially in Andalusia, among the lower orders. A stag's horn is considered a good safeguard, and on that account a small horn, tipped with silver, is frequently attached to the children's necks by means of a cord braided from the hair of a black mare's tail. Should the evil glance be cast, it is imagined that the horn receives it, and instantly snaps asunder. Such horns may be purchased in some of the silversmiths' shops at Seville.—*Borrow.*

Witchcraft Charms.

The charms by which witches worked were short rhymes at the different stages. In the fifteenth century an old dame was tried for using witchcraft in curing diseases, when the judges promised to liberate her if she would divulge her charm. This she readily did, and informed the court that the charm consisted in repeating the following words, after the stipulated pay, which was a loaf of bread and a penny—

> "My loaf in my lap,
>   My penny in my purse,
>   Thou art never the better,
>   And I am never the worse."

That was ludicrous indeed. Here is a "Charme for a Thorne"—

> "Christ was of a Virgin born,
>   And he was pricked with a thorn;
>   And it did neither bell nor swell,
>   And I trust in Jesus this never will."

For "A Burning":—

> "There came three angels out of the East:
>   The one brought fire, the other brought frost—
>   Out fire—in frost,
>   In the name of the Father, and Son
>   And Holy Ghost. Amen."

A Mountain Highway.

During the occupation of Java by the English in May, 1814, it was unexpectedly discovered that in a remote but populous part of the island a road leading to the top of the mountain of Sumbeng, one of the highest in Java, had been constructed. The delusion which gave rise to the work had its origin in the province of Banyunas, in the territories of the Susunan, and the infection spread to the territory of the Sultan, and thence extended to that of the Europeans.

On examination, a road was found constructed twenty feet broad and from fifty to sixty miles long, and it was wonderfully smooth and well made. One point which appears to have been considered necessary, was that this road should not cross rivers, and in consequence it wound in a thousand ways.

Another point as peremptorily insisted upon, was that its course should not be interrupted by any private rights, and in consequence trees and houses were overturned to make way for it. The population of whole districts, occasionally to the amount of five or six thousand laborers, were employed on the road, and, among people disinclined to active exertion, the laborious work was nearly completed in two months—such was the effect of the temporary enthusiasm with which they were inspired.

It was found in the sequel that the whole work was set in motion by an old woman who dreamed, or pretended to have dreamed, that a divine personage was about to descend from heaven on the mountain in question. Piety suggested the propriety of constructing a road to facilitate his descent; and it was rumored that divine vengeance would pursue the sacrilegious person who refused to join in the meritorious labor. These reports quickly wrought on the fears and ignorance of the people, and they heartily joined in the enterprise. The old woman distributed to the laborers slips of palm-leaves, with magic letters written upon them, which were charms to secure them against sickness and accidents. When this strange affair was discovered by the native authorities, orders were issued to desist from the work, and the inhabitants returned without a murmur to their usual occupations

A Buffalo's Skull.

Nowhere has superstition a greater power over the human mind than among the inhabitants of Java. Mr. Crawford relates that some years since it was accidentally discovered that the skull of a buffalo was superstitiously conveyed from one part of the island to another. The point insisted upon was never to let it rest, but to keep it in constant progressive motion. It was carried in a basket, and no sooner was one person relieved from the load than it was taken up by another; for the understanding was that some dreadful imprecation was denounced against the man who should let it rest. In this manner the skull was hurried from one province to another, and, after a circulation of many hundred miles, it at length reached the town of Samarang, the Dutch governor of which seized it and threw it into the sea, and thus the spell was broken. The Javanese expressed no resentment, and nothing further was heard of this unaccountable transaction. None could tell how or where it originated.

Superstitious Notion of the Number One.

The Bedui, a people found in the interior of Bantam, Java, have a superstitious notion of the number *one*. It is an established rule among them to allot but one day for each of the different successive operations of husbandry,—one day for cutting down the trees and underwood; one day for clearing what has been so cut down; one day for sowing the grain; one for weeding the field; one for reaping; one for binding up the grain; one for carrying it home. If any part of what has been reaped cannot be carried home in one day, it is left to rot in the field.

Thunder and Lightning.

Thunder and lightning have been fruitful sources of superstitious terror. The ancients considered lightning as a visible manifestation of Divine wrath; hence whatever was struck with it was considered to be accursed and separated from human uses. The corpse of a person struck by lightning was never removed from the place where it fell; there it lay, and, with everything pertaining to it, was covered with earth and enclosed by a rail or mound. In some parts of the East, however, it is considered a mark of Divine favor to be struck by lightning. In England, formerly, during storms, bells were rung, and the aid of Saint Barnabas was invoked, in abbeys, to drive away thunder and lightning.

The bay-tree was commonly believed to afford protection from lightning. It was also believed that if a fir-tree were touched, withered or burned by lightning, its owner would soon die. It was customary to place a piece of iron on the beer barrel, during a storm, to keep the beer from souring.

Manna Marked with the Number Six.

In the *Calaba*, the number *six* was considered to be one of potent mystical properties. The rabbinical writers assert that the manna, when it was found, was marked with the Hebrew *vau*, the equivalent of number six. As the world was created in six days; as a servant had to serve six years (Exodus xxi. 2); as the soil was tilled for six years (Exodus xxiii. 10); as Job endured six tribulations—so this number was typical of labor and suffering. Consequently it was impressed on the manna not only to show the Israelites that it fell but on six days, but also to warn them of the miseries they would undergo if they dared to desecrate the Sabbath day.

The Seventh Son of the Seventh Son.

Grose remarks as a popular superstition that the seventh son of a seventh son is born a physician, having an intuitive knowledge of the art of healing all disorders, and sometimes the faculty of performing wonderful cures by touching only.

It is recorded as a superstition in Yorkshire (1819), that if any woman has seven boys in succession, the last should be bred to the profession of medicine, in which he would be sure of being successful.

In an article on "Fairy Superstitions in Donegal," published in the *University Magazine* for August, 1879, are the following statements respecting the seventh son: "It is not generally known that a particular ceremony must be observed at the moment of the infant's birth, in order to give him his healing power. The woman who receives him in her arms places in his tiny hand whatever substance she decides that he shall rub with in after life, and she is very careful not to let him touch anything until this shall have been accomplished. If silver is to be the charm, she has provided a sixpenny or threepenny bit; but as the coinage of the realm may possibly change during his lifetime, and thus render his cure valueless, she has more likely placed meal or salt upon the table, within reach. Sometimes it is determined that he is to rub with his own hair, and in this case the father is summoned and requested to kneel down before his new-born son, whose little fingers are guided to his head, and helped to close upon a lock of hair. Whatever substance a seventh son rubs with must be worn by his patients so long as they live."

Virtue in the Number Seven.

In the manuscript on Witchcraft, by John Bell, a Scottish minister (1705), he says: "Are there not some who cure by observing number? after the example of Balaam, who used magiam geometricam (Numbers xxiii. 1), 'Build me here seven altars, and prepare me here seven oxen and seven rams,' etc. There are some witches who enjoin the sick to dip their shirt seven times in south-running water. Elisha sends Naaman to wash in Jordan seven times. Elijah, on the top of Carmel, sends his servant seven times to look for rain. When Jericho was taken they compassed the city seven times."

Not only the ancient Jews but the heathens regarded this number of great efficacy. in religious ceremonies. Apuleius says: "Desirous of purifying myself, I wash in the sea, and dip my head in the waves seven times, Pythagoras having thought that this number is, above all others, most proper in the concerns of religion."

The Bektashi dervishes of Turkey have many superstitious beliefs in connection with their girdle, cap and cloak. One ceremony with the stone worn in the girdle is rather striking. The Sheikh puts it in and out *seven* times, saying: "I tie up greediness, and unbind generosity. I tie up anger, and unbind meekness. I tie up ignorance, and unbind the fear of God. I tie up passion, and unbind the love of God. I tie up the devilish, and unbind the divine."

In Lane's "Modern Egyptians," mention is made of a ridiculous ceremony for the cure of a pimple on the edge of the eyelid. The person affected with it goes to any seven women of the name of Fa't'meh, in seven different houses, and begs from each of them a morsel of bread; these seven morsels constitute the remedy.

A curious French manuscript belonging to the latter part of the thirteenth century has a singular illustration of the number seven. It is a miniature,—a wheel cut into seven rays, and composed of seven concentric cordons. The rays form seven compartments divided into as many cordons, containing in each cordon one of the seven petitions of the Lord's prayer, one of the seven sacraments, one of the seven spiritual arms of justice, one of the seven works of mercy, one of the seven virtues, and one of the seven gifts of the Holy Ghost.— *William Jones, F. S. A.*

Onomancy.

The notion that an analogy existed between men's names and their fortunes is supposed to have originated with the

Pythagoreans; it furnished some reveries for Plato, and has been the source of much wit to Ausonius. Two leading rules in what was called Onomancy were, first, that an even number of vowels in a man's name signified something amiss in his left side; an uneven number, a similar affection in the right; so that between the two perfect sanity was little to be expected. Secondly, of two competitors, that one would prove successful the numeral letters in whose name, when summed up, exceeded the amount of those in the name of his rival; and this was one of the reasons which enabled Achilles to triumph over Hector.

Mystic Gifts.

Chrysostom says that the three gifts of the three Magi—gold, myrrh and frankincense—were mystic gifts, signifying that Christ was king, man and God.

Exterminating Vermin.

In France it is believed that water from the well of the Church of St. Gertrude of Nivelles will drive away rats and mice if sprinkled about the house. Earth from the tomb of St. Ulric, at Augsbourg, is believed to possess the same virtue. In Scotland it was the custom to paste the following rhyme against the wall of the house—

> "Ratton and mouse,
> Lea' the puir woman's house;
> Gang awa' owre by to the mill,
> And there ye'll a' get ye'r fill."

The Bulgarians beat copper pans all over the house on the last day of February, calling out at the same time, "Out with you, serpents, scorpions, fleas, bugs and flies!" A pan held by a pair of tongs is put outside in the courtyard.

Perforated Stones.

Creeping through perforated stones was a Druidical ceremony, and is practiced in the East Indies. Barlase mentions
a stone in the parish of Marsden, Cornwall, through which
many persons have crept for pains in their backs and limbs,
and many children have been drawn for the rickets. He adds
that two brass pins were carefully laid across each other on
the top edge of this stone, for oracular purposes.

St. Helena Coins.

Among amulets in repute in the Middle Ages were the
coins attributed to St. Helena, the mother of Constantine.
These and other coins marked with a cross were thought
especially efficacious against epilepsy, and are generally found
perforated for the purpose of being worn suspended from the
neck.

Weighing a Witch.

At Wingrave, in Buckinghamshire, in 1759, a case occurred
of the old popular witchcraft trial by weighing against the church
Bible. One Susannah Hameokes, an elderly woman, was
accused by a neighbor of being a witch. The overt act offered
in proof was, that she had bewitched the said neighbor's spin-
ning-wheel, so that she could not make it go round either one
way or the other. The complaining party offered to make
oath of the fact before a magistrate, on which the husband ot
the poor woman, in order to justify his wife, insisted that she
should be tried by the church Bible, and that the accuser
should be present. The woman was accordingly conducted
by her husband to the ordeal, attended by a great concourse
of people, who flocked to the parish church to see the cere-

mony. Being stripped of nearly all her clothes, she was put into one scale and the Bible into another, when, to the no small astonishment and mortification of her accuser, she actually outweighed it, and was honorably acquitted of the charge.

Poetry of Omens.

Omens constitute the poetry of history. They cause the series of events which they are supposed to declare to flow into epical unity, and the political catastrophe seems to be produced not by prudence or by folly, but by the superintending destiny. The numerous tokens of the death of Henry IV. are finely tragical. Mary de Medicis, in her dream, saw the brilliant gems of her crown change into pearls, the symbol of tears and mourning. An owl hooted until sunrise at the window of the chamber to which the king and queen retired at St. Denis, on the night preceding her coronation. During the ceremony, it was observed, with dread, that the dark portals leading to the royal sepulchre, beneath the choir, were gaping and expanded. The flame of the consecrated taper held by the queen was suddenly extinguished, and twice her crown nearly fell to the ground. The prognostications of the misfortunes of the Stuarts have equally a character of solemn grandeur; and we are reminded of the portents of Rome when we read how the sudden tempest rent the royal standard on the Tower of London. Charles I., yielding to his destiny, was obstinate in the signs of evil death. He refused to be clad in the garments of Edward the Confessor, in which all his predecessors had been arrayed, and he would be attired in white velvet. Strongly did the Earl of Pembroke attempt to dissuade him—for the prophecy of the misfortunes of the *white king* had long been current; but his entreaties were in vain, and Charles was crowned invested with the raiment which indicated his misfortunes.—*Quarterly Review.*

House Crickets.

It is singular that the house cricket should, by some weak persons, be considered a lucky, and by others an unlucky, inmate of a dwelling. Those who hold the former opinion consider its destruction the means of bringing misfortune on their habitations. "In Dumfriesshire," says Sir William Jardine, "it is a common superstition, that if crickets forsake a house which they have long inhabited, some evil will befall the family—generally the death of some member is portended. In like manner, the presence or return of this cheerful little insect is lucky, and portends some good to the family."

Sitting Cross-Legged.

Sir Thomas Browne tells us that to sit cross-legged, or with our fingers pectinated or shut together, is accounted bad, and friends will dissuade us from it. The same conceit religiously possessed the ancients; but Mr. Park says: "To sit cross-legged, I have always understood, was intended to produce good or fortunate consequences. Hence it was employed as a charm at school, by one boy who wished well for another, in order to deprecate some punishment which both might tremble to have incurred the expectation of. At a card-table I have also caught some superstitious players sitting cross-legged, with a view of bringing good luck."—*Brand.*

The Death-Watch.

This name has been given to a harmless little insect which lives in old timber, and produced a noise which somewhat resembles the ticking of a watch. It is simply the call of the insect to another of its kind, when spring is far advanced.

The general number of distinct strokes in succession is from seven to nine, or eleven, and the noise exactly resembles that produced by tapping moderately with the finger nail upon a table, and, when familiarized, the insect will readily answer to the tap of the nail. The noise used to be regarded as an omen of death in the family, and is mentioned by Baxter in his "World of Spirits." Swift ridicules the superstition as follows:—

> "A wood worm,
> That lies in old wood, like a hare in her form,
> With teeth or with claws it will bite, it will scratch,
> And chamber-maids christen this worm a death-watch;
> Because, like a watch, it always cries click:
> Then woe be to those in the house that are sick!
> For, sure as a gun, they will give up the ghost,
> If the maggot cries click when it scratches the post.
> But a kettle of scalding hot water injected,
> Infallibly cures the timber affected;
> The omen is broken, the danger is over,
> The maggot will die, the sick will recover."

Sundry Rural Charms.

For good bread—

> This I 'll tell ye, by the way:
> Maidens, when ye leavens lay,
> Cross your dow and your dispatch
> Will be better for your batch.—*Herrick.*

To make the butter come—

> Come butter, come,
> Come butter, come,
> Peter stands at the gate
> Waiting for a butter'd cake,
> Come butter, come.

Scattering wash-water—

> In the morning, when ye rise,
> Wash your hands and cleanse your eyes.
> Next be sure ye have a care
> To disperse the water farre,
> For as farre as that doth light,
> So farre keeps the evil spright.—*Herrick.*

There is mention of older charms in "Bale's Interlude Concerning the Laws of Nature, Moses and Christ," 1562—

> "With blessynges of Saynt Germayne
> I will me so determyne
> That neyther fox nor vermyne
>   Shall do my chyckens harme;
> For your gese seke Saynt Legearde,
> And for your duckes Saynt Leonarde,
>   There is no better charme."

> "Take me a napkin folte
> With the byas of a bolte,
> For the healing of a colte
>   No better thynge can be;
> For lampes and for bottes
> Take me Saynt Wilfrid's knottes,
> And holy Saynt Thomas Lottes,
>   On my life I warrande ye."

Charm against Dogs.

On the 22d of November the sun enters Sagittarius. According to an old magical manuscript of the fourteenth century, an aspect of "Sagittary" seems to have dominion over dogs. "When you wish to enter where there are dogs, that they may not hinder you, make a tin image of a dog, whose head is erected towards his tail, under the first face of *Sagittary*, and say over it, 'I bind all dogs by this image, that they do not raise their heads or bark;' *and enter where you please."—Fosbroke.*

Barnacles.

An extraordinary belief was long current that the barnacle, which is found adhering to the bottom of ships, would, when broken off, become a species of goose. Several old writers assert this, and Holinshed gravely declares, that "with his own eyes he saw the feathers of these barnacles hang out of the shell at least two inches." Giraldus Cambrensis gives similar ocular testimony. "Who," he says, "can marvel that this should be so? When our first parent was made of mud, can we be surprised that a bird should be born of a tree?" The following lines occur in Isaac Walton's quotations from "The Divine Weekes and Workes" of Du Bartas—

> "So, Sly Boots, underneath him sees
> In the cycles, those goslings hatcht of trees,
> Whose fruitfull leaves falling into the water
> Are turn'd (they say) to living fowls soon after.
> So rotten sides of broken ships do change
> To barnacles! O, transformation strange!
> 'Twas first a green tree, then a gallant hull,
> Lately a mushroom, now a flying gull!"

In a description of West Connaught, Ireland, by Roderic O'Flaherty (1684), the barnacle is thus mentioned: "There is the bird engendered by the sea, out of timber long lying in the sea. Some call these birds *clakes*, and solan'd geese, and some puffins, others barnacles; we call them *girrinn*." Butler tells us, in "Hudibras," of those

> "Who from the most refined of saints
> As naturally grow miscreants,
> As barnacles turn soland geese
> In the islands of the Orcades."

The numerous tentacles or arms of the animal inhabiting the barnacle shells, which are disposed in a semicircular form and have a feathery appearance, seem to have been all that could reasonably have been alleged in favor of this strange supposition.

Odd Way to Discover a Dead Body.

In the "Gentleman's Magazine" (February 8th, 1767), is a curious notice of the mode of discovering the body of a drowned person: "An inquisition was taken at Newbury, Berks, on the body of a child nearly two years old, who fell into the river Kennet, and was drowned. The body was discovered by a very singular experiment. After diligent search had been made in the river for the child, to no purpose, a two-penny loaf, with a quantity of quicksilver put into it, was set floating from the place where the child, it was supposed, had fallen in, which steered its course down the river upwards of half a mile, before a great number of spectators, when the body, happening to lay on the contrary side of the river, the loaf suddenly tacked about and swam across the river, and gradually sunk near the child, when both the child and the loaf were brought up with grabbers ready for that purpose."

The Salagrama Stone.

In India the "salagrama" stone is supposed to possess extraordinary powers. It is about the size of a billiard ball, of a black color, and usually perforated, as if by worms. It is believed to be found only in the Gandaki, a river in Nepaul, which, according to the followers of Vishnu, flows from the foot of that deity, but, according to the Saivas, from the head of Siva. The fortunate possessor of this stone preserves it in a clean cloth, from which it is frequently taken and bathed and perfumed. The water with which the ablution is performed acquires a sin-expelling potency, and it is therefore swallowed and greatly prized. This stone possesses many other mysterious powers, and in death it is an essential ingredient in the viaticum. The departing Hindoo holds it in his hand, and, through his confidence in its influence, hope brightens the future, and he dies in peace.

Charm for the Cramp.

Coleridge tells us of a couplet that it was common to repeat in his boyhood, to relieve the foot when asleep, or to cure the cramp in the leg. The sufferer pressed the sole of the foot hard on the floor, and said—

> "The devil is tying a knot in my leg!
> Mark, Luke and John, unloose it, I beg!"

Fisherman's Luck.

The fishermen of the Firth of Forth believed that if they chanced to meet a woman barefooted, who had broad feet and flattish great toes, when they were proceeding to go to sea, they would have "bad luck," and, consequently, need-not go out in search of fish. It was also considered unlucky to sell fish for the first time in the day to a person having broad thumbs.

The Swedish anglers say that if a woman strides the rod, no trout will be caught that day. Tackle, they say, stolen from a friend or neighbor, would bring better luck than that bought with money.

In Forfarshire there are fishermen who, on a hare crossing their path, while on their way to their boats, will not put to sea.

It is unfortunate, on starting out, to sneeze to the left side; the print of a flat foot in the sand is considered unlucky.

Fishermen, while standing or walking, consider it unlucky to be numbered, or to be asked where they are going. A pin picked up in church, and made into a hook, brings luck.

Luck of Birthdays.

In the west of England the fortunes of children are believed to be much regulated by the day of the week on which they are born—

"Monday's child is fair in face,
Tuesday's child is full of grace,
Wednesday's child is full of woe,
Thursday's child has far to go,
Friday's child is loving and giving,
Saturday's child works hard for its living;
And a child that's born on a Christmas day
Is fair and wise, good and gay."

Sleeping on Stones.

Borlase, in his Antiquities of Cornwall, mentions, as a relic of Druid fancies and incantations, the custom of sleeping on stones, on a particular night, in order to be cured of lameness.

Spilling Salt.

In Scotland there exists a common belief that it is unlucky to spill salt at table, but that the luck can be changed by taking up a pinch of the spilled salt and throwing it over the left shoulder. To spill salt on Friday is considered especially unlucky.

"Help me to *salt*,
Help me to *sorrow*,"

Is a saying among the Highlanders, and they always decline salt with a wave of the hand. The popular superstition of this accident being unlucky is said to have originated in the celebrated picture of The Last Supper, by Leonardo da Vinci, in which Judas Iscariot is represented as overturning the salt. Among the Italians, to spill oil at table is regarded as an omen of the worst import.

Charm for the Ague.

This charm for the ague, on "St. Agnes' Eve," is recited up the chimney, in England, by the eldest female in the family—

> "Tremble and go!
> First day shiver and burn;
> Tremble and quake!
> Second day shiver and learn;
> Tremble and die!
> Third day never return."

Ancient Practice of Medicine.

The blood of an innocent child, or of a virgin, was believed to cure the leprosy; that of an executed criminal, the falling sickness. The hearts of animals, because the seat of life, were held to be potent drugs. The Rosicrucian physicians treated a case of wounding by applying the salve to the weapon, instead of to the wound itself.

Amethyst Amulets.

The ancients imagined that the amethyst possessed the property of preventing intoxication, and persons much addicted to drinking therefore wore it on their necks.

Preservative against Toothache.

In some parts of England it is believed that carrying suspended round the neck a molar-tooth taken from some grave in the church-yard, is a preservative against toothache.

Mixed Moons.

The dim form of the full moon seen with the new moon was considered an evil sign by the sailors of the sixteenth and seventeenth centuries—

> "I saw the new moon late yestreen,
> With the old moon in her arm,
> And if we go to sea, master,
> I fear we'll come to harm."

The Blood of the Martyrs.

During the horrible persecutions of the primitive Christians at Rome, the blood of the martyrs was esteemed a talisman of especial power.   A sponge saturated therewith was sometimes worn as a sacred relic.   Prudentius describes the spectators of the martyrdom of St. Vincent as dipping their clothes in his blood, that they might keep it as a sort of palladium for successive generations—

> "Crowds haste the linen vest to stain,
> With gore distill'd from martyr's vein,
> And thus a holy safeguard place
> At home, to shield a future race."

The First Sale for the Day.

In London, in the street market-places, amongst the stall-keepers, it is considered unfortunate to refuse a "first bid" for an article.   It brings bad luck on the day's selling, and it is better to get the first sale over, even at a loss.   In all such places, much to the stall-keeper's exasperation, there are to be found mean folks who are known as hansel (first-sale) hunters, and who are early at market, on the alert to take advantage of the poor vendor's superstition.   The latter is well aware of the paltry device to obtain goods at less than cost price; but though he may swear somewhat, he will rarely turn away the "first bid," and "chance" it for the day. When he has taken hansel money, he would as soon think of throwing it into the road as putting it into his pocket without first "spitting upon it."

Arsenic as an Amulet.

During the severe visitation of the plague in London, amulets composed of arsenic were very commonly worn in the region of the heart, upon the principle that one poison would drive out or prevent the entry of another.   Large quantities of arsenic were imported into London for the purpose.   Dr. Henry, in his "Preservatives against the Pestilence" (1625), wrote against them as "dangerous and hurtful, if not pernicious to those who wear them."   The wearing of arsenic in the way of an amulet, common in olden times, is said to have arisen chiefly from ignorance of Arabic, the word in the Arabian authors which is rendered *arsenic* properly signifying *cinnamon*.

Red Tape a Protection against the Plague.

Taylor, in his "Account of the Rebellion in Wexford," relates a curious story of the amuletive properties of *red tape* as a protection against the plague: "Before the rebellion broke out in Wexford, all the red tape in the country was bought up, and more ordered from Dublin. It was generally bought in half-yards, and all the Roman Catholic·children, boys and girls, wore it round their necks. This was so general and so remarkable as to occasion some inquiry, and the reason given was this: A priest had dreamed there would be a great plague among all the children of their church under fifteen years of age; that their brains would boil out at the back of their heads. He dreamed also that there was a charm to prevent it, which was to get some red tape, have it blessed and sprinkled with holy water, and tie it round the children's necks till the month of May, when the season of danger would be past. The Protestants suspected that it was intended as a mark to distinguish their own children, like the blood of the Paschal Lamb, when the Egyptian first-born were to be cut off.''

Owl's Claws.

The Russian Non-conformists (Raskolnics) are in the habit of carrying about with them, in rings and amulets, parings of owl's claws, and of their own nails. Such relics are supposed by the peasantry in many parts of Russia to be of the greatest use to a man after his death, for by their means his soul will be able to clamber up the steep sides of the hill leading to heaven.

Witch-ridden Horses.

In olden times it was believed that witches took from their stalls the horses, and rode them through the night. Aubrey, in his ''Miscellanies,'' mentions the practice and publishes a remedy: ''Hang in a string a flint with a hole in it by the manger; but, best of all, they say, hang about their necks, and a flint will do that hath not a hole in it. It is to prevent the nightmare, viz: the hag or witch from riding their horses, who will sometimes sweat all night." Herrick says—

> " Hang up hooks and shears to scare
> Hence the hag that rides the mare,
> Till they be all over wet
> With the mire and the sweat;
> This observed, the manes shall be
> Of your horses all knot-free."

A Smuggler's Talisman.

The following was found in a linen purse on the body of one Jackson, a murderer and smuggler, who died in Chichester Goal, February, 1749—

> "Ye three holy kings,
> Gaspar, Melchior, Balthasar,
> Pray for us now, and at the hour of death."

"These papers have touched the three heads of the holy kings of Cologne; they are to preserve travelers from accidents on the roads, falling sickness, fevers, *sudden death.*" He was struck with such horror on being measured for his irons, that he expired soon afterward. His talisman failed him.

Rubbing with a Gold Ring.

Pegge, in his "Curialia," alludes to the superstition that a wedding-ring of gold, rubbed on a stye upon the eyelid, was considered a sovereign remedy, but it required to be rubbed nine times. In Beaumont and Fletcher's "Mad Lovers," reference is made to the practice. In the West Indies the explanation of the merits of the gold wedding-ring used for this purpose is, that it is something which, once given, can never be taken back; and the Barbadians believe if you give anything away and take it back, you are sure of a stye, or "cat-boil," as they call it.

Divination of the Bible and Key.

This was long popular, and is still practised. A case was tried before Mr. Ballantine, an English magistrate, as late as June 10th, 1832. "A person named Eleanor Blucher, a tall, muscular native of Prussia, was charged with an assault upon Mary White. They lived in the same court, and Mrs. White having lost several articles from her yard, suspected the defendant. She and her neighbors, after a consultation, agreed to have recourse to the key and Bible to discover the thief. They placed the street door-key on the fiftieth Psalm, closed the book, and fastened it very tightly with a garter. The Bible and key were then suspended to a nail; the prisoner's name was repeated three times by one of the women, while another recited the following words—

> 'If it turns to thee thou art the thief,
> And we all are free.'

The incantation over, the key turned, or the women thought it did ; they unanimously agreed that Mrs. Blucher had stolen two pairs of inexpressibles belonging to Mrs. White's husband, and severely beat her."

Visions of Destiny.

A singular mode of divination practised at the period of the harvest moon is thus described in an old chap-book: "When you go to bed, place under your pillow a prayer-book, opened at the part of the matrimonial service 'With this ring I thee wed;' place on it a key, a ring, a flower and a sprig of willow, a small heart-cake, a crust of bread and the following cards—

the ten of clubs, nine of hearts, ace of spades and the ace of diamonds. Wrap all these in a thin handkerchief of gauze or muslin, and on getting into bed, cross your hands and say—

> "Luna, every woman's friend,
> To me thy goodness condescend;
> Let me this night in visions see
> Emblems of my destiny."

Selecting an Avocation.

A writer in "Notes and Queries" mentions a species of divination (sent him from Northamptonshire) of the leading events in a man's life, or rather of future employment, drawn from the last chapter of the Book of Proverbs. This consists of thirty-one verses, each of which is supposed to have a mystical reference to each of the corresponding days of the month. Thus, a person born on the 14th will be prognosticated "to get their food from afar." This was so fully believed in by some, that a boy was actually apprenticed to a *linen*-draper, for no other reason than because he was born on the 24th of the month, the twenty-fourth verse of the chapter mentioning "fine linen."

Spitting for Luck's Sake.

Spitting for "luck's sake," and as a charm against all kinds of fascinations, was regarded with importance by the ancients. Theocritus says—

> "Thrice on my breast I spit to guard me safe
> From fascinating charms."

Among the Greeks it was customary to spit three times into their bosoms at the sight of a mad man, or one troubled with an epilepsy. Children were lustrated with spittle by their nurses or relations; the old grandmother, or aunt, moved around in a circle, and rubbed the child's forehead with spittle, selecting her middle finger, to preserve it from witchcraft. Persius alludes to this custom—

> "See how old beldams expiation make,
> To atone the gods the bantling up they take
> His lips are wet with lustrous spittle; thus
> They think to make the gods propitious."

Spitting, as an Irish luck superstition, is noticed by Camden: "It is by no means allowable to praise a horse or any other animal, unless you say, 'God save him,' or spit upon him. If any ill-luck befalls the horse three days after, they hunt up the person who praised him, that he may whisper the Lord's prayer into the animal's right ear."

Spitting for good luck has still its votaries among hucksters, pedlers and others. The first money received for the day is spat upon by dealers in England, Scotland and Roumania.

A Yorkshire custom to secure luck when a rainbow appeared was marking a cross on the ground and spitting on each of its four corners.

May Marriages Unlucky.

It is a common notion that May marriages are unlucky, and the superstition is as old as the time of Ovid. An old saw says, "The girls are all stark naught that wed in May;" and another saying was

> "From the marriages in May
> All the bairns die and decay."

An ancient proverb, cited by Ray, says, "Who marries between the sickle and the scythe, will never thrive."

In the rural districts of France a marriage contracted in May or August is unlucky. In the "Almanach des Laboureurs," it stated that a woman marrying in these months will put her husband under a yoke.   The superstition of the month of May being unlucky for marriages still prevailed in Italy in 1750.

Pin Superstitions.

It used to be considered lucky for bridesmaids to throw away pins on a wedding-day. In Brittany the young girls who visit the bridal chamber secure the pins used in fastening the bride's dress for a lucky marriage.

Randolph, in his "Letters," writing of the marriage of Mary Queen of Scots to Lord Darnley, says that when the queen, after her marriage, went to her chamber to change her clothes, she suffered "them that stood by her, every man that could approach, to take a pin." The Bretons throw pins into certain wells for good luck. The following saying is connected with pins—

> "See a pin and pick it up,
> All the day you'll have good luck.
> See a pin and let it lie,
> All the day you'll need to cry."

Superstitions about Children.

A superstition used to exist that a child which did not cry when sprinkled in baptism would not live long. The same would be the case if the children were prematurely wise. Shakespeare puts this superstition into the mouth of Richard III.

Bulwer mentions the tradition concerning children born open-handed, that they will prove of a bountiful disposition and frank-handed. A character in one of Dekker's plays says: "I am the most wretched fellow; surely some *left-handed* priest christened me, I am so unlucky." The following charms for infancy are taken from Herrick—

Bring the holy crust of bread,
Lay it underneath the head;
'Tis a certain charm to keep
Hags away while children sleep.

Let the superstitious wife
Near the child's heart lay a knife;
Point be up, and haft be down,
(While she gossips in the towne);
This, 'mongst other mystic charms,
Keeps the sleeping child from harmes.

Digging for Water.

The divining rod is not the only superstition connected with the digging for water. In the country of the Damazas, in South Africa, before they dig, the natives offer an arrow, or a piece of skin or flesh, to a large red man with a white beard, who is supposed to inhabit the place; at the same time they repeat a prayer for success in finding water. To dig for it without this ceremony, they say, occasions sickness and death.

Wolf Superstition.

In Normandy a phantom in the form of a wolf is believed to wander about at night amongst the graves. The chief of the band of phantoms is a large black wolf, who, when approached, rises on his hind legs and begins to howl, when the whole party disappear, shrieking out, "Robert is dead! Robert is dead!"—*Nimmo.*

Stanching Blood.

The ancients firmly believed that blood could be stanched by charms. The bleeding of Ulysses is reputed to have been stopped by this means ; and Cato the Censor has given us an incantation for setting dislocated bones.   To this day charms are supposed to arrest the flow of blood.

> " Tom Potts was but a serving man,
>   But yet he was a doctor good;
>   He bound his kerchief on the wound,
>   And with some kind word he stanched the blood."

Sir Walter Scott says, in the "Lay of the Last Minstrel "—

> " She drew the splinter from the wound,
>   And with a charm she stanch'd the blood."

Arab Charms.

The Arabs have many family nostrums, and are implicit believers in the efficacy of charms and mystic arts.   No species of knowledge is more highly venerated than that of the occult sciences, which afford maintenance to a vast number of quacks and impudent pretenders.   The science of *Isen-Allah* (or Name of God) enables the possessor to discover what is passing in his absence, to expel evil spirits, cure diseases, and dispose of the wind and seasons as he chooses.   Those who have advanced far in this study pretend to calm tempests at sea by the rules of art, or say their prayers at noon in Mecca, without stirring from their own houses in Bagdad !   The *Kurra* is the art of composing billets or amulets which secure the wearer from the power of enchantments and all sorts of accidents.   They are also employed to give cattle an appetite for food and clear houses from flies and other vermin.

Superstitions among the Bretons.

In the district of Carhaix is a mountain called St. Michael, whither it is believed all demons cast from the bodies of men are banished. If any one sets his foot at night within the circle they inhabit, he begins to run, and will never be able to cease all the rest of the night.

In one of the districts is a fountain called Krignac. To drink three nights successively of this at midnight is an infallible cure for intermittent fever. In other districts there are fountains into which, if a child's shirt or shift be thrown, and it sinks, the child will die within a year. If it should swim, it is then put wet on the child, and is a charm against all kinds of diseases.

The *Ar cannerez nos* are ghostly "wash-women," who ply their trade at night, washing their linen while they sing quaint old ballads. They solicit the assistance of people passing by to wring the linen. If the assistance be given awkwardly, they break the person's arm; if it be refused, they pull the "refusers" into the stream and drown them.

Blessing of Beasts.

On St. Anthony's day the beasts at Rome were blessed and sprinkled with holy water. Lady Morgan says that the annual benediction of the beasts at Rome, at a church dedicated to St. Anthony, lasts for some days: "For not only every Roman, who has a horse, a mule or an ass, sends his cattle to be blessed at St. Anthony's shrine, but all the English go with their job horses and favorite dogs; and for the small offering of a couple of *paoli*, get them sprinkled, sanctified and placed under the protection of this saint. Coach after coach draws up, strings of mules mix with carts and barouches, horses kick, mules are restive, dogs snarl, while the officiating priest comes forward from his little chapel, dips a brush into a vase of holy water, sprinkles and prays over the beasts, pockets the fee, and retires." Dr. Conyers Middleton says, that when he was at Rome he had his own horses blest for eighteen pence, as well to satisfy his curiosity as to humor his coachman, who was persuaded that some mischance would befall them during the year, if they had not the benefit of the benediction.

Moles.

In "The Husbandman's Practice; or, Prognostication Forever," 1658, there is much to show what moles on various parts of the body denote. For example: If a man have a mole on the place right against the heart, it denotes him to be undoubtedly wicked. If a mole in either man or woman appear on the place right against the spleen, it signifies that he or she shall be "much passionated and oftentimes sick." In "A Thousand Notable Things," we find that moles on the arm and shoulder denote great wisdom; on the left, debate and contention. Moles near the armpit signify riches and honor. A mole on the neck is commonly a sign that there is another near the stomach, which denotes strength. A mole on the neck and throat denotes riches and health; a mole on the chin, that there is another near the heart, and signifies riches. A mole on the right side of the forehead is a sign of great riches both to men and women; on the left side, quite the contrary. Moles on the right ear denote riches and honor; on the left ear they signify the reverse.

Whipping Toads to Produce Rain.

At one time the natives of Venezuela worshipped toads. They regarded the toad as "the lord of the waters," and treated it with much reverence; though, as has been the case with other idolaters, they were ready, in times of difficulty, to compel favorable hearing from their pretended deities. They whipped their imprisoned toads with little switches when there was a scarcity of provisions and a want of rain.

The First Butterfly.

A superstition prevails in Devonshire, England, that any individual neglecting to kill the first butterfly he may see for the season, will have ill-luck throughout the year.

Child-Stealing Elves.

According to Irish as well as Scottish fairy superstitions, the elves, though in the main harmless, or at most tricky, have the bad reputation of stealing children from the cradle and substituting for them a changeling who bears a resemblance to the stolen infant, but is an ugly little creature, and never thrives. On such a theft of a female infant, who is carried to Fairyland, but in the course of years returns to her parents, James Hogg founded his fine ballad of "Kilmeny" (Queen's Wake).

INDEX.